Memories

of Maggie

Memories of Maggie

Martha Raye: A Legend Spanning Three Wars

Noonie Fortin

LANGMARC PUBLISHING • San Antonio, Texas

Memories of Maggie

Martha Raye: A Legend Spanning Three Wars

By Noonie Fortin

Editors: Debra Innocenti and James Qualben, Ph.D.
Cover: Michael Qualben

First Printing: 1995
Printed in the United States of America

Published by
LANGMARC PUBLISHING
P.O. Box 33817
San Antonio, Texas 78265

Library of Congress Cataloging-in-Publication Data

Fortin, Noonie, 1947—
Memories of Maggie : Martha Raye—a legend spanning three wars / Noonie Fortin.
p. cm.
Discography: p.
Filmography: p.
Includes bibliographical references.
ISBN 1-880292-18-1
1. Raye, Martha. 2. Entertainers—United States—Biography. I. Title.
PN2287.R248F67 1995
792′ .028′ 092—dc20
[B] 95-49178
CIP

To all

the men and women who have served our country
in the Armed Forces since its birth,
those who gave their lives during armed conflict
around the world,
the Gold Star Mothers, Fathers and siblings,
the POW/MIA'S still not accounted for
and especially to the eight women whose
names are etched in the Wall

In memory of
Hap, Elaine, Dad, Gram, and Tom

"I love truth. I believe humanity has need of it. But assuredly it has much greater need still of the untruth which flatters it, consoles it, gives it infinite hopes."

Anatole France, *La Vie en Fleur*

CONTENTS

FOREWORD

I first met Noonie Fortin at Fort Bragg, North Carolina during my Mom's funeral service. At that time I was not aware of the tremendous effort and time she had put into promotion for the Presidential Medal of Freedom presented, at last, to Mom.

Shortly afterwards we befriended each other and have stayed in constant touch. When she told me about this book I was thrilled, to say the least. After the wonderful responses I received (to my open letter following Mom's funeral) from many service women and men, I decided to send Noonie the ones that related their encounters with Mom from World War II through Vietnam.

Knowing that Mom had touched thousands during her military experiences all over the world and that (because of short notice) they never got a chance to say their final good-bye [to her] I felt this book would be a definite winner.

Memories of Maggie will help keep Mom's spirit alive forever. All those who loved her will be able to relate to this history of documented military experiences. To Mom these events were her happiest and best of times, which she constantly related to everyone including the entertainment industry.

This special relationship Mom had with the military was one of mutual, unconditional love.

Noonie, thanks for hanging tough and persevering to get this memorable book out there. I love you for it.

Melodye Condos

PUBLISHER'S PERSPECTIVE

Most were teenagers. Most had been drafted. Many had to surrender their school books when America's political leaders ordered them out of the country to a place called Vietnam. There, "in-country," most tried to do their best to live up to what was expected of them. Tens of thousands died doing so; many more were wounded and watched buddies die.

As the tragic dimensions of our leaders' miscalculations swelled, rather than take responsibility for their policies' outcomes, most dodged it. That left troops to feel like they were the national wash hung out to dry when they came home.

Martha Raye may have seen it coming. We do know she organized her own life around a phenomenal compassion for our military personnel throughout the Vietnam War years. If her compassion may be likened to a jewel, this book describes the lights which shone from its many facets into the lives of individual American troops.

So we share Noonie Fortin's commitment to present these stories of Veterans who saw or met Martha Raye. Perhaps through this book, their own personal experiences with "Colonel Maggie" will be multiplied as they read of fellow troops' encounters with this extraordinary and—we believe—historically significant woman!

James Qualben, Ph.D.
Senior Editor

PREFACE

The fabric of this book is woven with a few threads from Martha's personal life and more from her career; but most threads come from Martha Raye's wartime experiences. I could not write about this extraordinary comedienne, singer, and actress without sharing some facts about her career, which began in Vaudeville at three, nightclubs by her early teens, progressing to stage, television, and movies. At a tender age, she had fame—but her generous heart lured her to the battlefields of three wars spanning fifty years and into operating rooms to assist with the wounded.

I skim over her personal life, however; Martha played that hand very close to her chest and, frankly, I wasn't inquisitive about it. Writing her personal biography can be done better by a member of her immediate family.

Although her family, friends, and Veterans of World War II and Korea knew her as Margaret or Martha, Vietnam Era Veterans knew her as "Colonel Maggie." That is how she wanted to be remembered. *Memories of Maggie* is not Martha Raye's biography. This is, above all, our *Veterans'* story of what Colonel Maggie did for them over five decades and through three wars.

Subject matter is arranged in chronological order, rather than by themes. This should make it easier for a reader to follow—and appreciate—the "juggling act" she kept up to be with "her" troops. It is also my hope that Veterans especially will consider this book a touchstone that connects their children and grandchildren with their military years, by contrast with history books' often-impersonal character.

With that in mind, I have toned down often-earthy language in some Veterans' letters whenever possible. Few people with very quick minds have mouths that can keep up with their brains. Martha did. Her "Big

Mouth" was a fast mouth—very fast—which became a hallmark of her comedic and conversational style. When Martha was on stage, radio, screen, or television, her language followed whatever script she had. When she was in the public's eye, she presented herself as a lady. But when she was with the troops, her language could take on their own purple hue. She was committed to her contexts!

Martha seldom gave interviews, so it has been difficult to distinguish fact from legend. If an interview was with someone from Hollywood, she would talk about show business. If an interview dealt with her devotion to the Armed Forces, she would talk about those experiences. She seemed determined to promote a distinct show business *persona* known as Martha Raye in order to support her driving, passionate mission with our troops. Her Hollywood career and personal life were a universe apart from the time she spent with our Armed Forces personnel.

My interest in Martha Raye's relationships with Veterans began October 1987 when I joined the Tri-County Council Vietnam Era Veterans in Albany, New York. A retired Veteran mentioned that the Special Forces Association was attempting to get Martha honored by President Ronald Reagan. He asked for the Council's help. During the next two years I surveyed Martha's endeavors, sensed something of her mission, and decided it was worth pursuing. Belle Pellegrino worked with me during that initial research phase.

Our original goal was to have Martha honored with more medals than just the Presidential Medal of Freedom. That meant acquiring an overwhelming body of substantiating material that would override Maggie's stateside image as a brassy, big-mouthed comedienne. Without such materials, bureaucratic inertia could smother any prospect of honoring her extraordinary personal mission with tens of thousands of American troops.

Belle and I were named co-chairs of the newly-named Medals for Maggie committee of the Tri-County Council in November 1989. We requested—and received—many personal stories about Martha (whom we came to know as Maggie). We learned much about Veterans' organizations and about how the Pentagon, Congress, and the White House operated on such matters.

I first spoke with Martha in February 1990. After many telephone conversations, Belle and I visited her in California during August and September of 1990 and Arden Davenport and I visited her again in 1991. In the presence of witnesses, Martha orally authorized this book with the request that I tell the truth as she had verified it. At one point, Martha stated that I probably knew her experiences with our Veterans as well as she could remember them. Martha's daughter, Melodye Condos, also authorized this book in November 1994; she has written its Foreword, provided photos of her mother's family, and shared additional information about her mother.

We hit many snags along the way. But on November 2, 1993, I received a telephone call from the White House to inform us that President Bill Clinton had approved and was signing the Presidential Medal of Freedom for Martha Raye's humanitarian efforts spanning fifty years. On November 15, 1993, the Medal was presented to her at her Bel Air home by Congressional Medal of Honor recipient Master Sergeant Roy Benavidez, United States Army Special Forces (Retired) and Major Leo Mercado (President Clinton's United States Marine Corps Liaison).

I gathered information from library references, magazines, newspaper morgues—most of it verified by Martha. Where pertinent, I tried to show that some reference material seems to contradict what Martha herself recalled. Given her astounding memory, one cannot automatically assume official records should take precedence. Many of the letters I received and stories I heard are included. Each letter told about how Martha affected people she met. Some folks wrote only a couple sentences, while others wrote pages about significant feelings or remembrances of her and the high-risk places to which she traveled to be with our troops. Names and locations of those who wrote have been used, except for a few people I could not locate to secure publication permission. Photos used throughout the book have been loaned by museums and individuals who shared their memories.

Enemies at war de-personalize each other, demolish their enemy's very humanity, reduce armed opponents to mere "targets" or "Geeks."If there is one theme—a singular thread—woven through the hundreds of experiences volunteered for this book, it is this: Martha Raye's core mission with our troops was to underline their real humanity in the twilight zone of firebases and foxholes—if only for a few hours or minutes.

With Martha, rank and military function faded in favor of the person's identity in the Real World: son or daughter, husband or wife, parent, family member. Through her personal contact, Martha tried to connect the soldier with his or her existence as a *person* with a name and beloved relationships beyond the tragic craziness of war. In America's history, few fulfilled this mission as well—or as passionately—as Martha Raye did!

BLESS YOU, COLONEL MAGGIE!

Noonie Fortin

ACKNOWLEDGMENTS

Thank you to those Veterans who shared their most personal memories of Colonel Maggie. Throughout this book, I capitalize the words Veterans and Vets because they seem almost "God-like" to me.

Thanks to the Tri-County Council Vietnam Era Veterans and their families in Albany, New York, for their support and assistance while the "Medals for Maggie" project was in full swing—especially Belle Pellegrino, our committee co-chair whose research assisted in obtaining the Presidential Medal of Freedom for Martha "Colonel Maggie" Raye, to past president Joe Pollicino , to Lieutenant Colonel Frances Liberty, and to Larry Wiest.

A heartfelt thanks to Arden Davenport, without whom these recollections about Maggie wouldn't have been pulled together for this book.

Jimmy Dean provided information and pictures which the Special Forces Association had gathered during their organization's eight-year endeavor to have Maggie honored prior to our committee's start. Also, Roxanne Merritt at the John F. Kennedy Special Warfare Museum at Fort Bragg, North Carolina provided photos and stories about Maggie.

Thanks to Congressman Mike McNulty (D-NY) and his aide Jim Glenn, to Senator John Seymour (R-CA) and his aide Alan Poff. Jim and Alan wrote the House and Senate Resolutions and kept in contact with the White House. Thanks to Colonel Kenneth Deutsch and his Pentagon staff for acquiring recommendations from Secretaries of Defense Dick Cheney and Les Aspin. Also to Deputy Secretary of Veterans Affairs Hershel Gober who provided valuable assistance throughout this project.

Special thank you to Susan Christiansen, who helped me realize the difference between fact and legend, and to Congressional Medal of Honor recipient Master Sergeant Roy Benavidez, who was the first person to endorse the "Medals for Maggie" project.

Thanks to Benita Zahn who gave our project television notice, to Grace O'Connor whose Albany *Times Union* article got our efforts national coverage, to Dana Lynn Singfield for her articles in the Schenectady *Daily Gazette;* to Eve Baker at Twentieth-Century Fox and LuAnne Williams for sharing information about Maggie's career in stage, film, music and television; to Don Smith of Albany and Photowave in Killeen, Texas whose professional eyes helped with photo reproduction.

Thanks to museum curator Ceilia Stratton and the Second Armored Division of Fort Hood for World War II photos and stories about Maggie's tours in North Africa; to Marvin and Kathy Sorensen of Butte, Montana; to Kevin Hargrove of the Navy Recruiting Office in Killeen for his assistance; to Kathi Hansen-Nauert of Copperas Cove, and Janet Olin Altschuller of Niskayuna, NY, for assisting with travel arrangements.

Those friends whose support and encouragement have meant so much to me and who offered comments on the manuscript, especially Ann Kahle, Robin Evon, Sue Naccarato, and Sara Wiest; Al Hemingway of Waterbury, Connecticut, who helped me keep my head above water during this project, and Bruce Jones of Sacramento, who helped me through final stages prior to the publication process.

Special thanks to LangMarc Publishing, Michael Qualben for designing the cover, and my editors Debra Innocenti and Dr. James Qualben.

Thank you, Melodye Condos, for providing valuable dimensions of your mother's personal life and career.

Martha "Colonel Maggie" Raye was a national treasure and a true American heroine, who will be greatly missed by all who knew her, especially by the Veterans of our country.

Noonie Fortin

INTRODUCTION

There aren't many "firsts" left for me at this stage of life; however, writing the introduction to this book is one of them. I never thought I'd be so privileged as to be asked. When Noonie did, I fretted for months: How could I do Maggie the justice she deserves?

Then I remembered an admonition Maggie always gave as she waved her finger and told me, "Don't worry about what you put in print, Susan," she added firmly, "as long as it's the truth."

I don't remember exactly when I first met our Colonel Maggie. Like many of you, as soon as I met her, I felt I'd known this woman forever.

One of our later encounters took place at the Bonaventure Hotel in Los Angeles, 1987. There was an enormous Veterans' Convention going on. Colonel Maggie was there, every day, just "one of the guys." This woman was the center of attraction in the lounge.

Day after day, you couldn't help but notice a blind man, quietly standing outside the lounge, his dog stoically beside him. Many Vets asked if he needed assistance. He always quietly declined. Finally, a group of nervous Veterans asked me to intercede.

I walked up to this man and asked what he was waiting for—all those days.

"I'm waiting for Colonel Maggie to have a moment to see me, Ma'am. I don't care to disturb her." Something about the guy got to me and I sent Chuck, Maggie's escort, to go get her.

Maggie strode right over to the man. "What's up, Soldier? You wanted to see me?" Even his dog stood at attention as he replied, "Yes, Ma'am!"

"Well, I'm here. What is it?"

"I served in Vietnam in..." Maggie finished his sentence by providing the place she'd met him—once he'd mentioned the year.

While others standing around us showed pure awe at Maggie's capacity for memory of detail, I only smiled; it's her trademark.

While Maggie and the man (we never asked him his name) reminisced, the blind soldier's face glowed with joy. Finally, he said what he'd waited twenty years to say, "Colonel Maggie," he began, "when I was hit, you stayed in that foxhole, holding me, singing to me till the medevac came. I wasn't so scared, with you there, and all." They were staring deeply into each other's eyes. Somehow, we knew they were both seeing a time and place they'd shared long ago, and in this, his blindness was unimportant. It was suddenly quiet enough to hear footfalls 16,000 miles away.

"When Doc went to bandage my eyes, you stopped him," with a choke, he continued, "you looked me right in my eyes and told me 'Someday we'll see each other again.'"

"Well, back in The World, when they unbandaged me, they told me I'd never see anything ever again. I wasn't depressed. I knew I could live with this," he pointed to his sightless eyes, "because the last thing I ever saw—was the most beautiful sight I could ever live to see. You."

Maggie took him in her arms and we onlookers had a good cry. The Veteran? His eyes were glowing with a sight from within. Maggie? Once again, she gave that man exactly what he needed—when he needed it.

This story is not only true—it epitomizes the Colonel Maggie I've been fortunate enough to call "Friend" for the last two decades—at least.

When I met Noonie and Belle, they painstakingly explained years of frustration in trying to obtain the coveted "Presidential Medal of Freedom" for Colonel Maggie. Shame on me! I never realized she'd not received it! I suppose it was so obvious she was more than entitled, that I couldn't imagine administrations from Roosevelt on not recognizing the agonizing contributions Maggie had made.

I suppose that's another anomaly of Maggie's life; while Veterans from World War II, Korea, Africa and Vietnam were well aware of what Maggie had been doing for our military in combat, she was so low key about federal administrations that never really understood the full scope of her contributions!

Maggie didn't publicize her trips into combat. She usually used her own money to finance them. She was whatever the troops needed at any given time, under whatever circumstances existed. If a surgical nurse was needed, Maggie was up to her elbows in blood. If a Corpsman was needed, Maggie was, in uniform, on the front lines. If an entertainer was required, Maggie sang, danced and joked until the tears were ones of laughter—not fear.

Most important of all, Colonel Maggie was wife, mother, sister, daughter to any who needed her to be.

Every life she touched experienced her unconditional love. Troops as old as my grandfathers and as young as my sons knew this.

It's just our United States government that was unaware.

Noonie, Belle, and Veterans groups allied for the impossible quest of correcting this tragic oversight.

In doing so, these two women put their own lives on hold and dedicated themselves to the matter at hand. And Veterans responded from every walk of life, spanning decade after decade of fond memories

Finally, while the dedication of "The Vietnam Woman's Memorial" occurred in Washington, D.C., in November, 1993, Colonel Maggie did indeed, receive The Presidential Medal of Freedom.

Due to Maggie's failing health, the highest civilian honor in our land was awarded to her at her home,

"Maggie's Team House" in Los Angeles. Noonie, Belle and I were in Washington, D.C. at the time.

The last time I was with Maggie, I asked her how and why this medal was important to her. Taking my hand in hers, she said, "To be close (united). I've done so much running around, I don't stay put long enough to get close. My friends, you, Noonie, Belle, all of you working on getting me the medal—I don't want to disappoint you."

And that's who Maggie was and is to me. After all she'd been through, all the thousands of American troops she'd touched, much of the time at great personal cost, and in her declining years, her worry was that she'd disappoint us by not receiving the medal.

This book is Maggie's story. The story she refused to have published until she was again joined with troops from long ago, so as not to be embarrassed or embarrass anyone else.

I don't think—knowing and loving Maggie—that she ever truly realized how great a person, how beloved, she really was—and is. This book stands to tell The World just that.

And I feel honored to have been a part of it, in any small way. Because to be touched by Maggie was to be blessed by an Angel.

Susan M. Christiansen
Veteran Correspondent
California, 1995

Chapter 1

From Charity Ward To Celebrity

"What a great girl, movie star,
and lover of humanity."

Sam Patton, M.D.
(Macon, Georgia)

Little Margy Reed

Montana—1922: L-R: Melodye Reed, unknown friend, Bud Reed, and Margy Reed. Photo contributed by Melodye Condos.

-1-

Margy Reed was born in the charity ward of Saint James Hospital in Butte, Montana, on August 27, 1916. Butte's most visible feature is a gigantic semicircular strip mine in the center of town, a copper mine in the middle of "Big Sky Country." Hardly a "showbiz" capital!

With such an inauspicious start in life, her immigrant parents, Peter Reed and Maybelle Hooper, would have been surprised that by mid-century their daughter would be a legend, beloved by many of her countrymen, admired by some colleagues, scorned by others. Nor could they have guessed that thousands would know their newborn infant as "The Big Mouth" or "Old Lady of the Boondocks."

Fans got the impression Margy was of Irish or Italian decent. But, according to her birth certificate, her father came from England and her mother from Montana. Her death certificate, however, listed her father from Ireland and her mother from Wisconsin.

Whatever her family's actual roots, it was to her advantage that people thought she was Irish. She was a master at belting out Irish songs at "pubs" in the most unlikely places!

Out of Diapers...Into Show Business

She was only three years old when Margy began performing with her parents in vaudeville. Maybelle played piano while Peter sang and danced. They were called "Reed and Hooper" or "The Red Hooper Revue." She had a sister named Melodye and a brother named Bud. Margy attended public schools in Montana, Roman Catholic parochial schools in Chicago, and the Professional Children's School in New York City. Like so many children in show business at that time, she never completed high school.

Between 1919 and 1929, Margy also performed with the Benny Davis Revue, the Ben Blue Company, and the Will Morrissey Company. In 1929, when she was only thirteen, Margy began singing with Paul Ash's orchestra.

How did she get the name Martha Raye? Margy's baptismal name was Margaret Theresa Yvonne Reed. In her early teens she searched a telephone book for possible stage names. She chose: *Martha Raye.*

By the time her family finally settled in Great Falls, Montana, the acting bug had bitten Martha, and she set forth on a career of her own. She wasn't about to become a nurse, teacher, or secretary. She had already been around too much to settle for one of *those* jobs (as she told me).

At fifteen, Martha performed the comedy lead in a children's act that included Jackie Heller, Hal LeRoy, and Sonny O'Day, along with Buddy and Vilma Ebsen. That year she also sang at the Paramount in Chicago. Between 1931 and 1935, Martha frequently joined Eddie Cantor on "The Chase and Sanborn Hour," his NBC weekly radio program.

Throughout her long career, many show business colleagues had high regard for Martha's abilities as a singer. When Martha was sixteen (1932), she recorded her first record. One side was "I Heard" and the flip side had "How'm I Doin.'"

R.L. Romez remembered working with young Martha when he played trumpet at the Frolic's Club in Miami Beach in 1933. Louis Kraft of El Cajon, California recalls a cold night in February 1934 when he caught Barbara Blaine and seventeen-year-old Martha coming out of Chez Paree Club in Chicago, where Martha was appearing. Both women signed his fraternity paddle as they chatted amicably with him.

Martha headed back to the Big Apple that year for her New York vaudeville debut at Loew's State Theater.

She frequently joined Bob Hope for NBC's half-hour weekly radio program, "The Bob Hope Pepsodent Show."

At eighteen, Martha made her Broadway stage debut at The Hollywood in Lew Brown's "Calling All Stars," which opened in December 1934, but closed only thirty-six performances later.

Throughout 1935, one could catch Martha's performances with Jimmy Durante at the Casino de Paris, with Louis Prima in New York City clubs, at the Casanova Cafe, and the Ben Mardene Riviera in Fort Lee, New Jersey. She sang and cracked jokes on the weekly NBC radio program "The Rudy Vallee Show." That same year, nineteen-year-old Martha appeared in another Broadway show at the Winter Garden Theater in Earl Carroll's "Sketch Book."

Martha's big break came in 1935 when she made a guest appearance one Sunday night at The Trocadero in Hollywood. That evening she was "discovered" by Norman Taurog, who signed her on the spot for the movie *Rhythm on the Range.*

Oh yes, this teenager was indeed getting around! Now a star on stage-screen-radio, Martha Raye's career was launched!

Martha Raye sang, danced, acted, and joked her way into America's heart. By the time she was nineteen, this five-foot three-inch, 122-pound pack of dynamite with a cavernous mouth was a seasoned trouper in vaudeville, on stage, radio, and in record studios. She was making a name for herself as a jazz and cabaret singer, band vocalist, and even more as a comedienne.

Between 1935 and 1939 she appeared frequently on "The Eddie Cantor Pabst Blue Ribbon Show," a weekly program on CBS radio. These performances helped earn her The Susie Award (also known as The Eddie Cantor Award). Martha also was a regular on Al Jolson's half-hour show that aired weekly on CBS radio between 1936 and 1939.

In 1936, Martha appeared at The Famous Door in New York City and later at the Century Club in Los Angeles. She often appeared on "The Edgar Bergen and Charlie McCarthy Show," an NBC radio program. But, she wanted more.

On to the Silver Screen

Martha's screen career began in the Paramount film *Rhythm on the Range*, an easygoing musical comedy with a Western background. This 1936 release also starred Bing Crosby, Frances Farmer, and Bob Burns. Martha portrayed Emma and knocked the socks off moviegoers when she sang "If You Can't Sing It, You'll Have To Swing It (Mr. Paganini)." According to some film critics, Martha stole every scene she was in. This three-star movie also was a stepping stone for "The Sons of the Pioneers," led by Roy Rogers.

Even for someone becoming as famous as she was, show business pay during the Depression was meagre. When Martha needed income during slack periods, she worked as a waitress. She also received training as a nurse's aide at Cedars of Lebanon Hospital in Los Angeles, where she volunteered her time in the wards when she was not waiting tables, appearing on stage, or making movies.

Martha portrayed Patsy in Paramount's *The Big Broadcast of 1937*, a three-star musical comedy about a radio station manager who was having trouble with his sponsors. Her costars included Jack Benny, George Burns, Gracie Allen, Bob Burns, and Ray Milland.

Paramount next signed Martha to play Helen Flint in *Hideaway Girl*, a two-star musical about a girl who was suspected of stealing a necklace. Shirley Ross and Robert Cummings costarred.

Martha's last film of 1936 was Paramount's *College Holiday*, a musical comedy about a group of bright young people who were invited to spend a summer with a female hotelier who just happened to be interested in selective breeding. Stars included Jack Benny, George Burns, Gracie Allen, and Martha, who played Daisy Schloggenheimer.

Now nationally popular, Martha concentrated on making films that were presented by Adolph Zukor for Paramount. *Waikiki Wedding,* a musical about a press agent in Hawaii who promoted a Pineapple Queen contest, starred an up-and-coming cast of Bing Crosby, Bob Burns, Leif Erickson, Anthony Quinn, and Martha as Myrtle Finch. This movie received a three-star rating when it was released in 1937.

Marriage Number One

At twenty, Martha met twenty-one-year-old Hamilton "Buddy" Westmore, a makeup artist at Paramount Pictures. Born in New Orleans in 1918, Buddy was the youngest of five Westmore brothers, all makeup artists. Some sources claim that Buddy Westmore's given name may have been George Bud Westmore or Wallace Westmore, and that he also may have been a cosmetics manufacturer.

After promising Martha's mother that they would wait two years before marrying, the pair eloped. Their Las Vegas wedding was attended by actress Noreen Carr as maid of honor and Hollywood physician, Dr. Frank Nolan, as best man. Judge Marion B. Earl performed the ceremony on May 30, 1937. It was the first marriage for both. Martha wore a blue chiffon evening dress with a black velvet wrap. Three months after the wedding, Martha's attorney, Vincent Marco, announced that Martha was filing for divorce, charging Buddy with "extreme cruelty."

That same year, Martha and Bob Burns starred in *Mountain Music,* a two-star musical comedy about a hillbilly running from a marriage and losing his memory.

Martha performed a zany routine in *Artists and Models*, a 1937 musical about an advertising executive's search for the right girl to be the marketing symbol for a silverware company. This three-and-a-half-star movie had a great cast, which also included Jack Benny, Ida Lupino, Ben Blue, Hedda Hopper, and Judy Canova.

A musical comedy called *Double or Nothing* centered on a group of beneficiaries who, under a trick will, must double their bequests or lose them. In this 1937 film Martha portrayed Liza Lou Lane. Bing Crosby, Andy Devine, and William Frawley rounded out the cast. Songs such as "It's On, It's Off," "Don't Look Now," and "All You Want To Do Is Dance" helped make this two-star film worth watching.

Career Crossroads

Martha had built a prominent career, but she still had to wait tables to make ends meet. In those days, it was unusual to take more than a week or so to shoot a film. With her varied show business venues, she was not trapped in Hollywood studios' "contract system" and was paid per film. Nonetheless, she volunteered more of her time as a nurse's aide. Martha later said that she wanted to become a registered nurse but did not have the time, money, or education to do so. She was torn between her dreams of becoming a star and her burning desire to become a nurse. How could she possibly integrate these two diverse interests?

In 1990, Dr. Sam Patton of Macon, Georgia told us about his introduction to Martha in the Charity Clinic of Cedars of Lebanon (now Cedars-Sinai) Hospital in 1937. Brothers Sam and Joe had traveled to Los Angeles to visit James, their brother, and Gene Hopp, Sam's former classmate.

> This charming and very affable lady in white greeted us at the hospital. Gene introduced us to Miss Martha Raye. We were so pleased to meet a real movie star!

> James did not believe us when we returned home. He said, "I have been here two years and have never seen a real live movie star, and you meet one in just twenty-four hours!"
>
> Martha was very professional in helping the interns, house officers who were internists, surgeons and others. She assisted in preparing patients for examination and treatments. Here was this busy movie star helping with those less fortunate sick people. What a great girl, movie star, and lover of humanity.

Martha returned to Paramount to make more films presented by Adolph Zukor. *The Big Broadcast of 1938* was a musical comedy about a steamship owner engaged in a transatlantic race while his practical-joking twin brother hampered his efforts. The great W.C. Fields starred in this film as both twins (T. Frothinghill Bellows and S.B. Bellows) and Martha portrayed Martha Bellows. The movie included Dorothy Lamour, Ben Blue, Leif Erickson, and Bob Hope, who made his movie debut in this three-star film.

College Swing was a musical comedy about a feeble-witted girl who must graduate from college so that the school can inherit a fortune. Starring in the movie were George Burns, Gracie Allen, Bob Hope, Edward Everett Horton, Ben Blue, Betty Grable, Jackie Coogan, John Payne, and Martha. Robert Cummings appeared as a radio announcer. Despite this star-studded cast, *College Swing* received only a one-star rating.

Next came *Tropic Holiday*, a Paramount musical about a Hollywood scriptwriter who found romance in Mexico. Martha played Midge Miller; Dorothy Lamour, Bob Burns, and Ray Milland also starred. Bob Burns and Martha staged a memorable bullfight comedy scene in this two-star film.

Martha's last movie of 1938 was *Give Me a Sailor*, a musical comedy about two sisters who became involved in a "beautiful legs" competition. They meet two brothers

(Bob Hope and Jack Whiting) who are in the Navy. Martha played the role of Letty Larkin, and Betty Grable portrayed her sister, Nancy. Betty Grable wasn't the only star with beautiful legs! Martha's great legs were evident in this two-and-a-half-star movie.

Marriage Number Two

During 1938, while filming her musicals and performing on two radio programs, Martha met composer and orchestra leader David Rose. At the time, he was conductor for Tony Martin's radio show. David was born in London in 1910, but had studied music in the United States. He and Betty Jean Bartholomew were married on December 28, 1928; they had two daughters, Melanie and Angela. David worked for NBC from 1938 to 1942. He was handsome, kind, quiet, self-contained—and he fell hopelessly in love with Martha. They were married on October 8, 1938. This was the second marriage for both of them.

Between 1938 and 1939, Martha made many personal appearances. Edward Baron of Houston, Texas remembers that he first met her at the Shubert Theater in Detroit.

> After the show, she introduced herself, extended us a handshake and joined us for lunch. That meeting confirmed my belief that she was a great person. I've met many stars in the theater, stage and movies. I still consider Martha tops.

First Fan Club

Irving Davidson of Brooklyn knew Martha well and formed her first fan club—a sometimes overly-spirited group. He said, "There isn't a nicer person in this world. In 1938 she gave me my nickname 'Schnitz.' She will always be in my heart. I have some nice memories of her."

Martha and Irv's relationship was described in "The Mayor of 44th Street," an article written by Luther Davis and John Cleveland that appeared in the December 14, 1940, issue of *Collier's Magazine*. They stated that Martha gave Irv his trademark nickname when he hung out by the Paramount stage door. "I think I'll call you 'Schnitz,'" Martha said, "that's the way you look. Sort of schnitzy."

Schnitz organized Martha's fans into choral groups who stood across from the theater. They would sing to her whenever she stuck her head out the window. These impromptu glee clubs kept the area police quite busy.

Schnitz and four other fans followed her to the Metropolitan Theater in Boston. Martha bailed them out when they were jailed for vagrancy and then proceeded to register them at the Ritz-Carlton. Five more fans arrived when Schnitz telegraphed, "COME AT ONCE STOP MARTHA NEEDS YOU."

But her patience must have been at the breaking point when Schnitz and his friends climbed on stage at her final show to present her with a handsome token of their regard—their bill charged to her account!

While Martha performed in Providence, Rhode Island, Walter Rochette caught her act.

> My first experience with Martha was in the late thirties. Between my own shows, I skipped over to the other theater to catch her act and as usual she was brilliant. She was a top vaudeville star doing singing and comedy.
>
> She certainly showed the true meaning of "star," just a fantastically funny lady with a voice—and mouth—that wouldn't quit, as well as a perfectly delightful body and a pair of legs that she wrapped around her microphone stand for laughs. I still remember parts of her act and her puns about singing "Mr. Paganini."

Martha acted in two Paramount films in 1939. *Never Say Die* was a comedy about a millionaire hypochondriac (Bob Hope) who is convinced he is dying. Martha and Andy Devine rounded out the cast. Martha sang "The Tra La La and the Oom Pah Pah;" however, the story lacked interest, had too few laughs, and critics gave it only one and a half stars.

Martha's second film in 1939 was *$1000 A Touchdown,* a routine two-star comedy about a college trying to start a football team. Martha, Joe E. Brown, Susan Hayward, and Eric Blore played the main characters.

On the Brunswick label that same year, Martha recorded four songs: "Stairway To The Stars," "Ol' Man River," "If You Can't Sing It, You'll Have To Swing It (Mr. Paganini)," and "Melancholy Mood." David and his orchestra accompanied her. She also performed on a radio program "The Tuesday Night Party."

Between making movies and recording songs, Martha found time to appear on stage. Beginning August 7, 1939, she headlined a show for a week at the Palace Theater in Albany. Appearing with her were the dancing Condos Brothers, the Six Willys jugglers, comedian Jackie Miles, and dancers Martells and Mignon. Years later she would marry "my beloved Nick" Condos, who also became her manager.

A month later, Martha recorded four more songs with David on the Columbia label: "Jeanie With The Light Brown Hair," "Body And Soul," "It Ain't Necessarily So," and "I Walk Alone." In October, they recorded "Once In A While," "Gone With The Wind," "Yesterdays," and "Peter, Peter, Pumpkin Eater."

The 1940 version of *The Farmer's Daughter*, a film comedy about a stagestruck country girl who tried to horn in on a Broadway musical rehearsal, earned a two and a half star rating. Martha starred as Patience Bingham, along with Charlie Ruggles, Richard Denning, William Frawley, and William Demarest. The film had few laughs; unfortunately, Martha's funniest scene had her falling down.

Martha's first film for Universal was *The Boys From Syracuse,* a musical comedy about two sets of twin brothers in ancient Greece, one pair aristocrats and the other slaves, all of whom were separated at birth. Martha played Luce. This three-star movie had some great songs.

Martha costarred with Al Jolson, Eunice Healey, Bert Gordon, Jack Whiting, Jinx Falkenburg and Gil Lamb in the Broadway musical *Hold on to Your Hats,* which opened on September 11, 1940, and continued for one hundred fifty eight performances. One number was "Don't Let it Get You Down." Martha portrayed Mamie both in this production and in a later one at The Shubert Theater in Detroit.

KISS THE BOYS HELLO

Camp Upton, NY—1940: Sergeant Orlando "Lonnie" George and Martha Raye entertaining members of the 198th Coast Artillery (AA) Regiment of Delaware. Photo contributed by Thomas Lodge and the 198th Coast Artillery Association.

During September of 1940, Martha took time off from the stage and visited United States troops. Thomas Lodge of Wilmington, Delaware recalls her visit to Camp Upton on Long Island. There she entertained members of the 198th Coast Artillery of the Delaware National Guard. They had just been federalized.

She brought down the house when she danced to Sergeant Orlando George's accordion accompaniment.

That same year Martha appeared in Miami. Dan Lamb was serving aboard the USCG *Mojave*. He and his lonely shipmates met Martha one afternoon at the Port-of-Call, a small cafe near the harbor where they were docked. Martha treated them to hamburgers, hot dogs, and beer; she even sent food to the guys who were on shipboard duty. The *Mojave* had to depart unexpectedly and the crew missed her show at the Five O'Clock Club. Several months later, when Dan and his shipmates were back in Miami Beach, they ran into her again. He said, "What impressed me most was that she remembered our names and our ship. What a classy person!"

Martha's first film for Warner Brothers was *Navy Blues,* a 1941 musical comedy about Navy personnel getting into trouble in Honolulu. The star-studded movie included Ann Sheridan, Jack Oakie, Martha as Lillibelle, Jack Haley, Jack Carson, and Jackie Gleason. It opened with a comedic song and dance routine by Martha and Ann Sheridan; Martha wore a flowered top with a short hula skirt. They sang "I've Got The Navy Blues." Martha also danced on top of a bar and spun in circles hanging from a ceiling fan.

When Jim Hanig was a sailor in 1941, his platoon was used as background during the filming of *Navy Blues.* Sailor Frederick Mawhinney also was aboard the USS *Curtiss.* He remembers that the ship's entire crew was asked to be part of that movie. He was in many scenes shot on the pier with the ship as backdrop. Frederick says he did not have the chance to see Martha after that, but he was aware of her many visits to Pacific battle areas.

The United Services Organization (USO) was chartered on February 7, 1941. It was—and still is—providing welfare, social and spiritual services, as well as recreation and entertainment for members of the American Armed Forces. The USO brought live shows to overseas military commands and to Veterans Administration hospitals in the United States.

A Divorce and Marriage Number Three

Martha divorced David Rose on May 19, 1941, after only thirty-one months of marriage. Soon after their divorce, David married Judy Garland; their marriage lasted from 1941 to 1943. Less than five weeks after Martha's divorce from David, she surprised everyone when she married hotel manager Neal Lang on June 25, 1941. He was a former captain in the United States Army.

In 1941 Universal lured Martha back for three more films. *Keep 'Em Flying* was a two-star comedy musical about two Army Air Corps incompetents becoming involved with identical twin girls. It starred Bud Abbott, Lou Costello, and Martha, who portrayed both twins, Barbara and Gloria Phelps.

When *Keep 'Em Flying* was completed at Cal-Aero Academy in Ontario, California, Martha, Bud, and Lou attended the Academy's graduation ceremony. Lieutenant Colonel William Hutchinson was there for his brother's graduation.

> My brother had organized the band at Cal-Aero and had been named "Outstanding Cadet." As such, he was in the picture being taken of all the stars for posterity's sake. It is etched in my memory because he stood between Martha and Lou Costello. Lou was determined to make him laugh. At the same time, my brother

was determined not to lose his decorum. It was a most amusing incident.

Hellzapoppin, also released in 1941, was Martha's third Universal film. This well-known comedy was about two inept comics trying to make a movie. Martha starred as Betty Johnson, with Ole Olsen and Chic Johnson. It was filled with laughs and music; many people believe this three-star movie was Martha's best film.

Later that year Martha appeared in the stage revue *Hold on to Your Hats* at Loew's State in New York City.

By Martha's twenty-fifth birthday, she had already made a name for herself on stage and radio, in night clubs, and films. Between 1934 and 1941, she had acted in nineteen movies and recorded fourteen songs. And she was already on her third marriage.

With such a diverse and promising career, what more could she do that would be rewarding, but not anti-climatic?

Chapter 2

On the Road in World War II

"Some of them were busted up pretty bad. Anyway, when Martha came into that ward with her words 'Hi Ya Fellows,' it was like someone turned on a bright light."

Arthur Horne
(North Platte, Nebraska)

MARTHA RAYE IS NOW A CAPTAIN IN U.S. ARMY

Martha Raye of stage, screen and radio fame, and now a full-fledged captain in the Army Air Corps, Special Services Department, U.S. Army, paid a surprise visit to Colonel Johnson's base and gave an impromptu performance that will long be remembered by soldiers here.

Captain Raye, returning from an overseas mission where, with Marlene Dietrich, Mitzi Mayfair, and Carole Landis, she spent several months entertaining soldiers, won over her air base audience and had them in continuous guffaws doing her brief but entertaining program. Later she visited the Service Club and spent more than an hour visiting with the soldiers.

One of the first celebrities to begin entertaining in service camps, Captain Raye had the soldiers at a momentary disadvantage when they learned of her commission. The soldiers didn't know how to address her. But, with deft tactfulness she put them at ease by becoming one of them.

Captain Raye, who said she came up through the ranks the "hard way," first a private first class, then lieutenant, then captain, arrived dressed in her captain's uniform but for her personal appearance she changed to a summery street frock, looking more glamorous than the best of a Hurrel portrait. Her impersonation of Lana Turner dancing with a sailor at the Hollywood Stage Door Canteen, and Miss Turner's answer to the gob's query about her v-neckline started the short show off with a bang.

Her singing of "Blues in the Night," unaccompanied, brought down the house, and was a thing of sheer beauty, even for the most creditably musically minded.

Captain Raye's appearance was brief, but it will long be remembered by everyone at this base. Before leaving she said she hoped to return to the Caribbean area sometime in the near future.

Clipping by Harry N. Scott

-2-

Although many nations were involved when it started in 1939, the United States did not officially enter World War II until the day after Japan bombed Pearl Harbor on December 7, 1941. The United States soon had troops in Europe, England, Africa, and throughout the Pacific Ocean allied with other nations to retaliate against Japan and Germany.

By this time Martha Raye was an accomplished—and famous—singer, actress, dancer, and comedienne. She had learned to speak French, Yiddish, Greek, Italian, and Spanish. She also felt an overwhelming urge to do something special.

Martha visited troops at Pearl Harbor shortly after the bombing. Donna Reed of Selkirk, New York tells of her father-in-law's recollections.

> He met Martha while he was stationed at Pearl Harbor. She had gone there to entertain the troops to try to help them get their minds off what had happened. During her performance Martha went over to my father-in-law, sat down on his lap, and planted a great big kiss on him.
>
> He never forgot that day. He always told his children—and now his grandchildren—about his encounter with Martha. Even now, though he has Alzheimers, he vividly recalls that day in Hawaii.

Martha also visited troops stateside. She went to Nebraska to see the troops before they were sent overseas. Thomas Hoke, a Springfield, Missouri resident, was one of the first two hundred troops to be stationed at Grand Island Army Air Base in Nebraska during January 1942. "We were entertained by Martha in the mess hall. It is very heartwarming to know that she continued entertaining small groups in isolated places throughout her career."

In the British Isles

Arthur Horne of North Platte, Nebraska was seventy-seven years old when he first contacted us. He was a member of Company C, 133rd Infantry, 34th Red Bull Division out of Cedar Rapids, Iowa. Arthur broke his back shortly after arriving in the European Theatre in Belfast, Ireland in January, 1942. Martha came to visit while he was a patient in the Fifth General Hospital in Belfast. In his ward were several young British aviators and Canadians who had been wounded in action. "Some of them were busted up pretty bad. Anyway, when Martha came into that ward with her words 'Hi Ya Fellows,' it was like someone turned on a bright light."

Interviewed at age seventy-three, retired Lieutenant Colonel Jack Orton, formerly of Alexandria, Virginia, remembered Martha's visit to England in early 1942. He was with Headquarters, VIII Bomber Command. Martha and a small USO troop performed on a makeshift stage. They were in a Nissen hut on the grounds of a girls' school in High Wycombe. Jack said, "It became the Roxy for us that night. I'll never forget the joy she brought to a bunch of lonely guys."

Stateside

On March 20, 1942, in New York City, Martha joined ex-husband David Rose and his orchestra to record the songs "Pig Foot Pete" from the film *Keep 'Em Flying,* along with "My Little Cousin," "Three Little Sisters," and "Oh! The Pity of it All" for Decca Records.

Martha made her way to Louisiana and Florida. Major Rudy Bittman, a retired Marine, recalled attending an induction ceremony of Naval Cadets at the New Orleans City Park Stadium around June 1942. Martha was on the reviewing stand where she congratulated the cadets and gave each one a kiss. Rudy saw her again in October at the Pensacola Naval Air Station Officers Club. She was dancing with someone else when he cut in.

John Kappas saw Martha when a USO troupe appeared on Oahu, Hawaii. He remembers troops already calling her "The Big Mouth." The last time he saw her was when he was stationed on a Polynesian island. Her plane had to refuel, and she put on a small show for the troops there.

Stuart Bibb of Keswick, Virginia was in the Bermuda Islands in late 1942 when he met Martha and Dinah Shore.

> I was to fly back to Fort Benning on transfer. We loaded on a PanAm in the middle of the night in a driving rain on Hamilton Island. After a struggle to get airborne, the plane settled down. So did we, almost.
>
> The soldier sitting next to me had no buttons on his GI blouse. Martha and Dinah Shore were sitting behind us; they offered to sew on the buttons but I had just about completed the job. Dinah noticed that my buddy was unstable. She handed me a pint of Canadian Club to give him. Martha took me to the rear of the plane to meet the other members of the USO show. Again, a never-to-be-forgotten experience.
>
> Bob Hope once said, "When Martha would smile, she would disappear completely." She was one of our greatest assets ever, smiling or not.

The Pentagon turned to Hollywood for entertainment for our troops. Martha readily volunteered for the USO. Many other Hollywood personalities also responded. Entertainers who helped at the Hollywood Canteen included Dorothy Lamour, Ann Southern, Donna Reed, Joan Bennett, Eleanor Powell, Loretta Young, Claudette Colbert, Betty Grable, Joan Crawford, Rita Hayworth, Jane Russell, Marlene Dietrich, and

Lauren Bacall—just to name a few. Al Jolson, Merle Oberon, George Murphy, Margaret Whiting, Joey Bishop, Bing Crosby, Bob Hope, Danny Kaye, and Dinah Shore also went to the war zones.

England—1942: Martha checks her schedule with unidentified soldier. Photo contributed by Special Forces Association.

On one tour, Martha joined Kay Francis, Carole Landis, and Mitzi Mayfair as they left California for England. Their appearance schedule was kept secret until they arrived at their destination. They left the U.S. on October 25, 1942, expecting to head directly to England. However, they flew south on a Clipper plane to Bermuda, where they entertained troops on Darrell's Island. They continued on to Hamilton Island, where they performed at the Pan-American Club of Cedars Lodge and the USO Club at The Flatts, and then to Castle Harbour, St. David's Island, and Cooper's Island at Turtle Hill.

From Bermuda, the women flew to the Azores, where they appeared at the Pan-American Club in Horta and then on to the Hotel Aviz in Lisbon, Portugal. Their tour continued northward. They performed in Foynes, Limerick, and Shannon. Finally they flew to England where they performed in Bristol, then in London at the Savoy, at Pastories in Victoria, and at The Four Hundred Club. On some occasions they were hosted at a sumptuous country manor.

England—1942: L-R: Martha Raye, unidentified soldier, Kay Francis, and Mitzi Mayfair. Photo contributed by Special Forces Association.

Around Britain

Their grueling schedule included anywhere from one to five shows per camp, at one to three different camps—the same day! They were honored to give a Command Performance at Windsor Castle for Queen Elizabeth, Princess Elizabeth, and Princess Margaret. Later they performed on British Broadcasting Company (BBC) Radio.

When Carole was hospitalized with an appendicitis attack, Martha, Kay, and Mitzi went on to Scotland to visit the troops. W.L. Moore's unit was located in Glasgow when a USO Show arrived. He was leaving his room when Martha and her group came out of the Company Commander's office. She saw him about twenty feet away, gave him one of her beautiful smiles and waved.

The weather in England was often cold, damp, and rainy. Wherever performers went they were required to wear military helmets and carry raincoats, galoshes, and gas masks. Mitzi was hospitalized with pneumonia. Meanwhile Martha, Carole and Kay returned to Ireland by ship. They performed at the Grand Central Hotel in Belfast and then went to Northern Ireland. They returned to England in a B-24 Liberator bomber.

Jack Dymek of Ocala, Florida said the foursome was at his base in Chesveton, England in November 1942 while he was with the Eighth Air Force. He went on stage as a "straight man" in their routine. The band started playing. The audience stood and began singing with gusto, especially members of the Royal Air Force. Recognizing the tune, Jack started singing as loudly as he could. After a couple of bars, Martha, who stood next to him, started tugging at his hand. She gave him a terrible frown. He suddenly realized that everyone else was singing "God Save the King" while he was singing "My Country 'Tis of Thee."

Cora Jacobson saw Kay, Mitzi, Carole, and Martha in her hometown of Rushden in Northamptonshire in 1942. They were the only stars who visited Rushden that year. Cora attended their performance with Special Service Officer, Captain Wells. Former Army Nurse Corps First Lieutenant Ruth Long of Kenmore, New York was assigned to a station hospital in Winchester in early 1943 when the foursome entertained its patients. Both Cora and Ruth commented that England was under heavy bombardment at the time.

On to North Africa

After New Year's Day 1943, the troupe was told they were going to Africa. On January 8, 1943, all four women boarded a B-17 Flying Fortress bomber and refueled in Gibraltar where they visited with entertainer Beatrice Lillie.

They proceeded first to Algiers and played nightly at the American Red Cross Club, where the performers experienced an air raid. The women were determined to be where the action was; they even persuaded General Eisenhower to let them go closer to the front lines. General Doolittle provided them with transportation. Accompanied by Spitfires, they flew on transports from one airfield to another; then they traveled across the desert in jeeps or on camels. They went to Oran in Algeria, Casablanca in Morocco, and to other military places throughout the Sahel (Sahara Desert) region. At one desert camp the women met photographer Margaret Bourke-White, who took their pictures with some troops.

Daytime was hot but evenings were cold, especially in the desert. The performers were asked to help at some of the hospitals. All pitched in—cleaning instruments, scrubbing floors, or helping shorthanded doctors and nurses. Martha felt right at home and put her nurse's aide skills to work. Years later, she commented that the other "gals" did not especially like the hospital work.

Biskra, North Africa was another stop for Martha, Kay, Carole and Mitzi. They visited a P-38 air base there. Jack Ilfrey of New Braunfels, Texas was serving with the Ninety-fourth Fighter Squadron, First Fighter Group, Twelfth Air Force. He recalled Martha's rendition of the song "Queenie—the Cutie of the Burlesque Show."

Biskra, North Africa—1942: Martha signs an autograph on Major Glen Hubbard's back while he shakes hands with Carole Landis. Photo contributed by Fred Wise.

Scripps-Howard roving correspondent, Ernie Pyle, spent six months in North Africa. In his book, *Here is Your War,* he wrote of his encounter with Martha.

> Four good soldiers, who had already done more than their share in the war, unexpectedly turned up over here. They were Kay Francis, Martha Raye, Mitzi Mayfair, and Carole Landis.
>
> Some people may have taken lightly the contributions of Hollywood folks to the war effort, but I didn't. Those gals worked themselves to a frazzle. They traveled dangerously. They lived and worked under mighty unpleasant conditions. They didn't get a dime. They were losing a lot and they had nothing to gain—nothing material, that is. But surely they went home with a warm inner satisfaction, knowing that they had performed far beyond the ordinary call of duty.
>
> The quartet of stars had been away from America since October of 1942. They had flown the Atlantic by clipper, toured the camps in Northern Ireland and England and, despite the gloomy predictions to the contrary, had come to Africa by Flying Fortress. They had heard bombs fall, and they knew about army stew. They averaged four hours sleep a night. Each of them had had a bout with the flu. They had done all their own washing, because there was no other way to get it done. Yet if they had chosen they could all have been in California lying on the sand.
>
> When they went out to one of our far desert airdromes they put on their performance on the flat bed of a big wrecking truck out in the mid-afternoon sun, surrounded by soldiers sitting on the ground. They spoke the first English from a woman's mouth these soldiers had heard in months. To say they were appreciated is putting it mildly.
>
> Martha Raye was really the star of the troupe. The soldiers went for her crazy brand of slapstick. She wound up the program in practically a riot. When it was all over the four girls came out and sang the French, British and American national anthems. [1]

Roy Rogers, Jr. served with the Seventeenth Bomber Group in North Africa. He remembers Martha fondly.

> We had just returned from a devastating raid on the harbor at Tunis and already all the guys were assembling for our first USO show. Kay Francis was the emcee, along with Carole Landis, Mitzi Mayfair, and the irrepressible Martha Raye.
>
> She brought the house down with her mirth and songs. Our spirits, which had been at an extremely low ebb, were catapulted into the sky that afternoon. I fell in love with Martha Raye that day, and I have been carrying on that admiration ever since.
>
> Her "Mr. Paganini" should be put into a Hall of Fame somewhere. I can still see her on the back of a semi-flat bed doing her routine.

Trouper With the Troops

Five months had passed since the four women left the United States. Although they were not eager to return home, changes had to be made. Kay had torn ligaments in her ankle and Mitzi had badly infected teeth, so they both headed back to the States. Carole wanted to be with her new husband, Captain Tom Wallace, so she returned to England where he was stationed.

Martha went on alone, first to Casablanca, then Biskra, Marrakech—anywhere she could get transportation. Eddie Bigham of Rosemont, Pennsylvania, who had been in Algiers in January when the foursome entertained his group, played piano for her. A photograph of Eddie and Martha appeared in the March 1943 issue of *Life* magazine. Lieutenant Colonel Frank Walsh of Jackson, Mississippi appreciated Martha and Eddie stopping to entertain the troops in their primitive living conditions at a B-26 medium bomber air base in North Africa.

As a member of the Sixty-eighth Observation Group, U.S. Army Air Corps, Lieutenant Colonel Leon Brooks of Biloxi remembered Martha showing up at Oujda Air Base, French Morocco. Their intelligence had advised them that they were under an air raid alert. Martha insisted that if the airmen had to stay there, she would remain with them. And she did! He also remembered that before she left his unit, she posed in the nose section of an A-20 aircraft. With a big grin on her face, she sat spread-eagled showing off her "long johns."

Benny Powell recalls Martha's visit to the 154th Observation Squadron, U.S. Army Air Corps, at Oujda Air Base in February 1943. Instead of performing she spent most of the day visiting and listening to what troops had to say.

In March, Martha stopped by the hospital in Accra (Gold Coast). She played black jack with some of the patients. One of those lucky guys was Master Sergeant James Winstead of Austin, Texas.

Andrew Johnston of Portsmouth, Virginia was on the USS *Arkansas* in the harbor near Casablanca when Martha came aboard. She gave a performance on top of their twelve-inch gun turrets. Andrew said that other entertainers were supposed to come with her but opted not to because of nearby invasion fighting.

Chief Warrant Officer 4 Hyatt Moser of El Paso believes that Martha was the first celebrity to entertain his unit. He was a member of the 286th Joint Assault Signal Company of the First Engineer Special Brigade at Arzew, Algeria.

Former Lieutenant Charles Moyer of Montour Falls, New York says that Martha came alone to his unit near Oran in North Africa when he was serving with the Second Armored Division in 1943. She put on a solo show with no music or backup. She joked, sang, and danced her way into the hearts of all those men. Charles believes she was the only woman to fly from England to this part of Africa to give the boys a treat that year. Emory Jeffares also served with the Second Armored

Division in North Africa. Martha entertained his group in the Cork Forest. "I never forgot her and what a wonderful entertainer she was, even better than Bob Hope."

Cork Forest, North Africa—1942: Martha stands in chow line with members of the Second Armored Division. Photo contributed by Ceilia Stratton, curator, Second Armored Division Museum, Fort Hood, Texas.

Robert Ruvere of Brick, New Jersey was in Aim Taya, North Africa on guard duty. "I was thrilled to see her walking towards me. She asked me how I was doing. I requested her autograph on a *Readers Digest*. After she left, an officer came to my post and what a chewing out I received! Plus, he took the *Readers Digest* with her signature."

Colonel Adolph Tokaz of Columbia, South Carolina served with the 340th Bomb Group flying B-25 bombers. He saw Martha in Accra, Gold Coast. "Meeting Martha Raye was an unforgettable experience. She was there to entertain the boys, and she put on a good show in her inimitable way. I also got her to sign my short snorter bill."

Edna Martin of Riverside, California recalled that her husband had a soft spot in his heart for Martha because she went on to entertain the troops by herself when the others in her group became ill. Leonard Martin served with the 304th Maintenance Squadron Mobile Unit near Marrakech.

Marrakech, North Africa—1942:Martha with members of the 304th Maintenance Squadron. Next page: Martha with four officers of the 304th Maintenance Squadron. Photos contributed by Edna and Leonard Martin.

The hospital ship *Arcadia* picked up patients all along the North African coast. Muriel Westover formerly of Auburn, New York was on board and said, "Many times Martha Raye with Bob Hope and others made our lives much happier. She was a great trouper."

Many people saw Martha throughout the European Theater of Operations. Lucille Ball joined Martha in France for a time. Joseph Croce of Massapequa, New York was a member of the 505th Medical Detachment, Eighty-second Airborne. He remembered getting up on stage and dancing the Lindy hop with them. When the dance was over, they both kissed him on the cheek. Another airborne soldier recalled going to Luxembourg to pick up the piano Martha had left there. He delivered it to his mess hall in Chalons, France where Martha entertained his unit. Commander Lorraine Friedman of Kentwood, Louisiana served with the Navy during World War II and recalls that Martha was out there cheering and supporting sailors, as well. Her tour was cut short when Martha was stricken with yellow fever and anemia, forcing her to return to the States.

Career Crossroads Clarify

About this time, Martha Raye realized that being with our troops had become—and would remain—one of her life's highest priorities. She expected no reward for her efforts to entertain the troops. She gave it all she had. But, she gave even more when asked to help in field hospitals. She progressed from cleaning to nurse's aide duties, to being pressed into service as an assisting surgical nurse on combat front lines. With a bit of medical knowledge and experience and with a movie career dangling within her reach, Martha Raye decided to go right down the middle—she would mix her entertainment career with performing for our troops. This would prove to be a heart-wrenching decision.

Once her health improved, Martha picked up her career where it had left off. She appeared at the RKO Theater in Boston in early 1943. Command Sergeant Major William Ryan of Melbourne, Florida met her there when he was working as an usher. She was singing with the Charlie Barnett Band. After the last show, Bill was assigned to help her with her baggage as she headed to South Station for the train ride to New York. In the middle of the concourse, she stopped to buy some vodka. As Bill handed the filled shopping bag to Martha, she said, "I can't take these train rides without a little something to relax me."

Don Stonebraker of Huntington Beach encountered Martha in Hollywood around April 1943. He was assigned to Marine Corps Air Station in El Toro and was looking for a ride back to the base.

> As I passed Costello's Band Box, people were coming out in droves. I asked someone where I could catch a streetcar downtown. A gentleman, whom I recognized as Lou Costello, approached me. He asked if I had a problem. I said I needed to get downtown to catch the Red Car (an electric car system discontinued long ago)

to Santa Ana. He said, "Wait here." Mr. Costello returned and led me over to a lady he said would take me downtown. I recognized Martha Raye and I followed her to a large black sedan, where a gentleman was waiting.

Miss Raye had been to North Africa in 1942 and was in several combat areas. I told her about my time at Guadalcanal. We could sympathize with one another on how it felt to be shot at and bombed. In no time we were at the terminal in downtown Los Angeles. I bid her good night and a very appreciative thank you for her kindness.

A Divorce...and Marriage Number Four

On January 3, 1944, Martha went to Juarez, Mexico where she filed for divorce from Neal Lang. Her extended trips had troubled their marriage. The divorce was granted on February 3, 1944.

A month later Martha again stunned the entertainment world when she married dancer Nick Condos. Nick toured frequently with the dancing Condos Brothers and had known Martha for several years. Nick's home was in Miami Beach, where he and Martha often appeared on stage together.

Nick became her personal manager for the rest of his life. Martha went back and forth between agents. Sometimes she was with the William Morris Agency and other times she used the Ruth Webb Agency.

In 1944 Martha joined Kay Francis, Carole Landis, and Mitzi Mayfair at the Twentieth-Century Fox studios. They made the musical *Four Jills in a Jeep,* based on their adventures in England and Africa; the script followed a book of the same name written by Carole Landis. The movie starred Jimmy Dorsey and his Band, Phil Silvers, John Harvey, and Dick Haymes in his screen debut. Appearing as themselves were Alice Faye, Betty Grable, Carmen Miranda, and George Jessel. Martha sang her famous rendition of "If You Can't Sing

It, You'll Have To Swing It (Mr. Paganini)." Mitzi danced to "How Blue the Night" sung by Dick Haymes. Carole sang "Crazy Me." Kay performed the role of announcer, mediated arguments, and kept everyone on schedule.

Certain lines in the movie portrayed exactly how Martha felt. In the film she said, "I hate to hear them sign off. I wish I could be there with all those boys. If I were a man like Joe E. Brown or Al Jolson, well, I'd be over there right now tramping in the mud with them up at the front."

Martha also appeared in Twentieth-Century Fox's film *Pin-Up Girl,* based on a story by Libbie Block. This two-star musical comedy depicted a Washington secretary who became a national celebrity when she became involved with a Navy hero. It starred Betty Grable, John Harvey, Martha as Molly McKay, Joe E. Brown, and the dancing Condos Brothers. Martha sang a snappy rendition of "When The Red Red Robin."

Motherhood with Melodye!

Melodye Raye Condos was born on July 26, 1944. She was named after Martha's sister. Although Martha loved entertaining the public and the troops, she hated leaving Nick and Melodye. This created an occasionally stormy relationship among the three of them. Some of our correspondents believe that Martha also had a son who was killed in Vietnam. This became a hot topic for speculation, especially when the film *For the Boys* was released. The truth is that her only child is Melodye.

That same year Martha found time to perform at the Palace Theater in Albany. Ruth Endlar Cyphers recalls that her younger sister was a patient in Memorial Hospital, which was directly across the street from the Palace Theater. Ruth could see Martha in her dressing room. She sent a note to Martha asking if she could possibly visit her sister, who was dying of cancer. Martha did visit Ruth's sister and even gave her a beautiful bed jacket. Ruth said that Martha was "absolutely wonderful—so friendly and gracious."

Martha continued entertaining and visiting American military personnel wherever they happened to be. Between 1944 and 1945, Martha returned to Bermuda where Walter Rochette now was serving as the Army Special Services Officer for the Bermuda Base Command. He was ordered to take good care of Martha for the ten days she was on the islands.

> On a cold blustery night, I delivered Martha into the hands of the officers at the U.S. Submarine base officers' club at St. George's Harbour and I stood close by. As an Army officer, I was about as welcome there as the flu in a conjugal bedroom. The off-duty submarine officers were really enjoying their bar on this miserable night and in the fun, Martha was asked if she'd like to board a submarine and see how they lived at sea. Being a good sport, she said, "Yes!"
>
> She blithely ran through the downpour as every one of the officers tried to cover her up with his personal raincoat. She got safely through to the deck of one of our subs tied up at the dock. Martha was wearing a dress. Every gob on duty who got the word headed straight for the hatch that led down from the conning tower into the control room.
>
> I'll bet there are still strained necks in the ranks of retired submariners from that episode! Martha knew full well what she was doing to them, and she got as much of a charge out of it as they did. They'd nearly forgotten what panties looked like!
>
> I got her out of there as soon as I politely could, before that crowd of women-starved undersea Ensigns finished deciding they'd like to "dump the Army" and take her back to the hotel themselves. Fortunately, I outflanked them, spirited her out of there, and got her safely to where she was staying.
>
> Martha enjoyed the whole experience, and we laughed about it at breakfast the next morning.

PTO Pal

Next, the USO sent Martha to entertain troops in the Pacific Theater of Operations. Lieutenant Commander Archibald Seabrook of Beaufort, North Carolina saw her several times in the South Pacific.

LeRoy Hackett saw Martha while he was on Saipan. Conditions were miserable, which endeared her to those GI's all the more. By doing her "thing" in such a setting, she was affirming somehow their own daily performance under similar conditions.

> I have a vivid recollection of her performing in the rain. It was pelting her, causing her clothes to cling to her body, but she kept going.
>
> She was just wonderful and an inspiration to us lonely GI's so many miles from home. We all stood and gave her a thundering applause. She was a lovely person demonstrating her love for our country and the GI's.

Former sailor Donald Blair of Simi Valley credits Martha with helping him keep his sanity while he was a Prisoner of War.

> I met Martha Raye after a USO show in the forties when I was a young sailor. She came down front and personally talked to us. She singled me out, probably because I was a very shy seventeen-year-old. While looking me straight in the eye, she placed her hands on my shoulders. She told me that I was doing a great job. No one had ever told me that before. It made a big difference; it boosted my ego and gave me tremendous confidence.
>
> I went on to distinguish myself on the submarine chaser PC-803 and eventually wound up in North China as the *last* prisoner of war in WW II. Her words "you're doing a great job" kept me from cracking through all the torture, starvation and beatings I endured as a POW. God bless Colonel Maggie!

Touring the Trainees

Victor McClurg fondly remembers having coffee with Martha at the Hollywood Canteen while she was entertaining stateside troops.

Robert Setchfield formerly of Schuylerville, New York saw Martha during the fall of 1942 when he was in Missouri. She was hanging out a window!

> I was wearing my Reserve Officer Training Corps uniform. As I walked down main street of Rolla to the Rolla Hotel, the only hotel in this town of 20,000, I noticed several people with their heads turned upward. They were looking at two individuals leaning out of a third floor window of the hotel.
>
> One was waving frantically and hollering "Hello." It was Martha Raye. Her extensive grin and ample bosom were in evidence as she hung out the window, her body sort of jumping up and down.
>
> "Martha Raye's here to entertain the troops," someone said. The troops were the thousands of recruits pouring into the newly built Fort Leonard Wood, located about forty miles west in the heart of virgin Ozark country.
>
> It is my opinion that Martha was lending her talent to entertaining the troops far in advance of the USO and Special Services Organizations. Martha was a front runner. Seeing the need to bring a few laughs to the boys, she was there on her own, doing what she could.

Captain George Villielm from Ulster Park, New York served with the Army. In the spring of 1943, his unit (Company L, 136th Infantry, Thirty-third Division) moved from the relative comforts of Fort Lewis, Washington to the Mojave Desert, where they trained for desert warfare. Martha was touring the area. She was escorted to the top of a tank, into the turret, and back out. Judging from the look on her face when she came out, George surmised she did not enjoy the confinement.

Joe Rybak of Haines City, Florida saw Martha while he was stationed in Arizona. He remembers her saying, "The colonel asked me if I would like to mess with the officers. I told him Yes! Then all we did was eat." Her sense of humor really hit the spot with GI's.

Gerald Rucker of Lebanon, Oregon said that Martha entertained his unit while he was at Mitchell Field in New York. After the show, she visited individually with both officers and enlisted men.

Jean Hayes of Seattle met Maggie during World War II. "She came to the base where I was serving—The U.S. Coast Guard Barracks and Recruiting Station in San Francisco. I was in the Coast Guard SPARS. The mess hall was packed, standing room only. Maggie sang 'Accentuate the Positive' and brought the house down. You had to know the song to understand its impact. Everyone loved her."

Mildred Janisch of St. Louis wrote us about her husband Joe's encounter with Martha in Hollywood in 1943. He was staying in a Los Angeles hotel for two months while attending school after being stationed at Muroc Air Base (now Edwards).

> Sunday was their only day off, so Joe and two other GI's went to a lounge to relax. They were unaware that Martha and her manager were there. Herb was standing in line to make a phone call and Martha's manager was behind him. He asked Herb if he could go ahead of him. Herb said, "Sure."
>
> Captain Martha had just returned from Africa and had been interviewed by NBC Radio across the street. She wanted to find out from her mother if she sounded nervous. When her manager finished the call, he invited Herb to come to meet Martha. Herb said he had two friends at the bar. The manager said to bring Joe and Charles, too.
>
> They had several drinks together, and then they were invited to come with them to Costello's Bar (of Abbott and Costello). There was a long line of people waiting to get in. The guys were impressed that Martha

could enter ahead of the crowd and bring three GI's with her. They wanted to buy drinks but Martha refused. Instead, she said she was having a party at her house the next Sunday and invited them to come, which they did. Two weeks later they were shipped out to Europe.

Looking over Joe's pictures this evening brought back such good memories of Martha and her genuine hospitality and love for servicemen. While this was not as dramatic as some of her efforts in the war zone, it certainly made these three GI's happy.

L-R: Maggie, Joe Janisch, Maggie's Secretary outside Costello's Bar. Below: Herb Cohen. Contributed by Mildred and Joe Janisch, St. Louis.

Mildred refers to Martha as "Captain Martha." When entertainers joined the Special Services Department or the USO, they were issued service numbers, identification cards, and dog tags to provide proper identification and to assist recovery personnel should they be lost, injured, or killed—like any other service member. The entertainers were usually given honorary ranks or titles. The clipping by Corporal Harry N. Scott was one of many that made it appear Martha was in the regular Army. It hung on Martha's "Team House" wall. (Portions are printed on page 18)

Chapter 3

Career, Korea...and Back

"This woman went from bunk to bunk and spoke to each of the wounded, caressing them, holding their heads and talking to each in turn to soothe their fears and distract them from their pain. She seemed to know that someone badly wounded needs to be touched....One of the two corpsmen remarked to me that he never saw anything like it. That woman was Martha Raye."

Lieutenant Colonel Frances Liberty
(East Greenbush, New York)

During the Berlin Airlift—1948

Grafenwohr, Germany—1948: Martha entertaining troops during the Berlin Airlift. Photo contributed by Mario Leslie Orsetti.

-3-

When World War II ended, Martha's involvement with our service personnel did not stop. An ex-Prisoner of War, Robert Reppa of Alexandria, Virginia saw Martha at the Roosevelt Hotel in New York City on January 14, 1946. She was the guest of honor at a POW reunion. Robert observed that she left a warm spot in many more hearts than his. However, in Hollywood it was a different story.

Blacklisted by the Hollywood Herd

In 1947, Charlie Chaplin asked Martha to play Annabella in his movie *Monsieur Verdoux,* which he produced and directed. This comic crime drama was about a bank cashier who married and murdered rich women to support his real wife. The film starred Charlie Chaplin, Martha, and others.

This was Martha's first real dramatic role although, frankly, I found her performance amusing. This mediocre movie was released by United Artists. Unfortunately, Martha's association with Chaplin, who was under suspicion for his alleged communist affiliations, got her unofficially blacklisted for some time in the film industry. In fact, she did not make another film until 1962—fifteen years later. Martha was distressed by this blacklisting, but she got on with her life and career. She returned to the stage and continued to spend more time with the troops wherever they were. She certainly wasn't on *their* blacklist!

Vice Admiral Thomas Weschler of Portsmouth, Rhode Island remembers how Martha played a very important and happy role in his life at a crucial time; both he and his wife hold her in the highest regard.

> I was aboard the cruiser USS *Macon*, which docked in Baltimore for Navy Day, October 1947. Over that weekend our first child was to be born. I was "blue" about being away, but I bumped into Martha at a club where she was performing. Between numbers she talked to me for nearly half an hour and really boosted my morale! Our lovely baby daughter was born that night, and we have always thought of Martha Raye as a special godmother to her.

On March 29, 1948, Martha made her variety show debut at London's Palladium.

Berlin Airlift

In June of that year, Soviet troops blockaded food and supplies from getting into Berlin. Western allies began the Berlin Airlift. Shortly thereafter Martha made an appearance for our troops in Germany. Gil Young of Brookline, Massachusetts and Leslie Orsetti of Round Lake, Illinois both saw Martha when she performed in Grafenwohr. Leslie sent photos of her.

Grafenwohr, Germany —1948: Martha rests before a show during the Berlin Airlift. Photo contributed by Mario Leslie Orsetti.

Colonel Jack Emerson, formerly of Battle Creek, Michigan recalls that Martha also appeared in Wiesbaden while the Berlin Airlift was in progress.

> After presenting her scheduled show, she insisted on going to Base Operations where she spent over an hour

giving the on-duty people an impromptu show. I was lucky enough to enjoy her full performance. Her manager kept trying to get her to move on, but she insisted on telling jokes and stayed there for over an hour.

It was quite evident she came there to entertain. And entertain she did!

Throughout the late forties Martha was performing on both coasts of the United States. Ed McDonald of San Francisco met Martha at the Circus Room of New York's Hotel Capitol; it was a reunion for both of them. They talked about their Montana heritage; Ed was raised in Great Falls. He recalled that around 1939 Martha was in Great Falls to visit her sister, Melodye. Ed stopped by her family's house and got her autograph. A teenager, he was thrilled to meet a movie star. Martha's film *Big Broadcast of 1938* was released at their local theater. He remembers her as a "truly lovely person."

The Naval Air Station at Los Alamitos was where Lieutenant Donald Bost formerly of Suffolk, Virginia met Martha.

"The Bob Hope Radio Show" was scheduled to appear on stage at the base. I was assigned to assist the lighting and sound people. The day before the show, I sat with the professionals midway in the seating area to check the sound and lighting. Martha was sitting in the row in front of me.

The Officers Club sent over a large buffet and set it up on the stage. The Officer-in-Charge announced that all the "show people" were to come up on the stage and partake of the food.

Martha knew that the enlisted men did not have time to go to their mess hall. She immediately stood up and said, "I will not eat a bite of this food unless all of the enlisted men can eat too!" They were then invited.

I was never able to thank her personally for that warm thoughtful gesture. I have never forgotten her kindness.

Talents Transfer to Television

It is said that Martha Raye and Lucille Ball were among the few stars who successfully transferred their comedic talents from radio and films into television. Television was just becoming popular, and Martha had the opportunity to be on several shows. Viewers could now see a face to go with the voice they had heard over the radio. Martha often joined Milton Berle on "The Texaco Star Theater" between September 1948 and June 1953. Berle's show became something of a national ritual each Tuesday night it was broadcast.

While stateside, Martha also became a frequent guest on NBC's "The Colgate Comedy Hour." This hour-long TV program was on the air for five years from September 1950 until December 1955.

"Anything Goes," a sixty-minute musical special on NBC, aired in October 1950. Based on a Broadway musical, it was about a nightclub singer who helped a man romance an English heiress forced to marry someone she did not love. Martha portrayed Reno Sweeney. Four years later, Ethel Merman and Frank Sinatra starred in an NBC remake of the same show.

Martha was one of numerous guest hosts of NBC's "The All-Star Revue," which ran from October 1950 until April 1953. This weekly variety show rotated Martha's program with those of Victor Borge, George Jessel, the Ritz Brothers, Danny Thomas, Jimmy Durante, Ezio Pinza, Jack Carson, Jane Froman, Tallulah Bankhead, Phil Foster, Spike Jones, Bob Hope, Paul Winchell, Olsen and Johnson, and Ed Wynn.

From 1949 to 1953 Martha owned the Five O'Clock Club in Miami Beach. She frequently performed there with her husband, Nick Condos. Jim Coppeler remembers his good fortune to catch "The Big Mouth" when she also appeared at The Big Red Barn in Miami.

By the time Martha was thirty-two, she owned a cottage in Nassau, a house in Kings Point, Long Island,

and a penthouse in Miami Beach. And, she was on her fourth marriage. She had performed in twenty-two movies and had recorded eighteen songs. During 1951 Martha recorded the album "Martha Raye Sings."

She enjoyed her stage performances, which continued to keep her active. When she had time off, deep-sea fishing on her forty-four-foot cruiser in Florida was a source of pleasure. Decorating her homes was another favorite hobby.

But Martha was disillusioned with Hollywood. Whether it was because she was still "blacklisted" or because she was outside the "in-network," film offers were not forthcoming, despite her television popularity.

Performing in a "Police Action"

Meanwhile, unrest was building in a small country called Korea. Communist North Korea was threatening its southern neighbor. America edged closer to another war. Martha packed her bags once again. She was happy to return to entertaining the troops and helping out in military hospital areas. Friends knew she felt a sense of fulfillment when she was with our military men and women.

Throughout America's involvement in the Korean "Police Action," Martha frequently toured military camps with the USO. Entertainers George Gobel, Raymond Burr, Bob Hope, Frances Langford, and Joey Bishop were among those who also visited our troops in Korea.

Official temperatures ranged from thirty to seventy degrees in Korea. Rain or snowfalls often measured from one to eight inches; in mountainous areas, conditions could be especially trying. So, it is not surprising that many Korean Vets' memories of Maggie also mention miserable weather conditions.

Joe Ed Spargur served with Easy Company, Second Battalion, Fifth Marines, Second Platoon in Korea. He commented that Martha put on a show for his outfit under very trying circumstances. It was cold and slushy, hardly the most ideal conditions for a show. He recalls that the lift she gave those Marines helped keep them going.

Train Duty

Lieutenant Colonel Frances Liberty of East Greenbush, New York is a retired Army nurse. Friends know her as "Colonel Lib." She served our country through World War II, Korea, and Vietnam. She remembers seeing Martha several times.

> During the summer of 1952 while serving in Korea, I was assigned "train duty" on a troop train bringing wounded Marines and soldiers from the Demilitarized Zone to Inchon where they were to be transferred to a Navy hospital ship. No one was assigned train duty for too long because it was too emotionally and physically draining.
>
> Prior to the start of this train ride, I was approached by a tiny woman with red-brown hair and dressed in Khakies too big for her. She asked me if she could bum a ride. I said, "Yes, if you don't get in the way." She asked, "Can I help?" I directed her to go to the next car and try to calm the boys down in there, since all of them were severely wounded and many were moaning or crying. She responded, "That's right up my alley" and entered that car with two of the corpsmen. The car was outfitted with a number of three-tier bunks that held at least twenty-four Marines.
>
> This woman went from bunk to bunk and spoke to each of the wounded, caressing them, holding their heads and talking to each in turn to soothe their fears and distract them from their pain. She seemed to know that someone badly wounded needs to be touched. The moaning and wailing quieted down in short order.

They were all just kids, really, scared to death, realizing that here was someone who cared. They reminded me then of infants in distress being soothed and comforted by a loving mother.

The stench in these trains I still remember. It was hard to tolerate even for those of us accustomed to this duty. It would make an "ordinary" person sick if they were in there for any length of time. Yet, this woman stayed with them throughout the entire three-hour trip.

A couple young Marines were so severely wounded that I never expected them to last the trip, and this woman chose to devote much of her attention to them. I don't know what happened after their transfer to the hospital ship at Inchon but they survived that train ride solely, I'm convinced, because of the tender care given them by her.

One of the two corpsmen remarked to me that he never saw anything like it.

That woman was Martha Raye.

Some people who met Martha in military settings during World War II saw her again during the Korean Police Action. She was a pillar of support for those she visited. George Rogers, Jr. of New Bedford, Massachusetts said that the time she spent with troops in the Pacific will never be forgotten. George served with Task Force Fifty-eight. James Bardin of Garden Grove, California remembered her well from World War II and Korea. He saw her while he was in the Pacific and again in the San Diego Naval Hospital, as well as in Korea. He said that she was a truly marvelous person. Others remembered seeing Martha both in Korea and Vietnam. Their stories will be shared later.

In 1953, the Korean Police Action ended. Due to exhaustion, Martha's final trip to Korea was cut short. Back on American soil, she recovered and returned to her career.

Back to Earning a Living

During the summer of 1952, Martha was back in Miami Beach starring as Annie Oakley in *Annie Get Your Gun*. Her daughter, Melodye, joined her on stage as one of the youngsters in the cast. In September Martha went to New York City and performed at the Latin Quarter.

Martha continued making a name for herself on TV as a comedienne. She appeared seven times on NBC's "The Bob Hope Show," which first aired in October 1952.

She was nominated for the 1952 television EMMY award for Best Comedienne along with Lucille Ball, Joan Davis, Eve Arden, and Imogene Coca. What an outstanding group of comediennes from which to have to choose only one! Lucy received that EMMY.

During the Korea era (1950 through 1953), Martha also recorded on the Discovery label: "Ooh, Doctor Kinsey!," "After You've Gone," "Miss Otis Regrets," and "Life's Only Joy." She also recorded on the Mercury label "Blues in the Night," "Close to Me," "That Old Black Magic," and "Wolf Boy."

On June 17, 1953, Martha and Nick Condos were divorced on grounds of cruelty. As years passed, it became obvious they dearly loved each other, but it had been a tumultuous marriage. Nick wanted her to be either at home or pursuing her career, while Martha also wanted to be with the troops.

Melodye was caught in the middle. With joint custody, Melodye spent time with each of her parents on both coasts. Although divorced, Nick remained Martha's manager and years later moved back into her home with her. Melodye and her mother had a good relationship until 1988, when Nick passed away.

Chapter 4

Clown Princess of Comedy

"She gave so unselfishly of herself for her 'boys.' Her spirit was indomitable. During a time when soldiers felt alone and unsupported by the folks back home, Martha was there..."

Lieutenant Colonel Philip Choate

Blending Career and Troop Entertainment

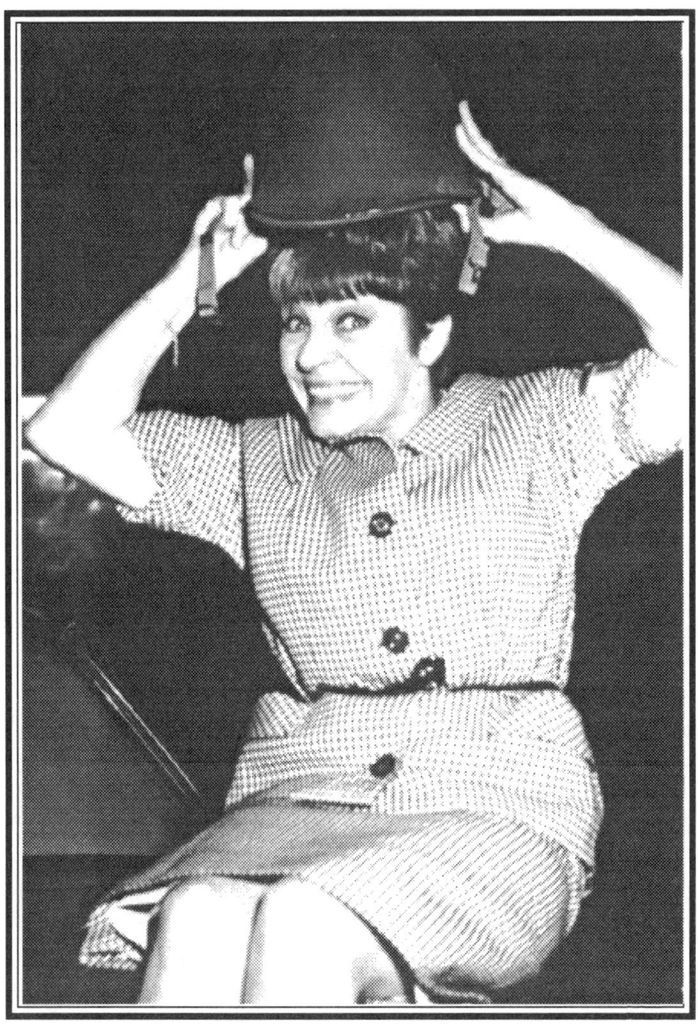

Los Angeles, California—1964: Martha tries on a helmet before boarding plane to Vietnam. Photo contributed by Tony Petrello.

-4-

Martha's shows on "The All Star Revue" were the stepping stone for yet another triumph. NBC's "The Martha Raye Show" premiered December 26, 1953, and aired an hour per week. Its program format included musical productions, songs, dance, and slapstick comedy sketches. Frequent guests on the show were Rocky Graziano and Margaret Truman, President and Mrs. Harry Truman's daughter, who later became a successful mystery writer. Martha's relationship with Margaret Truman was exceptional. They became close friends. When I visited Martha in 1990 and again in 1991, I was not surprised to find a photo of Margaret Truman Daniel on her dresser.

In 1954, *Somebody Up There Likes Me,* a book about Rocky Graziano was published. Former boxing middleweight champion of the world, Rocky spoke of the friendship among his wife Norma, Martha, and himself. He said Martha often helped him with his lines for her show and sometimes covered for him if he missed a cue.

"The Martha Raye Show," which rotated with "The Chevy Show" and "Texaco Star Theater," was rated in the top ten for the 1954-1955 season. Martha was reported to be the highest paid female comedienne at the time. Columnists called her the "Clown Princess of Comedy."

Hugh Holt remembered her television days and wrote, "I had the great pleasure of working with Martha Raye at NBC-TV during the time of her television show. Such a pro, a trouper with a warm and generous heart for those around her. What happiness she brought to those who saw her every week."

In 1953, Martha was again nominated for an EMMY. The category was "Outstanding Personality." Other prestigious nominees were Edward R. Murrow, Bishop Fulton Sheen, Arthur Godfrey, and Jack Webb. That EMMY went to Edward R. Murrow.

Marriage Number Five

In 1954 she found her next husband. Edward Thomas Begley was a dancer on Martha's TV show. Edward, thirty years old, became Martha's fifth husband; Martha, then thirty-seven, was his first wife. Martha and Edward flew to Elkton, Maryland where they had planned to be married, only to learn that Maryland required a forty-eight-hour waiting period for marriage licenses. They then flew to Alexandria, Virginia, drove to Arlington, and got their marriage license. On April 21, 1954, they were married in a double-ring ceremony performed by Dr. Arthur Maiden, a retired minister, in the courthouse across the Potomac River from Washington, D.C. They pledged to be "true and loyal." Martha was overheard saying, "This time it's for good." In attendance were Carl Eastman, a talent scout from Westport, Connecticut, and his wife. The happy couple then left for a honeymoon in Connecticut.

In September 1954 Martha performed at The 500 Club in Atlantic City. Martha recorded the album "Here's Martha Raye" on the Epic label. She appeared on "Dateline," an NBC ninety-minute production, which aired in December 1954. It was a musical tribute to the Overseas Press Club as it dedicated its memorial building in Manhattan in honor of the men and women who had given their lives for the cause of a free press. Hosted by John Daly, "Dateline's" guests included Martha Raye, Fred Allen, Elsa Maxwell, Bob Hope, Robert E. Sherwood, Richard Rodgers, Sid Caesar, Milton Caniff, Eddie Fisher, Perry Como, Marian Anderson, and Carl Sandburg.

"The Big Time" was cohosted by Martha, Milton Berle, and Ray Bolger. This lavish ninety-minute musical revue featured songs, dances, and comedy sketches; it aired in February 1955 on NBC. Their guests included the Bill and Cora Baird puppets.

Martha separated from Ed Begley and alleged that he had threatened her life. She hired private detective Robert O'Shea of Westport, Connecticut to guard her and her home. In April 1956 Martha received notice that she was being sued by Robert's wife, Barbara Ann, for $50,000, alleging alienation of affection. Mrs. O'Shea charged that Martha was showering Robert with gifts and claimed she "captivated" Robert and stole his affection.

At thirty-nine, Martha was at the height of her career. About the same time, tabloids ran stories about Martha's personal life including tales of nervous breakdowns, marital difficulties, adultery, and suicide attempts.

Because of the bad press she was receiving, "The Martha Raye Show" ratings began to drop. NBC executives quoted a "morals clause" in her contract, and her show was canceled on May 29, 1956.

Martha initially failed to obtain a divorce from Ed Begley when in August 1956 Circuit Judge Stanley Milledge dismissed her petition on grounds that she had not fulfilled Florida's one-year residence requirement.

Pressures Take Their Toll

Later that month, Martha was hospitalized in Miami Beach for an overdose of sleeping pills. She had arrived at her Miami Beach home less than thirty minutes earlier when her maid found her unconscious and called Martha's physician, Dr. Ralph Robbins. Martha was listed in critical condition when she was admitted to the hospital. Dr. Robbins stated that she had been despondent for about a week; later he said that she was in very poor condition.

Martha survived, picked up the pieces, got on with her life...and another divorce. In Juarez, Mexico October 6, 1956, Martha was granted a divorce from Edward Begley. The lawsuit by Mrs. O'Shea was settled several months later in Bridgeport, Connecticut. Barbara O'Shea reportedly received about $20,000.

In 1957, Martha was rushed to Doctors Hospital in New York and spent a night in an oxygen tent. Her manager reported that she did not feel well and was going in for a checkup. She was released a couple of days later.

In October 1957, Martha performed at the Copacabana in New York City. In January 1958, she became a regular on "The Steve Allen Show," an hour-long variety music and comedy series, which aired weekly on NBC-TV from September 1959 to June 1960. Martha sang, danced, and joined Steve Allen in comedy skits.

In February 1958, Martha returned to New York City where she helped with a WABD-TV telethon on behalf of the Association for the Help of Retarded Children. While in New York, she appeared at City Center in *Annie Get Your Gun*. She soon left the show due to an undisclosed illness.

Columnist Dorothy Kilgallen reported on June 19, 1958, that Martha would vacation in Europe with former husband Nick Condos and new beau, ex-cop Robert O'Shea. The unusual trio was planning a July cruise aboard the *Queen Mary*.

Marriage Number Six

On November 7, Martha, now forty-two, married Robert O'Shea, thirty-one. This was Robert's second marriage and Martha's sixth. The ceremony took place in the home of Mayor August Hannibal in Teaneck, New Jersey; Joan Crawford was matron of honor. His first wife had divorced O'Shea on grounds of intolerable cruelty after her attempt to sue Martha.

In February of 1959, Martha appeared on WNEW-TV in New York City, where she again assisted with a nineteen-hour telethon for the Association for the Help of Retarded Children. She helped raise $352,000 in pledges.

Troubles!

On February 19, 1959, a newspaper reported that the government had filed a $46,038 tax lien against Martha's property. The Federal agents charged that Martha owed taxes for 1957. Ten months later the U.S. Government notified Martha of another income tax lien of $30,922 against her and former husband, Nick Condos.

More Troubles...

On February 27, 1959, Dorothy Kilgallen reported that Martha had suffered a severe case of trichinosis. At the time, she was negotiating a deal with TV producer Bernard Schubert to play the title role in a video production of *The Marie Dressler Story*; she never did play the role.

In October of 1959 Martha was back in the tabloids. Rumors flourished that she was having second thoughts about her marriage to Robert O'Shea. By the end of that month, they were separated. Stating that he still loved her and had not abandoned her, Robert threatened to sue Martha for $100,000. He had already filed a $21,000 suit for "services rendered" as her bodyguard. Martha divorced him in 1962. According to newspaper reports, before the divorce was final O'Shea cleaned out Martha's house right down to the carpeting.

From 1959 to 1960, a ninety-minute TV variety show called "The Big Party" aired weekly on CBS. Several hosts and hostesses held informal gatherings of celebrities at their homes. Greer Garson hosted one with guests Martha Raye, Sal Mineo, Walter Slezak, Mike Nichols, Elaine May, Peter Lind Hayes, and Mary Healy.

In December of 1960 Martha was back on stage at the Drury Lane in Chicago in *The Solid Gold Cadillac,* playing the part of Laura Partridge. In February 1961 she portrayed Carol Arden in the stage production of *Personal Appearance* at the Sombrero Playhouse in Phoenix. Later she appeared as Pam in *Separate Rooms* and was once again joined on stage by her daughter Melodye. During the summer of 1961, Martha starred as Calamity Jane in the Pittsburgh Light Opera production of *Calamity Jane.* Roles in four plays meant a lot of lines to learn in a short period of time! This corresponds with her uncanny ability to recall troops' names, places, and dates at the drop of a hat.

Powers of Recall

Martha's incredible memory was a gift that amazed many troops over the years. Lieutenant Colonel Philip Choate remembers that when Martha was entertaining in Maine, he was a college student working at a resort in Lakewood. Martha was the star performer for a week at a nearby summer theater and Philip spoke to her daily. He was impressed with how down to earth she was. When the week ended, Martha and her supporting cast moved on to another theater. Time passed and he did not think about Martha except when he saw her on TV.

Six years later, Philip was a captain assigned to the First Brigade, 101st Airborne Division. His unit arrived in Chu Lai, Vietnam for a stand-down. Martha was there with a troop of young dancers and singers performing *Hello, Dolly!* He attended her show and went backstage after the performance. As Martha came out of her dressing room, he said, "Hi, Martha. Remember me?" She looked at him a few seconds, flashed her famous smile, and in true Martha Raye fashion exclaimed, "Lakewood, 1961! What in the hell are you doing here!"

> She gave so unselfishly of herself for her 'boys.' Her spirit was indomitable. During a time when soldiers felt alone and unsupported by the folks back home, Martha was there with a kind word, a joke, a hug, and a pat on the back. When one considers the entertainers who have been there time and time again, Martha Raye rated right up there with Bob Hope.
>
> I will never forget her and will always hold a special place in my heart for her.

On March 26, 1962, Melodye and her father, Nick Condos, found Martha unconscious on a deserted beach near her home in Malibu. She was revived by a county fire department rescue squad, treated at the Malibu Emergency Hospital, and transferred to the Hollywood West Hospital. Her physician, Dr. Morris Katz, said she evidently collapsed from exhaustion. He said she was in good condition otherwise, but kept her in the hospital for observation another two days.

Return to the Silver Screen

After fifteen years since her last film, *Monsieur Verdoux,* Metro-Goldwyn-Mayer and Jimmy Durante brought Martha back to the big screen to portray Madame LuLu, a fortune teller, in *Billy Rose's Jumbo. Jumbo* was a musical about the daughter of a circus owner trying to prevent a takeover bid. The movie starred Doris Day, Jimmie Durante, Stephen Boyd, and Dean Jagger. During the circus parade Martha wore a lion's suit and sang part of "Circus on Parade" with Jimmy and Doris.

One scene showed her preparing to be shot from a cannon—only to pop out the other end when it backfired. Martha joined Doris for the song "Why Can't I?" In another scene she hung from a mouth-strap in a butterfly costume—then fell into a catch net and broke it. During the finale she performed on the trapeze, rode horseback, and dressed as a clown with a very exaggerated chest and butt. She joined Jimmy, Doris, and Stephen in singing "Sawdust, Spangles and Dreams." The film's producers were Joe Pasternak and Martin Melcher. Music and lyrics were by Richard Rodgers and Lorenz Hart.

When I was at her home in 1990, Martha told me that she really enjoyed making the film and working with Doris and Jimmy. Movie posters for this film hung in her guest bathroom.

In August 1962, Martha returned to the stage as Wildcat Jackson in *Wildcat* at the Westbury, Long Island music festival. The cast toured on the Guber-Ford-Gross stage circuit.

Generosity at The Stork Club

Master Sergeant Timothy Doherty shares this story about meeting Martha with members of the U.S. Army Drill Team, part of the Honor Guard Company of the First Battle Group, Third Infantry Regiment (The Old Guard). They had been invited to perform on "The Jimmy Dean Show." After traveling by bus to New York from Washington, D.C., the team arrived at the studio for the taping session. At the end of a very frustrating day of rehearsals, tapings, waiting, retapings, and more waiting, the team members were impatient to be released.

Martha Raye walked in. As she greeted them, she managed to make each soldier feel special. She realized that their day in the studio had been long and tiring. Martha asked if they had eaten. Twenty-four soldiers replied almost in unison, "No, ma'am!" "Well," she said, "I haven't eaten, either, so let's get some supper."

Martha quickly arranged for taxis to take the entire team to The Stork Club. They could not believe they were actually at *The Stork Club,* nor could they believe the dinner to which they were treated. Timothy said, "Because of Miss Raye, twenty-four soldiers experienced one of the most memorable evenings of their lives."

The Stork Club, New York City—1962: Martha took members of the U.S. Army Drill Team to eat. She is seated next to Timothy Doherty, who contributed this photo.

In 1963, Martha portrayed Sally Adams on stage in *Call Me Madam!* She toured the Guber-Ford-Gross circuit with this production.

Martha appeared as a guest on NBC's hour-long "The Bob Hope Show" on April 14 and October 25, 1963. The April show also starred Dean Martin and Lucille Ball. Guests on the October broadcast included Andy Griffith, Jane Russell, Connie Haines, Beryl Davis, Don Drysdale, Sandy Koufax, and Tommy Davis.

"Colonel Maggie"

Since 1955, Martha had been aware that American military advisors were going to a small yet little-known country called Vietnam. They were there to "train" the South Vietnamese people to protect themselves. Through Martha's contacts in the military and government, she was kept apprised of our nation's overseas military actions. Some of this information was classified, but she knew America's involvement with Vietnam in personnel and equipment kept increasing.

By the end of 1963, Martha's information about the U.S. troop buildup was confirmed. She felt that this generation of soldiers needed her, so she donned fatigues and went in search of our military personnel.

Vietnam is where her love affair with the U.S. Army's Special Forces began. She was given many nicknames such as "The Sweetheart of Vietnam," "The Old Lady of the Boondocks," and "Maggie Drawers." However, she became known to most soldiers as "Colonel Maggie," a nickname cited frequently throughout the rest of this book.

From January of 1964 until February of 1970, Martha frequently appeared as a guest on ABC's weekly variety show "The Hollywood Palace." She appeared with Tony Randall, Jack Jones, and Groucho Marx on NBC's "The Bob Hope Show" in April 1964.

Chris Barker, formerly of Independence, Missouri, tells of his experience at the Marine Corps League national convention in Kansas City. The farewell banquet at the Muehlebach Hotel was graced with dignitaries such as Bob Hope, General Lewis Walt, Lee Marvin, and Martha Raye. Martha had a high fever and could not attend the pre-banquet cocktail party. But she insisted on attending the banquet itself.

> I tried to get her to remain in bed. Her reply was. "I owe it to those people to make my appearance."
>
> I'll never forget the fire of dedication in her eyes as she said that. She was quite a woman, entertainer, and American!

Victor Marchese of Lakeside, California is a recording artist on the Metro-Goldwyn-Mayer label. Although he never met Martha, he reminisced about an evening he was in a show called *Saucy Scandals* at the Fontainebleau Hotel in Miami Beach. As he sang "Maria" from *West Side Story*, there was only a pin-spot shining on him. He was back in a corner while two dancers on center stage were the main attraction. When the scene was over, the audience gave the dancers a standing ovation. Martha was in the audience. After everyone sat down, Martha stood up. She pointed to Victor and applauded. The audience rose and gave him a standing ovation as well. Victor said, "What a wonderful lady. I shall never forget that moment in my career and shall talk about it forever. I tried to thank her, but she was mobbed and I couldn't get near her."

Several people sent us tapes about their encounters with Martha. Tony Petrello of Murrieta, California first wrote me a note saying, "What would you like to know about my pleasure of meeting Martha Raye?" A few months later he sent a tape and photographs. Stationed with the Los Angeles Recruiting Command in 1965, he drove Martha to the airport to join a tour for the troops in Vietnam.

Los Angeles—1964: Martha clowns around before departing for Vietnam. Photo contributed by Tony Petrello.

Los Angeles—1964: Martha and Tony Petrello, who contributed this photo.

They discussed some of the old days when she played in the movies with Joe E. Brown. Martha told him that she was a grandmother and talked about her grandson. Tony added, "Every time the Public Relations office in the Los Angeles Recruiting Command asked Martha to participate in anything (whether it was a dinner or speech or whatever), she never failed to come through for us."

Family Matters

Martha bought a home in the Bel Air section of Beverly Hills. This would be her last real estate investment. That home was (and still is) located at 1153 Roscomare Road. Little did anyone know at the time just what her home would come to mean to many of our military Veterans!

Martha's daughter Melodye, then twenty years old, had married Edmond Lancaster. Using the name Melodye Condos Lancaster, she began to pursue a singing career. Melodye gave birth to a son on January 28, 1965; they named him Nicholas, after her father. He was baptized at Holy Trinity Church in New York City on March 27. Although the relationship among mother, father, and daughter was strained, Martha and Nick Condos attended the ceremony, where the Reverend Papadeas officiated.

The baptismal ceremony was Greek Orthodox and because neither Edmond nor John Paul "Cappy" Capobianco, the Godfather, were Greek, Nick applied the baptismal water to his grandson's head.

Following Nicholas' baptism, pictures were taken in the church with Martha holding her grandson. The reception was held at The Stork Club. John Paul and his wife, Pauline, of Bronxville, New York provided this information by phone and sent us the photos. They wanted Nicholas to know where they live and hoped to see or hear from him and his mother. They had not been in touch in many years.

What a thrill it was in late 1994 to be able to provide the long-lost addresses so Melodye and Nicholas and John Paul and Pauline could communicate once again.

Three Generations

Holy Trinity Church, New York City—1965: Martha holding her grandson, Nicholas, with her daughter, Melodye, looking on following Nick's baptism. Photo contributed by John Paul and Pauline Capobianco.

Chapter 5

Sweetheart of Vietnam

"For a short time, she allowed me to escape the lousiness of war and drowned me in laughter. I had a newborn son whom I had never seen and thought that I possibly might never see. Colonel Maggie was the only 'sane' person over there; she brought us all the sanity of laughter in an otherwise insane situation."

Julio Rodriguez
Warner Robins, Georgia

A Christmastime Sweetheart at the "PlayBoy Club"

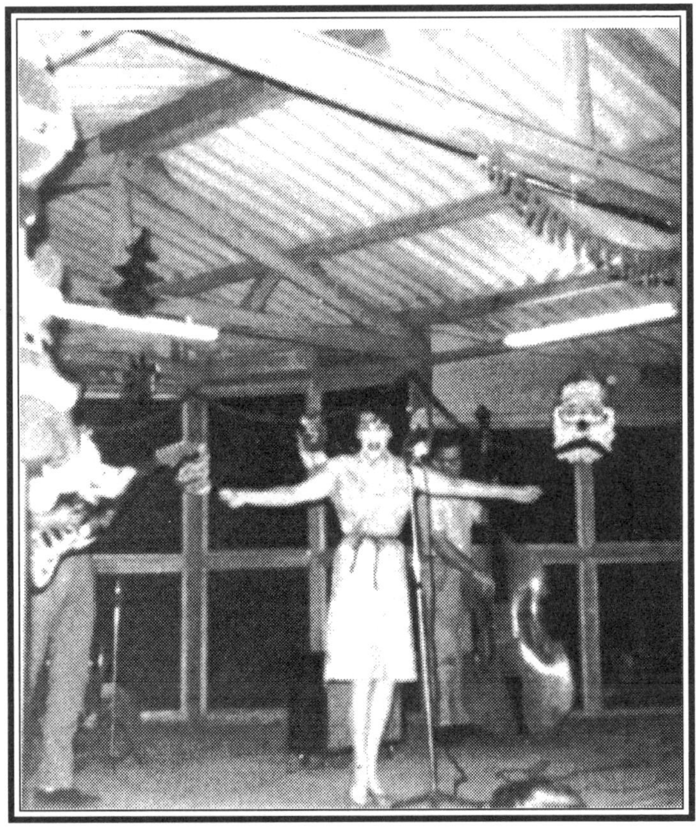

NhaTrang, Vietnam—Christmas 1965: Maggie entertains at the Special Forces "PlayBoy Club." Photo contributed by John Sullivan of Rochester, New York, who was there.

-5-

From 1964 to 1973, Martha traveled from camp to camp in isolated areas throughout Vietnam. She would stay "in-country" from four to six months at a time—usually at her own expense—to be with the troops she so dearly loved. She used the nurse's aide skills she learned back in the 1930s and surgical techniques she picked up during World War II to help treat the wounded. Whatever her official nursing qualifications, her assistance was often needed and very much appreciated. Her presence, whether as entertainer or as nurse, helped to make life bearable for so many enlisted troops and officers.

Lieutenant Colonel Warren Henderson of Clovis, New Mexico remembers Martha in Vietnam sometime between June 1964 and June 1965. He was the Air Liaison Officer with the Twenty-first Army Republic of Vietnam (ARVN) Division stationed at Bac Lieu, and he lived with an Army Advisory Unit. During that year, only two "name" entertainers visited his group—Raymond Burr and Martha Raye, both of whom came through on more than one occasion. Martha used one of their "hootches" (simple huts or dwellings common throughout rural Vietnam).

While at Bac Lieu, Martha paid visits to their Regimental Headquarters. She also flew into outlying locations in resupply helicopters. Warren said that he was personally involved in one large operation near SocTrang, during which Vietnamese Army forces had many wounded. Martha worked at the hospital for forty-eight hours straight helping with those injured troops! He said it was a privilege to meet such a "high-caliber lady" who donated her time to help both morale and medical caregiving.

Saigon, Vietnam—1965: "Colonel Maggie," arrives at the airport and is greeted by two members of the USO. Photo contributed by Special Forces Association.

With the USO in Vietnam

In May 1965 Martha began the first of her eight USO tours in Vietnam, visiting military camps and outposts. On May 24, she arrived in Manila for a series of performances at U.S. bases in the Philippines. She was accompanied by Earl Colbert, a guitarist, and Ollie Harris, a bass fiddle player. From Manila she went on to visit Thailand and South Vietnam. During one of her shows, she performed with Johnny Grant, Eddie Fisher, and John Bubbles. Johnny Grant later became an emcee on Channel-5 KTLA-TV in Los Angeles and also the "honorary" Mayor of Hollywood. That May tour lasted three and a half weeks.

In October that year, Martha was back in Vietnam with the USO for another six weeks. Until America's withdrawal in 1974, Martha toured in Vietnam at least annually, sometimes with the USO (1965-1970) but most often on her own and at her own expense.

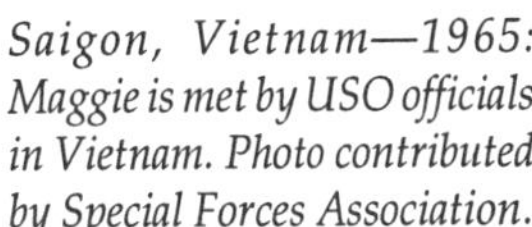

Saigon, Vietnam—1965: Maggie is met by USO officials in Vietnam. Photo contributed by Special Forces Association.

Some soldiers recall exactly when and where they saw Martha; others knew where but could not provide exact dates.

Maggie opened the Cobra Lounge in Takhli, Thailand. She also stopped in Korat and visited the Ninth Logistics Command. Sergeant First Class Harold Ward said he worked with the public address system for all events. "When Maggie said she was the 'Big Mouth,' she sure was. I saw her on stage stick a big microphone in her mouth."

James Ryhal, Jr. of Hubbard, Ohio was in Vietnam in 1965. When he landed at Red Beach on March 8, his unit set up camp one and a half miles from the Danang Air Base at the foot of Hills 327 and 268. It took them about thirty-three days to set up a decent camp of ten-man tents with generators for electricity. He saw Maggie twice and remembers her well.

> We had the use of some old French structures for a mess area and went from C-rations to B-rations. I figure it was in April or May when Martha Raye came out to talk to us and tell a few jokes. She had no escorts and no truckbed to use for a stage, and we had no bleachers or seats. She wore an old sleeveless dress; I guess they

were called "shifts" that you could picture your Mom wearing. There were only about thirty of us gathered around her in a semi-circle. We drank water from gerry cans, water buffalos, and Lester bags.

We went out at night and stayed in foxholes around the perimeter of the air base. There were a few times the enemy got into the air base and blew up planes. There were times you could hear small arms fire nearby. I want you to know she came out in remote areas like ours to entertain a few men...and I love her for this.

I also saw her in November of 1965. I was taken from Charlie Medical Battalion on Hill 327 to Danang Air Base to be evacuated to Clark Air Force Hospital. The plane was full of wounded. I only had an infected kidney that was taken out a month later. I was able to sit up; most were on stretchers. There she was, dressed in colonel U.S. Army fatigues. We were Marines, so I was a little surprised—but not offended. She walked down the aisle and talked with us and then, after a few words, she would go up to one of the men on a stretcher and visit. We got off at Clark Air Base and so did she. That was the last I saw of her.

I could be wrong, but I doubt if Bob Hope ever went out in the boonies to entertain a handful. It seems he was at Saigon and larger areas where he entertained hundreds and maybe thousands at one time. I greatly admire him also—so no hurt intended.

In Harm's Way

Gil Woodside, Jr., of Seekonk, Massachusetts was a nineteen-year-old Marine stationed at Chu Lai. His unit's area was unsecured, and their perimeter was being hit or probed every night. They were building a combat airstrip the Viet Cong did not want completed. It was a very dangerous area. Gil recalls Maggie's visit.

> Five or six weeks after our landing at Chu Lai, some of us were detailed to help move some equipment and set up a makeshift stage for a show to be given by a Hollywood personality. We didn't know who it was going to be, but recognized her instantly as Martha

Raye. I remembered her from "The Milton Berle Show." As we worked, a Marine officer came up to Ms. Raye and told her that the small knoll that she had chosen for the stage site was in an area that would expose her to enemy fire and that the area had been the site of several sniping incidents. Ms. Raye looked around and said, "But this is the spot where more troops will be able to relax and enjoy the show."

At great personal risk Martha Raye gave the first formal *celebrity* performance to American combat troops in Vietnam. After the show—which, by the way, was stupendous—she walked among the troops, signed autographs, took pictures with us, and had chow with us.

You will never know what that visit did for the morale of hundreds of Marines, sailors, and Seabees who were fortunate enough to be able to be there with her.

Chu Lai, Vietnam—June 1965: Maggie visits Marines. L-R: standing—Schrader, Maggie, Coleman, and Lopez; sitting—Boyd, Mosher, and Woodside. Photo contributed by Gil Woodside.

Only those touched by her and her troupe could ever understand the feeling of love, respect, and gratitude we have for her.

We all appreciate the efforts and risks taken by many of America's entertainers and sports celebrities but FEW have taken the risks or gone to the lengths to bring a little comfort and "home" to the troops that Colonel Maggie has. How many wear the Purple Heart? Colonel Maggie wears *two!*

Major General Ellis Williamson of Arlington, Virginia organized the 173rd Airborne Brigade (Separate) on the island of Okinawa in 1963 and commanded it for three years. These were among the first Army ground combat units to enter Vietnam in May of 1965. Ellis remembers Maggie well.

Martha Raye entertained our troops during our first year over there. She made the remark to me that she thoroughly enjoyed entertaining troops and, except for wanting to see her grandchild every now and then, she would be willing to stay over there indefinitely. I asked her why she did not stay longer. She said that her contract was running out and that although she did not need the money, the band needed to be paid. I asked if she would stay if we of the brigade furnished her backup music. Her answer was, "Of course." I called General Sternberg [the personnel officer in Saigon] who said that it was okay with him.

A flock of musicians volunteered to play her backup. We had only a few limitations. The group had to be small enough to ride in one helicopter, and I insisted that my men wear Army uniforms and show our unit patch.

We had many more volunteers than we could accept. Martha listened to many of them and selected three or four. She later told me that she could have used several times that many. Their first performance was on a U.S. Navy Aircraft carrier.

She was a good trouper, and all of us loved her dearly.

While serving with Company B, Third Battalion, Third Marines, Sergeant Fred Olinger landed at Hue Phu Bai in April 1965. A few months later his unit was notified that there was a USO show forty miles away. They were expecting to see Ann-Margret. Instead they found Maggie.

> But believe me we weren't disappointed—Miss Raye put on a wonderful show. I had seen her on television, so I was familiar with her. She was really great.
>
> I *had* to go to Vietnam because I was in the service; Miss Raye didn't have to come but she *did*. God bless her. I will never forget the joy and laughter she brought us.

Evening Dress and...Combat Boots?

Marine Private First Class James Cutler was also in Hue Phu Bai in 1965. He felt lucky to have been chosen to guard Maggie when she visited his area to put on a show. "She was a breath of fresh air." He heard that she had been hit by mortar fragments during an enemy attack. His commander ordered the unit not to say anything because it would mess up other USO shows. Jim mentioned this to Maggie and she said, "Mum's the word." Later he was stationed at Lake Mead Base near Las Vegas and had the opportunity to see Maggie.

> I had my first flashback of Vietnam. Martha Raye was at the Sahara. I was thinking, will she remember me? How is she feeling about the war now?
>
> It took me a while to get to see her at the Sahara. I went one night with Jerry McCabe, a fellow Vietnam Vet. I wrote a note asking if she remembered me and if I could talk to her. We went in full dress tropics, ribbons, badges, and a glow! We got to the room where she was playing. It was full—not even standing room. I thought I'd come back another night. I gave the headwaiter the note I wrote to Maggie, and we were leaving when he stopped McCabe and me. He seated us at a table, front row and center stage.

Martha came on stage, just the way I remembered her—what an angel. Her show was the best.

The last part of her show, she came out in a full length evening dress. She sang a song, talked about Vietnam and our people in the war and how much she wanted everybody to get behind our troops in Vietnam. She said, "I am. One hundred percent, in fact!" She lifted up her full length dress. She had combat boots on. I felt real good!

Then she said, "If you don't believe me, just ask these two gentlemen down here" pointing at McCabe and me. She gave me my welcome home....We stood up for about ten minutes of applause. I didn't even think she'd know me; what a pro she was!

We were invited to her room after the show. That's when she told me to call her "Maggie." I gave her a set of bush greens with my name and hers on it, got some pictures, and had a great time!

Maggie appeared at large bases, too, such as Danang, NhaTrang, Pleiku, Saigon, and SocTrang. As battle conditions deteriorated, our military leadership usually limited big-name performers to these more secure areas for their own safety. Nonetheless, Maggie went most often to small obscure outposts where only handfuls of soldiers worked and which were often under threat of attack.

She was never taped, recorded, nor paid for her Vietnam television specials. She also refused to be photographed, except by the troops themselves and usually as they posed with her. She felt the people back home wanted to know about their sons and daughters—*not* about her. She did not want publicity about her time with them.

Julio Rodriguez of Warner Robins, Georgia attended a show in the Fifth Special Forces Camp PlayBoy Club at NhaTrang Air Base in 1965. The show featured "The Old Lady of the Boondocks," another nickname given to

Maggie, and her performance brought hysterical laughter to the audience.

> Her antics on stage were in the true sense of "above and beyond." Few people would have had the courage to put themselves in the position of self-humiliation, but she did it just to make us laugh!
>
> After the show Ms. Raye was signing autographs. I only had a Military Pay Certificate for paper, but she signed her name on a five-cent note, which years later I would lose. I no longer have her signature, but she and her show are locked away in my memories.
>
> For a short time, she allowed me to escape the lousiness of war and drowned me in laughter. I had a newborn son whom I had never seen and thought that I possibly might never see. Colonel Maggie was the only "sane" person over there, and she brought us all the sanity of laughter in an otherwise insane situation.
>
> A few days later, the club was the target of rockets and mortars and, though it was destroyed, Colonel Maggie and her memories live on.
>
> She touched many lives, and I am thankful that she touched mine. I have only one regret...losing my Military Pay Certificate with her signature. She was every serviceman's link to the joy of life and laughter.

Flying Economy Class: Gunship

Robert Wetherbie of Alexandria, Virginia saw Maggie when he was stationed at SocTrang with the 121st Aviation Company.

> Martha had more talent in her little finger than the entire U.S. presence in Southeast Asia. On several occasions I flew her and one of her escorts to some very dangerous outposts where she would entertain only a few troops. To my knowledge, she was the only civilian that ever flew with an armed helicopter platoon. Due to the mission, weight limitations, and rigid training requirements, no other non-crew members ever flew on the gunships. During her stay, she endured several mortar attacks.

Serving with the Marine Corps in Danang, Master Gunnery Sergeant T.C. Allen said that Colonel Conley had promised them steaks, corn on the cob, strawberry shortcake and some entertainment.

> The entertainment came in the form of Martha Raye. At least a thousand to twelve hundred troops were packed into the mess hall. When the colonel introduced Ms. Raye, the crowd went wild. Then the colonel had Ms. Raye turn around and bend over; the flight suit she was wearing had "Property United States Marine Corps" stenciled right across her rear end.

Herb Herther was also in Danang during the summer of 1965. It was hot there, but at least they had a place where they could go to relax—Colonel Conley's pride and joy, the MAG-11 Officers Club. It even had a little pond near the front entrance and a raggedy palm tree. It was more of a mud hole, really. Everyone called it the officers' swimming pool.

> The club rules, even in that makeshift, rough-sawn, canvas-sided, nailed-together club, were the same as stateside. "He who enters covered here, shall buy for all, a round of cheer." Of course in 1965 we hadn't begun to feel politically-correct pressures. "He" meant "She" and everyone else.
>
> Well, wouldn't you know it, in came Martha Raye, escorted by Colonel Bob Conley, purported to be an "old Friend." She had her hat on and was dressed in uniform. It was some sort of Army or Air Force flying suit.
>
> There were about forty-five officers in the club, mostly from the four Marine fighter squadrons stationed there. The volunteer bartender rang the traditional bell and Ms. Raye had to buy the round of drinks. Of course, drinks were only ten cents, so it cost her about $4.50. I think Bob Conley picked up the tab. She sang a few songs and we joined in.
>
> I told her I had read the book, *Four Jills in a Jeep* [Carole Landis wrote the book in 1943 about the four

> women's trip overseas]. She seemed very surprised, joking that I was the only one she'd ever met who had. She was a helluva nice lady.

Peggy Adams of Prince George, Virginia was an Army nurse stationed with the Eighty-fifth Evacuation Hospital near Qui Nhon from August 1965 through August 1966. She retired from the Army Nurse Corps as a captain. Peggy saw Maggie on two occasions. Maggie spent the night with the nurses in the Military Assistance Command-Vietnam (MACV) compound where they were temporarily housed while redeploying. They shot the breeze with her until late one evening.

Peggy met Maggie again at a show in a warehouse at Qui Nhon near the airfield. Maggie was fielding questions from the audience when one young trooper expressed his deep concern over the antiwar protesters. Maggie replied that she could understand how it must hurt to see people destroying the flag but, she said, "Son, remember one thing. Those people are not good enough to wipe the mud from your boots."

Peggy has never forgotten those words. "She dressed like us, ate what we ate, and was no cleaner than we were. No fancy quarters and VIP treatment. Just one of the gang."

Maggie Becomes One of the "Green Berets"

Colonel Tom Bing of Nokomis, Florida was a Senior Transportation Advisor to the IV Corps in the Delta area of Can Tho. He sent an enlightening audiotape about his encounters with Maggie.

> We went out to Rach Gia, where Maggie put on a show. We had lunch in their command building. This was for the Senior Area Advisor and his people.
>
> After lunch, Maggie was to go up to Chi Chi to a little Special Forces camp—out in the middle of a rice paddy—horrible place. So we flew up this canal—dodging back and forth so they [the Viet Cong] couldn't

take potshots at us. At Chi Chi they had a chopper pad big enough for one, but we managed to get two choppers on it. There weren't two inches between the tips of the rotor blades; we landed these two helicopters down on that pad, which was just plywood they had anchored to the ground.

Anyway, you can't believe how bad it was there; it was monsoon season. They were pumping out water to keep that area accessible. They built a triangular dike up around it and pumped to keep the place from going completely underwater.

Martha was in old regular GI fatigues that had her name on it. She was a lieutenant colonel in the Nurse Corps, so she was in uniform and tropical boots. But she slugged up through the mud to this camp and went to the tent where the Detachment Commander and his people were. They had a bunch of Cambodians/mercenaries there that they paid. She put on a show.

When the show was over, the Cambodians, the kids, GI's, officers, and the others who watched the show gathered outside the tent. The captain said, "Miss Raye, I've been authorized to make you a member of Special Forces United States Army." She said, "Oh boy, what an honor!" She stood up and the captain held the Special Forces badge in his hand. Martha threw her left bosom out and said, "Well, pin it on captain!" The captain turned red and said, "Um, ah, um." Finally, she said, "Captain, pin it on. Anybody in your position should have that much courage." The captain lifted the lapel of the flap of the pocket on her shirt and pinned the badge on it. I remember crying—I was laughing so hard.

Martha had a place with a U.S. Army helicopter battalion north of Can Tho: SocTrang, right on the edge of the river. These guys had really been her buddies. They had a hootch there for her, so she could come and go anytime she wanted. They never knew when she was going to come in, and she'd stay there in that hootch.

The next time I saw Martha, she had been out somewhere in the boondocks entertaining the guys. Those

> guys in the helicopter battalion would take two gunships with somebody riding shotgun and take her anywhere she'd want to go. She looked for the worst places.

An Air Force Forward Air Controller, Captain Norman "Pete" Peterson of Whispering Pines, North Carolina was to report to Quang Tri at the Demilitarized Zone (DMZ) in August or September 1965. He had been waiting for three days for a plane to fly him to Dong Ha. Quang Tri did not have a runway at that time. His new boss, Major Shugart, was getting impatient. Pete checked with Base Operations at Danang and a C-123 two-engine cargo plane was flying north to Dong Ha at noon, but it was reserved by a woman.

> I thought, what a way to fight a war. I was to ask this woman for a ride—I did not know who she was. About 11:30 A.M., in she came, colonels with her, airmen loading her baggage. I recognized Maggie immediately and asked her for a ride, stating I was three days late for going to war. She happily said, "Get aboard, we'll keep each other company." No truer words spoken.
>
> The C-123 is very noisy in back. She sat on one side, and I sat on the other; she motioned for me to sit next to her. We were the only ones in the back of the plane. She told me a dirty joke even before we took off. Enroute about one hour, it was dirty jokes, drinking from her flask—bourbon, I think—and her hand on my leg. Yes, I thought, what a way to go to war!
>
> Only two entertainers came to Quang Tri while I was there—Martha and Robert Mitchum. The seven mile drive from Dong Ha to Quang Tri was not too safe—snipers. Martha had guts.

Lieutenant Colonel Mel Rupp, of Port Richey, Florida was a newly-promoted captain serving as an advisor in Advisory Team Fifty-nine located at Cau Mau, An Xugen Province, in the IV Corps area. Cau Mau is at the tip of the Mekong Delta.

There were no roads beyond Cau Mau and everyone arrived and departed by air. It was fall of 1965 when Martha was scheduled to visit the twenty or so members of Team Fifty-nine. It had been raining for several days, and we doubted she could get in. But shortly after lunch a helicopter landed. She and her accompanist, an older fellow with gray hair and a beard or goatee and carrying his guitar, had arrived.

One problem during the rainy season was that the four "crappers" would stop up and overflow. Three of the four were not operating when Ms. Raye arrived and the fourth was in continuous demand. I was the lucky occupant of that lone crapper when she entered the Military Assistance and Advisory Group compound loudly proclaiming her need of a toilet.

She was ushered into the latrine by my boss, Major Hamp Dews, who jokingly ordered me to cut it short because we had a VIP who needed that crapper! She stood outside the stall wisecracking about what all would happen if I didn't hurry. I did cut it short and have ever since modestly boasted of having "shared a crapper with Martha Raye."

She got a real kick out of my "short-timers" chart—I only had about a month to my rotation home. The chart was a series of footprints, each representing one day, leading to a crapper where on the last day the individual "flushed" himself out of the country.

Martha also met and admired our mascot, a twelve-foot python that we called "Big John." Years later, I heard her joke on a TV show about "Big John" turning out to be "Big Joann" after it laid some eggs.

She talked with each of us, sang, and told jokes for about an hour and was a welcome relief from our normal routine. I particularly remember her rendition of *The Girl from Ipanema.* We all really appreciated her, not only for her talent but for caring enough to brave the elements and putting up with the hardships just to entertain twenty GI's at a remote post in the middle of a war.

On 14 November, I was wounded during an attack on our compound and after treatment in-country, was medevaced to the Philippines on 16 November. As eleven of us litter patients were waiting on a bus on the flight line at Ton Son Nhut to be loaded on a C-130, who should come aboard but Martha Raye! She was wise-cracking and reassuring each of us that we were going to be okay and that she ought to know because she was a nurse! When she got to me she remembered the "crapper incident" and "Big John." It was a joy to see her again, and it reinforced a respect that I shall have for her the rest of my life. She was truly a great person and a compassionate human being.

Maggie in her Green Beret with parachute backdrop. Cover photo of Colonel Maggie copyright, Radix, 1989, reprinted with permission from "The Green Beret Magazine," Volume V (1970), available from Radix Press, 2314 Cheshire Lane, Houston, TX 77018, (713) 683-9076; original photo by James Fisher, Georgetown, Texas.

Letter of Commendation

During the same Christmas season tour, Lewis Walt, the Commanding General of the Third Marine Division (Reinforced), Fleet Marine Force, presented the following Letter of Commendation to Maggie on December 16, 1965.

> It is with the utmost pleasure that I take this opportunity to commend and thank you for your selfless devotion as a true American to the improvement of the morale of the fighting men of the Third Marine Division.
>
> Whereas the appearance of an American lady in a combat zone one time in the normal course of events is more than we would expect, you have most assuredly placed yourself on the rolls of those who have gone above and beyond the call of duty in making your third appearance in Vietnam during the last six months. These appearances have not been confined to the rear areas, but have been made to our front line units where the need is the greatest. On each occasion you have braved danger, tirelessly endured the discomfort of heat, rain and mud, to deliver the style of entertainment for which you are world renowned and the style we Marines appreciate most.
>
> Your superlative performance, "can do" attitude and calm demeanor in the presence of potential danger, reflect the highest credit upon you and your profession. Your actions were in keeping with the finest traditions of the United States of America.

P.S. Maggie, we love you!

Major General L. W. Walt, USMC

Chapter 6

Welcome Back Maggie

"Hundreds of wounded in tent hospitals and thousands whose names appear etched in stone on the Vietnam Memorial were beneficiaries of her deep and abiding concern for her fellow man. She brought love and laughter and left it behind in abundance."

James Carr

Binh Thuy Air Base

Binh Thuy Air Base, Vietnam—1965: The 22nd Tactical Air Support Squadron decorated their building for Maggie's return. Photo contributed by James Binnicker.

-6-

During the summer of 1965, Maggie was stateside and appeared at various theaters across the United States portraying Opal in a stage production of *Everybody Loves Opal.* She also appeared on "The Bob Hope Show" with Tony Randall and Jack Jones that aired in November 1965.

Five days later, "The Comics"was shown on NBC. This hour-long comedy special spotlighted the talents of a select group of comedians. It was hosted by Danny Thomas, and the guests included Maggie, Bill Cosby, Tim Conway, Spike Jones, Jr., and the Three Stooges (Moe Howard, Larry Fine, and Joe DeRita). While these shows were airing stateside, Maggie was back with our troops in Vietnam.

When he was stationed at Binh Thuy Air Base (IV Corps) with the Twenty-second Tactical Air Support Squadron, James Binnicker met Maggie. He said that of all the visitors that came to town, Martha Raye did more for morale than all the rest put together. "She was real, sincere, and genuine." James first wrote to us while he was serving as the Chief Master Sergeant of the Air Force stationed at the Pentagon. He is now retired and living in Universal City, Texas.

Binh Thuy Air Base—1965: Maggie talks with soldier as they are followed by guitarists. Photo contributed by James Binnicker.

Panning Those Protestors...

During December 1965 Maggie was accompanied by Specialist 4 Chuck Langmack, a machine gunner, on bass; singer Private First Class Tom McGlockin, an assistant machine gunner, on guitar; and Private First Class Dick Swan, a chaplain's assistant, on drums. They were members of the 173rd Airborne Brigade. Maggie was in Danang following an eight-day schedule of fourteen shows, both ashore and afloat, in the Danang and Chu Lai areas. She also visited the Seventh Fleet.

Pacific Stars and Stripes quoted Maggie as saying after each performance, "I just want to leave you with two little thoughts. First about those demonstrators back in the States—they are a kooky, illiterate minority group. And second, they could not possibly shine your boots and don't you ever forget that."

Maggie was distraught over what protesters were saying about the men and women who served in Vietnam and elsewhere. She also was upset that the United States was not doing more to either support the troops or end the war.

The Navy enjoyed appearances by Danny Kaye, Vicki Carr, Maggie, and others. Sailors aboard the USS *Enterprise,* USS *Kitty Hawk,* and the USS *Stormes* were thrilled by Maggie. She often made the perilous "highline" trip from one ship to another. Bill Wooding of Wilson, North Carolina remembers her taking those highline rides from a carrier to other ships. After a show on the USS *Stormes,* she and her companion were lifted by a lifeline sling seat into a helicopter that took them back to the carrier. Bill was a machinist mate aboard the *Stormes.*

Rear Admiral William Sizemore recalls that Maggie spent two days aboard the *Enterprise* performing several shows on the hangar deck. According to Richard Whalen, she used the captain's quarters during that visit. Lawrence Hardegen was a Chief Electrician's Mate aboard the *Enterprise.* He said that it was unusual for the escorting ships to get entertainers aboard but Martha, in her unselfish manner, made the trip.

Captain James Mulligan of Allerton, Iowa was the Executive Officer of VA-36 "Roadrunners," an A4C squadron aboard the *Enterprise.* In 1990, he recalled how Maggie's visit to his ship impacted his life.

> Another memorable visitor was of lesser rank, perhaps, but certainly sported one of the biggest smiles in the South China Sea. On 20 December 1965, Martha Raye arrived by air to conduct a holiday show for the crew. The following day she highlined over to our accompanying destroyers, demonstrating her true showmanship and good sportsmanship.
>
> Ms. Raye was dog tired from shows she did in Vietnam. I don't know how she held it all together. When I saw her at breakfast, I saw how fatigued she was and did not want to intrude. A mistake on my part, for some weeks later I was shot down and captured: I remained a POW for almost seven years.
>
> It was a long lonesome war for me, and her appearance on the *Enterprise* was one of the highlights I could remember and enjoy.

Special Forces Camp, Vietnam—mid 1960s: Maggie with members of Special Forces. Photo contributed by Special Forces Association.

Temper Triggers

Marge Davis remembers Maggie's temper. Marge was married to Lieutenant Colonel R. N. "Stormy" Davis, now deceased. Stormy had served in all three wars. He had been assigned to escort Maggie while he was in Vietnam in 1964-1965. Maggie knew that Stormy's pet name for Marge was "Butch." Marge wrote us about several meetings with Maggie.

> My late husband, "Stormy" fell in love with Maggie as all that knew her did. Stormy's letters told of his pleasure escorting Maggie. I had never met her, but I fell in love with her also. Why? She was not only entertaining our loved ones; she was *there* for them. She was giving her time, almost her life, a bit of extra love and comfort that a wife could only write in letters or communicate via tapes.
>
> After Vietnam his duty station was Lake Mead Base near Las Vegas. He was Commander of the Marine Barracks for nearly three years.
>
> Maggie came to the Sahara Hotel to perform. Stormy called her and that is when I met "The Great Lady!" She became a dear friend.
>
> Have you ever seen her mad? During her performance on stage—if a heckler made light of our flag, or showed a lack of respect for our Armed Forces, our country or men, *then* our "Colonel Maggie" stopped the show. After she finished with the heckler, she'd receive standing ovations from her audiences! That is when I saw Maggie mad, and the heckler or hecklers were no longer around. She'd smile, pick up her show and didn't miss a beat!
>
> Colonel Maggie wasn't a phony. She was so full of love and compassion for our country and military regardless of branch or rank. She was the same at all times.

Marge Black of Rantoul, Illinois remembers what her late husband, Specialist 5 Jon Robert Black, told her about Maggie. She said that Jon served in Korea before she met him in 1957. Her husband of eight years then served in Vietnam in 1965 and 1966. She has been a widow for over twenty years.

> Over the years I've told my children how much their father loved and admired Martha Raye and Bob Hope. So many times my husband told me how he and the troops loved Martha, and how she came out on the stage and told jokes, sang and was *there* for them! That is what was so important—she apparently never showed fear for herself. His absolute favorite thing she ever said was "Look at me—I may not be young and I may not be cute, but look real close guys—I've got *round* eyes." He always thought this was so funny because he said while you were over there, you saw only "slant-eyed" females and almost forgot what American "round-eyed" women looked like!

Robert Scheidig was living in Paris, France when we heard from him in 1990. In 1965 and 1966 he was part of a U.S. Advisory Team assigned to the Army Republic of Vietnam's (ARVN) Twenty-first Infantry Division stationed at Bac Lieu. Robert was advising the Vietnamese Forty-second Ranger Battalion. Maggie often visited remote outposts and his was just that kind of place.

> Maggie actually lived with us and had her own "hootch." She used our location as a springboard for visiting other more isolated camps. The attack on SocTrang was just up the road. The firefight in Tay Ninh was some distance from our operational area, but it does not surprise me that she found herself in the thick of things there. That was just her way. She always wanted to be where the troops were and most of them were not in the Saigon area! Like most advisory camps, we were not big and important enough to warrant the visit of Bob Hope and the other big, star-studded shows. So, to us at Bac Lieu, these other happenings didn't matter since we had our own star living among us...and she was there when we needed her! She managed to have one or two other performers come see us.

> I will never forget Maggie and Edgar Bergen (with Charlie McCarthy) performing for us at Christmas 1965. They used only jeep headlights because our generators went out. It was one of the best moments our team spent at Bac Lieu!

Sergeant First Class Stephen Woodman of East Lebanon, Maine saw Maggie near Danang in late 1965. One day during noon chow, a jeep pulled up with three drenched people in it—Maggie and two men. They entered the mess hall and Maggie introduced herself and her companions. She said they were very hungry and that they would try to earn their lunch by entertaining them for a while. She stood in the pouring rain and told jokes and sang a few songs. She then asked if her group had earned their meal. All the troops gave them a hearty applause. Maggie and her friends then went through the chow line and each of them sat with the soldiers. Stephen said, "They ate the same slop we did under the same conditions. After finishing their meals, they prepared to leave. Martha thanked us for allowing her to eat with us. She said she had other GI's to see and must go. The three of them got into their jeep and left."

"She's Amazing, Doc"

In 1990 Michael Hirsh was preparing to make a documentary film for television about Maggie. He interviewed Dr. Carl Bartecchi of Pueblo, Colorado who was a flight surgeon assigned to a "dustoff" helicopter unit in the Mekong Delta during 1965 and 1966. The doctor explained:

> Martha was one of the boys. The impression that some of us had about star-type people was that they mingled with the officers, the higher-ups or the upper echelon. Martha wouldn't do that. She was off with the "grunts," as they were called. The officers didn't need so much of what she had to offer. But the boys did. Martha seemed to know how to touch that little nerve to get those men laughing and singing.

It's hard to believe that the celebrity I heard so much about was all of a sudden able to switch roles and become somebody helping you in tough situations that were difficult even for some of our medics. We had bleeding wounds; we were tying off arteries that were severed, and cleaning up burns that smelled terrible. Yet there she was doing a good job.

Units in my area sustained heavy casualties when they found themselves surrounded by a Viet Cong battalion. The casualties came to my dispensary.

I was in the operating room. I heard this female voice—a sound that was somewhat unusual for our area. I looked at the name tag and it spelled Raye. I obviously was very surprised. She said, "Don't worry, I know what I'm doing." We were moving people along. We were cleaning out wounds. She seemed very skilled. We did this for probably a couple of hours.

At one point I noticed that she walked out. Later on, I heard the moment that she left, she donated a pint of blood to one of the fellas we were working on who needed blood at that time. We didn't have a storage of blood at the base. But she came right back and continued to work. We kept working on people and periodically she'd leave. Then I would hear laughter. She'd help clean up and sterilize instruments and did a fantastic job.

I understood later that Martha was cracking a lot of jokes and keeping everybody's spirits up. I went to our front room where we had all these casualties. Martha was moving from stretcher to stretcher teasing, cajoling, and kidding with these people and lifting their spirits in one way or another. A lot of these young fellas hadn't experienced these many casualties.

From that experience I learned that adding a little humor to a serious situation is very helpful. It made it a lot easier for the young medics to work in this setting. The team worked better.

Very few entertainers came down to our area. It took somebody special to come and stay overnight because at night we'd be mortared. But Martha was there several days.

> I remember the show and I remember that she brought down the house that evening. I remember Martha Raye. I think it's because all of a sudden she'd become something special to the people on our base. I didn't know then that she was at other locations in the Mekong Delta, in places where you usually didn't go. Yet, these are the places that people like Martha were most needed, and there was nobody who could pick up your spirits like Martha Raye.
>
> She knew how to make you feel good. The words that came back from my medics and my men who were working were, "She's amazing, Doc. You oughta see her."

William Chase Jr. of Stevensburg, Virginia served two tours of duty in Vietnam. The first was in 1965 and 1966 as an advisor to a Vietnamese Infantry Battalion; the second was in 1969 and 1970 with the U.S. 173rd Airborne Brigade.

> During my first year Martha came to Tam Ky for us. She put on a tremendous one-hour show in the room we used as a chapel. She talked and joked with us for another hour. The most remarkable part is that she did all of this for only eight or nine of us advisors. I felt so grateful that she would do all of this for so few of us.

Stationed with a small group of Americans in Quang Ngai, Geoffrey Hancock provided support to the Second Vietnamese Infantry Division.

> We seldom saw any entertainment or visitors due to our remote location and small number of Americans. Martha Raye *did* visit us! She spent about an hour in the officers club and several hours in the Non-Commissioned Officers/Enlisted Men's shack buying drinks, telling stories, and cheering everyone up.

Donald Collins from Manchaca, Texas was stationed with the Ninety-third Evacuation Hospital at Ben Hoa.

He was a Mess Sergeant when Maggie visited the hospital.

> She worked in the operating room with our doctors and nurses during a critical period when our operating room was overflowing with wounded soldiers of the 173rd Airborne Brigade. Martha worked side by side with our hospital staff for hours on end to help the numerous patients who were brought into the emergency room. Ms. Raye also radiated a genuine feeling of caring and support to both the patients and hospital staff.

Tex and Wayne

Sergeant First Class Edwin "Tex" Sellers of New Boston, Texas was also stationed in Bac Lieu.

> Maggie spent approximately five months, on and off, at Bac Lieu, Vietnam and this was her headquarters. She was made an honorary member of the Vietnamese Twenty-first Infantry Division, known as "The Paddy Rats." We were located in the Mekong Delta with Advisory Team Fifty-one.

In February 1990, I was at home answering piles of mail we had received about Maggie and her exploits. Accounts about our project to have Maggie honored with the Presidential Medal of Fredom had been in newspapers nationwide two weeks earlier. The phone was ringing off the hook because my number had appeared in many publications.

There was a knock at the kitchen door. A Colonie (New York) police officer introduced himself and said he had an emergency phone call for me. The caller had been trying unsuccessfully to reach me by phone and had contacted the local authorities. The officer handed me a slip of paper with the person's name and number. Since I did not recognize the name, all kinds of thoughts ran through my head. As a First Sergeant in the Army

Reserves, I envisioned that one of my soldiers was in trouble. I was worried that a family member or friend had passed away. I thanked the officer for the message and dialed the number he had given me.

Master Sergeant Wayne Sexton answered the phone. He wanted to tell me about his brief but exciting encounter with Maggie.

Wayne served from 1965 to 1966 at Bac Lieu with Advisory Team Fifty-one. Maggie stayed at his camp a couple days a week, sometimes a week at a time. When she entertained his group, she had a two-piece combo with her from Saigon.

He suggested that we try to contact Colonel Spellman, the senior advisor of Wayne's team and the Twenty-first Division of the ARVN. That name rang a bell. Tex Sellers also had suggested that we locate the same man who was known to all his troops as "Bull Moose." Both Vets felt that the colonel could provide me with more background on Maggie. To this day, however, we have been unable to reach him.

I recognized similarities between Wayne's and Tex Seller's stories. I asked if he knew "Tex." He certainly did: they were old teammates, and Wayne had no idea that Tex was even alive. I gave him Tex's address and phone number. What a joy to share information to bring together these two friends from so long ago!

Julius Crane of Strafford, Missouri saw Maggie in March 1966. Serving with Detachment B-Thirty-three, Fifth Special Forces Group in Hon Quan, Binh Long Province, he received a radio message that Maggie was flying in by chopper. He could not believe she would come to this unsecured remote camp to see only ten Special Forces troops. But Maggie arrived, performed, sang, and talked with them.

> She spent the night and never complained about the poor sleeping accommodations and our borrowed, well-

> used mosquito net. She flew off the next morning. Our morale had been greatly lifted, and we all just felt great that she cared enough to come out to see us. She made my day!

Just Deserts

William Doherty served with the Marines' D-First of the Ninth, D-First Reconnaissance. He was impressed that Maggie not only was an accomplished entertainer, but that she voluntarily endured the dangers and discomforts of the war zone where lines between front and rear were often invisible. William feels Maggie deserved the Legion of Merit medal and the Vietnam Civilian Service medal. He is not alone.

Sergeant Major James Carr formerly of Orange, California believes that Maggie should have earned the Humane Services Medal and the Air Medal. He also feels she should have been promoted to the rank of full colonel in the Army Reserves.

> Martha is, was, and always will be a very special lady in the hearts of Vietnam Veterans. Hundreds of wounded in the tent hospitals and thousands whose names appear etched in stone on the Vietnam Memorial were beneficiaries of her deep and abiding concern for her fellow man. She brought love and laughter and left it behind in abundance.
>
> Martha, wearing jungle fatigues and the leaves of a lieutenant colonel, Army Nurse Corps, appeared out of the dusty skies of the combat zone via a helicopter and invaded Advisory Team Ninety-five in mid-1966, at the height of the Vietnam War. She came fully equipped with her wonderful smile and dynamic personality to put on a show for our small group of American troops. There were no conveniences, no stage, no speakers. However, she proved that her brand of talent, wit, and extraordinary humor didn't require any props. She was the only entertainer our team was to see during the entire year, but her presence has long remained.

After the show, she sat with us to discuss her visits to isolated Special Forces teams in War Zone D. She remarked about my earning the Combat Medical Badge. My immediate thought was that my efforts paled in comparison to hers. Here was a talented actress and expert Army Nurse who freely gave of her time, money, and self to literally aid and comfort the wounded while uplifting the spirit and morale of those who continued to carry out the mission at hand.

Does Martha Raye deserve a medal? She deserves a whole truckload!

Colonel Maggie got her hands dirty, helped in aid stations, bravely—and repeatedly—moved in harm's way, and gave up creature comforts to be with her troops.

In 1966 while serving with the "Swift Boats" at Monkey Mountain, Danang Harbor, Chief Petty Officer Carl Jay saw Maggie. His group, PCF-102 and YR-71, also covered Coast Guard Division Twelve. He remembered that Maggie left the Admiral's Headquarters, which was on the river at the White Elephant Building in Danang. She entered the harbor on the Admiral's Barge and crossed to Jay's base.

In 1966 things were pretty hot. While she was there, we had a red alert. The Viet Cong fired rockets but pretty much were off target. The sky was lit up with flares and red smoke. It was something that we were used to. Martha was real cool, calm, and collected, but I could tell she was scared.

She toured all the boats, visited with all the crew members, cracked jokes, and told us all how much she loved us. I remember the Admiral's Aide trying to get her to leave and scurry back across the Bay to relative safety—which was not really true in those days. Anyway....she said, "Hell No...I came to see these guys and I'm here, and I'm gonna stay." And she did....

There were a lot more celebrities who came out there. But they stayed in the safe spots. Martha Raye will always be special to me.

A Longtime Friend

Joe Bristol of Potterville, Michigan corresponded with us for several years. We finally met at Maggie's funeral. He had a special relationship with Maggie that began in 1966.

> Martha Raye and I met in Vietnam in 1966. Another marine and I were sneaking to Danang from Hill Fifty-five. The road was shut down for a mine sweep so we stopped at an army camp to get some hot chow. Colonel Maggie was there in her fatigues doing a vaudeville act with a ukulele player accompanying her, singing songs, and telling jokes. She stayed for hours entertaining and signing autographs on soft covers, helmets or whatever.
>
> I got out of the Marine Corps in 1968. Several years later I went to see her in Flint, Michigan in the musical *Little Orphan Annie.* I was able to meet with her after the show. We partied until four A.M. We laughed and we cried. She gave me one of her rings to remember that evening. A few months later she sent me tickets to see her Chicago performance in the play *Everybody Loves Opal.* It was a very special time for us. In the middle of the night we went down to the lobby and took the marquee with her picture in it off the wall so she could give it to me.
>
> We kept in touch several times a year. I flew to Los Angeles to see her at Cedars-Sinai Hospital after her stroke.
>
> I think of her as a second mother to me. She will always be a special person in my heart.

James Turner of Pleasant Valley, New York was with the 819th Red Horse Squadron in 1966. His Air Force engineer unit was building what was to become the Phu Cat Air Base. He said that they were surprised that anyone would come to entertain them out in the boondocks, a far cry from the usual entertainer's circuit. But he soon learned this was Maggie's style.

Phu Cat Air Base, Vietnam—1966: Maggie signs autographs for members of the 819th Red Horse Squadron. Photo contributed by James Turner.

Combat Boots Two-Step

"China Beach" was both a television show and an actual place. Some nurses claim the TV production was nothing like the real thing, while others say it was somewhat similar. Gunnery Sergeant William Robinson of Omaha was with the Third Marine Division in Danang, just a few miles from China Beach.

> One day when I was at China Beach walking around looking for some buddies, I noticed several guys sitting by a shelter hut. They looked pretty tired and hot. I could tell by their expressions and dirty worn uniforms that they had just come in from the bush. I asked what they were waiting for, and they replied that someone was going to put on a show soon. They did not know who. Being curious, I waited around too. Within a short time a lady came out in combat fatigues and started talking to us. I recognized Martha Raye. You could

sense that she was disappointed that there were not more servicemen to perform for, and I think she probably would have liked to have had a stage.

After chitchatting for a few minutes, she said, "Well, I thought there were going to be more men here, but what the hell, I said I was going to give a show and that is what I am going to do." Accompanied by a tape recorder, she proceeded to tell jokes, sing and dance (in combat boots!) for about forty-five minutes in the hot sun. During the show, men would walk by, attracted by the tape recorded music. Some would stay and others would keep walking.

In spite of the very hot weather, the working area, the small crowd, poor conditions, men milling around, she performed like she was on Broadway for the entire show. At the end of her show, which she concluded with her famous big smile, she looked as if she had just run a twenty-six-mile marathon. There were only about three or four of us who were there at the end, but we rose to our feet and gave her a standing ovation.

I will never forget that moment as I experienced dual emotions: embarrassment, because she did not have a larger audience to appreciate her efforts, and immense admiration because regardless of all the elements, she showed why she was called "the grandest trouper of all."

He Never Saw His Twentieth Birthday...

Infantry trooper Marion Hattabaugh of Roann, Indiana was serving with B-2/502nd, 101st Airborne Division when he and his eighteen-year-old friend were wounded and sent to a field hospital in Tuy Hoa. Maggie performed for less than fifty men.

> Her music was great and her humor even greater. She had a gift for lifting your spirits and truly knew how to entertain you.
>
> My friend never saw his twentieth birthday. I know that Miss Raye's performance was one of the very few highlights in his young life.

They Blew Her Stage Away

Sergeant First Class Samuel Muoio of New Albany, Indiana was sixty-seven years old when we corresponded. He was a veteran of World War II, Korea, and Vietnam. He saw Maggie in 1966 in the Tuy Hoa area of II Corps.

> I was an advisor with the Vietnamese Infantry. We had a rear area of approximately one hundred American troops of which about seventy-five percent were administrative. We were in the rear area on a break when she came with a bass guitar player and another gentleman. Before the show was over, we were called to duty and loaded three Vietnamese battalions on choppers for what we thought was a small operation but, as usual, our information was very off. We were hit by the first North Vietnamese Regulars that had entered the war.
>
> We handled the Viet Cong okay and secured the area. We had only ten Americans on this operation. All of a sudden we got a call to secure a school house that was in the area, that we were getting visitors. In came three choppers, two of them were gunships. We couldn't believe it: coming out of the chopper in fatigues and a lieutenant colonel emblem, was Martha Raye and her crew. She put on her show in the schoolhouse with no power, but she didn't need any. The area was still taking enemy fire.
>
> I don't know if she ever found out, but approximately two hours after she left, we were overrun by the North Vietnamese. We lost three of our ten Americans.
>
> That lady has more guts than a lot of men I know. My hat is off to her!

Chapter 7

Above and Beyond the Call

"After fifteen straight hours of work, we finished treating the wounded. I walked out into the cool of the night to smoke a cigarette. That same nurse asked for a spare cigarette. She removed her surgical mask, and I recognized Martha Raye.

No entertainer has accomplished what this woman did. She not only entertained, but worked as a nurse to help treat the wounded. To the men of Vietnam, she was a Saint!!"

Joseph Garrigan, Jr.
(Marina, California)

UNITED STATES ARMY
CERTIFICATE OF APPRECIATION
FOR
PATRIOTIC CIVILIAN SERVICE
TO
MISS MARTHA RAYE

For meritorious service from 18 to 19 October 1966 while Miss Raye was entertaining United States military personnel at SocTrang, Republic of Vietnam, a great number of casualties were brought to the military hospital for emergency treatment. Realizing that the medical personnel were overburdened, Miss Raye volunteered her services. Throughout the evening and early morning hours, she labored tirelessly to help relieve the suffering, she donated blood, cleansed wounds, prepared patients for surgery, and applied dressings. In her well-known jovial manner, she circulated throughout the hospital, talking and joking with the patients and staff, and succeeded in raising and maintaining the morale of all during a period of extreme stress and anxiety. Miss Raye's unselfish, humanitarian actions were of immeasurable benefit to the health and welfare of personnel involved and reflect great credit upon herself and the entertainment profession.

9 NOVEMBER 1966
GENERAL WILLIAM C. WESTMORELAND

-7-

Maggie cohosted "The Mike Douglas Show" in Philadelphia during part of 1966, but her heart was in Vietnam. In September she went there again on her own. After returning stateside for a brief visit, the USO sent Maggie back to Vietnam...for fifteen weeks!

Former Army Captain Philip Dvorak of Davenport, Iowa was at SocTrang in September that year.

> Martha had entertained the troops with her USO show. The following day was for her a rest day, which she chose to spend at SocTrang. That day our aviation companies ran into stiff Viet Cong resistance. We suffered casualties. Friends died.
>
> During the daylong vigil, we awaited the engagement's outcome. It was during this time that Maggie added her fellowship of cheer to help raise morale. She donated blood that day. I was particularly touched by this poignant act.

While serving with the First Battalion, Third Marine Regiment, Third Marine Division at Khe Sanh in the fall of 1966, Royden Pearson of Ormond Beach, Florida had the pleasure of meeting "Colonel Maggie."

> On one occasion when she was about ready to put on a show at the Third Medical Battalion, they had incoming wounded. The show waited while she assisted with their care. She was truly a professional both as nurse and an entertainer. I do not know of any other entertainer that cared the way she did.

The "Black Patches"

Hershel Gober, Deputy Secretary of Veterans Affairs during the Clinton Administration, was an Army captain who carried a rifle and a guitar during the Vietnam conflict. He was ordered to form the first all-soldier entertainment troupe consisting of two guitarists, a bass player, a drummer, and a saxophonist. They called themselves the "Black Patches" for the black identification tags, chevrons and such worn by soldiers in combat areas. The "Black Patches" crossed trails with Maggie several times.

> In the fall of 1966, our "Black Patches" group flew to Danang to entertain the Marines. We were met by a three-quarter ton truck and a captain who took us to an open bay barracks with no way to secure our instruments—really a miserable place. We were combat troops so we normally would not have complained; however, my guys would do four or five shows a day and never complain. I went to the officer in charge and asked if perhaps we could have a better place. He was upset that we would even ask. I believe his IQ was equal to, or less than, an ice cube.
>
> I knew Martha Raye was in Danang and that she was a good friend of Lieutenant General Lewis Walt, the Senior Marine in Vietnam. I called her and she had us moved into the villa where they normally put civilian performers, regardless of how bad they were. As the group's leader I guess what upset me the most was that you could be a *civilian* entertainer and be treated well. Because we were "Grunts," we weren't treated that well.
>
> After returning stateside, I was assigned to Recruiting Command and sent around the country. While I was in New York, I called Martha. She was starring in *Hello, Dolly!* I could hear her attendant tell Martha who it was. Martha grabbed the phone and began bubbling at a hundred-miles-an-hour. She put me front row center. In the middle of her biggest scene—where she made her entrance—she stopped and introduced me to the audience.
>
> A great lady, a great patriot, and a friend to the guys and gals who make America great and keep it strong.

What, Me Worry?

Master Gunnery Sergeant J.R. Todd, a Naval Aviation pilot, met Maggie under high-risk circumstances.

> The lady was my passenger on the run from Chu Lai to Danang on 30 October 1966. We had taken one hit going in and I related this to Martha. Her reply was, "Those S.O.B.'s couldn't hit the broad side of a barn" or words to that effect. She wasn't in the least bit worried.

While stationed with the First Special Forces Group on Okinawa, Joseph Garrigan, Jr. of Marina, California received Temporary Duty orders to the Fifth Special Forces in Vietnam in September, 1966. He was assigned to the Mike Force at Pleiku as a medic.

> Around 1 November 1966, we were heavily engaged against North Vietnam Regulars and sustained heavy casualties among our Montagnard troops. We evacuated the wounded to the C-team infirmary. A doctor and the C-team medics were tending to the wounded.
>
> While treating a young "yard" with a serious arm wound, an American woman dressed as a nurse approached me and asked to assist. She helped with the debridement and bandaging of the wound. I was grateful for her much needed assistance.
>
> For hours she continued to assist us in treating the wounded. I remember her going from table to table. She obtained needed instruments and supplies, assisted with the debridement and suturing of wounds, bandaged wounds and assisted with the application of casts.
>
> After about fifteen straight hours of work, we finished. I walked out into the cool of the night to smoke a cigarette. That same nurse asked for a spare cigarette. She removed her surgical mask, and I recognized Martha Raye.
>
> No entertainer has accomplished what this woman did. She not only entertained, but worked as a nurse to help treat the wounded. To the men of Vietnam, she was a Saint!!

Troops' Personal Courier

Patricia Fisher of Las Cruces, New Mexico was one of many wives who received a phone call from Maggie. In the fall of 1966, she was a twenty-five-year-old Navy wife and mother of five living in San Diego. Her husband was in Vietnam assigned to Navy Seal Team One. She recalls what led up to the phone call.

> I was expecting our sixth child when in November I developed complications with the pregnancy and was told that the baby would not make it. Mail was not something I got a lot of as my husband, Ray, was in-country and security did not allow a lot of outside contact. The Red Cross sent a telegram, but I had no way of knowing if he got it. Needless to say, Christmas of 1966 is not one of my better memories.
>
> As I became more and more depressed, I felt very much alone until one day in January 1967 my phone rang. I was asked my name and if Ray was my husband; well, it was Martha Raye. She had been in-country in Vietnam and had appeared at Ray's camp.
>
> She personally talked to each man, took phone numbers, and promised to relay messages. Ray told her about the baby, and true to her word she took time out of her busy schedule and called me right away. In fact, she not only called me to let me know Ray got the telegram, but talked to me for almost half an hour.
>
> I will always have a special place in my heart for Martha Raye for taking the time to do this on her own for someone she had never met. She talked to me like a sister and not like someone just relaying a message. Her kindness and sisterly attitude really helped me get through this tough period in my life.

Compulsion to Care

Maggie was entertaining aboard the USS *Constellation* when the USS *Oriskany* had an explosion. Zalin Grant was there and kept a journal, which he turned into a book called *Over The Beach.* He mentions Maggie as willing to risk her life to assist the wounded.

> No one had to say it. Every man understood. The *Oriskany* was fighting for her life. Reports began flowing to the bridge. The ship's Senior Medical Officer was dead, as was the chaplain. Casualties were mounting. Men were trapped in their rooms, sure to die if not rescued soon. Captain Tarrobino radioed the USS *Constellation* to ask the carrier to send all available doctors. Martha Raye was visiting the "Connie" and wanted to go to the *Oriskany* as a nurse—she was turned down. The fire continued to spread. [2]

Chief Journalist George Marshall also remembers Maggie that fatal day. He was serving as the assistant Public Affairs Officer aboard the "Connie" in the Gulf of Tonkin.

> Maggie was aboard to entertain the five thousand-plus sailors and Marines. She was doing a "handshake" tour and the night before had visited the crew in messing and work spaces, the ready rooms, the ship's hospital, etc. Maggie was preparing for the short hop by helo for the "Big O" just about breakfast time. We had closed to about a half mile to make a quick ride for Miss Raye when the alarms went off.
>
> The flare locker, located amidships on the *Oriskany,* had exploded, injuring and killing a number of sailors. We immediately moved closer so our fire-fighting equipment would be available to assist if needed. Our doctors and medical personnel got ready to helo over for the massive job they knew they would be called upon to do.
>
> The first, of course, to volunteer (actually demand, plead, beg permission) to go was "Colonel Maggie" Raye. People were injured, dead, or dying. She was a nurse. She *was* going!
>
> It took an admiral, several captains, and assorted officers, chiefs and medical personnel to finally convince her that, as much as she wanted to assist, because

of her celebrity status, she would only be more of a hindrance than a help.

In tears, she relented—but she made hundreds of *real* friends that day. Not because she was Miss Martha Raye, the entertainer, but because she was "Colonel Maggie," the nurse with the biggest heart we knew.

Fort Martha Raye

Staff Sergeant Barry Sadler wrote the song, "The Ballad of the Green Berets." In his book *I'm A Lucky One,* Barry mentioned that Maggie visited the Eighth Field Hospital at NhaTrang when he was a patient there, and she made a big hit with everybody. She made quite an impression on him, especially that she toured Vietnam posts in a tiger camouflage suit. He mentions that a bunker at Bac Lieu was named Fort Martha Raye.

About this time, another pre-taped program aired on CBS-TV. "Clown Alley," a one-hour variety special, was hosted by Red Skelton. The show was a tribute to circus clowns. Guests included Maggie along with Robert Merrill, Amanda Blake, Jackie Coogan, Audrey Meadows, Vincent Price, Bobby Rydell, and Billy Barty. Meanwhile, Maggie continued her mission throughout Vietnam.

Keith Hall was attached to a Marine photography unit. His group was located at Chu Lai, about sixty or seventy miles south of Danang. He had just returned from two weeks in the bush. All he wanted were a shower, clean clothes, a "warm" beer, any food he could get "not in a can" and then some sleep. But first he had to turn in his film and captions. He heard that Maggie was performing for the troops in the mess hall. Her visit was unexpected. He grabbed some fresh film, loaded his camera, and headed there.

> There she was, sporting tiger fatigues and a matching jungle hat that must have been provided by the Army. Marines in 1966 didn't rate camouflage. We're forever donning green, unless the Army has a garage sale.

Raye's set was simple: a mike, a beat-up speaker system checked out of Special Services, and a male accompanist with a guitar.

What immediately grabbed you was the wide mouth and the unmistakable smile. All she had to do was beam that smile and all knew we were in the presence of Martha Raye.

She opened her show by telling us that America was proud of our dedication and sacrifice in the name of freedom. Usually, we scoffed at such banter. But, her words were sincere and it was obvious she believed what she was saying. Raye didn't have to come to this hole in the wall in the middle of the monsoon season to perform before a bunch of teenagers whose only recollection of her accomplishments was from "The Late Show" movies. But, there she was, and we admired her for being there.

Her opening dialogue segued into a series of songs popular to a generation or two before these teenagers. But, we were in the presence of an institution and that's all that mattered.

Raye ended the show by introducing her accompanist and making another heartrending speech about how wonderful we were to be in Vietnam.

The public relations troop performed a perfunctory interview; I snapped a few frames and Raye's visit to Chu Lai was over. A chopper was waiting on the pad to fly her to Danang.

The rain fell harder as we exited the mess hall. The Public Relations marine left to file his story, and I dashed back to the lab, desperately trying to keep the camera dry. The gunny'd kill me if I ruined the camera.

All I could think of as I sloshed through the mud was, "Gosh, so that was Martha Raye. Who'd have guessed?"

Hollywood Bowl, East—*Far* East

Colonel Arthur Kelly of Frankfort, Kentucky was a lieutenant colonel with the First Battalion, Seventy-seventh Artillery, First Cavalry Division when he visited Colonel George Casey's Second Brigade.

In November of 1966 when Martha Raye touched down at Landing Zone Oasis, south of Pleiku in the Ia Drang Valley area, during November, 1966, she looked exhausted. Colonel Casey asked, "What do you need that we can help you with?" "A latrine, a shot of bourbon, and a place to clean up in—in that order," she said.

In a preshow ceremony, Colonel Casey expressed the gratitude of all the men and women in Vietnam for her tireless effort to entertain so many in Vietnam. The men watched to see how she would respond to their little surprise.

Colonel Casey proclaimed the natural bowl theater, the "Martha Raye Bowl Theater," and he unveiled the well-finished engraved concrete marker. First a smile crossed her lips, then she cried. And the men in their combat attire had to wipe their eyes as best they could without being noticed.

Her weariness dissolved when the show started and again she evoked laughter from the men fresh out of the jungle where belly laughs were hard to come by.

As she departed in the bright moonlight night, she turned and in a loud voice said, "Be careful Colonel Kelly." Two steps farther she turned again and said, "And beat the crap out of them."

Vietnam—November 1966: L-R Specialist 4 VanHook, Maggie and Rennie Grant. Photo contributed by Rennie Grant.

Many chaplains saw Maggie. Chaplain (Captain) Robert Witt of Capistrano Beach was assigned to the First Battalion, Third Marine Regiment, Third Marine Division. Their assignment was to protect a small airfield and the ARVN camp at Khe Sanh, a few miles east of the Laotian border and the Ho Chi Minh Trail, about ten miles south of the DMZ. Robert remembers the U.S. Marine Corps birthday, November 10, 1966.

> With only a brief notice of her arrival, Miss Raye and party arrived by helicopter, along with steaks and soft drinks for our birthday celebration. Without much hesitation, she hopped upon a hastily (and shakily) erected platform of C-ration cartons and artillery shell carriers.
>
> After an excited crowd of Marines gathered around, Miss Raye began her marvelous and hilarious routine. Her rapid-fire delivery and outlandish facial expressions produced round after round of laughter and cheers for the first time in months.
>
> It was obvious that she was not just another performer, but that she really cared about us being so far from home.

Round Eyes

During the Vietnam War the troops seldom saw women. When they did, the women were usually Vietnamese. The rare times when troops saw American women were if they were injured and sent to an evacuation hospital or if they happened to catch a USO show somewhere. The troops referred to any woman from America as having "round eyes." Colonel Peter Vogentanz formerly of Wheaton, Illinois was a major when he saw Maggie. The occasion stuck in his mind. It was the week before Christmas 1966 just west of Plei Djerang.

> I remember her telling the soldiers that she had already entertained their fathers and in some cases their grandfathers in World War II and Korea, but that the only

> redeeming physical assets she brings to the task in spite of her being an "old bag" were her "round eyes." Well let me tell you she brought more to me than round eyes!

Another soldier was recovering from malaria at a hospital outside Saigon. Maggie showed up to entertain and lift the hospitalized troops' spirits. Sergeant Major Marshall Anders describes his encounter.

> I will never forget her opening line. After coming on stage, all smiles, she suddenly got very serious, looked at a young soldier in the front row and said, "Honey, I know I'm not young or pretty, but look at my eyes, Baby—they're *round*." She went on to perform a show I'll remember always.

In March 1966, Colonel James Gueydan of Houma, Louisiana assumed command of the NhaTrang Air Base, just north of Cam Rahn Bay in the II Corps area. Maggie's visit followed a very busy night.

> In December of 1966, Martha Raye was scheduled to visit our base. The commander at Danang sent a message saying she would be delayed. The next day he called and told me that she was not at all the loud-mouthed buffoon she pretended to be in her act.
>
> He told me that when she landed there, they had just been attacked again and had many casualties. When Maggie heard this, she asked to be taken to the operating room. Some people thought she was grandstanding, but she scrubbed, asked how she could help and worked hard and competently for about fourteen hours nonstop. She was a skillful Operating Room nurse. I understand that she was a Reserve Corps Nurse but I am not certain of that. I am certain, however, that she greatly impressed the people at Danang.
>
> After her stint in the OR, she cleaned up, did her act and came directly to NhaTrang. She did her "thing" there after having had no sleep the night before. When she finished her performance, she turned to me and said, "I've checked: you have an air-conditioned trailer—

> *OUT*! I need some sleep." She promptly crashed, got back on schedule and was on her way.
>
> Though there was no doubt in my mind that she was going to evict me, her demeanor when not performing was quiet, soft spoken, courteous, friendly. She was a delight to all who met her.

Her Beverage of Choice: Vodka

Colonel Leo Ehmann was the Commander of the 535th Troop Carrier Squadron in Vung Tau (Cape St. Jacques). The squadron was formed from an Army Aviation Group of CV-2 "Caribou" Aircraft (U.S. Air Force C-7's). Effective January 1, 1967, the Air Force took over and operated these Army aircraft, much to the Army's chagrin. Colonel Ehmann was on Army duty during the transitional period.

By the official changeover date, the airmen had begun to operate an Air Force Officer's Club in Vung Tau at the small hotel they took over as an aircrew housing facility. Maggie had been flown to Saigon on one of their aircraft to appear for the Army. An enterprising pilot asked her to come to Vung Tau and enjoy the hospitality of their small Club. She accepted and, with her guitar player, arrived in Vung Tau just after Christmas 1966.

> You must be aware of Maggie's penchant for vodka—at least at that time. In conjunction with her guitar player, Martha serenaded us into the wee hours while consuming vodka by the water glass. To our amazement, she maintained her professionalism and voice.
>
> A small group of Air Force C-7 Caribou pilots will never forget her appearance at our small, practically unknown, outpost in the Port of Vung Tau over twenty years ago.

Many people commented about Maggie's love for vodka, and I saw her put away quite a bit of it each time I visited her. Her home had many different varieties of alcoholic beverages in it, but she usually drank vodka.

Surrogate Swilling

A retired Marine, Major Charles Olson of Havelock, North Carolina commented that Maggie will always be one of his favorite people. Since the forties, he had enjoyed her performances on stage, screen, radio, newsreels, and television. Although he noted that her entertainment achievements were known to most Americans, knowledge of her dedicated service to our country was not widespread. He suspects this was due to her reluctance to capitalize on the publicity. In her own words, she was "just doing my job." From 1965 to 1967 Charles spent most of his time in the I Corps area from Quaing Ngai to Dong Ha. He met Maggie in Dong Ha in late 1966.

> While exchanging scuttlebutt and sea stories with my counterparts at the headquarters level, I heard stories about Martha being in Vietnam, not only as an entertainer, which some said was the initial purpose of her stay, but as an expert nurse. Holding the rank of lieutenant colonel, she was doing amazing things in hospitals in the southern Corps area with the Army, Special Forces, and the Air Force. The Marines told these tales reverently, with almost parochial interest, confiding that Martha was "one of our own." It seems that is a common feeling among members of all branches of service.
>
> Martha was a gracious and charming guest at dinner at the O-Club. She treated everyone as if they were very special, encouraged an informal atmosphere in the Wardroom and at the bar, and kept the conversation light and lively. She moved away from the bar to a table located by one of the shuttered side windows, and Marines stumbled over each other bringing her drinks. They tried to keep up with her, but the drinks went to her table in conspicuous amounts, prompting the Marines to marvel at her ability to keep up with them, and even surpassing some thirsty officers' capabilities. What they *didn't* know was Martha kept handing those drinks

out the side window to enlisted Marines standing outside!

It was a bonanza for the troops, since they were limited to about two beers a day, when it was available, and that wasn't very often. The party inside the Club was almost as cheerful as the surreptitious party going on outside. The young Marines loved it. The officers thought Martha had to have a hollow leg, earning her a reputation for drinking along with the best of the party group that evening.

Months after the fact, Marines at Danang were still talking about the evening and several officers were most happy to point out the table where Martha had been sitting. They boasted about how she had taken care of the troops waiting outside the window.

Major Olson recalled seeing Maggie again when, during a recon mission, a helicopter was shot down near the landing zone. A Quick Reaction Force was sent to protect the aircraft mechanics while they repaired or destroyed the chopper. Flight operations were curtailed, requests for artillery support increased, and there were requests for medevac choppers. The tension was broken when he noticed Maggie.

I don't know how long Martha had been standing on the small veranda of the French barracks just down from the Commanding General's quarters. She was wearing a black nightgown with her field jacket or utility shirt over her shoulders. The nightgown wasn't revealing, but it did have a covering of lace. Her hair was tousled but appeared neat, nonetheless. She couldn't sleep because there was no way of keeping the hordes of mosquitoes out of her temporary sleeping quarters. She had patiently waited for a break in operations to ask for some insect repellent—"bug juice," as she put it. One of the Marines gave her his bottle, and she cheerfully bade us "good night" as she went back to her room.

I guess we were dumbfounded by her appearance when we realized who she was. All of us had silly smiles on our faces, but they were relaxed smiles. After all the worry and anxiety of the hours before, Martha's appearance did more for all of us than I could ever describe. Fears disappeared, the situation was well in hand, and it was a new ball game.

I don't know if it was the way it seemed completely normal to have Martha Raye standing in a nightgown asking for insect repellent, or the way she appeared to be so casual about the whole thing, or if her touching our lives at that time brought a softness, a missed femininity, to the harsh world of stark realities. Whatever it was, it was just the right touch for the moment. It had a terrific, calming effect on all hands.

Major Olson had helped a squad out of a scrape and they "adopted" him as their own. This recon squad had spent a great deal of time behind enemy lines.

One of the lads, a corporal, had a reputation for being expert in the recon business. He was deadly serious, had the coldest "killer eyes," flat and gray, and was coldly impersonal with most folks he met. He didn't like officers, but went along with the rest of the squad in my case. Without exaggeration, whenever I talked with him, the hair on my neck stood out. His sergeant saw me come in and wanted me to meet the squad's special guest that evening. He was as excited as I had seen him, and I wondered what the squad was up to this time.

He led me over to the table where the rest of the squad was seated, and I almost choked when I recognized Martha Raye sitting with them. She was sitting right next to the corporal with the killer eyes! I immediately worried about what might come of her meeting with this squad of recon Marines. The sergeant introduced me to her, and after a brief exchange of pleasantries, I went back to the bar to think of what I could do to get her away from that table. I really didn't need to worry. She had the whole situation under control; the Marines were on their best behavior, as good as school boys, and she appeared to be enjoying herself immensely.

The sergeant was talking, occasionally looking over his shoulder toward me, and it was obvious I was the topic of conversation. Bless her heart! Martha got up and walked over to where I was leaning against the bar. She said the lads thought a lot about me, and she felt I should know that. I was flattered for several reasons, but I was impressed with Martha's kindness in passing on a compliment simply because she knew it would be important to me. I couldn't think of anything to say, but I wanted to do something for her for all the things she had done for so many folks, and what she was doing in Vietnam.

As you've read, my chance meetings with Martha weren't anything spectacular, but they were then—and still are—priceless memories. I will always have a warm spot in my heart for her.

Who Was Maggie's "Son"?

Melvin Bell, Jr. was with the Nineteenth Support Command Headquarters and Headquarters Company when he contacted us. He served in Vietnam near the DMZ at Phu Cat. In late 1966, he saw Maggie.

> At that time, it was still a very dangerous place, and we were just a bunch of GI's crowded into a small, dimly lit tent. Ms. Raye simply talked for a little while and left. She thanked us for being there and mentioned something about a son being stationed in Vietnam.
>
> I am sure there are thousands of other Americans whose spirits were lifted by her visits over the years. I believe she is a very generous and courageous woman.

Maggie's only child is her daughter, Melodye. Many people think she also had a son. During one of our conversations, she mentioned that she felt as though all the troops—both male and female—were her children and would refer to them as such. Perhaps that is where folks got the idea she had a son.

Senior Chief Petty Officer Frank Cirino of Virginia Beach saw Maggie while he was in Vietnam from 1966 to 1967 in Mobile Construction Battalion Forty, The Fighting Fortieth Seabee Battalion based in the I Corps, Chu Lai, Camp Shield. During late 1966 and early 1967, the Ninth Engineer Battalion, Fleet Marine Force was living in an austere field cantonment area. They supported the First Marine Division and later the Americal Division of the U.S. Army situated in Quang Tin Province. Major Edward Lifset of Oceanside, California remembers that his unit was honored with two extended visits by this great lady.

> Due to the adverse effects of both the tactical situation and winter monsoon rains, no suitable stage could be erected. Maggie was forced to spend two nights at our encampment with absolutely no amenities save a field shower that could only be reached by traversing a paddy covered by an eight-inch deep muddy Laterite quagmire. No other celebrity ever visited our units during this time frame due to our deployed situation, hostile activity, and the prohibitions of weather and terrain.
>
> Maggie made it a point to visit the marines and sailors from all seven of our companies. She focused special emphasis on the lower-rated personnel—often called "grunts." She continually exhibited genuine interest for the men, their unique equipment, as well as their activities. On one occasion she remained with a few of us well into the wee hours as we awaited the return of a combat patrol. She did not cower when a few incoming eighty-two millimeter mortar rounds exploded close by.
>
> There was no question as to the positive value of her visits on the morale of all personnel of the Ninth Engineer Battalion, Fleet Marine Force. Her cheerful, humorous, but sincere attitude truly served as an inspiration to us all, as well as providing a valuable memory.

Joe's Derby

Joe Powers of Prunedale, California also had a memorable experience with Maggie when he was with Advisory Team Fifty-one in Bac Lieu, headquarters for the southernmost part of the Mekong Delta. It was in what troops called "Marlboro Country."

Joe's job was to visit small villages and hamlets to conduct sick calls among the Vietnamese. Maggie went with him on a couple of those challenging trips; they had to travel mostly by sampans on small canals that ran throughout the Delta. When Joe was off duty he ran the small bar that they had at their MACV Compound. He was also well known for card tricks he could do.

Joe had uniforms made in Bac Lieu for his bar duty. He had black pants, a white shirt with a black bow tie, and a black vest. He wanted a black derby hat to go with the outfit but was unable to find one in Vietnam. He had men who went to Japan and the Philippines on R & R try to find one for him, but none could. That is where Maggie came into the picture.

> While Maggie was with us, I told her about the trouble I was having trying to find a derby. She said, "No problem. What size do you wear?" I told her the size, and she swore when she returned home she would send me a derby. Well, when she went back stateside, I thought that would be the end of the story. But it was not.
>
> About two months after she left, I had just come back from being out on patrol and the Unit mailman said to me, "You better get over to the mail room. I got a big box with a cowboy hat in it for you." The reason he thought it was a cowboy hat is because the return address on the box was from the Western Costume Company. I was wondering what was in the box, too.
>
> I opened the box and found the most beautiful black derby that I have ever seen. I am sure that it was expensive; it was from Dobbs Hat Company of New York. It was the hat that Maggie said she would send to me. I still have that hat today and the box it came in, and I will cherish it forever.
>
> When I received my orders to rotate back to the States the guys in the outfit asked if I was going to leave the derby with our unit. I said, "No way. The address

on that box said Sergeant First Class Joseph A. Powers and it is going home with me."

The Grunts' Gal

Colonel Harlan Jencks, Ph.D., of Monterey remembers seeing Maggie several times.

> In the spring of 1967, I was in Can Tho passing through Company D, Fifth Special Forces Group on my way to the U.S. for extension leave. Maggie was scheduled to put on a show that night, but canceled because more important needs came up. An American helicopter assault up in III Corps had run into a very "hot" landing zone, and there were so many casualties that all the hospitals in III Corps were swamped. Lots of overflow casualties were sent to the hospital in Can Tho. Maggie heard about it, went to the hospital, and went to work as a nurse. I heard later that she was in surgery for over twelve hours that night, but I can't vouch for that part.
>
> In 1984, I was commanding the Third Battalion, Twelfth Special Forces Group, U.S. Army Reserves. In May, one of my soldiers, Master Sergeant Bill Meranda, was killed in a helicopter crash. Maggie attended the funeral, providing a little extra comfort to Bill's family and his buddies.
>
> Maggie had always been there for us, especially when it was unpopular, when other show business people were making money by ridiculing and denigrating American soldiers. She specially remembered the guys who lacked publicity value, the isolated advisory and Special Forces detachments the ostentatiously "patriotic" stars never bothered with.
>
> She had no personal C-141, no air-conditioned trailer, and spent minimum time in the big secure base camps. She rode in dusty choppers and jeeps; lived, ate, and slept the way we did. She put on shows for tiny handfuls of guys out in dirty bug-infested places the rest of the world never heard of. Nor am I aware of any multimillion dollar TV specials exploiting her grand tours to "entertain the troops."
>
> She just made us happy and proud to be American soldiers, and I guess that was enough for her.

Chapter 8

"Focus on the Troops!"

"Maggie placed her career in jeopardy when she went to entertain the servicemen in Vietnam. Her career suffered tremendously because of her trips. However, she never flagged in her efforts to bring a little bit of 'home' to the troops."

Lieutenant Colonel John Forde, Jr.
Carlsbad, California

DEPARTMENT OF DEFENSE
MILITARY ASSISTANCE COMMAND, VIETNAM
CERTIFICATE OF APPRECIATION
TO
MARTHA RAYE

For your outstanding contributions to the morale and welfare of the United States and other free world military assistance forces in the Republic of Vietnam while touring the command, entertaining personnel of all military services. Your willingness to extend your tour has been appreciated deeply by the many thousands of men of all services. Because of your personal desire to present your show for the men at the more remote locations, these men serving under hardship conditions have had the rare pleasure of seeing and talking to a personality who is loved and respected by all and needs an introduction to none. Once again your tour has been characterized by a sincere desire to bring cheer to the fighting man wherever he is, and you have achieved another successful tour. The significant and lasting impression you made enhanced the morale of all fighting forces and reflects great credit upon yourself and your profession.

19 JANUARY 1967
GENERAL WILLIAM C. WESTMORELAND
SAIGON, VIETNAM

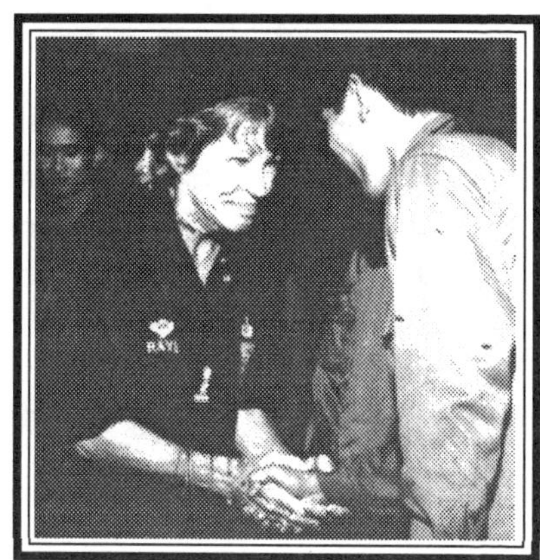

Danang East near Marble Mountain—1968: Maggie visits Fifth Special Forces camp, Forward Operating Base 4. Photo contributed by Robert L. Lawson.

-8-

We received more letters and phone calls from military personnel who saw Maggie in different areas of Vietnam at different times during 1966 and 1967. Whether they were enlisted personnel or officers, everyone fondly remembers their encounters with Maggie. Major General Donald Gardner saw Maggie while she was visiting the III Marine Amphibious Force.

> Ms. Raye has made an exceptional contribution to our servicemen in the interest of world peace. As a Vietnam Veteran, I recall, as if it were only yesterday, Ms. Raye's 1966, 1967, and 1972 visits to Danang. She was completely dedicated to keeping morale high.
>
> Her songs from *Hello, Dolly!* and *September Song* could always bring a smile to a tired Marine's face. Her shows were a touch of home for so many of us! Martha made the day brighter for us when we were wet, tired and far from home. She always received a standing ovation. In peacetime or wartime, she was a real pro.

Although I never met Lieutenant Colonel John Forde, Jr. of Carlsbad, California I feel that I know him. It was his article in a military newspaper in 1988 that triggered my own commitment to help Maggie be honored by our country. John believed Maggie had served our nation "above and beyond" through the three wars, and he was upset that she had not been publicly acknowledged. He noted that Maggie had already been in-country for a total of eighteen months before Bob Hope made an appearance in Vietnam!

> Maggie Raye, a qualified nurse and a lieutenant colonel in the Army Reserve, entertained anywhere and everywhere there was a soldier, sailor, airman, or Marine.

Miss Raye asked her assigned escorts to shelter her from the media. Maggie did not want attention focused on her—only on the American servicemen who were in-country.

Shows for Sapper Survivors

Lieutenant Colonel Forde holds Maggie in high regard. He cited two occasions where she indeed went "above and beyond the call of duty."

In early November 1966, I was assigned to be the escort for Martha Raye while she was in the First Marine Division Tactical Area of Responsibility, Danang and Chu Lai.

I met her at the First Medical Battalion's helicopter pad. When her helicopter approached and hovered a few feet off the pad, the helicopter was waved off to make room for a medevac helicopter bringing in wounded. Maggie jumped off her helicopter as it began to acknowledge the order to clear the pad. She waited for the medevac chopper to land.

She accompanied a badly wounded Marine sergeant into Shock and Debridement, and subsequently into the emergency operating room. She scrubbed up and spent the next two and one-half hours in the Emergency Operating Room. When she finally finished, she asked to walk through the wards (although they were not on her schedule) and talk with the doctors, nurses, and corpsmen. It was getting late in the evening and she was obviously tired, but she insisted that we carry out her schedule before she returned to her assigned quarters in downtown Danang.

On 10 November 1966, (the 191st Birthday of the founding of the Marine Corps), we helicoptered into Colonel Don Mallory's First Marine Command Post. The night before, the regimental CP had been struck by Viet Cong sappers with twenty-four Killed In Action and about forty wounded. Colonel Mallory felt that entertainment was the last thing his Marines wanted. Maggie convinced him otherwise. She put on a one-hour show for the bulk of the troops—then waited while the company guarding the perimeter was relieved on site and could gather for a second show. Both performances were well received by the troops. As we were breaking down the public address and Bill Bryant's amplifying system, a platoon-size patrol returned to the CP. Maggie put on a "mini-show" for them.

When we arrived at the chopper pad to be lifted back to the First Marine Division CP at Danang, Maggie walked down the ranks of the rifle company providing security at the helo pad. She talked to every man, taking names, addresses, and phone numbers of wives, mothers and sweethearts with a promise to call them when she returned to the United States—a promise she kept! While the chopper pilots were getting nervous about sitting on the pad and being taken under sniper fire, Maggie just said, "Be cool! I'll tell you when I'm ready!"

Maggie placed her career in jeopardy when she went to entertain the servicemen in Vietnam. Her career suffered tremendously because of her trips. However, she never flagged in her efforts to bring a little bit of "home" to the troops.

Like a Favorite Sister

Joseph Wuertz of Washington, Indiana was a Marine captain flying F-4's at Chu Lai in 1966-1967. He recalls that they kept two fighters on five-minute strip alert at the end of the new concrete runway. The "hot pad" tent was close to the transient facility which measured sixteen feet by thirty-two feet, had a phone, a crude deck, a rudimentary schedule board, and was minimally functional. There was little room, however, to accommodate passengers waiting for air transportation. So usually they stood around outside waiting for time to pass.

> On one occasion Martha Raye was one of those passengers. She came to where I was standing outside the hot pad, close enough to hear the scramble phone. We chatted for at least an hour about everything under the sun. I knew who she was, although I had not been able

to catch her performance. She had the ability to put me at ease and the result was something like a long visit with a favorite sister whom one hadn't seen in a long time.

We had been standing in the rain for some time. It made little difference to me, because with full flight gear, the high temperature and humidity, I was just as wet inside as I was on the outside. But to someone who did not normally live that way, I considered it remarkable for her to not seem to notice how wet she was.

There are a lot of bad things written about the Vietnam War...but I happen to be one who did see some good from time to time. And Martha Raye's contribution to that good was substantial!

Don't Burn that Bra, *Wave* It!

One of many who saw Maggie in Pleiku is my dentist Ken Kelman from Albany. He remembered that she was waving her bra at some of the medical staff as she was hanging her laundry out to dry!

Sergeant First Class Walter Moraski also met Maggie at Pleiku while he was Wardmaster of the Post-Operation ward at the Eighteenth Surgical Hospital. "She gave me her signature, which I asked for, on the back of a prescription pad. She was visiting and talking with all the patients there. She was wearing fatigues with her lieutenant colonel rank patch."

Vice Admiral Thomas Weschler of Portsmouth, Rhode Island encountered Maggie numerous times in various places. He tells of his second and third encounters with her.

In 1966, when I was a Rear Admiral assigned to Naval Support Activity in Danang, Martha Raye arrived as a visiting "star" to boost troop morale. She was a first-class lady. She understood soldiers and Marines, and she didn't demand special treatment. She would visit units in the field by six or seven A.M., go all day, play poker with a group at night, and then be ready to go again the next day! She did just what she came for—make everyone feel better, be a little more proud of oneself and be ready to fight a little harder.

> It was my pleasure to see her at General Walt's Headquarters, to have dinner with her at my quarters, and to see her often in the field. We hated to see her go!
>
> During the summer of 1967, my wife and I went to the Marine Corps Commandant's quarters for a major reception. We were stationed in Washington. As we walked out of the Commandant's house toward the garden, this bouncy figure came rushing toward us. It was Martha Raye, renewing greetings from Danang and meeting my wife for the first time. What a happy occasion, and one I will never forget."

Maggie appeared in Kontum with George Jessel and Chuck Connors. She also showed up in Duc My with Roy Acuff and his band. Master Sergeant Byron Williams of Arroyo Grande, California and Sergeant First Class John O'Connor of Sparta, Georgia saw her when she entertained troops and advisors of Military Assistance Command-Vietnam (MACV).

Sergeant First Class Benny Robertson of Seale, Alabama recalls that Maggie came to Fort Campbell, Kentucky in 1966. The Second Field Artillery unit gave her a demonstration about an emergency mission. She also visited his unit in Vietnam the following year.

A Mother's Memory

We received several calls and letters from women with loved ones who served in Vietnam. Mrs. Virginia Pauley of Orchard Park, New York wrote about her son's meeting with Maggie.

> Our son, Peter T. Pauley, was stationed in Vietnam from 1966 to 1967 with Mobile Construction Battalion Six. He sent home a snapshot of him serving Martha in Officers Mess. He said while she was at Danang there was some kind of trouble and she worked in surgery like a "regular guy." I remember him saying if anyone ever said a bad word about her, they would have to answer to him! He was very impressed with her.
>
> Peter [who survived his tour of duty in Vietnam] was killed by a drunk driver in 1972.

Danang—1966: Peter Pauley was serving Maggie breakfast with members of Mobil Construction Battalion #6. Photo contributed by Virginia Pauley.

Like a Proud Mother or Aunt

Colonel John Welch recalls Maggie and several helpers entertaining a small contingent of U.S. Forces stationed at Qui Nhon. He was a forty-six-year-old lieutenant colonel who was delighted that Maggie did her best to make the younger enlisted people feel good about what they were doing for their country. She assured them that others genuinely appreciated their sacrifices.

> After her regular show was over, she stayed and talked with the young guys one-on-one, as though she were each one's proud mother or aunt. Naturally their response was enthusiastic.
>
> Of all the entertainers I have seen visiting the troops, she came across as the most genuine. I had the feeling she'd be glad to come out and put on a show for just one person and would want to get to know and hug him.

Jim Gravino of Houston, Texas served with I Company, Third Battalion, Fifth Marines. He saw Maggie in Vietnam—perhaps it was at Tam Ky.

> She came into our Enlisted Club wearing her Green Beret, a *very brassy lady!* Coming into a Marine "grunt"

> company wearing that damn Green Beret!! Very brassy. She earned my deepest respect right then and there! At any rate, since we were not allowed to wear a "cover" inside a building, she had to buy the first round.

Henry Lazzaro of Wadsworth, Illinois served with the Marine Corps in Vietnam in 1966 and 1967. He said that it was on a particularly miserable, cold, and rainy night at a place called Marble Mountain that he caught Maggie's performance.

> Because of the weather, the show could not be held outdoors, as was the custom. Rather than cancel the show, Ms. Raye opted to perform in the mess facilities so that the show could go on. Her performance was magnificent. I remember that evening with true fondness and appreciation.
>
> What set that show off from all the others was the sincerity, concern, and love that Ms. Raye showed for a bunch of cold and lonely Marines who were a long way from home. She clearly was there for the sole purpose of bringing a little joy to the lives of her fellow Americans and she succeeded. She had absolutely no ulterior motives.

More Blood—From Maggie

In 1966 and 1967, Commander Ray Betson of San Diego was assigned to a Navy surgical team caring for American troops and also wounded Vietnamese people in provincial hospitals.

> Martha Raye visited our camp in the Mekong Delta at SocTrang. We were caring for casualties from a firefight with the Viet Cong. These casualties were Americans. One American had received a chest wound and needed not only a chest tube but also a blood transfusion.
>
> Martha Raye heard this and, since she was the same blood type as the wounded trooper, she immediately volunteered to donate blood for him. That wounded American was stabilized due to her compassion and sacrifice. He was then sent to a hospital near Saigon for further care.

> All the individuals in my outfit who were involved in this incident were amazed and gained a great respect for Martha Raye.

Neither Rain, Mortars, Nor Small Audiences...

Maggie would entertain one person or groups of any size. She would perform in the rain or sun. She would not be put off by enemy activity. She put her life on the line many times. Master Gunnery Sergeant Tom Ryan speaks fondly of Martha's efforts at the Dong Ha Combat Base near the DMZ, where she disregarded bad weather, enemy activity, and how she might have felt.

Colonel Charles Mizell of Annandale, Virginia commanded the Fifty-fourth Artillery Group headquartered in Xuan Loc, Long Khanh Province. He said that Martha Raye was the *only* entertainer that ever visited and performed at their camp during his Vietnam tour. "She traveled the extra mile time and time again to entertain our servicemen with dedicated performances through the years."

Monsignor Charles McDonnell of New Jersey spent a year and a half in Vietnam as Chaplain for Fifth Special Forces between 1966 and 1968.

> On a number of occasions I met Ms. Raye at our Special Forces sites, often when they were in danger of attack. She was then—and still is—a person admired by our soldiers who served in Vietnam. She was singularly responsible for raising the morale of those who served on the frontiers of freedom. This was one great lady.

In 1967 Maggie taped an appearance on ABC's "Dateline" program. Meanwhile, Armed Forces personnel continued to see her in Vietnam. As a young Green Beret captain in Vietnam in 1967, George Massey had the pleasure of seeing Colonel Maggie perform for two hours one very hot afternoon in Duc Hoa. She took extra time to be photographed with each individual there.

George said that what really impressed him was her reaction to Rear Echelon staff who kept trying to hurry her back to Saigon.

Duc Hoa—1967: Maggie with then Captain George Massey, both wearing their Berets. Photo contributed by George Massey.

> Colonel Maggie asked if there were any other Green Berets in the area. We told her that there was a camp located out near the Cambodian border. She said, "Great, let's go see the boys out there!" One of the strap hangers said they needed to get back to Saigon. Colonel Maggie, in her inimitable way said, "To hell with Saigon, I'm going where the real war is!" And she did.

Wars May Change But Not the Warriors

John Patrick of Tacoma was an experienced Hospital Corpsman attached to grunt infantry companies of the Third Marine Division, Fleet Marine Force in 1967. He said that he had just joined a new company but found the same old problem of inefficient resupply.

> It had been my habit to scrounge any necessary medical gear from sympathetic corpsmen and doctors of the Third or Fifth Medical Battalions. Whenever my platoon was allowed a rest between patrols, I would bum a lift on anything crawling, red-balling, or flying from

our "rear area" to the nearest facility to stock up on the goods of my trade.

One morning I was slogging through the mud trying to hitchhike south for supplies. Two Marines in their six-by truck stopped to offer me a lift. As we bounced and spun our way down the road, they mentioned a show of some kind was being held that afternoon at some in-country R & R spot on a nearby beach. Normally, I would return to my outfit the following morning, but I felt I could stretch my luck a bit, take in the show, and rejoin my people without anyone the wiser. The six-by dropped me off at a crossroad a short distance from the show site. After another slog through the mud, I arrived in the R & R camp.

I learned that Martha Raye was going to present a one-woman show. The crowd was getting larger, so I planted myself within a few feet of center stage. Soon a truck and a few other vehicles arrived and musicians began setting up their drums and sound system. An officer who couldn't seem to stop grinning introduced Ms. Raye...then she took over. Memories were made that day that are beyond priceless to me.

I enjoyed Martha Raye in her Hollywood movies when I was younger. Yet here I was, a nineteen-year-old Marine, looking at a woman who had been a favorite of my *father's*!

Colonel Maggie had magic that day. She had the magic of one who believes in herself and the job she's doing. First I asked myself, "Is this how the men in the Second War or Korea felt?" I had never met a celebrity before.

Then her words began to make sense. *The wars may change but not the warriors.* Her joking had us all laughing and eager for more. The day became timeless. For a brief time we weren't in Vietnam. Somewhere else, anywhere else, but not Vietnam.

Ms. Raye used all her talents for us that day. Her famous large-mouthed comedy, her dancing with fine-looking legs that I can never forget, and her words of encouragement for us against the protesters and draft dodgers back home. After *all* she had done in her life, I felt embarrassed when she told us how she felt about us.

After her performance, Maggie gave out autographs and more encouragement. I had no paper for her to sign since paper lasted zip in the monsoon season. Shyly, I mumbled that if she could sign my jungle rainhat, I'd be forever grateful. She hesitated a second, then smiled and signed it.

As I made my way back to the medical battalion, it was business as usual for me except I had to keep looking at that signature. I was very proud of that hat. Weeks later while on patrol, I noticed that the rain had finally erased all but a smudge of her autograph.

Within a few more weeks, I, along with most of my platoon, was injured again. My wounds were multiple and fairly serious. But one that has proved upsetting over the years has been an almost total inability to recall dates, places, times, or any events from Vietnam.

I share nightmares with thousands of others. Yet I cannot recall the vast majority of details that were my life in 1966 and 1967. There must be a reason I recall much of the afternoon I met Martha Raye.

I am not sure why things are the way they are. But I treasure the gift that she gave me that day. I will never forget her.

It's One Way to Slash Your Clothes Budget

Jerry Brophy of Oneida, New York was stationed with the Marines in Chu Lai in 1967 when he met Maggie.

She was so dynamic a personality that I had to wait after the show to see if I could just tell her how much I enjoyed her performance. She performed in the same uniform we wore—Marine utilities. There was no wardrobe traveling around with her.

She was in somewhat of a hurry to get back to the station "hospital," which was apparently her usual practice. Return, not to entertain, but to help out in any way her capable hands could, while lightening the spirits of those around her. Luck was with me, and I

> was able to meet Maggie. She was just as warm and delightful in person as she seemed on stage.

Felix Rivera, Jr. of Farmingdale, New York said that while recovering from wounds in the base camp at Dau Tieng, Martha put on a one-woman show that pulled him out of a profound despair that nobody back home cared about the troops. He doesn't recall any other entertainer visiting that camp in 1967. "She's my hero. God bless her."

First Sergeant Norris Ridgeway of Blythewood, South Carolina says that in 1967 Martha Raye made an unscheduled visit and performed for troops of the Fourth Division at a newly-opened firebase on a French rubber plantation known as Dau Tieng. Performing alone, Ms. Raye's comedy, singing, and a little two-step entertained them for well over an hour.

Springtime once again found Maggie in Vietnam for both Army and Air Force personnel. Lieutenant Colonel Franz Cone said that Maggie arrived, unannounced, by helicopter at the Kramer Compound, home of Advisory Team Two, MACV.

> With her was one man, apparently a sound man/accompanist. She was wearing jungle fatigues with a lieutenant colonel's leaf and a Green Beret given to her, I understand, by the Fifth Special Forces Group at Danang. She put on a little show for the troops in the compound; then, accompanied by one of our advisors, proceeded to chopper out to *all* of our sector, subsector, and battalion teams. The Battalion A-teams consisted of one captain and only one noncommissioned officer.
>
> One battalion team was on a hilltop accessible only by air due to Viet Cong interdiction. All of us were amazed that she had shown up! She was the only celebrity I saw in Vietnam. Bob Hope got to Danang, but that was many Viet Cong-filled miles away. Advisor teams were sort of the U. S. Army's stepchildren in Vietnam.

Martha Raye went to see everybody. In fact, it was sort of a standing joke in MACV: "I was so far back in the boonies that Martha Raye never got there!"

Funny? Ehh...Friend—Yes!

Brigadier General Richard Toner was a young captain at Bien Hoa Air Base in 1967 when Maggie made a lasting impression on him. He had never cared much for her style of comedy, but since meeting her, she has been high on his list of extraordinary human beings.

For some forgotten reason I was alone as I headed to the club/dining hall door. I saw a female Green Beret approaching on a collision course. I didn't think that this could be—a *female* Green Beret, that is. But I had seen many strange things in the previous six months, so there was no reason not to believe this. I recognized Martha Raye and saluted (she had on lieutenant colonel insignia along with her Green Beret).

In the club, she asked me if I could join her for a drink before lunch, which I did, and she seemed to be very subdued and pensive. As it turned out, she was feeling a little down. Understandably, the pressures of doing two or three shows a day, along with all her hospital activities, listening to hundreds of stories from kids who were lonesome and war-weary and all the while, maintaining a cheery smile and a stiff upper lip. Perhaps she was a bit homesick herself. She didn't feel like being the center of attention that day nor did she want a crowd of people around.

Instead, she just wanted to talk and to be herself for a little while. She was warm and polite to those who stopped by where we were sitting, but she soon made it clear she wanted to return to the "private conversation" she was having with me. We talked about everything under the sun those few hours that we spent together—her experiences assisting in triage at first echelon aid stations, the attitudes of the public back home about what was going on in Vietnam, my wife and three little ones back in Kansas, her family and her famous and not-so-famous friends at home—but most of all, the deep love and respect that she had for all of us who were "doing our time."

Finally, she said that she had a show to do at an outdoor theater on the other side of the base. I offered her a ride there in my jeep, and then I sat in the front row as she brought laughter and tears to nearly a thousand pairs of eyes. As the crowd of autograph-seekers and grateful admirers thinned, she spotted me and came over to where I stood. She started to extend her hand, but then came closer and hugged me, hard. With what appeared to be just a slight glint of a tear in her eye, she thanked me for giving her "morale a much needed boost." Little did she realize that it was *she* who had been the morale booster that day.

The memory of Martha Raye that hot Easter Sunday afternoon is as fresh today as if it were just this past Easter. Of all the entertainers and celebrities who gave time and effort for the troops, no one gave more or more selflessly than Martha Raye.

I may still not like her style of comedy very much, but I love the woman.

Friends in the White House

Maggie had been a guest at the White House several times. She received a special invitation to attend a White House luncheon to honor General William C. Westmoreland on April 28, 1967. President Johnson introduced Maggie as he read the following statement:

> General Westmoreland is not the only hero of Vietnam with us today. Nor is he the only high-ranking officer.
>
> We also have a colonel in the Marine Corps, and a lieutenant colonel in the Army's Green Berets. In fact, they are one and the same person. And although the ranks are honorary, they are also richly deserved. They are held by Miss Martha Raye.
>
> Miss Raye has been to Vietnam three times. She has spent many long months there. She has entertained our troops out on the firing lines. The Green Berets have made her the only person outside this elite corps who may wear their proud symbol.

> One night in the Delta, Miss Raye was to entertain the men of two helicopter units. But they ran into a heavy fight that day, and as Miss Raye arrived, the wounded began to pour into the dispensary.
>
> Miss Raye is a former nurse. So, without hesitation, she put on Army fatigues, administered blood and prepared the wounded for surgery. The show didn't go on that night, but as the *Army Digest* wrote, "Those who benefited from her nursing care remember a Martha Raye performance no stage show could ever duplicate."
>
> Ladies and gentlemen, I am proud to present a great artist and a great American: Miss Martha Raye.
>
> Lyndon B. Johnson

Maggie personally knew several of our Presidents. She was friends with John and Jackie Kennedy (who gave her their private phone number in Hyannisport), as well as Dwight and Mamie Eisenhower, and Richard and Pat Nixon.

This typewritten note was sent from Austin, Texas.

> Dear Martha:
>
> Whatever the season or circumstance, a message from you always makes me feel better. Thank you once again for being thoughtful and concerned.
>
> Sincerely,
> LBJ

He added this handwritten line:

> And thank you again for all you have done for *our* Country.

Raymond W. Gimmler from East Rockaway, New York was the chairman and director of a group called "We Supported Our Men in Vietnam, Inc." He produced a film entitled *At Home with Honor.* The film's topic was a May 13, 1967 parade that showed how New

Yorkers appreciated, supported, and saluted the Armed Forces serving in Vietnam. The parade lasted nine hours and had 250,000 marchers. Chuck Connors, star of "The Rifleman" series, carried a flag and Maggie Raye was in her fatigues, Green Beret, and wearing her military rank and ribbons. Maggie was interviewed that day on film by WPIX-TV (New York's Channel 11).

Q. How much time have you spent there, Martha?
A. In Vietnam, 14 months.
Q. 14 *Months?*
A. Yes, Sir.
Q. Are you disturbed about the demonstrations like we had a month or so ago against our participation?
A. I just don't pay attention to them anymore. We've got too many *good* Americans.

There were more parades held in New York City to honor our troops. A Loyalty Day Parade was held there on April 29, 1967, and Maggie was present. A picture of her giving a hand salute appeared in many newspapers across the country. She was at a four and a half hour "Welcome Home" Parade that took place on March 31, 1973. Maggie attended every Veterans parade she could, no matter where or when it was.

John Colgan of Dumont, New Jersey says "What a girl!"

> I marched with Colonel Maggie and Local #46 Metallic Lathers, New York City, in a parade to support the guys, etc. in Vietnam. We were supposed to march behind the New York Police Department who were on horseback, which meant walking in the horse droppings. Well, not Maggie—we ran ahead, and they rode alongside us, not in front. What a girl!

USO's "Woman of the Year"

In May of 1967 at New York City's Rainbow Room, the USO presented Maggie with their "Woman of the Year" award. This USO award recognizes a woman who has contributed significantly to the Armed Forces, either by entertaining service personnel or in another capacity through the local USO operations. Maggie certainly deserved that award. Prior recipients were Mary Martin and Joan Crawford. Other notables who have received it since 1967 are Pearl Bailey, Gypsy Rose Lee, Mamie Eisenhower, Louise (Mrs. Douglas) MacArthur, Helen Hayes, Kitty Carlisle, Delores Hope, and Betty Ford. Shortly after that presentation, Maggie returned to Vietnam for the summer.

A Full-Bird (from the) Colonel

That summer Chief Warrant Officer 4 Charles Boyle was assigned as a Chief Engineman to the U.S. Coast Guard's *Point Caution,* which was part of Coast Guard Division Twelve out of Danang.

> Miss Raye was an enlightenment for the spirits of the eleven men who manned this patrol boat. Our boat was only eighty-two feet long and after many days on patrol within shouting—and shooting—distance of the beach, Maggie did everything she could to make sure that we got our minds off the conflict going on around us.
>
> Everyone who had a camera on board had their picture taken with her. The amazing thing she pulled off was to be sure she gave the camera the bird in every picture. I was never able to pin down whether the signal was for me, or to the folks back home!

Victor Arce, Jr. remembers that Martha Raye was the only major celebrity he saw during his stay at NhaTrang in 1967. He recalls a full-bird colonel introducing her show with comments about Maggie being an officer in the Army Reserves.

Captain Dennis Dee of Amherst, New York arrived in Saigon and eventually was sent to Kelper Compound, where he met Maggie by accident in late September of 1967.

> With one exception, I knew no one and was a little disoriented, having arrived at four A.M. By the time I awoke that same morning, everyone in my assigned quarters had left for parts unknown; I didn't have the opportunity to meet them and wish them well. New "in-country," I didn't really know what to expect. Everything was totally foreign to me—until I looked out the window slats and saw this woman in fatigues walking by. I thought I knew her from back home, but I was having difficulty placing her. I called out to her and tried to explain my embarrassment and predicament. She just laughed and hugged me. She introduced herself and simply stated that we were, one and all, in this together.
>
> Rather strange: all of a sudden I felt "at home" and I wasn't so distant from those whom I had left behind. I grew to love Vietnam, despite all of its tragedies, especially those with whom I served and suffered. I knew I was only one screen star away from home.

Maggie went stateside for a little while. She appeared as a guest on "The Jerry Lewis Show" in August of 1967. A month later she was part of "The Carol Burnett Show" premiere. Carol's show ran until 1970, and Maggie was an occasional guest on it. Following her performance with Carol, Maggie recorded a record album with her on Tetragrammaton, "Together for the First Time."

Freedom Foundation's National Service Medal

Maggie received the Freedom Foundation's National Service Medal that same year. This Foundation annually honors Americans for "significant contributions toward making this nation a better country for all of us." Other recipients of this award were Bob Hope, Lawrence Welk, Red Skelton, and John Wayne. Maggie's plaque read:

> For her unconcealed love of the United States of America and its Armed Forces.

> For her dauntless, mirthful spirit and enthusiastic support of our gallant men in the honored uniform of our country on the battlefield, on ships at sea, and in hospitals.
>
> For her lighthearted entertainment giving cheer to lonely patriots far from home.
>
> We salute this gallant lady who loves God and country so much she gives her talent unstintingly without concern for fatigue, health or risks.

Broadway in Vietnam

In February of 1967, Maggie had taken over Ginger Rodgers' role of Dolly Gallagher Levi in the Broadway production of *Hello, Dolly!* at the Saint James Theater in New York City. When her six-month contract was completed, the USO asked her to take the show to Vietnam. She, along with nineteen top-rated actors, singers, and dancers, left New York for Saigon on October 2, 1967. For thirty-three days they toured base camps and airfields with the show. This road show version of *Hello, Dolly!*, produced by David Merrick, was directed and managed by Maggie Raye. Maggie starred in the title role as Dolly Levi.

During one of her outdoor performances before an audience of about two hundred soldiers at Camp Davis, a U.S. Army logistics center a couple miles from Saigon, Maggie collapsed from heat exhaustion. After resting only a day, she was back on stage.

Bill Herndon was serving with the Seventy-first Evacuation Hospital at Pleiku when he saw Maggie's *Hello, Dolly!* production.

> There was an actor named Bill Herndon from New York in the play. I noticed his name on the program and, since I have the same name, I went backstage to meet him. He was very nice.
>
> I met Colonel Maggie the next day when she toured the Seventy-first. I worked in the Emergency Room. I

> have thought about the two-hour talk I had with her. I will always love that "Big Mouth Lady." She was a personal encouragement to me.

Jim Eldridge of West Lafayette, Ohio was in Danang when Maggie's *Hello, Dolly!* troupe performed at Freedom Hill (Hill 327).

> Ms. Raye and her entourage stopped and talked with us before and after the show. They all posed for group and individual pictures, whether for privates or majors. Several of my Marine buddies and I went to the show one afternoon. There were several performances scheduled. A short time later Bob Hope was to put on his Christmas Show in the same open air theater. Only one show!

In the December 1988 issue of *The Vietnam Veteran,* an article was reprinted that had appeared twenty years earlier about Maggie visiting troops of the Americal Division at Chu Lai. She had performed *Hello, Dolly!* at the Chu Lai Amphitheater for over five thousand Marines, Seabees, and soldiers. Between performances Sondra Lee, Amelia Haas, and Maggie visited the Second Surgical Hospital and the First Marine Hospital, bringing smiles to many faces.

According to a newspaper report from United Press International (UPI) filed in Saigon, a *Hello, Dolly!* performance was interrupted one afternoon by a Viet Cong attack. Maggie and two other performers were plucked to safety by helicopters, one of which was flown by First Lieutenant Gerhard Weis and Warrant Officer Richard Bashline. This troopship helicopter had monitored the emergency call to rescue "some VIPs," who remained nameless so the Communists wouldn't hear that Maggie was one of them. According to many Veterans, the Viet Cong had a price on her head because she brought so much cheer to the troops and was so effective in boosting morale.

The Viet Cong hated Maggie as much as they loved Jane Fonda. Jane neither visited nor entertained our own troops. Instead, she went to Hanoi and visited the North Vietnamese. There was no love lost between Maggie and Jane.

Regardless of how Maggie felt about the war itself, she believed in helping these young American men and women, personally, as best she could. This entertainer would not be satisfied with just putting on shows. Perhaps she was motivated by the nurse in her. Perhaps it also was her stated gratitude to the American Dream that had welcomed her immigrant parentage.

While too many Americans can become so obsessed with an "issue" that they ignore the *people* it affects, Maggie could not—and would not—do so. Her mission with our troops cut through the stateside politics over Vietnam and centered on caring for our troops as *individuals*.

Go to The Wall at the Vietnam Memorial if you would understand Maggie's compulsion to be with her troops. All those *names*—mostly teenagers or barely older—of individuals. Thousands of them had met "Colonel Maggie" before their final tragedy. Mothers have asked if we have actual knowledge her son had been with Maggie before his death, because knowing he had would be comforting.

If Maggie's spirit dwells anywhere on earth these days, we can be sure it is not in Hollywood and show business. Rather, her spirit would likely still be "there" with her troops, especially at The Wall. I can almost picture her fingertips lightly tracing each name and her amazing memory recalling when and where she had talked with him or her, and what about....

Bullets were flying as they were lifted off Nui Ba Dan Mountain, the site of a Special Forces detachment and a radio relay station for the U.S. First and Twenty-fifth Divisions. The mountain is about fifty-five miles northwest of Saigon, near the Cambodian border. Maggie was wearing her tiger-striped combat clothes and Green Beret. By this time she was an honorary Lieutenant Colonel in the Special Forces and had visited Vietnam more than any other prominent entertainer.

Richard Seymour, a nurse from Abilene, Kansas, recalls a performance Maggie gave at Dong Tam for the Ninth Division and his meeting with her.

> Later she came by the hospital and talked for over an hour with me. I had not been able to attend her performance, as I was working in the hospital. She is truly a lady I will never forget!
>
> Early the next morning the Viet Cong mortared the camp, and I was called back to the hospital to work in the emergency room taking care of the wounded. I was surprised when Ms. Raye showed up to assist me. She helped me take care of the wounded for over two hours and was never in the way! The wounded responded to her so well, and they couldn't believe she was taking care of them.
>
> I must admit, I really don't think of her as a comedienne, but rather as a wonderful, caring person who helped a young nurse care for the wounded that night in Vietnam.
>
> Comical Coverup—
>
> 31 October 1967 I wrote in my diary: And now for the rest of the story...we talked for over an hour discussing the idea of having a nurse general for the Army Nurse Corps; she was against it and I was for it. She stayed in the nurse's quarters, and when she had come into the emergency room to help me she had on this pretty, frilly, bright red negligee. It did not for one minute take away from the work she was doing! The funny part was that the Chaplain kept trying to get her to put on his field jacket. She was busy working, and he was chasing her around trying to get this jacket on her.

Marianne Reynolds was fresh out of college. She was twenty-one years old and in Dong Tam running a service club. She recalls the area being hit by incoming rounds the night after Maggie's group arrived.

> Since I lived with the nurses, we all shared a bunker. I'd risen from a sound sleep and was fighting back fear-induced nausea. In the dim light of the bunker I saw two little tiny legs in a baby doll nightie say, "Anybody want a beer?" I laughed, for as the alarms sounded Maggie must have scooped it out of the base commander's quarters—her temporary home. I'll never forget her bringing me "back" that night with a joke and a smile.

Steve Hadlock remembered being in the enlisted mess hall at Phu Bai in the fall of 1967 during a dismal monsoon rain.

> I sat down to a powdered egg breakfast, and I asked the Marine sitting next to me to pass the salt and hot sauce. It was cordially handed to me by none other than Martha Raye!
>
> We spent our breakfast time chatting about my home state of Texas and, to this day, that very brief encounter was one of the most memorable ones I ever had. In this Marine's mind, she made a difference that I will always carry in fond memory.

Going to Her Grunts

Gary Hall was serving with the Fourth and Americal Divisions, Detachment A, Long Range Patrol, when he crossed paths with Maggie.

> I cannot put in words the profound effect she had on us. In a world of terror and loneliness, a world of Hanoi Jane Fonda types, we had Martha Raye. Thank God for her courage and sacrifice. I will never forget her as long as I live.
>
> In late fall of 1967—I think—we were operating in a hotly contested border area of the Highlands. Food was bad, weather awful, and casualties very high. Most of

> us were bummed out because of the conditions and the approaching holidays.
>
> As grunts we expected the worst. While the brass in Saigon got all the "bene's" and USO shows—we got crap! That is until one hot afternoon when Martha Raye and company paid us a visit. No one else cared about a bunch of dirty grunts except her!

General Westmoreland was well aware of Maggie's efforts throughout the Vietnam era. He had already presented her with two prestigious awards. He summed up his feelings about her in his book *A Soldier Reports* when he called her "the grandest trouper of all." He observed that she had visited Vietnam time after time, once for five months. Maggie had begged him to let her extend one of her visits over the Christmas holiday; she said that she had no family to celebrate with at home. "These gallant men were her family."

He stated that sometimes she appeared with an accompanist, other times she would get help from the soldiers. He recalled her collapse during *Hello Dolly!* Later she pitched in to help with those who were wounded when the Viet Cong attacked SocTrang with mortars.

General Westmoreland said, "Nobody contributed more of herself than that wonderful, generous woman."

Chapter 9

...Trying to Do the "Right Thing"

"Maggie had the ability to see this war the way it really was—about people. We were mostly teenagers trying to do the right thing, and we did our best."

Larry Lamb
La Jolla

My Green Beret Padre

"Whenever we crossed paths at an A-site or at NhaTrang, she would 'hit' me for another supply of St. Christopher Medals."

NhaTrang, Vietnam—1968: Maggie with Chaplain (then Captain) Michael Ortiz. Photo contributed by Michael Ortiz.

-9-

Maggie went stateside for a few days of rest after the exhausting USO *Hello, Dolly!* tour throughout Vietnam. In November 1967 she returned by herself on a USO tour that lasted twelve weeks and was divided between troops in Pacific area hospitals and the jungles of Vietnam. Sergeant Rocky Kelley served with the Ninth Infantry Division at the Bear Cat base camp. He met Maggie before Christmas of 1967.

> The evening of her performance was very, very hot. Halfway through her act, she became faint from the weather. Maggie was helped off the stage and a gentleman stated that she had become fatigued from all the shows she had put on. Before he could finish with the apology, she was back on the stage. She blew us all a kiss and finished her performance.
>
> After the show was over, she came out into the crowd and I can remember introducing myself to her. I told her that I had enjoyed her performance and I asked her if she was feeling well. She said, "Honey don't worry about me, just keep your head down." Then she hugged and kissed me.

"Maggie" Co-opts "Kilroy"

Commander John Lepore of Coronado, California served in Vietnam as a Marine chaplain from 1967 to 1968. Maggie stood out in his mind as the most dedicated and bravest of all the celebrities. He went on to reminisce about both of their missions.

> One of my main missions in support of the Marines in "I" Corps (northernmost area in South Vietnam) was to visit and minister to some small remote outposts. The

crude roads leading in and out of these outposts were extremely dangerous by day and impossible by night. Yet these were the very roads Ms. Raye traversed. So often when I reached these places, I would hear, "Guess what Chaplain, Martha Raye was here!" It reminded me of "Kilroy" from another war.

The only time I actually saw Ms. Raye was Christmas week 1967 along the road from Marble Mountain, Danang to a place euphemistically called the "Riviera"—on the coast above Hoi An. The road had been blown up several times that week, and my driver and I were negotiating our way home very cautiously, when barreling down the road came two Marine jeeps heading for the Riviera. In the rear seat of the second jeep was the indomitable Ms. Raye with her famous grinning smile. We both waved as they passed, and it was a heartwarming moment.

I was impressed that someone from the States cared enough to visit us during Christmas week, and at such risk, especially since the war was so unpopular at home that even the politicians who sent us there were beginning to disown us.

I also remember feeling angry that someone would send such a patriot as Martha Raye along so perilous a road until I learned that she would have it no other way.

Looking back on the effect Martha Raye had on my Marines, I would say that they were most impressed, not by what she said or the goodies and cheer she left with them, but rather by the fact that she braved personal danger just to be with them. That counted the most in their book, and in mine.

"Maggie Drawers"

Captain Orville Wolf, writing from Khamis Mushayt, Saudi Arabia, recalled Maggie's tour that took place shortly before the Viet Cong "Tet Offensive." He was a pilot in command of a CH-47 Chinook helicopter of the 200th Assault Support Helicopter Company. Their group was called "The Pachyderms" and were based at Bear Cat near Long Binh.

I received the mission to transport Martha and her group to several remote artillery bases in our operational area. We came to lovingly know her as "Maggie Drawers." I'll never forget her down-home personality, heartfelt compassion and wonderful big smile in spite of the rigors and horrors of combat all around her. She was one fantastic lady in my book.

The last trip out with us was to a tiny artillery camp on top of a mountain called Gia Ray. We often carried ammunition to this location, always in cargo nets on a long sling cable. The area was so tiny it was very difficult to land a big Chinook there. But knowing it would be undignified to carry Maggie's troupe in there in a cargo net, we did our best. Even though we were hanging off the mountain on both ends, we managed to land at the camp. After the troupe disembarked, we went to a nearby helicopter gunship and 155mm artillery base called Blackhorse to wait until it was time to pick them up again.

As the afternoon wore on, the weather began to deteriorate as low clouds moved inland from the coast. We also received intelligence reports that a company-sized Viet Cong unit was moving in the vicinity of Gia Ray. To us, this meant that the Viet Cong probably intended to use the weather as cover for one of their frequent mortar attacks on the Gia Ray mountaintop artillery base. The base was in an excellent strategic location for shelling any Viet Cong units for miles around.

We decided to get up to the top of the mountain early, in case it would be necessary to take Martha and her troupe out ahead of schedule.

Arriving at Gia Ray, we found that the low clouds had already enveloped the lower slopes of the mountain and the top was sticking up like a small island in a white sea.

The noise and rotor wash of our landing brought everyone out to see what all the commotion was about.

We discussed the weather and Viet Cong situation with the commanding officer who had already been informed by radio, and we agreed that it would be wise to take Martha and her group off the mountain a little early. Of course, she wanted to stay and visit a while longer, but we insisted, and left the camp thirty minutes earlier than scheduled.

As we departed, the clouds began to close in over the top of the mountain, and we heard on the radio that five minutes after we left, the first Viet Cong mortar rounds began coming in.

Arriving back at Bear Cat, Miss Martha, our "Maggie Drawers," gave all of the flight crew—including me—a big hug and kiss and thanked us for taking good care of her and her group for the two days she was with us.

Yes, I remember Miss Martha Raye, "Colonel Maggie," "Maggie Drawers," and there will always be a special place in my heart for her.

Bruce Jones of Sacramento served in Vietnam where he had two very special encounters with Maggie. He related those occasions in his book *War Without Windows*. He even dedicated his book to her, as well as to the memory of Colonel Gains B. Hawkins.

PRE-TET/1 NOVEMBER 1967-29 JANUARY 1968:
THANKSGIVING:

On Thanksgiving Day, I had a late afternoon call from my old classmate, Lieutenant Swandby. He and a buddy were coming into Saigon and they needed a bed and some R & R. They'd meet me at the Meyerkord Hotel.

I waited outside and saw them roar up in a jeep. Covered with red dust, M-16s slung over their backs, sporting flak jackets and camouflaged helmets, these spooks looked like honest-to-God soldiers. We were climbing the stairs while I wondered where to put them up.

As we got to the second floor, coming out of a room with an ice tray was Colonel Maggie, the Old Lady of the Boondocks—*aka* Martha Raye.

"Hi, men! Just in from the field? You look muddier than a rice paddy! I was just borrowing some ice from the colonel, but he doesn't know it! He's asleep! Now that I've got it, maybe you'll join me for a drink!" Her delivery was a staccato of high energy, making each sentence seem funny.

This was the second time I'd seen her at the hotel. A few days earlier I had come into the lobby to find a second lieutenant with a stunned expression saying to no one in particular, "I didn't know the Special Forces had women!"

I looked at him strangely until around the corner came Martha Raye in her beret and tiger suit with Special Forces insignia and a lieutenant colonel's silver leaf. Her special love of the Green Berets had earned her the honorary rank and uniform from her men. She'd even made a parachute jump with them! In her extended annual trips to Vietnam she was the only entertainer who went to the smallest bases way out in the boonies. She had been under fire many times and legend had it that the Viet Cong had a price on her head. For her bravery in the field, including often working as a nurse in medic tents during attacks, she was lovingly called the "Old Lady of the Boondocks." It was a title she cherished.

My guests were stunned by the encounter. I had the great pleasure of making the introductions, and I learned you did not refer to her stage name. In Vietnam it was only Maggie. All Irish, to us she was Maggie Theresa O'Reed. "Martha Raye" was some other person who had had one of the hit variety shows during the Golden Age of television, who made movies, and who was one of the great jazz singers. Here in Vietnam she was mother and friend to thousands of troops just as she had been for the men in Korea, where my father had seen her, and in World War II.

Maggie moved us into the USO lounge, the closest thing to luxury my guests had seen since we had arrived in Vietnam, with a bar, refrigerator, TV, carpets. She stacked their weapons in a corner and proceeded to make us honored guests. The enlisted jeep driver, a polite country boy from the Midwest, had probably thought the Saigon trip was going to be just another drive; he wound up in Maggie's shower with a drink delivered by herself. Then he just sat in the lounge with a series of drinks and grinned. He asked me more than once, "Is this for real, sir?"

I asked Maggie where she lived and she replied, "Vietnam!" Her trips were three months out of every year with only per diem pay of some twenty dollars for compensation, so it was almost true. She continued, "My house is in Bel Air near Beverly Hills, but I'm only there TDY!"

She arranged food and beds and offered to give up her own if the men needed a nap. The evening was one of songs and laughter, but we never once left the topic of the war, the men, the military. She'd been everywhere and knew everyone and her stories were incredible. We were amazed that she had been trying to get to Dak To and earlier, to Con Thien to be with the troops under fire. We were satisfied to be drinking booze in Saigon with the Old Lady of the Boondocks.

HOLIDAYS:

Christmas came and went and, except for Miss My's surprise "all-night party" on Christmas Eve, I hardly noticed it....

Then came New Year's Eve. At 2300 hours I pulled on my fatigues after a nap and then went dejectedly down the stairs to sign in, draw my pistol and put on the officer-of-the-day armband. From my room I had heard a vigorous party rocking out on the roof. All the roundeyes, including Colonel Maggie, were going to be there. I trudged up the stairs to inflict more punishment on myself by watching the party until I had to start my watch. On my arrival, everyone stopped dead in mid-dance. I realized with dismay that they thought I was there to quiet down the party.

Quickly I yelled that it was only coffee I wanted, that they should, please, have a good time! They carried on, but I felt like a jerk for having dampened the celebration. I drank my coffee and stayed in a corner. Maggie had seen me and waved. As midnight neared, the Old Lady of the Boondocks yelled at me, "Hey, you! Lieutenant! Come here!"

I jumped to it and found myself dancing with her to the applause and cheers of the crowd. Then someone announced it was midnight and she planted on me a huge Martha Raye kiss! More cheers from the crowd. Blushing red, I thanked her profusely, waved good-by to the party, and took off for my guard post on the sixth floor.

About two hours later I was surprised by the approach of feet behind me. It was Colonel Maggie and her officer escort, delivering a sandwich and a cup of coffee, with more best wishes and a hug.

Nowhere, ever again, will I have such a joyous New Year's Eve.

Bruce's EPILOGUE:

Until I left the Army in 1969, I was assigned as an advisor to a wide variety of reserve units in southern California....My only respite from the tedium of the job was Colonel Maggie. I wound up living in west LA near her house in Bel Air, where I was often invited for dinner and to play Scrabble (until dawn, and she always beat me).

Each year during her stateside TV and stage appearances, Colonel Maggie asked relatives of GIs to write her so that she could deliver letters in person to their sons and husbands. I created a filing and index system for the five hundred or so letters she had received. I was pleased that during her 1969 trip, Colonel Maggie was able to find up to three hundred of the men. [3]

I spoke with Bruce several times following Maggie's funeral. He reiterated his love for her. He also had been trying to have Maggie honored nationally. He gave us the letters he had been sending to the White House since early 1969 and the form letter responses he received.

The Dickie Chappel Award

In 1967 Maggie received The Dickie Chappel Award from the Marine Corps League for her work in Vietnam. Dickie Chappel, a female correspondent for *Reader's Digest*, was killed while visiting a dangerous area in Vietnam. Female military and civilian nurses, Red Cross workers and other women were being injured, killed or listed as Prisoner of War or Missing in Action (POW/MIA) in Vietnam; but, that did not stop Maggie from going back there again and again.

More letters were received from military personnel who saw Maggie in Vietnam and stateside during 1967,

1968 and later. Major Roger Pierson of Marina, California flew Reconnaissance Team Support with the "Tiger Hounds."

> Lieutenant Colonel Raye was on Active Service Reserve Duty with our adjacent unit, Special Forces Advisory Team B-Twenty-four, Kontum City, Kontum Province. She assisted some of the Reconnaissance Teams (RT) on the ground and had to fly in to get to the area of the RT position—a highly dangerous mission.
>
> I have heard reports that Lieutenant Colonel Raye received the Purple Heart Medal for injuries/wounds sustained in action against enemy forces, and the Combat Medical Badge, awarded for excellence in performance of medical duties while under hostile enemy fire, and of her medical assistance to U.S. forces personnel wounded in action.

Code: Number One!

Captain Robert Siebenmargen of Warner Robins, Georgia was a helicopter pilot who flew Colonel Maggie around the IV Corps, Mekong Delta area. He piloted for the Outlaws out of Vinh Long and his call sign was Outlaw Nineteen.

> I recall an incident when we picked Maggie up at the Tan Son Nhut airport. When flying VIPs, a code number is used with flight following service to indicate the priority of the passenger(s). A code book lists various numbers assigned to VIPs. The lower the number the more important the passenger is. "Code 1" was for the President of the United States.
>
> After we had picked up Maggie and were flying out of Saigon, I contacted the traffic controller for flight following service. He asked if we had a Code on board. I said we did, but I wasn't sure what number she was assigned; my passenger was Martha Raye and in my book she was "Number One." The flight operator laughed, agreed with my code number assignment, and cleared us on our way.

R.L. Harris remembered Maggie staying in Ban Me Thout with Special Forces B-Twenty-three in late 1967 or early 1968.

> When she came in, she stayed for dinner and that turned into an all night poker session. Since I tapped out early, I sat around, watched and just enjoyed Maggie's storytelling. During the card game, Maggie had to go to the latrine. Unless you were fortunate enough to be in Saigon or some other major city, it was no use looking for an indoor water closet. At B-Twenty-three they had a burnout two-holer. I had the honor of being Maggie's escort. On the way to the latrine we talked about many things. I recall her invitation to visit her when I returned to the states.
>
> The one thing she was definitely afraid of was snakes. While we were walking, she held onto me; she wanted reassurance that there were no snakes around. When we got to the latrine, she wanted me to double check it for snakes, which I did; I assured her there were none, not even two-legged types. While she was in the latrine she kept up a line of conversation to keep herself from thinking about snakes. When she came out, she said, "That was the fastest pee I ever had." Maggie said whatever came into her mind, which was refreshing.
>
> The next morning when she left, she diverted her chopper to pick up some wounded and was subsequently wounded herself, taking shrapnel in her butt—from what was put out on the chopper's radio.

Specialist 4 Brian Donnelly of Sloatsburg, New York served with the 588th Combat Engineers at Dau Tieng. He believes Maggie was an unsung hero. He said that the most memorable time they had was when Maggie asked their commander if their escorts could take her to areas in Vietnam where the USO rarely went.

> One day on top of Black Virgin Mountain, Maggie and our group put on a show of songs and a lot of comedy. Everyone had a great time. But, just as we were leaving, a patrol was hit by the Viet Cong! Maggie would not

leave the mountain until she knew that all the boys were safe. When *all* returned we boarded a Huey; upon leaving, we took on automatic rifle fire. Fortunately, no one was harmed.

This *Lady* in Wet Greens

While serving as a Seabee, William Brown saw Maggie when he was with the Ninth Battalion a few miles south of Danang, between Marble and Monkey Mountains.

> One day we were told to come back to base camp. A USO show was coming. We were in monsoon season. Twelve hundred men sat in the mud and rain waiting two to three hours for this USO show. Finally a three-quarter ton truck pulled into camp and this lady in soaked greens got out by *herself.* We had a couple of boxes—planks for a stage and a tarp over it.
>
> Maggie got up on our stage and told us the USO troupe would not come out in this downpour; but, she said we deserved something—so she came alone. For the next three hours, this *lady* in wet greens, wet hair and running makeup made us the happiest guys in the world. When she spoke, twelve hundred men listened—God love her.

Larry Lamb of La Jolla also served with the Seabees. He was located at Khe Sanh when Maggie showed up there.

> Martha Raye visited my unit on two different occasions. The first was at Red Beach north of Danang, and the second at a firebase somewhere along the DMZ that separated South and North Vietnam.
>
> She placed herself in danger both times, and she will never be forgotten in my heart. She never gave up on us, and we never gave up on America.
>
> Maggie had the ability to see this war the way it really was—about people. We were mostly teenagers trying to do the right thing, and we did our best.

Mike Scott contacted us from Kingston, Ontario, Canada. Although he is a Canadian, he served with the U.S. Army for nine and a half years. During that time, he spent thirty-seven months in Vietnam. Mike met Maggie while he was assigned to the Fifth Special Forces Group, MACV Special Operations Group, Project Delta, from 1967 to 1969. He saw her again during 1970 to 1972 when he was training Cambodians out of Bien Hoa.

> Maggie came through Danang, NhaTrang, and Bien Hoa several times. I believe she was involved in a couple of camps that were assaulted when she was there and she performed nursing duties.
>
> Her trips to the A-camps were received with open arms. She was one of us, not a woman who had to be pampered. As a Korean Vet, she knew what was up. She is still on my mind as a bright spot in a tough situation.

One on One

John Swizer of Vacaville, California was a young helicopter pilot with the 128th Assault Helicopter Company. He was based at Phu Loi from 1967 to 1969 when Maggie came.

> On two occasions I have had the opportunity to see her show and experience the joy she brought to me and my colleagues. During one of her visits, our company returned to Phu Loi after her performance had concluded. After learning that we missed her show, she put on an additional show for our unit and spent time with each of us.

David Fawcett recalls that Maggie "dropped in" on him in 1968 when he was on a hill in the Central Highlands, not far from Dak To while serving with the Fourth Infantry.

> We got word that a VIP was inbound on a "bird." Nothing more about who or for how long. The chopper

landed and out she stepped. Our hill had been attacked regularly, as recently as one or two nights before. She turned to the pilot and gave the "cut off" sign across her throat. I could see the pilot shaking his head. Martha repeated the sign and again the pilot shook his head. Finally she, of course, won out and the pilot shut down his engine on a hill he obviously felt was not too safe.

For the next several hours, this wonderful woman went from bunker to bunker talking, joking and letting us know we were important and not forgotten at home. She also wrote down many of our addresses and home phone numbers. I know that she called many parents and wives at her own expense when she got home.

Years later—1980, I believe—I saw her in a play in Orlando and after the last curtain I introduced myself to her. She said she remembered the hill and our visit and gave me a hug and said, "Welcome Home." It was easy to see that she really cared.

Maggie—Queen of the Boonies

One person who crossed paths frequently with Maggie was Chaplain (Colonel) Michael Ortiz. When he first contacted us, he was stationed at Fort Sam Houston in San Antonio. Michael is now retired and living in San Diego; however, he was a captain in 1968 and remembers his very good friend.

To the older generation, the name "Martha Raye" conjures up the comedienne who brought joy and laughter to millions of moviegoers in the sixties and seventies. She was the big-mouthed, loud, crazy movie star who attracted so many to theaters.

To almost any Vietnam Veteran the name elicits admiration for an American woman whose love and respect for troops made her undergo dangers and sacrifices in actual combat areas.

I met Maggie during my first tour in Vietnam (1968) as the Catholic chaplain for the Fifth Special Forces Group. Since there were over ninety A-sites, I was constantly traveling the breadth and length of the

Republic providing religious coverage to the Vietnamese, Montagnards and our own Americans.

There was hardly a Special Forces Camp I visited which had not already had a visit from Maggie Raye! If I were staying overnight, the Team Sergeant would bunk me in the shelter Maggie had just vacated; hence the joke around some of the sites that the chaplain usually "shared beds" with Maggie.

By the time our paths crossed I knew why she had been adopted by the Special Forces as "one of their own." She voluntarily came every year to spend months visiting service members without fanfare and publicity or an entourage. Her time in-country was mainly in the "boonies," usually at remote A-sites accompanied only by an escort officer.

I found her to be a spiritual person in spite of her funny-lady facade. She really cared for every soldier regardless of rank, color or belief. When Maggie found out that I always took along some "airborne (St. Christopher) medals" to distribute to the troops, she asked me for some. Whenever we crossed paths at an A-site or at NhaTrang, she would "hit" me for another supply.

When returning via California for a second tour, I decided to call her home in Beverly Hills. It was impossible to refuse her invitation to pay her a visit. It was during this visit that I again saw another side of Maggie and appreciated her all the more. We talked about her personal life, the adverse criticism she received from her peers because of her support for the troops, and her sincere desire to do everything possible to lift troops' morale. Maggie was so proud of being an honorary Lieutenant Colonel in the Green Berets.

We met again in 1970 and her energy and dedication hadn't diminished in the least. She continued to selflessly give of her time and would pay her own way to go anyplace where her soldiers requested her.

Michael said that he and Maggie exchanged Christmas cards every year. He would address hers "Maggie, Queen of the Boonies," Maggie would address his "To my Green Beret Padre." He said, "In my opinion, Martha Raye will always be remembered by Veterans with love and gratitude."

Danang East near Marble Mountain—1968: Maggie visits troops at Fifth Special Forces camp, Forward Operating Base 4. Photo contributed by Robert L. Lawson.

Senior Chief Yeoman Gerald Boryszewski of Sarasota was stationed with the Navy River Patrol Force for two tours from December 1967 to April 1972.

> I met Martha Raye in 1968 at Ben Thuey (Can Tho), Mekong Delta. She arrived at the base one day and made sure that she met all the troops. She took her time to have pictures taken with everybody.
>
> It meant a lot to me that she was there with us, and I have always treasured that moment. Martha Raye always had a kind word for everybody. I am glad that woman was on our side.

Grace for the Grunts

Colonel Harry C. Stevenson was a first lieutenant paratrooper in January 1968, and he was the Executive Officer for C Company, First Battalion, 327th Infantry (Airborne), 101st Airborne Division. His group was stationed at Song Be, about a hundred miles northwest of Saigon. He said that he "will never forget her kindness and love for the grunts of Vietnam."

First Lieutenant Ty Herrington had been a platoon leader with me in C Company and was now stationed in Saigon with the Fifth Special Forces detachment at Camp Goodman. Company C had a couple of our troopers in the hospital in Saigon, so I decided to go pay them at the end of the month and see Ty at the same time.

When I arrived in Saigon, I called Ty. He picked me up at the airfield and said we were going to Maggie's farewell party that night. I had just come out of the field with five weeks of red clay imbedded into every pore of my body and jungle rot on arms and neck. Ty called Maggie and she said to get me a shower if I could, but I WAS expected because she was there to see the real troops and not the Saigon generals. I got a hot shower at Camp Goodman, my first in weeks; Ty found me some spare civilian clothes and off we went to the top of a fancy hotel in downtown Saigon.

Maggie met us at the entrance and said she was glad I could come. I was scared to death of all the brass at the party and really impressed that Maggie would talk to the grunts. After about five minutes of small talk, I was convinced that Maggie knew as much about being a grunt as I did. Then she asked if I had ever met General Westmoreland. When I said no, she literally dragged me over to Westy and introduced me as one of "his" paratroopers. She said that I could tell him how the war was *really* going.

After that, she introduced me to most of the brass and much of the Hollywood staff and stars. By the end of the evening I was overwhelmed by Maggie's hospitality and graciousness. Her staff shared Maggie's priority—that the real "troops" were what counted most.

Needless to say I had a great time in Saigon. The next night Ty and I went bar hopping with several members of Maggie's tour, including James MacArthur. For a forty-eight-hour break from being a rifle company executive officer, nothing could have topped that trip.

A few months later, First Lieutenant Ty Herrington married Maggie's friend, entertainer Chris Noel. Everyone knew him by his nickname "Ty," but his given name was Clyde Berkley Herrington. Chris talked about her late husband "Ty" and their brief marriage in her book, *Matter of Survival.*

Karen Forte married a man who served in Vietnam in 1968. Although they were later divorced, she recalls that anytime someone would praise Bob Hope for all he had done for the enlisted men, Ray would let everyone know about Martha Raye and all she did—without the publicity.

In March 1968, Maggie received the USO Board of Governor's Special Award for Gallantry and for repeated USO tours of Vietnam in face of gunfire and personal danger in the "show must go on" tradition. More awards were to come her way over the next few years.

Jean Hersholt Humanitarian Award

At the 1968 Academy Awards, Bob Hope presented the Jean Hersholt Humanitarian Award from the Academy for the Motion Picture Arts and Sciences to his longtime friend, Maggie Raye. A very large photo of the happy occasion hung in Maggie's home next to her bar. The Oscar sat on a glass-covered pedestal in her den, which is better known to Veterans around the world as "The Team Room." When her drapes were open and the sun was shining, the golden Oscar had a special glow about it. It was the only piece of Hollywood memorabilia in that room, perhaps because of its ties to her troops.

Maggie would not stay in one place too long. She starred in *Good-bye Charlie* at the Mill Run Playhouse near Chicago during April 1968. She returned to Vietnam shortly thereafter.

Dan Laino is a former Marine who saw Maggie at the Mill Run that April. He was a drummer with the Marine Drum and Bugle Corps. They had an exhibition concert to honor her for what she had done for military personnel. He felt she was very appreciative for this small tribute. After the concert, they got to see her performance in *Good-bye Charlie*. They were all invited to join her afterwards in a lounge next to the Playhouse. She even bought a round or two of drinks for them. "She was a genuine, down to earth, beautiful woman, and after all these years I still consider this a high point of my life."

Lieutenant Colonel Darwin Edwards of Warner Robins, Georgia was an Air Force captain in 1968 and 1969. He was a helicopter pilot supporting the Green Berets. He saw Maggie at Ban Me Thout upon her return to Vietnam.

> Somewhere in my vast amount of accumulated junk, I have a photo of that "Old Lady of the Boondocks." She was not old and never will be to those of us that saw her in action and love her for it to this day.
>
> I can still see her. She was on a dimly lit stage improvised in the mess hall. Most of the light was behind her so her face was somewhat in shadow. The light lent a soft, golden glow to The Lady in her jungle fatigues and Beret. Things kind of stopped whenever she was at a camp and everybody truly felt her presence.
>
> It was wonderful how they [the Green Berets]—and we—carried on over her. I'm not sure that even Ann-Margret ever gave her any competition! Maggie filled a

void in such a wonderful way just by being there and showing she cared. We knew if she and old what's-her-face Fonda ever squared away, the starlet would come out on the bottom every time.

I don't know how many times Maggie came to Ban Me Thout between March 1968 and March of 1969, but it was wonderful each time—kind of like Thanksgiving, Christmas, and Valentine's Day all rolled into one. I was never fortunate enough to fly her, but I did envy the aircrews who had that honor.

I salute a real soldier—Maggie Raye!

A Pithy Pal

Command Sergeant Major James Trepoy of Salina, Kansas was the Command Sergeant Major of the Third of the Twenty-first Infantry, 196th Light Infantry Brigade, Americal Division from June 1968 to June 1969. His unit was located at Landing Zone Center in the mountains west of Tam Ky, and their mission was to sweep the trails, valleys, and Ho Chi Minh Trail. Although he did not see Maggie this particular day, his soldiers told him about her.

Martha Raye picked a day to visit our Landing Zone when the Battalion Commander and I decided to visit our wounded in the hospital back in Danang. It was quiet in our Area of Operations so it was ideal for us to go to Danang and for Martha to visit the LZ. We were not aware of her planned trip.

When we returned from Danang and learned of Martha's visit, we were disappointed that we had missed her. I talked to the troops on the LZ and the line company in bunkers surrounding the area to get their reactions to Martha's visit. Everyone was impressed with Martha and her down-to-earth conversations.

You may have heard how the troops in Vietnam printed quotations, sayings, and cartoons on their steel pot camouflage covers. I was told that some of these troops stayed in the background because they were embarrassed, but Martha picked out some of the troops with these more explicit printings and had her picture taken with them. She made them all feel at ease.

Frank Angarola of Madison, Alabama also missed her appearance, but he heard about what she had done and the places she had visited. Frank served with A Company, 229th Assault Helicopter Battalion, First Air Cavalry Division (Airmobile) in Vietnam from June 1968 through June 1969 as a UH-1 assault helicopter pilot. During the second half of his tour the division relocated from I Corps, up near the DMZ, to III Corps. His unit was stationed at a large firebase called Tay Ninh. The areas north, northeast and northwest of Tay Ninh were extremely "hot" areas, covering much of the territory the North Vietnamese used as supply and infiltration routes into the Saigon area.

> I cannot recall the name of the small firebase located on the Cambodian border north-northwest of Tay Ninh. Perhaps that is because it was one of those locations we didn't talk about much; maybe we thought we wouldn't draw missions up there if its name was not spoken.
>
> I recall flying one mission up to that firebase the morning after it had been attacked by a large unit of North Vietnamese Army regulars. Three hundred of the enemy were killed outside the LZ and on the wire. One of the soldiers who was working with us on the mission mentioned that Martha Raye had been giving a show just a couple of days prior to the attack.
>
> This was not the first time I had heard her mentioned as an entertainer who knew exactly where the front lines were, and who seemed to gravitate there.
>
> Of course, there were no real front lines in Vietnam, but there were areas where the likelihood of death from enemy action was greatest, and those areas are what I'm talking about. Martha Raye was, and is, a legend among the troops who fought in Vietnam. She should be recognized as such.

A Legend Among the Troops

Duc Hoa—1967: III Corps, Fifth Special Forces Group. Contributed by Lieutenant Colonel George Massey.

Chapter 10

Our Old Lady of the Boondocks

"Thousands of Vietnam Veterans and I love and would die for her. She proved in Vietnam that she would do the same for us. Rarely do history and God produce such individuals."

Edmond Orr
(McCool, Mississippi)

DEPARTMENT OF THE ARMY
MARTHA RAYE
IS AWARDED
THE OUTSTANDING CIVILIAN SERVICE MEDAL

For your outstanding contributions to the morale and welfare of the United States forces in the Republic of Vietnam. During your sixth tour of the command during the period 24 October 1968 through 7 January 1969, you further enhanced your record of selfless service and achievement in furtherance of the well-being of United States Servicemen serving their country in Vietnam. Your significant and lasting contributions to the morale and welfare of United States Servicemen in Vietnam and to the success of the US Mission is greatly appreciated and reflects the utmost Credit upon yourself and your profession.

CREIGHTON W. ABRAMS, GENERAL
United States Army

Unknown location: Maggie visiting Marines in Vietnam. Photo by Corporal A. C. Ferreira, USMC printed with permission of BRAVO Veterans Outlook.

-10-

By now, America was four years into the Vietnam War. The number of American troops sent there kept increasing—over one-half million by mid-1970— as did the number of casualties.

Concurrently, racial tensions were escalating across America. Riots in Watts, Detroit, Newark, during the 1968 Democratic Party Convention in Chicago, and elsewhere often displaced Vietnam events at the top of evening TV news coverage. And, of course, there were the antiwar protestors—whose actual effect on ending the war still divides historians. For many Americans it was too easy to forget the people whose very lives were obscured by the smoke of "issues." Maggie could not forget those people, especially American military individuals in Vietnam—and she did not!

Between 1968 and 1970, Colonel Maggie was in her middle fifties and highly visible throughout Vietnam as well as stateside. Some who wrote us knew exactly when and where they saw her; others could only narrow it down to within their tour of duty.

Sergeant Major Leo Tucker of Las Vegas was the Battalion Sergeant Major of the Second Battalion, First Marines. His units were located in the Danang area.

> One day a master sergeant from the Marble Mountain Green Beret compound arrived at our battalion operating base. He had a passenger who happened to be Martha Raye. After a short visit with the battalion commander, Lieutenant Colonel Glasgow, she asked for and received permission to spend a few days with the battalion.
>
> If memory serves me correctly, she spent three days and two nights with us, informally visiting with the

> troops. She occupied the battalion Executive Officer's hootch; he bunked with the Battalion Training Officer during her stay.
>
> One evening while she was there, we received some harassing fire into the compound. She immediately let it be known that she was a nurse and would offer any assistance that would be needed.

Maggie liked getting to know soldiers as individuals, especially those with special talents. Michael Dooley, one of these talented young men, was killed in August 1968. Maggie escorted his remains stateside for his funeral. His sister, Olive Justice of Proctor, Montana recalled that day.

> My younger brother, Sergeant Michael B. Dooley, was in the Army Special Forces. I don't know exactly how he met Miss Raye, but I do know that she sort of took him under her wing, along with a lot of others. He was a budding cartoonist in the style of Bill Mauldin, and she encouraged him in his work.
>
> He was killed at a place called Duc Lap in 1968. The day of his funeral, Maggie led the honor guard. She stayed long enough to comfort each family member and then left quietly. No fanfare, no reporters. Just another Green Beret doing her job. She must have done this for a lot of families.

When I talked with Maggie in 1990, she remembered his funeral as though it happened yesterday.

Juggling Dollars and Sense

Maggie walked a tightrope between intensely different worlds—the screams of war, the devastating loss of a beloved young soldier, and then back into the world that made it financially possible for her to carry out her mission with the troops: the world of "glitz" and nonsense, movies, and guest shots. She kept on juggling her stake in both worlds, an ongoing dilemma now entering its fourth decade.

In September Maggie received P.T. Barnum's "The Circus Honored Saints and Sinners Award" for entertaining troops through the USO. Maggie was also the fall "Gal-Guest of Honor" at the P.T. Barnum Tent luncheon where $3000 was presented to the USO in her name. Before year's end, Maggie also was named B'nai B'rith's "Woman of the Year" for her humanitarian efforts.

The USO called in October in 1968 and, once again, Maggie was on her way to Vietnam for thirteen weeks.

Lieutenant Colonel Harry Hilling, Jr. of Hampton, Virginia was in Vietnam from August 1968 to 1969 as the Commanding Officer of Special Forces, Detachment B-Thirty-two, located at Tay Ninh. He was responsible for six Special Forces A-Detachments in various jungle locations near the Cambodian border.

During the period, 22-25 November 1968, Martha Raye visited us in Tay Ninh, and together we flew by helicopter to each of the six A-camps and spent considerable time at each. Martha talked with all my guys, had pictures taken with them, visited the sick and wounded American and Vietnamese, and in several instances, displayed her nursing skills by administering help to the wounded and sick.

This picture of Martha and me was taken at Katum, the most desolate and bombarded camp that I had. We were standing in front of a heavy mortar bunker....I treasure it greatly....Our B-team's nickname was "The Dirty Few of B-Thirty-two." I could go on about Martha's exploits. Her visit and presence in these remote areas was an inspiration to all, and we owe her a great deal of gratitude.

I am a great fan of Bob Hope. Everyone appreciated his great contributions. He deserved the many awards he received for his work with the troops. However, if anyone should have received the highest humanitarian awards, it should be Martha Raye. No one that I know of got right down with the troops on their battlegrounds. She was there where the action was, not at some plush rear area giving a few shows while wining and dining with the brass.

Instead of Girlie Shows, We Got...Maggie

Major Ronald Winkles of Whitesburg, Tennessee met Maggie in 1968. He was a twenty-two-year-old Air Force sergeant assigned to the Twentieth Special Operations Helicopter Squadron and attached to the Fifth Special Forces Command and Control Center Headquarters at Camp B-Fifty. When he met Maggie at a Special Forces B-camp near Ban Me Thout in the Central Highlands about thirty kilometers from the Cambodian border, she was wearing her lieutenant colonel's uniform.

> Most entertainers clung to the large coastal cities and big military bases like Cam Ranh Bay, NhaTrang, and Saigon.
>
> Consequently, it was a big surprise to hear that Bob Hope and some of his girls were going to make a quick visit to our camp. Of course, everyone was excited. Our counter-insurgency missions into Cambodia and Laos were rescheduled to allow as many of the Special Forces Recon Teams and our helicopter crews to be in camp to see the show. Altogether, this amounted to only seventy to eighty people.
>
> Well, Big Bob never showed. Instead, Lieutenant Colonel Martha Raye was sent as the bearer of the bad

news that Bob Hope and all those beautiful girls were unable to come. She carried the situation off beautifully.

Maggie, as she told us to call her, was wonderful. She told us jokes and amusing stories about her past experiences entertaining the troops. She answered our questions about anything we asked, and she even told why Bob Hope really didn't come. Best of all, she just sat down and talked with us.

All this really made us feel special in a way the girlie shows we had come to see could never have done. Martha Raye was able to do this because she was truly special. The fact that she was a big time celebrity became less obvious and less important as she spent more time with us that afternoon.

We could see the Mother figure who sincerely cared. She was a senior field-grade officer who would shoot straight with you. Most of all, she came across as a real friend who meant what she said and said what she meant.

The Bob Hope Show had been scheduled for a one-hour stop, but Martha Raye stayed with us nearly four hours. Then she left because she ran out of audience. We had to run recon, and she had to go "where the troops are." We both had our jobs to do.

I was really lucky. I got in late for the show. If Bob Hope had come, I would have missed his one-hour stop. By staying late and being the last to leave, I got to spend about ten minutes one-on-one with Maggie.

We sat and talked in a very comfortable sort of way about her career and family, and about mine. She was able to make the war just disappear.

She was a real trouper and a real person. She could be as salty as any sailor or as caring and gentle as any mother, but in between these two extremes, she was a *friend.*

She left me with a lifelong memory of one person that really cared about us guys serving in Vietnam.

Sergeant First Class Robert Moro of San Diego served on an A-team near the Cambodian border with the Fifth

Special Forces Group. That's where he met Maggie in December 1968. There were nine Americans and approximately three hundred Montagnards at this camp. Maggie found the time to visit, to share drinks and jokes with nine Americans in an isolated camp in a very hostile area. She was protected only by the helicopter crew that provided her the needed transportation, her photographer, nine Americans, and their contingent of Montagnards. This was an act of uncommon valor, an act she was to repeat over and over again until she had visited all the A-camps. All were as isolated and vulnerable in hostile territory as this camp was.

> The generosity, kindness, and courage that this unselfish great woman has given us not only boosted my morale and helped me finish out seven more months of my tour in Vietnam, but has been an inspiration through the years afterward when the going got rough.

Robert went on to say that he has a picture of Maggie and himself. It sits on his desk where he now works.

Byron Adams was recovering from wounds in the Fourth Medical Hospital during Christmas of 1968. He served with the Fourth Infantry Division.

> Miss Raye came into the ward dressed in full jungle fatigues. Even more important than her humor, she stopped at each of our beds and in a compassionate way, she gave each of us a St. Christopher emblem to carry with us. I am not Catholic but that act of love meant more to me than can ever be known. She is most honored in my memories and thoughts.

Chaplain Ortiz kept supplying Maggie with these "airborne medals." Byron is but one of many troops blessed by Ortiz's and Maggie's generosity.

Signing Their Wall

First Sergeant Joseph Waskas of Pottsville, Pennsylvania saw Maggie several times. He was stationed at a remote Special Forces camp (A-241) in a small village called Polei Kleng. Shortly after the 1968 Tet Offensive, things were unsettled. He has fond recollections of two visits and, like many others who didn't get to see many USO tours, he felt that although Maggie may have been "only an honorary Lieutenant Colonel," she earned that silver leaf. After all, she spent more time in hostile territory than most field-grade officers.

> There weren't any other USO tours that reached us out there but that didn't seem to slow down our Martha Raye.
>
> Every one of her visits was preceded by the incoming radio message that a "VIP—Code Name Maggie" was inbound. She began her visits weeks before Christmas and didn't finish until weeks afterward. She didn't arrive with any fanfare or large troupe to support her. She came with just one escort officer from the Special Forces Operating Base, a Polaroid camera, a huge supply of film, and a few words to let us know that not all of the people at home were of Jane Fonda's ilk.
>
> She told us we were not forgotten and to come home safely. She had drinks with us, helped at the dispensary, dared the Viet Cong or North Vietnamese to try to stop her visits, posed for pictures of each of us alone with her—which I'll treasure always—and went on her way to the next camp.
>
> At Detachment A-241, she ended her visits by signing her name and dating it on a wall. There were already two of her signatures on that wall! They were never painted over; when I left there were four of her signatures—and no doubt more before it was all over.
>
> Like many others we worried about her and wished she would be more careful in choosing the camps she visited. As long as a helicopter would take her, she went. It didn't matter if the camp was under siege or not. Once as she was getting into the helicopter, I yelled at her to be careful—or she would become a feather in the Viet Cong's cap. Her response was, "If they get me, they're going to get a feather up their butt."

Joseph said that Maggie gave her address and phone number to many people in case they ever needed a friend to talk to or a place to stay while they were stateside. She wished them luck, threw a good-bye kiss, and she was gone to the next camp. He knows that she visited all of the Corps areas and as many of the remote camps as was humanly possible. He believes that for most of those people she never lost her cheerful disposition and was always there with a kind word.

> I haven't heard a whole lot [in the press] about what Maggie did for the troops. It seems that unless you had an entourage of dozens of musicians and entertainers, there wasn't any publicity. I can speak only for myself. I was in Vietnam for three tours and never had the pleasure of one of Bob Hope's shows. We were too isolated, there weren't enough of us to warrant a trip, and it was too dangerous. At least that seemed to be the case for everyone—except Martha Raye.

On December 27, 1968, Maggie flew into Plei Me from Duc Co with an escort officer and nine Montagnard women and children who had hitched a ride on her helicopter. Maggie had brought a case of beer to the troops of A-253, Company B, Fifth Special Forces Group. She hugged and hassled the nine soldiers; she told jokes and posed for pictures. Maggie then flew on to Pleiku. Later that day when she heard that Duc Co was under attack, she stayed by the radios for over three hours until she knew that the troops of A-253 were okay.

Wounded... *Where?*

Somewhere between 1968 and 1969, Maggie was rescued by medevac pilot Hugh McClure. While entertaining troops, she had been caught in a mortar attack and a piece of shrapnel hit her buttock. McClure flew her out at night in a storm. Wounded, but always thinking of someone else, Maggie gave him her business card! She also told him to write a screenplay but keep it out of Hollywood "because someone would steal it." She advised him to make the film himself. Finally in 1980, McClure made his movie entitled *M*U*S*T*: The Vietnam Years,* filmed at Fort A.P. Hill, Virginia. An article about McClure's endeavors and his encounter with Maggie appeared in the *Washington Post* on September 21, 1980.

Robert Boyce of Lakewood, California was in the Central Highlands from March 1968 into 1969. He served with D Battery, Fifth Battalion of the Sixteenth Artillery, which Maggie visited.

> We were at Firebase Six on the Dak Poko River. We had just been mortared, yet she came in. She talked with us and didn't leave until things heated up and the officers with her *made* her go. I appreciated seeing a kind face after so many months of being pounded by rockets and mortars.

Chief Master Sergeant Gary Jones of Albuquerque met Maggie in the passenger terminal at Bien Hoa Air Base, where she was trying to "cop a hop" on a plane going to the Danang-Phu Bai area. Gary said that having an opportunity to just sit and chat for a few minutes with Martha Raye was one of the highlights of his career.

> Her "Christmas Show" was a 365-days-per-year effort that will not be forgotten by those fortunate enough to meet her. I certainly don't mean to belittle Bob Hope, because his appearances meant so much to us all; but Martha Raye was there whenever and wherever she was needed...not just a few days a year and certainly not escorted by a horde of VIP's and security teams.

Edmond Orr of McCool, Mississippi saw Maggie at the Pleiku Air Base, where she was the guest of a Special Forces unit.

Ms. Raye was then—and still is—the most popular entertainer and leading morale booster of the entire Vietnam War. She had great compassion for the GI's and gave unselfishly of her energy and time. To be in her presence for five minutes was to feel loved by her and to personally love her.

Ms. Raye was playing the piano and singing to a club packed with GI's. She made us feel like our country was worth dying for. I recall telling Ms. Raye that I truly appreciated her contribution to the Vietnam [troops] and that I had been a fan of hers for years. She smiled as if she had never before heard such a compliment. Then she kissed me! A warm brotherly kiss that I shall cherish the rest of my life.

Thousands of Vietnam Veterans and I love and would die for her. She proved in Vietnam that she would do the same for us. It did not deter Ms. Raye that we were under daily enemy mortar and rocket attacks. I know she was doing what she wished to be doing. Rarely does history and God produce such individuals.

Nightmares...to this Day

Vietnam War military historians remember 1968 most because of the Tet Offensive. Veterans also remember that year with loving thoughts of Maggie, as they try to forget those war-torn days and nights. So many letters mentioned continuing nightmares about Vietnam experiences, about fighting in a countryside where—at least in daylight—it was often difficult to distinguish friendly Vietnamese from those who were the enemy. Worst, for too many Vietnam Veterans, are the awful memories of seeing buddies die and then to come home to so little understanding, so little support, so much suspicion and...blame!

The war was far from over. During 1969, Maggie was seen in Vietnam, Germany, and stateside—giving her best to her beloved troops. Stories continued to come in about her exploits that year.

Lieutenant Colonel Bill Shelton said that Maggie did not need an "honorary" title of Lieutenant Colonel. He had been told she held a commission as a bona fide lieutenant colonel, Army Nurse Corps, in the Army Reserve.

> I first met Maggie while working at Command and Control, North, at Danang in 1969. Much earlier, Maggie had "adopted" the soldiers of Special Forces. She knew that those young soldiers were doing some very risky and thankless jobs. When she visited with us, she seemed to sense that those young men were not looking to her for sympathy, but as an understanding friend. She didn't have time for the few complainers. She had a wonderful capacity for making the men forget the war for a while. Her talent and wit as a comedienne was always appreciated.

Sergeant Major Raymond Eaton was the Senior Non-Commissioned Officer of a Special Forces Camp named An Lac, known as a "split" A-team. Normally they had a force of six American Special Forces personnel and a force of Montagnard tribesmen. Colonel Maggie came into their camp late one afternoon by UH1-A Helicopter—the only way in or out—with a Special Forces officer escort. They had a great time talking the night away inside their bunker. That night their Detachment Commander received a head wound that required eighteen stitches to close—done by none other than *Maggie!* The chopper came back for her the next morning and took her on to another remote camp. Their Commander recovered fine, Raymond adds.

Edward Marvin of Tabb, Virginia was an Air Force Technical Sergeant stationed in Pleiku in 1969. He and his friend, Staff Sergeant Frank McPeek of Pikesville, Kentucky went to the Fifth Special Forces Club.

> While we were there, "Colonel Maggie" came in the club. I recognized her and told Frank she was there! He

> replied that he knew her! I said, "Frank, *everyone* knows her!" Frank said he really *knew* her! I said I would buy the beer for the night if he could prove that. Well, we started across the room but did not even get close before "Colonel Maggie" saw him and said, "McPeek, you sawed-off runt, where have you been?" Frank then invited her to sit with our group—and I bought a lot of beer.
>
> She really made the place light up. There was not a person in the place she didn't know by first name and with whom she had many "war stories" to swap.

That year, General Creighton Abrams presented Maggie with the Outstanding Civilian Service Award, which consisted of a bronze medal, a rosette, and a citation certificate. (The citation text is on page 172.)

After this extended Christmas-season tour ended, Maggie went stateside for a while. In February of 1969 she appeared on "The Joey Bishop Show," where she was presented with the Try a Little Kindness Award for giving so much to so many others.

Two weeks later Maggie appeared on NBC's "The Bob Hope Show," a program based on vaudeville routines. Bing Crosby, George Burns, Diana Ross and The Supremes, and Lisa Miller joined Maggie and Bob.

James Kapucinski of Bay Village, Ohio served with Headquarters and Headquarters Company Second of the Twelfth, First Air Cavalry at Firebase LZ Grant. Maggie visited his unit during the summer of 1969.

> LZ Grant was a remote firebase by Tay Ninh province. We lost many GIs there and many were wounded, so it was *no* cushy area. I was very surprised and pleased to see Martha Raye there. She was like a motherly figure; she also was honest and sincere.

Rescued from Rabble

Captain Robert Knowles, Jr. of Lilburn, Georgia was passing through the San Francisco International Airport in June of that year, completing a courier mission when Maggie crossed his path.

> As I plodded down the airport corridor, I turned a corner and found the hallway blocked by a group of long-haired, noisy, sign-waving antiwar demonstrators.
>
> Although it was standard procedure in 1969 to avoid getting entangled with antiwar protesters by wearing civilian clothes, my assignment had required me to wear Class A Army greens.
>
> I was trying to find a way around the demonstrators, when I felt a light touch on the big, gold and black, "horse soldier" patch on my right "combat" shoulder. A voice in my ear sang out, "First Cav!" I whirled around, expecting that the television lights stabbing my eyes meant I had been spotted and was about to become embroiled in an antiwar demonstration.
>
> Instead, I beheld a welcomed and wondrous sight: a petite Army Nurse, Lieutenant Colonel, whom I quickly recognized as Martha Raye in full uniform, including Green Beret, greens and spit-shined jump boots.
>
> Without even a sideways glance at the noisy sign-wavers, she took my arm, and she and the accompanying TV camera crews "broke trail" for me.
>
> The little gray-haired lady had the most dazzling smile I had encountered up to that (pre-Jimmy Carter) time. She asked me when and where in Vietnam I had been. Then the little green whirlwind, followed closely by whirring cameras and bright lights, vanished from sight around the corner.

Robert found Ms. Raye to be caring, quick on her feet, and fearless. She gladdened a tired young cavalryman's heart and made the ride back to his base seem a lot shorter!

Some Stateside Support!

Lance Corporal Clayton Hough, Jr. of Holyoke, Massachusetts served with Company I, Third of the Fifth,

First Marine Division. He met Maggie in 1969 when he was recuperating at the Philadelphia Naval Hospital from losing both of his legs above the knees while in Vietnam.

> The first night I met her was at her show in Cherry Hill, New Jersey. About twenty to twenty-five of us from the hospital went to see her show *Hello Sucker*. At the end of the show she gave her speech about the men and women serving in Vietnam and asked everyone to think of them and keep them in their prayers. She really hit home, but never got into the politics. Then she *really* got to us—she had the spotlights put on us and introduced us. We were not only given a standing ovation; most of the audience went out of their way to come by us and thank us and say "Hi." Just remembering, it still brings chills to my spine and tears to my eyes. What a difference from the boo's and jeers we had been getting—to now feel love and honor instead of hate and disgust.
>
> Maggie showed her generosity and big heart after the show by loading the cast and staff of the show into the hospital bus and van and treating all of us at a nightclub. You should have seen the looks on the faces at this club we went to as all the guys with arms and legs missing, in wheelchairs and on crutches, came through the door with Maggie and the show girls. Maggie picked up the tab for *everyone* from the hospital and the show. She made sure that everyone ordered something to eat and drink. She danced with the guys, and she spent time with each guy from the hospital.

Clayton said that was to be the first of many meetings with her. He later went to the D.C. area to see Maggie and was with her in Chicago for almost a week.

Wherever she went during the Vietnam years, Maggie made her speech after every stateside show asking her audience to remember those who were serving their country. It was Clayton's proud honor to know her for over twenty years, and he characterized her as the most patriotic and generous person he has ever met. She visited Veterans Administration facilities and military hospitals wherever she was and apparently never forgot any Veteran she met. In 1969 Clayton Hough began the "Martha Raye Nursing Scholarship" at his old high school. He contributes a hundred dollars a year toward a student's nursing education.

> When we went to D.C. to see her, she gave us guys her room because it was bigger even though she and her secretary, Trudi, had to move in with Mary and Roseanne.
>
> In Chicago, she and Trudi drove out to O'Hare to meet and take us to our hotel, then picked us up every day and brought us to her hotel and theater. She found out about a marine who was a triple amputee from the Chicago area who was home on leave from the hospital and was having a hard time adjusting. She called him, found out how to get to his home and picked him up; he stayed with us for a day. Every night we went to her show, *Everybody Loves Opal;* then we went to her penthouse apartment, had something to eat and drink, talked, and played Password.
>
> We had one very sad time that week. Maggie got a call from Chris Noel about the death of Chris' ex-husband, Ty. She said that there was a problem getting him a military funeral. Maggie got on the phone and made a few calls to a few Generals, got back to Chris, and everything was taken care of.

A Letter from the President

The White House was aware of Maggie's endeavors on behalf of the Veterans of our country and her visits to stateside hospitals. She received this letter dated May 28, 1969.

> It was with special pleasure that I read of your recent visit to the veterans at the Philadelphia Naval Hospital and I want to take this opportunity to express my

personal appreciation for the thousands of miles you have traveled to bring a little bit of home and happiness to our servicemen.

I know that no recognition for your efforts can match the warmth and personal satisfaction you must feel from seeing the wounded smile again and the men in the fields welcome you as 'Colonel Maggie.'

Mrs. Nixon joins me in expressing our heartfelt appreciation for your service beyond the call of duty to our men in uniform and the nation.

With our very best wishes.

Sincerely,
Richard Nixon

On July 18, 1969, *The Los Angeles Herald Examiner* ran a story by Tom Duggan about a television special featuring Bob Hope's trip to Vietnam. Referring to Maggie the article said, "There are other entertainers just as dedicated. We ought to make Martha Raye a full general. She loves her country and she proves it."

Summer stock drew Maggie to the Colonie Summer Theater in Latham, New York. Her role brought to life the personality of Texas Guinan, a famous nightclub hostess from the prohibition era, in the musical *Hello Sucker.* Although the plot was unimpressive, it got a shot in the arm from Maggie's vitality, warm good humor, and her rendition of the torch song "Nobody, Nobody Knows." The show played in twelve other theaters, including the Storrowton Summer Theater in Springfield, Massachusetts before making its way to Broadway...without her.

On July 29, 1969, the Albany *Times Union* reported that twelve Green Berets had gone to Maggie's hotel before opening night at the Colonie Summer Theater. They had flowers, a Special Forces arm patch, and a note that read *"The first best thing to happen to the Special Forces was the Green Beret. The second best thing was Martha Raye."* Although she was ill and unable to attend their reception, she arranged for them to be her guests at the opening performance.

Lance Corporal Hough also visited Maggie's home in California and saw her Oscar. A sign outside her front door welcomed all GI's to stop in "Maggie's Team House," as she called it. The sign was a gift from one of her "troops." It was still hanging there when I visited her in 1990 and 1991. The name is apt, given how many remote A-team outposts she visited in Vietnam!

Maggie called Clayton periodically to see how he was doing. When she played at The Chateau Deville in Connecticut, she invited him to attend so she could let her hair down and be herself.

In August 1969, Clayton and several other amputee Veterans from the hospital went to surprise Maggie on her birthday while she was starring in *Hello Sucker* at the Storrowton Summer Theater in Springfield, Massachusetts. (They partied for a *week*.)

Massachusetts' *The Springfield Union* reported the event. When the performance was over, servicemen carried a large birthday cake down the aisle while the Eighth Air Force Band played her theme song, "Mr. Paganini," and "Happy Birthday." Air Force Colonel Harold Ottaway, commander of the Ninety-ninth Bomb Wing at Westover Air Force Base, presented Maggie with a citation and a key to the air base. The citation and key recognized her total elapsed in-country time of over twenty-four months in Vietnam.

Clayton, twenty-one at the time, had been released two weeks before from the Philadelphia Naval Hospital and attended with fellow amputees from the hospital—Sergeant William Clark of Hart, Michigan; Lance Corporal William Cady of Jamestown, New York; Lance Corporal Gregory Cost of Vermillion, Ohio; Lance Corporal Michael Douglas of Anderson, Indiana; Lance

Corporal John Lythgoe of Philadelphia; Corporal William Perry of St. Louis; Corporal Robert Sheppard of Dayton, Ohio, and Corporal Donald Udies of Cleveland—all accompanied by Hospitalman First Class Richard "Tiny" Colavechio.

Gregory Cost later moved to Costa Mesa, California. He recalls the same events:

> After being medevaced from the Danang area, I was sent to the Philadelphia Naval Hospital to recuperate from my injuries.
>
> Although I was not as bad off as some of the others, I was in an amputee ward. The doctors were still trying to decide whether to try saving my foot and leg or to amputate. I was in the Naval Hospital from April 1969 to March 1970.
>
> One of the corpsman who took care of us—listened to our complaints, problems, hopes, fears, plans, and was our best friend, big brother, etc.—was a Petty Officer First Class by the name of Richard "Tiny" Colavechio. He got the nickname "Tiny" because of his size—about six-foot five-inches and three hundred pounds. Tiny was constantly doing things for us, arranging for nights out, special liberty, taking us to ball games, the movies, etc.
>
> During the summer of 1969, perhaps when some of our spirits were at their lowest point and protestors' sentiment against the war seemed to be at its highest pitch, a group of us got to meet Maggie. We were invited as her guests to spend a week with her in Springfield, Massachusetts. She was starring in a summer stock play called *Hello Sucker*.
>
> It was one of the most wonderful weeks of our lives, and one that we will always remember. The kindness and friendship that Maggie and the rest of the cast showed us is beyond description, whether it was taking us out for ice cream sodas or just sitting and talking with us.

Back with the A-Teams

October 1969, Maggie embarked on another six-week USO tour in Vietnam. Once again she focused on posts where other civilians would not dare to go.

Lieutenant Colonel Robert Leiendecker of Charlottesville was the Commanding Officer of the Eighty-fifth Explosive Ordinance Disposal Detachment based out of Pleiku between July 1969 and February 1970. Robert said this was the type of duty that required travel to many of the firebases and remote camps throughout the central highlands.

> On one occasion, a member of my unit and I had driven to Ben Het, a camp to the north of Pleiku. As we approached the camp we came under fire but drove through it. We arrived at Ben Het and while taking the edge off our nerves in the local club bunker, we learned that the camp had just been hit, and we had driven right through the enemy retreat.
>
> After sitting at the bar for a few minutes, I looked to my right and saw a woman sitting there. She was dressed in fatigues and talking with two junior enlisted men. Her words were filled with encouragement, compassion, and concern. She talked of the war, the hardships, home, politics, and a variety of other subjects.
>
> It was dark in the bunker; I could not see who she was, but I was close enough to hear the conversation. I wondered, first of all, what a woman dressed like a seasoned combat veteran was doing on a hot firebase, and second, where she got the compassion she was sharing with these young men.
>
> Only after the bunker door opened, when the men left and some light came into the bunker, did I recognize the face of Martha Raye. I was convinced that it must be an illusion, because the Hollywood people I had seen and heard of in combat zones traveled in well orchestrated and protected groups and only in "safe" areas. Curiosity overcame me, and I approached her.
>
> If beauty was the only criteria by which to judge people, Colonel Maggie would have been deported on

> that day. She was dirty, dusty, unkempt, and in general disarray, but she was also on her second unescorted day on one of the dustiest, driest firebases in the area.
>
> After a few minutes of conversation, however, I came to realize that she was sincere and felt strongly that she had to give some of her time to bring a little something different to men a long way from the states. She had flown in to spend a few days with the men isolated there and had experienced her second ground attack in about as many days.
>
> She was firebase-hopping with no fanfare, escort, or demands. She slept wherever there was an empty bunk—if indeed there was a bunk—ate what rations there were, pulled midnight perimeter duty with the guys, and generally conducted herself like she was honored to be there. There was not the slightest hint that she expected recognition in return.
>
> She made a standing offer to all she met to stop at her home in Hollywood on our way back through California. I talked to some who took her up on that offer, and they spoke highly of her hospitality.

Lieutenant Colonel Leiendecker said that Maggie was a rare and exceptional woman who was unconventional. He thought she preferred to share the remoteness, danger, and drama of the bush rather than the glitter of a Bob Hope-style stage show far from the action. "I admired her for her courage and her desire to give of herself so freely. She was a class act in my book."

Purple Prose

Sergeant Major Edward Komac of Maplewood, Minnesota spent three tours in Vietnam with the Fifth Special Forces. On his second tour, he was with an A-team at Ben Het from 1969 to 1970.

> In 1970, Maggie paid our team a visit. I normally would not walk five feet to visit, see, or talk to any celebrity—this is one exception to my policy. This was one fine lady! She made me feel at ease.

> I'm a major league swearer. When we were talking, she never batted an eye when I cut loose with some of my purple phrases. This instantly won me over. She holds a special place in my heart.

Rather than...Raquel?

Lynda Van Devanter was a nurse in Vietnam from June 1969 to June 1970 at the Seventy-first Evacuation Hospital in Pleiku and the Sixty-seventh Evac in Qui Nhon. She wrote about her encounter with Maggie in her book *Home Before Morning: The Story of an Army Nurse in Vietnam.* She recounted an incident from an Operating Room where they were working on a patient under local anesthetic. When the patient found out that Martha Raye was just outside the OR, he wanted to see her. She suited up and came to see him. Realizing he was Mexican-American, she conversed with him in Spanish. Lynda also commented that she thought Martha was someone more GI's would like to see than anybody else, including Raquel Welch.

Brigadier General George Dooley of Pauma Valley, California first met Maggie at Marine Corps Headquarters in Arlington. The story he sent happened at a later time and place.

> My story about her starts on the evening of 9 November 1969. I was serving as Chief of Staff of III Marine Amphibious Force in Vietnam. As you well know, III MAF was responsible for the First Corps Tactical Zone, the "I Corps."
>
> At about 1800 hours, Martha called me and said she was at the Danang airport and that she was supposed to have been met by some Special Forces folks. Apparently, there was a mix-up and she was stranded. She asked if I could put her up for the night.
>
> Of course, the answer was "yes." So we sent a driver to pick her up and return her to our compound. We held dinner for her in the Commanding General's mess.

After dinner, she left to entertain the troops in a club on the compound. But as she was going out the door, about 2000 hours, I stopped her. I told her that we would be having a small ceremony the next day celebrating the Marine Corps birthday and that we would be very honored if she would attend.

Her response was that she was leaving early for a visit to a Special Forces Base—Fire Support Base Blaze was the name I remember. She stated that if she returned in time, she would be happy to attend.

Well, she entertained the troops until about 0200 hours and then departed for Blaze at about 0400 hours. Our ceremony was held at 1100 hours. She returned at 1045 hours.

She was seated on the reviewing stand, and, as it happened, next to me. The ceremony was brief with token troop participation. The Colors passed in review and we all stood and saluted as the Colors passed.

I glanced over at Martha and she was standing at rigid attention. She was absolutely exhausted. Her fatigues were covered with the dirt accumulated on her visit to Blaze. Her jungle boots were covered with mud. Her fatigue cap was slouched on the side of her head. She was holding a West Point salute and the tears were streaming down her face. I thought, and the thought is vivid to this day, "Maggie, you and I are Buddies forevermore"— and we are.

I have told this story many times to service clubs, to groups interested in what really went on in Vietnam, and, in fact, to anyone who would listen. I always emphasized that Maggie made these trips at great expense to herself. No one back in the States knew what she was doing. There was no publicity. She didn't hang around the Officers clubs, Saigon, or other centers of comfort. But she was out at places like Blaze.

She was exposed to her share of incoming rockets and satchel charges. She went through the ordeal each week with the malaria pill, as did we all. She endured the heat and the cold, the rain and the humidity, the flies, rats, and other friendly creatures.

Slugged for a Slur

George adds a postscript to this story. That night, Maggie joined a group of officers in the Officers Club on the compound. Seated with her was an Army Brigadier (a member of the III MAF staff), one or two Marine Colonels, and two civilians who had arrived that day from Quantico. These civilians worked for the Marine Corps and had been sent to do a study on Marine Corps operations.

"During the course of the evening, one of these civilians made a comment that Marines were a bunch of glory hunters, and he attempted to add other derogatory remarks. But not for very long! Maggie got out of her seat, walked around the table to the culprit and slugged him! Right in the chops! No one was going to talk about her Marines like *that* in her presence!"

The next day both civilians were ordered out of the country. Brigadier General Dooley had the pleasure of sending a dispatch to the Commanding General in Quantico telling him that they were *persona non grata*. He is still not sure if Maggie ever knew of this aftermath. What he had done was to back up and reinforce what she did the previous evening. He stated that Maggie was a true and wonderful soldier and that she embodied all the best in an American. "What she did during all of those years was demonstrate her love for her country. And love it she did—and all the men and women who served in its cause."

Howard Miller was a Special Forces Medic at an A-camp—A-325 in Duc Hue—when Maggie visited their outpost around December 1969. He says she was dressed in jungle fatigues with the appropriate patches—including her "Raye" tag—of a Special Forces colonel, her Green Beret and jungle boots. She gave each one a Saint Christopher medal. He kept his to this day. "It was a great boost to my morale for her to risk so much to bring us some cheer and encouragement."

The years changed, but not Maggie. She continued her treks throughout Vietnam and across America. When Kenneth Howell wrote us, he was in Saint Andre De L'Eure, France.

> When one is in a foreign country far away from home and friends, and under extreme pressures, it is relaxing to meet and converse with an old friend.
>
> I was fortunate enough to meet Martha on a beach at NhaTrang, Vietnam in 1970. She was dressed in a jungle fatigue uniform and wore the rank of a lieutenant colonel. She was very congenial and entertaining. She had a special knack for answering everyone's questions and still not ignore anyone. The actor, Fess Parker, was with her, and he too was very congenial.
>
> At the time I was forty-two years old and ending my military career. I felt that, perhaps, I had a little more in common with Martha than did many of the younger servicemen.

Special Silver Helmet Award

In April 1970 the National American Veterans Association held their tenth annual Silver Helmet Award luncheon in Washington, D.C.. The award is presented to one of their own members who falls into one of the following categories: AMVET of the Year, Congressional, Civil Servant, Defense, World Peace, Rehabilitation, or Americanism.

The AMVETS also have a Special Silver Helmet Award. Since its inception in 1961, the special award has been presented only four times. This time they presented the award to Maggie for her compassion and involvement with the Armed Forces during World War II, Korea, and Vietnam. She became the first actress and only woman to receive this award. This prestigious award also has been presented to Bob Hope in 1961, Raymond Burr in 1973, and Frank Sinatra in 1982.

Jose Natal saw Maggie at Fort Bragg. He was an artist who was asked to draw Colonel Maggie on a giant billboard. Below her picture he was to put the statement: "LOOK OUT S.F. MAGGIE'S BACK IN TOWN." The assignment took him all night, but it was up the next day ready for Maggie's arrival with the post commander.

When Maggie arrived, Jose was introduced as the one who drew her on the billboard. She autographed his work, gave him a big kiss, and they had photos of themselves and the post commander taken in front of the billboard. Jose said, "Needless to say, that day was a very memorable one that has lasted up to this day."

Reassuring Revelation

Major Dale Brown commented that he was one of the thousands fortunate enough to have met and been enriched by Maggie during the Vietnam years. Although he claims he did not have any "incredible" stories to tell, these two are personally significant to him.

> I first met Colonel Maggie at the Fort Bragg NCO club in 1970. She was kind enough to invite a nineteen-year-old Special Forces buck sergeant and his wife to her table for a drink and some lively discussion. Her words and the obvious fact that she truly cared about us and our input gave two scared kids a significant confidence boost.
>
> Subsequently, I met Maggie three times in Vietnam, 1970 to 1971. The first time she presented me with an Air Medal during a ceremony held at our C-team in Can Tho. Later she enlivened my evenings at NCO clubs in NhaTrang and Danang. On each occasion Maggie's warmth and sincerity made me forget—for a time—the loss of friends, the fear of tomorrow, and the many miles to home. She also reminded me that not all Americans ostracized us, and that in fact many supported us, if not the war.
>
> She brought humanity and love to a place where those necessary commodities were in extremely short supply. Furthermore, during those brief moments of

contact she, unknowingly, assisted at least one young sergeant to make it through the most difficult period of his life.

She left a legacy in my mind and heart which I hope comes through in my attitude and interactions with others. My experiences with Maggie may not have been overtly dynamic or "incredible," but they were personally significant.

AnLoc, Vietnam—1969: Maggie prepares to board a medevac chopper. Photo contributed by John Mitchell, Sandy, Utah

Chapter 11

Meanest Mother in the Valley

"We got an unexpected call saying that 'Mean Momma One' is coming to our location; meet them at the helipad. We attempted to identify 'Mean Momma One' by our code sheets to no avail. We went to the pad as they landed...darned if she didn't look like Martha Raye!"

Master Sergeant William Miller
(Fort Worth, Texas)

Ban Me Thout

Ban Me Thout, Vietnam—1971: Maggie clowns by an armored truck that often transported her. Photo contributed by Kenneth Roberts.

-11-

During 1970, Maggie found time to make two films. The first was Warner Brothers' production of *The Phynx,* a story about a secret government agency forming a rock and roll band to infiltrate a Communist country and rescue American entertainers. Reviewed as a mediocre comedy, it starred Joan Blondell, Michael Ansara, George Tobias, and Maggie as Foxy.

The second film was a fantasy called *Pufnstuf,* which starred Maggie as Boss Witch, Jack Wild as Jimmy, "Mama" Cass Eliott (from the music group "The Mamas and the Papas") as Witch Hazel, and Billie Hayes as Witchiepoo. This two-star movie was about a dejected boy being led by his talking flute on a talking boat to a place called Living Island. The island was full of strange but friendly animals in fear of an incompetent witch. The movie faired best with young children.

Maggie returned to TV as a frequent guest on popular programs such as "The Ed Sullivan Show," which ran weekly for sixteen years from 1955 to 1971. She also frequented "The Red Skelton Show" and, occasionally, "The Lucille Ball Show."

Maggie portrayed Benita Bizarre in twenty-six episodes of "The Bugaloos," a children's TV comedy program on NBC. Benita's disastrous attempts to destroy the Bugaloos' "disgusting goodness" focused a thirty-minute show that ran weekly for nearly two years.

"The Bob Hope Show" that aired October 5, 1970, on NBC poked fun at women's lib. Bob was the only male star in this hour-long program. The rest of the cast was female, including Maggie, Ruth Buzzi, Teresa Graves, Nanette Fabray, Kaye Ballard, JoAnne Worley, Imogene Coca, Edie Adams, Phyllis Diller, Totie Fields, Zsa Zsa

Gabor, Virginia Graham, Sheila MacRae, Minnie Pearl, Connie Stevens, Irene Ryan, and Nancy Walker. Quite a line-up!

Momma to a Multitude

Maggie made her final USO tour to Vietnam in November of 1970 when the number of our in-country troops was near its all-time peak. Although this eight-week trip was her last for the USO, it was not *her* last tour in Vietnam.

Norman Barabash served at Headquarters of the Fifth Special Forces Group in NhaTrang from April 1970 to March 1971. Maggie visited them in November 1970; she returned stateside shortly after New Years Day, 1971.

> Colonel Maggie was in a class by herself. She is the most unselfish entertainer I have known. She never traveled with an entourage, press agents, or support staff. She could not care less if she made it on the evening news or if any network would turn her travels into a TV special; publicity was the last thing on her mind. Nor would she tolerate any handler or intermediary interposing himself between her and her boys.
>
> I had always known of her to be a very talented and very funny lady. Meeting her in person, I discovered her warmth, her decency, her big heart, and, yes, her courage in bucking the Hollywood herd.
>
> All her shows for us were done in intimate, indoor settings. A remote, elevated stage was never for her. Her first appearance before our enlisted ranks on that tour occurred in mid-November in the movie house on the Headquarters compound. Our commander introduced her to us as "The Meanest Mother in the Valley."
>
> After a month of visiting the base camps, Maggie returned to NhaTrang. She liked to hang out with us at the NCO Club where I took the photos. She talked to us, joked with us, drank with us, and danced with us. If our Filipino house band of the month or a wandering

> Australian musical group were playing, it would not take much to get her on stage doing her shtick. "I was married so many times, I got pock marks from the rice," was one of her lines.
>
> Bands found themselves improvising to accompany her songs. The aforementioned Aussies were awestruck at sharing the stage with a show business legend. In turn, Maggie paid them a humorous tribute. "I wish to say that these guys are the most tasteful group I've encountered here. They're never vulgar or give you any bulls***."

Norman pointed out that, to conclude each performance, Maggie would always tell them, "I may not be young or pretty, but my eyes are round and I love you!" Norman wondered if she were already packing her bags for Saudi Arabia. "Our guys there need her." His letter was written during 1990 when we were involved with Operations Desert Shield and Desert Storm.

Agnes "Scottie" McLennan was stationed in Saigon. She was secretary and receptionist to General Creighton W. Abrams from 1969 to 1971. In late 1970 she had the opportunity to meet Maggie.

> She was Special Forces! The Commander of the Fifth Special Forces at the time was Colonel (later Brigadier General) Michael Healy. Because he spent so much time in my office waiting to see General Abrams, we became friends.
>
> When Martha Raye came to Saigon, Colonel Healy invited me to his quarters to meet her, and it was quite an experience! I was so awed by her enthusiasm and energy, I spent the entire time in her presence nearly mute—her personality was overpowering and left an impression I'll never forget.

Major Eric Helfers of Glenn Dale, Maryland saw Maggie in early 1971 when she visited his Special Forces camp at Kontum, Command and Control Central.

As a morale builder, an officer, and a nurse, she was a real person and an officer in the true sense. She visited the hootches on base to see how we lived and she checked the dispensary.

No one else above the rank of captain, in or out of our organization, visited us during my seven months there.

USO Board of Governors Special Award

On March 25, 1971, Maggie attended the USO's annual awards banquet at the Shoreham Hotel in Washington, D.C. She received the USO's Board of Governors Special Award—for the *second* time—for her efforts on behalf of the USO and our troops.

Michael Burnes commented that he still remembers when Maggie came to the Orthopedic ward at the old Fort Ord hospital. She was the only person who ever showed any concern toward him as a Veteran before, during, and immediately after Vietnam. He was sent back to Vietnam a week after her visit near the end of August 1971.

The last time Maggie appeared on "The Bob Hope Show" was September 13, 1971. This sixty-minute comedy special celebrated Bob's twenty-two years on television with a parody on *The Planet of the Apes.* Bob played an astronaut who landed on a planet dominated by man-hating females. Besides Maggie, the cast included Edie Adams, Dr. Joyce Brothers, Imogene Coca, Linda Cristal, Angie Dickinson, Phyllis Diller, Nanette Fabray, Zsa Zsa Gabor, Sue Lyon, RoseMarie, Barbara McNair, Phyllis Newman, Jill St. John, Sally Struthers, Jacqueline Susann, Edy Williams, and JoAnne Worley. Maggie was again in great show business company!

Subbing for Santa...Again!

Maggie was back in Vietnam for another lengthy Christmas tour in 1971. One of many places she visited was the Bien Hoa Air Force Base. Senior Master Sergeant Jerry Watkins remembers her. He was with the Eighth Special Operations Squadron and had his picture taken with Maggie. Their photo appeared in his hometown paper. Chief Warrant Officer 4 Chris Kamerer also was there when Maggie stopped by headquarters at the Khmere Training Command.

> Certain entertainers who shall remain nameless have indeed brought smiles to GI's overseas. It was done with much fanfare and patriotic publicity, so as to reflect back upon their own fame and glory. Clever trick, good idea, but in my book somewhat egocentric! Not so with Maggie! Our funny Colonel did it all on her own, and certainly not in "pacified areas." I have a great deal of respect and admiration for Martha Raye. Somehow, she emanated a more genuine care for the boys. She demonstrated it by pushing into hostile territories, whereas the bigger names sought complete security, thus entertaining mostly rear echelon troops, or pacified major division Headquarters.
>
> Our sites that trained Cambodian regulars were located in not so friendly territories. That did not stop Maggie! And it lightened the stress brought on by my last tour in Vietnam.

Only a few soldiers were assigned to Advisory Team Eighty-eight during Christmas 1971. They were located in Kien Hoa Province. Master Sergeant William Miller of Fort Worth was in the Don Nhon District. Colonel John Haseman was in the Ham Long District.

It was a pleasant surprise to receive a note from William who grew up only five miles from Colonie, New York where I lived while working on Maggie's Presidential Medal of Freedom. He even put me in touch with his parents who still lived in Schenectady. Maggie visited his camp in the Delta.

> I served in the Delta, assigned to Advisory Team Eighty-eight from 1971 to 1972. I was assigned as an advisor to

the Phoenix Program and served with two other U.S. military types.

We got an unexpected call saying that "Mean Momma One" is coming to our location; meet them at the helipad. We attempted to identify "Mean Momma One" by our code sheets, to no avail. We went to the pad as they landed and there were a pilot, escort officer, and someone who appeared to be either a lieutenant colonel or major with a name tag of "RAYE." Darned if she didn't look like Martha Raye. It *was* Martha Raye! We went to our bunker, where she visited with us. I asked her, "What are you doing here visiting a couple of guys who live in a hole in the ground." She responded, "Honey, Bob takes care of the large crowds, I take care of the small ones." I knew then that my dirty face had tear streaks running down it. Here was a woman—an entertainer, a *legend*—chatting with us.

She kissed me on the cheek—the first officer I would have allowed to kiss me. I have never forgotten her and will never stop getting a "glitch" in my heart and tear in my eyes every time I think of that day. Before she left, she gave each of us her phone number in California and said that *anytime* we are going through that area, even if we were with our family, call and her people would put us up for the night. A couple of days later, in a mortar attack, I lost the number. But, in my heart, she is still there and will always be.

Ban Me Thout, Vietnam-1971: Maggie visits with three soldiers at their outpost. L-R: Robert Spana, Anthony Holtry, Maggie, and William Miller. Photo contributed by William Miller.

Colonel Haseman contacted us while he was stationed at the American Embassy in Rangoon, Burma.

> During that Christmas period there were only two of us at Ham Long— myself and our Team NCO. We received a radio message to meet an incoming VIP Chopper at our pad, with no word as to who the VIP was. We went out to the pad and, of course, our VIP was Martha Raye. She had taken the time to visit all eight of the District Advisory Teams in Kien Hoa Province. She could stay with us for only a short while. We shared some Vietnamese snacks with her and a good amount of "Christmas Cheer." She brought us that wonderful smile, a sense of humor, a very real spirit of care and concern for two lonely GI's who felt like they were a million miles from home at Christmastime.
>
> I'll never forget the visit. She hopped off the helicopter dressed in fatigues and wearing her cherished Green Beret given by appreciative Special Forces guys at another place in the Vietnam boonies. We had little to give in return except our love and appreciation to a person who has always cared deeply for our men in uniform in faraway places.

Break a Leg? No, an *Arm!*

Major Kenneth Roberts wrote about his first meeting with Maggie in 1971. He seemed to be following her wherever she went; but he always just missed her. First it was in Danang, then NhaTrang. He finally caught up with her in Ban Me Thout.

> There was a party planned for Maggie in the Team Room. She was bunking at the dispensary and had spent most of the day with the Doc and Montagnards. We didn't know until later that they were also having their own party at the dispensary.
>
> We had a hardened two and a half ton truck that was once used to escort convoys. The truck mounted an electric Gatling gun and had tremendous firepower to match its heavy armor. In her honor, the truck sported the painted title "Maggie—Meanest Mother in the Valley." From then on, Maggie refused to ride in any other vehicle.

Maggie and Master Sergeant Edgehill left the dispensary for the two-block drive to the Team Room. Somehow, the driver and Maggie were not paying attention to the road. The truck managed to tear up about one hundred meters of chain link fence. Edgehill's arm was broken.

Maggie walked Edgehill back to the dispensary where Maggie set Edgehill's arm in a cast. Finally Maggie, the dispensary staff, and Edgehill came to the Team Room to be greeted by the assembled guests.

The party was long and loud. Maggie wore jungle fatigues with lieutenant colonel Nurse insignia and a Green Beret. She was one of us and always will be! She made every soldier feel at home and helped us celebrate Christmas in style.

Lieutenant Colonel David Bungay of El Paso was in Pleiku with the Fourth Infantry Division from 1967 to 1968. While he was assigned to MACV Special Operations Group in Ban Me Thout as the Logistics Officer in 1971, Maggie paid an unexpected visit to the area.

About 20 December we received word that we were to send Marine Major Bill "Fox" Copperweith to Saigon to pick up Maggie. She had come into the country without U.S. Army-Vietnam or MACV knowledge. Bill met her, and they stayed in a Saigon safe house.

The next day we flew her to Ban Me Thout by "Black Bird" for her Christmas visit. While with us from 21 December 71 to around 3 Jan 72, she went to our people in Kontum and our north and south launch sites.

One evening while partying, the "Fox" fell and broke his arm. Maggie took him to the dispensary, X-rayed his arm, set it and applied the cast. We heard she is an Army Nurse Corps lieutenant colonel in the

Reserves. Yes, she is honorary Fifth Group, but guys told us she earned jump wings at Fort Bragg. She did get two Purple Hearts in Vietnam. You should ask her where she was hit. You'll enjoy it. If at a party, maybe she will show you the scars.

Kept Promises Can Go Awry

Maggie was known for requesting their home phone numbers and addresses from the troops. She promised each one she would contact his loved ones and let them know he was okay. She fulfilled that promise quite diligently. Sergeant First Class Paul Erickson recalls Maggie's visit to his Special Missions Advisory group at Christmastime.

When she arrived, we had a reception, and she talked to everyone there. First, I did not know she was a colonel and second, that she was the warmest person I would ever meet. I was able to sit with her for a half hour just talking about home and my family. I was eighteen, recently married, with a month-old son. Even though our talk made me homesick, she made me feel important and proud to be serving my country.

Since it was Christmas, I bought her a necklace. She put it on and later asked if she could call my wife and let her know I was doing fine. I gave her the phone number, but really didn't expect her to call. I was proud she thought about me.

About a month later I received a letter from my wife telling me that Maggie called. However, my wife didn't get to talk with Maggie because of a funny foul-up. She was staying with my parents when the phone call came in about 4:30 A.M.; my mother answered. Maggie asked if this was Mrs. Erickson, and my mom answered "Yes." Then Maggie proceeded to tell her that her husband was all right—and my mother hung up the phone!

About five minutes later, my mother started yelling and woke up the whole house. She realized that Martha

Raye was on the phone—one of my mother's favorite people—and that it was *me* she was talking about and not my father, who was in bed. When my mother told everyone, she couldn't apologize enough to my wife. Then she really got upset because she had *Martha Raye* on the phone and didn't ask any questions.

Colonel Michael Moehlenkamp of Warner Robins, Georgia was in NhaTrang on Christmas Eve 1971. He was the commander of Detachment Two, 1881st Communications Squadron at the time.

Maggie was as personal, unpretentious, and sweet as a grandmother. She made Christmas in Vietnam as warm and special as she could, spending the whole evening with us with no fanfare. She made us feel there was no better place for her to spend her Christmas than with us singing, talking, and having a few drinks in a hooch at NhaTrang.

Martha Raye's personal commitment to our troops stood in a different league. She made it her life.

During 1972, Maggie also was active in her stage career touring on various stages and cabarets across the United States. In July, for example, she appeared at the Shamrock Hotel in Houston. In October she performed at Minsky's Burlesque Theater in Newark. In November she replaced Patsy Kelly, as Pauline, in the popular Broadway musical revival of *No, No Nanette.*

Hollywood's prestigious Screen Actors Guild presented Maggie with their award for "Outstanding Achievement" on November 19, 1973. Sandwiched between her stateside performances and awards, she still managed to return to Vietnam.

Clean Socks for the Lady

Maggie visited many of the A-teams and soldiers back at NhaTrang. Frederick Thaler of Newville, Pennsylvania served with the Fifth Special Forces and recounted their meeting.

> I was fortunate to have her as my guest for my birthday party back at NhaTrang—and we even had steaks. Maggie mentioned that she had been on the go and had not had a change of socks for ages and it was time for a change. So I said, "If you don't mind, I can give you a clean pair." She accepted.

Colonel Duncan Thompson, Sr. was personally familiar with Maggie's dedicated service. He wrote that Maggie's mere presence in South Vietnam base camps would raise troop morale beyond belief. She performed and visited at great risk to her personal safety. He claimed that her individual feats were too numerous for him to list; but, he felt they equaled or exceeded those normally associated with combat soldiers.

He also noted that there is no way to know the number of American lives she actually saved through her individual morale-building efforts and nursing care! Duncan said, "Being a native Texan, I would liken Maggie's caliber of service in Vietnam to those Texas women during the siege of the Alamo in March 1836."

T. Homer Bohler of Middleburgh, New York spotted Maggie as he was overlooking the Valley of the Rocks at a fire support base twenty miles north of Xuan Loc. Chaplain Frank Vavrin of Asheville, North Carolina saw her while he was serving with the 173rd Airborne. Captain G.G. Pendas, Jr. of Albany recalls presenting her with a Battalion coffee cup as Maggie visited his unit, First Battalion, Seventh Marines, at Son Tra Bong .

Costly Up-Keep

Major Pat Coulter of Hollis, New Hampshire was a Marine public affairs officer who got to know Maggie while serving as Director of the Marine Corps Public Affairs Office in Los Angeles.

Son Tra Bong, Vietnam: Maggie entertains members of the First Battalion, 7th Marines with Marine Construction Battalion #8. Presenting her with a Battalion coffee cup is then Lieutenant G.G. Pendas, who contributed photo.

Our office was just a short distance from her home. I visited her on several occasions and worked with both Martha and her agent/husband, Nick, on a number of events in which she participated to support the men and women of our armed forces. Whenever we called, she would do all in her power to help us out.

One time she confided in me that she often wondered if the people who requested her attendance at events ever stopped to realize how much it cost a person like her to participate in these activities. She was expected to look her best, which often meant expensive clothes, complete makeup and all the treatment that was not paid for by anybody except her. She did not say that to discourage or to knock any of those organizations. She was not looking for anybody to pick up the tab. It was just a response to my comment on how she always looked so great when we went out.

Caring When It Counts!

Gunnery Sergeant Richard Stebbins of Temecula, California felt privileged to meet Maggie while he served with the First Marine Division. He was coming off a patrol.

> I was dirty and smelled like who-knows-what, when this wonderful lady came up to me, kissed me on the cheek, and said, "May God bless you." I can't express the feeling that came over me at that time.
>
> She took time out to talk to me, and I will never forget that moment for as long as I live.

Major Francis Farnsworth, Sr. served as a helicopter pilot in Vietnam. He had transported Maggie several times. He always got a great smile from her—and sometimes a kiss! Unfortunately, he was wounded.

> When I was medevaced from Vietnam, the aircraft I was on landed at Clark Air Force Base. There she was, with an escort, standing on the flight line in a monsoon rain in the middle of the night meeting each and every medevac flight. She came aboard and greeted each of us individually with that big infectious grin, a hug, a handshake, or a kiss, and an encouraging word. I remember very little of the previous chopper and evac flights or the subsequent flight to Okinawa, but that moment was and will remain bright in my memory.

An Loc—1969: Maggie visits with medevac pilot John Mitchell at Fifteenth Medical Battalion, First Cavalry Division. Photo contributed by John Mitchell.

John Donovan of Larchmont, New York served as a combat correspondent in the First Marine Division. He accompanied Maggie via helicopter to a remote hilltop battalion headquarters. Before taking off, they had to wait forty-five minutes in a jeep. It was a rainy morning and Maggie looked as if she had slept poorly and was not feeling well. But when they arrived at the hilltop, Maggie got up before those marines and put on a performance that said, "I feel terrific and I hope you do too." This was done not in so many words but with the verve and energy she communicated to some marines who needed someone to do exactly that.

Engraved Memories, Engraved Names

Retired First Sergeant Simon Sauceda was in Korea when he first wrote to us. He met Maggie three different times during his five years in Vietnam.

> She shared our meals, our loneliness, and our quarters while staying overnight with us in some remote outpost. She shared the pain and sorrow of our wounded soldiers by visiting them in hospitals throughout Vietnam.
>
> She made us laugh with her jokes and allowed us to forget the war for a few hours. When it came time to leave, she would always offer to take mail or anything else back to the States to be delivered. I can go on and on about this fine and wonderful lady, Ms. Martha Raye, but I will make it short and to the point.
>
> I made it back, thanks to God, but a few of my friends did not. Their names are engraved on the black granite of the Vietnam Memorial. I know that a memory each of them took to his grave was the wonderful moments he and Ms. Martha Raye shared.

Many people also recall seeing Maggie stateside during this year. First Sergeant John Hunt of Sherman, Texas remembered Maggie from her many trips to Fort

Bragg. Audrey Kesten of New York City met Maggie in Fort Lauderdale.

Parents also wrote letters about their memories of Maggie and how she affected their children.

William Lane of Franklin Square, New York recalled that his son, William Jr., met Maggie when he was a lieutenant in the Green Berets, and she visited his jungle outpost in Vietnam. A photo of the occasion was sent to Bill's parents. Years later Maggie was appearing in *Everybody Loves Opal* at their local dinner theater, and she accepted the Lanes' invitation to their house for a few hours after the show. They had a great time listening to her stories of growing up in show business starting on the stage at age three. They again had the pleasure of her company several years later in Atlantic City.

Clark Snook of Marietta, Georgia reported that his son was in Vietnam when Maggie visited his unit; he was one of her escorts. Clark also saw Maggie stateside.

> We have enjoyed Martha Raye for many years and were delighted to attend one of her performances in a dinner theater at Buckhead in Atlanta.
>
> I asked the usher if we could speak with Martha to thank her for her wonderful support of our servicemen. The usher did not give me any encouragement since Martha seldom allowed such visits. However, she did when she heard that my son had been in Vietnam. Her first remark to us was, "I do hope your son returned."
>
> Somehow you had the feeling of being in the presence of an old friend. She was looking forward to flying back to see her grandchild after the show.

Maggie was not the only entertainer to visit our troops in Vietnam and not get the recognition they deserved. Among others who went to Vietnam without much fanfare were Raymond Burr, Vicki Lawrence, Ann-Margret, Chuck Connors, Hugh O'Brian, Fess Parker, Roy Acuff, Roy Rogers and Dale Evans.

Although the war's end was officially signed on January 27, 1973, United States Armed Forces remained in Vietnam until the fall of Saigon in 1975. Between 1973 and 1975 our troops were returning to the U.S., back to "The World," back to a citizenry who seemed to blame them for their own politicians' and bureaucrats' mistakes in Vietnam.

Maggie began to pick up the pieces of her disjointed life, too.

Bel Air—1968: Captain Bruce Jones, Melodye Condos, Maggie, and Nick Condos in Maggie's back yard. Photo contributed by Bruce Jones.

Chapter 12

Winding Down

"My motivation in giving up my career for ten years was to do what I could to save the lives of our men in action, to let them know somebody cared."

Martha "Colonel Maggie" Raye
(August 1979)

Association of the United States Army Award

The Association of the United States Army is deeply aware of the continuing contribution made to the well being of the men and women of the Armed Forces by Miss Martha Raye.

Miss Raye has brought laughter, a touch of home and brief respite from the ever-present concerns of war to thousands of young men and women—soldiers, sailors, Marines, and airmen—through her many visits to the Republic of Vietnam since 1965. Forsaking the comforts and safety of the cities and major headquarters, Miss Raye constantly sought as her audience the combat troops in remote and dangerous firebases without thought of personal welfare or safety.

Pressed into service as a volunteer nurse on occasion, Miss Raye has contributed significantly to the morale of the American soldier over an extended period and is deeply deserving of the Association's gratitude.

13 OCTOBER 1971
EDWARD C. LOGELIN, PRESIDENT

Early 1980's: Maggie receives a parachuter's baton from Special Forces members. Photo contributed by Special Forces Association.

-12-

In January 1975 Maggie returned to her role as Opal in *Everybody Loves Opal* at Sardi's Dinner Theater in Franklin Square, New York.

The following year, she earned an EMMY nomination for "Best Actress in a Single Performance in a Drama or Comedy" for her portrayal of Agatha in "Greed," the final episode of "McMillan and Wife."

This highly successful series aired on NBC from September 1971 to August 1976. Rock Hudson starred as Commissioner Stewart McMillan, Susan St. James as his wife Sally, John Schuck as Sergeant Charles Enright and Nancy Walker as the housekeeper, Mildred. In "Greed," Agatha and Mildred had been named in a will as two of several beneficiaries who were being killed off one by one. Though an intended victim herself, Agatha went sneaking around looking for clues as to the killer's identity.

It was Kathryn Walker who won the 1976 EMMY for her performance in "The Adams Chronicles." Other contenders were Helen Hayes in "Retire in Sunny Hawaii Forever," Sheree North in "How Do You Know What Hurts Me," and Pamela Payton-Wright in "John Quincy Adams." Once again, Maggie was in great company!

Susan St. James and Nancy Walker decided to leave "McMillan and Wife" for other commitments. Their characters were written out of the show: St. James' character died in a plane crash and Walker's inherited a diner and moved back East. Rock Hudson asked Maggie to try out for the role of Agatha Thornton, replacing Mildred as the housekeeper. She was hired on the spot. The show was renamed "McMillan" and aired six times from September 1976 to August 1977. Agatha continually tried to get McMillan involved with women—"after all, it was time for him to get on with his life." Maggie appeared in all six ninety-minute episodes.

Maggie's television career received another boost in 1976 when she appeared regularly on "Steve Allen's Laughback," along with Jayne Meadows, Louie Nye, Bill Dana, Don Knotts, Pat Harrington, and Skitch Henderson. This ninety-minute weekly show highlighted Steve's career from the 1950s and 1960s.

A CBS ninety-minute television special, "Bing! A 50th Anniversary Gala," celebrating Bing Crosby's fifty years in show business aired in March 1977. Maggie appeared with Bob Hope, Paul Anka, Pearl Bailey, Rosemary Clooney, Sandy Duncan, Donald O'Connor, Bette Midler, Debbie Reynolds, Anson Williams, The Mills Brothers, and the Crosby family.

Maggie returned again to her role as Opal in *Everybody Loves Opal,* which was her only documented stage appearance in 1976 and 1977. Information is sketchy about her career activity the following two years. From 1973 to 1979, Maggie appeared on stage in two plays, on television at least nine times on four programs, and had a bit part in one movie.

Blacklisted...Again!

The Record Eagle, a Traverse City, Michigan, newspaper, ran a UPI article on August 24, 1979, reporting that Maggie was the only Vietnam War casualty in Hollywood: she had been secretly blacklisted as a "warmonger" for devoting ten years of her life, off and on, working with medics under fire in the field.

Her apparent crime was compassion for wounded American GI's. She found herself unemployed, branded as a "hawk" by Hollywood's power brokers. Maggie was quoted:

> Like the servicemen who fought in Vietnam, I'm a victim of prejudice. It took three years after the war to get my first TV guest spot. It was an unpopular war and anyone connected with it still is unpopular in this country today. The Veterans who come by to visit me are confused about the way they're discriminated against. Most of them were drafted. They didn't want to go out there and kill people. They were serving their country. It's shocking the way they are treated, like Jack the Ripper or murderers. There's tremendous hostility toward them.
>
> Some people still call me a warmonger. That's the reason I haven't been able to get work in this town. My motivation in giving up my career for ten years was to do what I could to save the lives of our men in action, to let them know somebody cared.

Maggie did just that. She had put her career—as well as her family—on hold to be with the troops. Now, Nick Condos moved back into her home and was managing her career. Melodye, in her mid-thirties and divorced, was busy working, singing, and raising her teenage son, Nick.

Maggie loved the troops as if they were her own children, brothers, sisters or husbands. She was there for them, loving them, caring for them, treating their wounds, and listening to their cries. When she returned stateside, she tried picking up the pieces of her own life, but acting parts were few and far between.

Silver Screen, Stage, and Small Screen

Maggie appeared briefly in Universal's air disaster film *The Concorde: Airport '79*. The fourth in a series of airborne disaster epics, this film was about various disasters befalling the new Concorde SST (supersonic transport) on its way from Washington, D.C. to Paris. Maggie's bit part was her portrayal of Loretta, a woman who frequented the rest room on the first leg of the trip and then decided to drink her way through the rest of it. Although the movie had a multi-star cast including Susan Blakely, Robert Wagner, George Kennedy, Eddie Albert, and John Davidson, it received only a two-star rating.

Rounding out the year was a NBC musical comedy special, "Skinflint," showing in December 1979. This two-hour Country-and-Western version of Dickens' *A Christmas Carol* was set in a small Tennessee town. Maggie appeared as the Ghost of Christmas Past. The cast included Hoyt Axton, Mel Tillis, Lynn Anderson, Barbara Mandrell, Larry Gatlin, Tom T. Hall, Daniel Davis, Dottie West, Julie Gregg, David Bond, Stephen Lutz, Byron Webster, and Carol Swarbrick.

Universal Television signed Maggie to do a two-hour TV movie drama called *The Gossip Columnist,* which aired on March 21, 1980. Maggie portrayed Georgia O'Hanlon, an on-the-skids club singer hoping for a comeback. The movie also starred such notables as Bobby Vinton, Robert Vaughn, Lyle Waggoner, Steve Allen, Jim Backus, Allen Ludden, Jayne Meadows, and Betty White. In a nostalgic touch, Maggie appeared in a film clip from her old movie *Never Say Die.*

Summer stock beckoned Maggie back to The Coliseum Theater in Latham, New York in September 1981. Replacing comedienne RoseMarie, Maggie joined Margaret Whiting, Helen O'Connell and Rosemary Clooney for the production of *4 Girls 4.* The show played to sold-out audiences for its five performances.

"One of the Last Genuine Clowns"

Ralph Martin's column in the September 3 issue of *The Knickerbocker News* reported that Maggie was clowning, leering, joking, laughing and generally carrying on in *4 Girls 4* like a frisky teenager rather than the well-traveled sixty-five-year-old that she was. Miss Clooney was quoted as saying, "Martha Raye is a legend. She is one of the last genuine clowns. She provides the comedy that makes the show go." Miss O'Connell added, "An utter delight. An unpredictable talent who can make you cry at one moment and laugh at the next. Only Red Skelton can touch an audience like Martha Raye."

Margaret Whiting—a superb singer and musician—also entertained our troops on USO tours around the world. She helped GI's make recordings to send their families. Miss Whiting also commented, "People tend to forget that Martha is a great singer. She was considered one of the greats of the thirties until she turned to comedy. She can still belt out a tune." Miss Whiting noted that Maggie was a TV soap opera addict. Instead of relaxing or shopping between or after shows, Maggie would sit in front of a television set watching the afternoon soap operas.

In 1981, Maggie joined Ben Vereen and William Katt on stage in the musical *Pippin*, which was based on the (mythically) mischievous medieval life of Charlemagne's son. The original mid-1970s Broadway smash established Bob Fosse's fame long before his roles in "Cabaret" and "All That Jazz." William Katt portrayed Pippin in this parable of a young man searching for meaning and truth.

The show, which had received five Tony Awards while on Broadway, was seen only on stage except for a filming done at the Hamilton Place Theater in Ontario, Canada. Ben Vereen's character moved back and forth—from the 1980s to the Middle Ages. Maggie showed her boisterous energy while portraying Berthe, Pippin's grandmother. Maggie sang "Still Good Looking" and was frolicking across the stage like a much younger woman. Her most notable line was "Men raise flags when they can't get anything else up."

At a dinner-dance in Alameda on March 31, 1982, Maggie was honored for her exceptional service to our nation's military personnel. In a *Contra Costa Times* article, Jan Goldberg reported that while wiping away tears of gratitude, Maggie said, "I'd give my life for them, any day, any time." That same day she helped raise a POW/MIA flag at Lafayette-Moraga-Orinda VFW Post 8063. Ethel Schneider of Walnut Creek, California was at the dinner following that flag raising. She said, "At the dinner a man who had known Maggie in Vietnam read a poem written about her. When he had finished, there were many tears. I got to talk with her about the Army Nurse Corps and nursing in general."

The New 4 Girls

In the summer of 1982, Maggie, now sixty-six, joined her friends Kay Starr, Rosemary Clooney, and Helen O'Connell for the stage production of *The New 4 Girls* (previously called *4 Girls 4)*. They performed at places such as the Sahara in Las Vegas, the Cal-Neva Lodge in Lake Tahoe, Storrowton in Massachusetts, and in Dallas.

Prior to the four women's appearance on November 13, 1982 at the John F. Kennedy Special Warfare Museum in the Cumberland County Auditorium at Fort Bragg, the *CC Outlook* ran a story about Maggie. It reported that she had an honorary commission in 1964 with the Special Forces that became official in 1967. The article also stated that she had made five parachute jumps.

Following their performance, Rosemary led the audience in singing a familiar song to honor Maggie. It was an Irving Berlin number that Bing Crosby and Danny Kaye sang to General Waverly in the movie *White Christmas.* With the help of Frank Ortega, the lyrics to "The Old Man" were changed to praise their good friend Maggie

Ron Staszcuk's article in *The Paraglide* reported that Special Forces Master Sergeant Jimmie Foster first met Maggie in Kontum, Vietnam in 1968 and recalled that

L-R.: Helen O'Connell, Kay Starr, Rosemary Clooney, and Maggie. This press photo was for their show "The New 4 Girls." Photo contributed by Special Forces Association.

when Maggie came to a camp, she took a personal interest in each individual just like a mother coming to see her children. "She was just like home folks...a really great person interested in people."

The Sandpiper

Reggie Hurd told of his many encounters with Maggie. He first met her in the early sixties when the problems of our Vietnam commitment were just beginning; the last time he saw her was in 1982.

> I was co-owner of the Sandpiper, a bar-restaurant in Laguna Beach. We were known as *the* unofficial Marine Corps Officers' Club. We were also the unofficial hangout for the Naval Flying Team "The Blue Angels." As the Vietnam war accelerated, our "to-and-from" Marine officer traffic increased. Unfortunately, we were *not* popular in our hometown because we were catering to the Marines' trade in an unpopular war. We persevered. Then came Maggie. The moment was ripe for her appearance.

During her many unselfish tours to the war-ridden area of Vietnam, Maggie kept hearing about the Sandpiper in Laguna Beach. The boys always intimated that it was their *last* home away from home. Maggie's curiosity was peaked, so one day she walked in, introduced herself, and enhanced our already famous image. In a way, she sort of became our official hostess.

Maggie was wonderful. Often she came down from her home in Bel Air to visit us and entertain the troops. I particularly remember one St. Patrick's Day party. Being Irish herself, she sat and sang Irish songs in Gaelic to a very impressed bunch of Irish young Marines. It was a real touch of home to them.

My birthday happened to fall on my partner's day off. I elected to work. Maggie showed up, complete with wrapped gift and bows. Quite tersely she said, "*Nobody* spends his birthday alone." I had no idea that she even knew it was my birthday. On that same evening my cocktail waitress did a "no-show," leaving me short-handed. Maggie substituted—quite admirably. She worked the full eight-hour shift—and even stayed to clean tables, wash glasses and ash trays. I think she really loved it, playing the part of a waitress. I loved her for it.

During those Vietnam war years, I wrote and published a weekly paper, the *Sandpiper Newsletter*, in which I tried to update news of our Marine customers both at home and overseas.

In her many trips to Vietnam, Maggie kept running across copies of the *Sandpiper Newsletter*—sometimes pinned on bulletin boards, once in an Officers Club in Danang that was named "Sandpiper-East."

One evening Maggie marched into my bar and placed a gold friendship bracelet on my arm. She wished it on me, saying "don't ever take it off. This is for what you have done for our boys over there. God Bless." To this day I have never removed the bracelet. Maggie will be with me forever.

Though we remained in touch, it has been over six years since I last saw Maggie. She, Rosemary Clooney, Margaret Whiting, and Helen O'Connell were doing a show *4 Girls 4* in Dallas. It also happened to be Maggie's birthday weekend. My sister and I drove to Dallas to see the show—and I brought along her birthday present. Unfortunately, we had just missed her afternoon performance, and she had already left the theater. I gave her gift to the Security Officer for I knew we would probably never be able to see Maggie after her evening show. My sister and I were about to leave the theater when the same Security Officer approached us. "You come with me," he instructed. He took us to a small room backstage.

"Wait here," he said. Then Annie, Maggie's personal secretary, appeared. I knew her and then realized that I'd be seeing Maggie again. After the next show, Maggie sent out for drinks—and we had a beautiful reunion—lots of small talk about Laguna Beach and mutual friends. My sister even got to be friends with Rosemary Clooney, two hopelessly dedicated grandmothers sharing pictures. I was delighted to share nearly an hour with my beloved Maggie.

When we left the dressing room, she escorted me to the door, where she was suddenly besieged by a crowd of waiting fans.

Seen on the Small Screen

Maggie obtained an occasional role in CBS's half-hour sitcom "Alice," which starred Linda Lavin as Alice and Vic Tayback as Mel. Maggie appeared six times between 1982 and 1984 in her role as Mel's mother, Carrie Sharples.

Maggie also was a ringmaster on the seventh edition of "Circus of the Stars." The two-hour show aired on CBS in December 1982 with show business personalities performing circus acts.

In March 1983 NBC aired a two-hour variety show, "Bob Hope Special: Bob Hope's Road to Hollywood," saluting Bob's film career. Maggie joined Dorothy Lamour, Jane Russell, Jill St. John, Rhonda Fleming, Lucille Ball, Virginia Mayo, Dina Merrill, Rosemary Clooney and George Burns as guests on the show.

National Sojourners

In 1985 Maggie was guest of honor at the National President's reception and banquet of the Mid-Winter Sojourners meeting. She received a walnut plaque from (then) President Chuck Folsom of Fremont, Nebraska with this inscription:

> LTC Martha Raye, USAR, Actress, Singer, Comedienne, Patriot, Lady. You were there when our need was greatest. With the most sincere appreciation of National Sojourners, Inc.—THANKS. MAGGIE, WE LOVE YOU!

Later, Chuck told us that Maggie was quite proficient at flipping her false teeth from her mouth into a glass!

Alice's Adventures

In December 1985 Maggie portrayed The Duchess in a musical adaptation of *Alice's Adventures in Wonderland*. The four-hour TV film featured a star-studded cast including Steve Allen, Scott Baio, Ernest Borgnine, Beau and Lloyd Bridges, Red Buttons, Sid Caesar, Carol Channing, Imogene Coca, Sammy Davis Jr., George Gobel, Eydie Gorme and Steve Lawrence, Merv Griffin, Sherman Hemsley, Ann Jillian, Harvey Korman, Steve Lawrence, Karl Malden, Roddy McDowall, Jayne Meadows, Robert Morley, Donald O'Connor, John Stamos, Ringo Starr, Jonathan Winters, Shelley Winters and many others. Maggie and Imogene sang "There's Something to Say for Hatred" as Maggie tried rocking a baby while Imogene threw dishes at the walls. It was a very funny scene.

The Distinguished Public Service Award

This is the highest award our Defense Department can bestow upon civilians. The award consisted of a gold medal, a rosette and a citation signed by Secretary Casper Weinberger.

Camp Mackall, North Carolina—1982: Maggie sits in a chopper. Photo contributed by Roxanne Merritt, curator, JFK Special Warfare Museum, Fort Bragg, North Carolina.

DEPARTMENT OF DEFENSE
UNITED STATES OF AMERICA
TO
MARTHA RAYE

for extremely meritorious service from 1942 to the present, during which time she contributed to the morale, health, and well-being of millions of service men and women in war and peace.

Miss Raye represented, for forty-four years, the very best in entertainment tradition and the very best among supporters of US Armed Forces publicly rallying to the cause of service members, veterans, prisoners of war, and those missing in action. In addition to entertaining and improving morale of service members in England, North Africa, Korea and Vietnam, she acted as a volunteer nurse—particularly in Vietnam—where she served at great personal sacrifice, risk, danger, and without regard for her own safety or comfort. Touring Vietnam annually for nine years (up to five months at a time), she visited the troops—not in the safety of the major cities—but in the outposts, firebases, and bunkers. She experienced enemy attacks—once receiving shrapnel from an exploding enemy mortar round—nursed American casualties in field hospitals and even donated blood to wounded soldiers.

A recipient of numerous citations and awards, Miss Raye has demonstrated a great and selfless devotion to the Nation and a great love of humanity, the United States Armed Forces, and the American way of life. Her patriotic service and devotion to her country and its Armed Services reflect great credit upon herself, her profession, and the United States of America. I take pleasure in presenting Martha Raye the Department of Defense Medal for Distinguished Public Service.

APRIL 1986
CASPER WEINBERGER
SECRETARY OF DEFENSE

I had read an article about Maggie in the *Star Presidian* and contacted the paper to learn more about the author and where he got his information. Kenneth Petrack was the Deputy Chief of Public Affairs of the Headquarters Sixth U.S. Army at Presidio, San Francisco. Kenneth had written the article from the documentation on which her Distinguished Public Service Award was based. She had been nominated for it by the Commanding General of the Sixth Army. Kenneth added:

> I got the information personally from Martha Raye when I visited her at her home in Los Angeles in 1985. She discussed her experiences and let me copy some of the citations from the various awards she received over the years—all on display in her den. She also reviewed the information, in draft form, for factual accuracy prior to its being submitted, so I assume all the information is correct.

Actress Chris Noel also spent time in Vietnam. She, like Maggie, traveled throughout the war-torn countryside to visit and entertain the GI's. The Viet Cong also had a price on her head as she became the female voice of the in-country Armed Forces Radio Network. Chris and Maggie's paths crossed often, and they became very good friends.

In her book, *Matter of Survival* (1987), Chris mentioned Maggie several times. She cited Maggie's frequent trips to Vietnam, her outstanding talent for singing, her honorary lieutenant colonel status, and her involvement with troops since World War II. She said "Maggie is a comedienne whose singing has been underestimated." They shared a room in Danang. Toward the end in Vietnam, Chris was amazed that Maggie could still wish the guys "God Bless You."

Finally Chris recounts a time that Maggie broke down and cried about a major she dearly loved who had died in Vietnam and how it hurt to see him dead.

At one point Maggie was honorary cochair, along with Bob Hope, of "The POW-MIA Bracelet" campaign on behalf of POW's. She was also the Honorary Reviewing Officer of the twentieth annual VFW Loyalty Day Parade in New York City.

The Four Chaplains Award

On February 3, 1943, the US Army Transport ship *Dorchester* was traveling from Newfoundland to Greenland. A German U-boat's torpedo struck the *Dorchester's* starboard side killing 672 of the 902 men aboard. Four chaplains aboard the *Dorchester* directed the terrified survivors to lifeboats and passed out life jackets. When all of the life jackets were gone, the chaplains gave away their own. When the *Dorchester* sank into the icy waters of the North Atlantic, the chaplains went with it. They gave the ultimate sacrifice—their lives—to save others. The four chaplains were First Lieutenants: Clark V. Poling, a minister of the Reformed Church in America from Schenectady; John T. Washington, a Roman Catholic priest from Arlington, New Jersey; George L. Fox, a Methodist minister from Gilman, Vermont; and Alexander D. Goode, a rabbi from York, Pennsylvania.

The Four Chaplains Award honors their memory. Veterans' groups present it each February to someone for their humanitarian efforts with our nation's Veterans. This was an award Maggie certainly deserved and sincerely treasured.

Distinguished Service Award

Maggie received another USO award from its Board of Governors on February 23, 1987. Their Distinguished Service Award honors outstanding individuals, groups or organizations that have rendered exceptional and substantive service to the men and women of the Armed Forces over an extended period. Although the award is normally a brass plaque on mahogany, Maggie's was made of etched glass an inch thick.

Susan Christiansen, a writer for various Veterans' publications, is on the Board with Chris Noel for Vetsville Cease-Fire House, Inc. in West Palm Beach, Florida and founder of L.O.V.V.E. (Ladies of Vietnam Vets Are Enterprising). She began and continues *Vet Forum*. Susan would be the only invited visitor to Maggie's home after Maggie's September 1991 marriage.

Susan became involved with Vietnam Veterans after marrying a soldier who was later listed as Missing in Action during the war. She helped locate him and continues to assist other Veterans today in whatever way she can. Susan's path crossed Maggie's frequently. They spent a great deal of time together through the years and shared quite a few memories.

Susan first wrote about the blind Veteran, cited in this book's Introduction, in her column for a 1987 issue of *BRAVO Veterans Outlook*. She tried without success to locate this Veteran for his presence for Maggie's seventy-fifth birthday party in 1991.

Final Career Performances

In the latter part of 1987, Maggie joined Milton Berle on "The Love Boat." As Zeke and Zelda, stowaways on board *The Pacific Princess*, they managed to con someone out of their room, ate dinner by using an ill couple's table, and signed for drinks with another passenger's name. When finally caught, they went on stage and did a dance number while singing "For Me and My Gal." It concluded with Zeke on his knees trying to hold Zelda, only dropping her to the floor. Afterwards, the crew invited Zeke and Zelda to be regulars for their stage show.

Maggie's final professional job was "The Polident Lady." Her television ads for the Block Drug Company, manufacturers of Polident, were the last contract that Nick Condos arranged for her. Peter Mann, who was the Senior Vice President of U.S. Consumer Marketing for Block, said, "Martha's great smile, her ability to charm the camera, her honesty as well as the way the public loves and responds to her, are key reasons for her popularity as an entertainer and her longevity as a Polident spokesperson." She was among the longest-running celebrity spokespersons in advertising history.

Chapter 13

A Quest Begins

"Her heroism and lack of concern for her own safety and life brought her to combat areas that were dangerous to an extreme. Her gifts as a comedienne are a national treasure for they are of the spirit and reality of the battlefield, as well as of our ideals of freedom and human dignity."

Bishop Howard Hubbard
(Albany, New York)

On My Wall

This cherished autographed photo hangs on my wall.

-13-

On August 27, 1987, Maggie turned seventy-one. She had retired from the entertainment business after twenty-six movies, twenty-six recorded singles, three record albums, and one movie sound track. She married and divorced six times. Though no longer married, Nick Condos and Maggie continued to share her home. By 1987, he was quite ill.

Maggie had subordinated her professional career and personal life to being with "her troops." She continued to make appearances at Veteran functions whenever and wherever she was asked. She had served her country voluntarily, far beyond duty's call. She undoubtedly deserved to be recognized by our President and nation for her phenomenal track record of service.

In 1987, I became involved in a broad-based Veterans' effort to honor Maggie with the Presidential Medal of Freedom.

What is the Presidential Medal of Freedom?

Who receives it? What does one have to do to merit it? Answers came after research in New York libraries and numerous phone calls to the Library of Congress, the Pentagon, and to the White House.

President Harry S. Truman originated this award as the Medal of Freedom in 1945. Its purpose was to recognize American civilians for meritorious war-connected acts or services. During his presidency and through 1963, nominations for the medal were considered by a panel of people who would recommend several individuals. The board then presented their nominations to the President, who in turn made his final selections. The award could only be approved by the President of the United States.

Originally, the award ceremony was held in the White House's Rose Garden on the Fourth of July. Award recipients were allowed to invite ten guests—including family members—to the ceremony. All invited individuals traveled to the White House at government expense. A luncheon followed the ceremony. In the event of inclement weather, award activities were held in the East Room of the White House.

In 1963, President John F. Kennedy reestablished the medal, renaming it the Presidential Medal of Freedom—the nation's highest *civilian* award for those who contributed to the quality of American life. No longer limited to war-related services, it is now awarded to persons who have made especially meritorious contributions to world peace, the security or national interest of the United States, or other cultural, public or private endeavors during wartime or peacetime.

President Kennedy made another major change: a board no longer selected nominees. All nominations went directly to the President. He would select recipients based on the criteria. Recipients have been astronauts, actors, singers, artists, politicians, diplomats, military personnel, theologians, writers, foreign dignitaries, and others.

Unfortunately, President Kennedy was assassinated before he had opportunity to present any of these medals. Lyndon B. Johnson began his Presidency by awarding the first Presidential Medal of Freedom (PMOF) posthumously to President Kennedy. Before President Johnson left office, he had presented eighty-nine Presidential Medals of Freedom. President Richard M. Nixon awarded twenty-seven; President Gerald E. Ford also presented twenty-seven; President Jimmy Carter thirty-four; and President Ronald Reagan gave eighty-two (including one to his favorite author of Old West novels,

Louis L'Amour). President George Bush presented thirty-five medals, two going to European leaders Margaret Thatcher and Lech Walesa. Although the medal originally was to be a civilian award, he also awarded the medal to Generals Norman Schwarzkopf and Colin Powell.

Variations in PMOF Presentation

If a recipient is too ill to travel to Washington, D.C., the Presidential Medal of Freedom has sometimes been presented at a person's bedside. Other times it has been presented posthumously. We hoped Maggie would be well enough to make the trip to D.C..

In recent years, the presentation date has been changed to accommodate scheduling problems. The medal is identical for both men and women, but the men's medal is worn on a long red, white and blue ribbon around the neck, while the woman's is pinned on with a bow-shaped ribbon. The large medal is accompanied by a miniature medal, a lapel pin, and a citation. The recipient is allowed to have ten guests at the award ceremony.

We discussed with Maggie whom she would want present if and when she was awarded the PMOF. She said she wanted the following people with her on that day: Susan Christiansen; Rolande "Frenchy" Amundsen; General William Westmoreland; General Michael "Iron Mike" Healy; Jim Spitz; Nick Nichols, a longtime friend; Marge Durante; Command Sergeant Major Ramon Rodriquez, her companion; Tony Diamond, Editor of *BRAVO*; her nurse, Oneata McDowell; Belle Pellegrino; and Noonie Fortin.

We contacted everyone to get their correct addresses, phone numbers, and social security numbers, which would be needed so White House security could run background checks before they could enter the White House.

The Birth of a Quest: 1987

At a meeting of our Veterans organization in Albany in October 1987, Tom O'Brien, a fellow Veteran from Gloversville, spoke about Martha Raye's work in Vietnam and the lack of national recognition for her efforts. At Tom's urging, the group agreed to write Congressman Sam Stratton urging his initiative in getting Maggie the recognition she deserved. Inspired by Tom's impassioned speech and our conversation after the meeting, Belle Pellegrino and I agreed to check into Maggie's background and qualifications for national medals. Several months went by with no response from Congressman Stratton's District or Washington offices.

For eight years prior to this, the Special Forces Association (SFA) had been working to have the Presidential Medal of Freedom (PMOF) awarded to Maggie. Largely through SFA efforts, House Concurrent Resolution 233 was submitted by Congressman William Dannemeyer, a California Republican in the House of Representatives on December 18, 1987. Unfortunately HCR 233 never got out of the Committee on Post Office and Civil Service, to which it was assigned.

"A Star for Maggie"

After reading Lieutenant Colonel John Forde, Jr's. letter to the Editor in the March 7, 1988, issue of *Navy Times*, our campaign to have Maggie honored shifted into higher gear.

> This letter is for all of the Army, Navy, Marine Corps, Coast Guard, and Air Force men who were entertained by Martha Raye during World War II, Korea, and/or Vietnam.
>
> I recently watched while Bob Hope, Sammy Davis Jr., Perry Como, and Bette Davis were awarded the Presidential Medal of Freedom—the highest civilian award bestowed by the President on behalf of the

nation. Each of these fine entertainers richly deserved the award.

However, "Maggie" Raye has been entertaining troops since World War II. She has been in Europe, the South Pacific, and aboard US Navy warships during WW II. She made the Korean conflict too. In Vietnam, "Maggie" not only entertained in Saigon, Cam Ranh Bay, Danang, Hue Phu Bai, and Chu Lai, but she spent months in the field with the guys, while most of the other entertainers remained in the safe areas.

I first met Maggie at the First Medical Battalion, Danang. She jumped out of her chopper as it hovered and was waved off to make room for an incoming medevac chopper. She assisted in the handling of a badly wounded Marine. Following hours of helping the wounded, she still carried out her entertainment schedule.

On the eve of the Marine Corps birthday, 1968, the command post of the First Marine Regiment was infiltrated by sappers with considerable loss of lives and equipment and many wounded. Maggie arrived early the next day and gave three shows. Before leaving the First Marines, she took the names, addresses, and phone numbers of wives, mothers, and sweethearts with a promise to call or write each of them—a promise she kept when she returned from Vietnam.

During her eighteen months there, she refused any attempts by the media to publicize her exploits. Her feeling was the media should tell the people back home that their men were "standing tall" under adverse conditions, and not what Martha Raye was doing.

If you believe, as I do, that Miss Martha Raye deserves to be honored for her patriotic efforts in World War II, Korea, and Vietnam, deluge the White House with cards and letters! Such recognition is long overdue!

John's published letter impressed on us—for the first time—that Maggie had done much more than just entertain the troops. We had thought of Maggie as chiefly an actress, singer, dancer, and comedienne. We again searched the libraries, this time for insights into her "Colonel Maggie" *persona*. Except for an occasional passing reference, we found little in books about her wartime exploits. Or, for that matter, about her professional career.

At the Special Forces Association Banquet

While attending the Special Forces Association banquet in Fayetteville, North Carolina (her beloved Fort Bragg is there) on July 7, 1988, Maggie received a letter from The White House.

> I am happy to join in the congratulations as the Special Forces Association honors you for your years of outstanding effort for America's service men and women.
>
> This tribute is fully well deserved. As an entertainer, nurse, combat veteran, and patriot, you've made your talents an invaluable asset to our Nation and those who shoulder its defense. From Europe to Korea to South Vietnam, you've always been there, bringing your sparkle and humor to some mighty lonely places. Ask those who fought in distant lands in the cause of liberty what your presence far from home meant to them, and they will say, "She made me laugh, and she made me proud." Maggie, on behalf of the American people, I am proud to salute you.
>
> Again, congratulations. Nancy joins me in sending very best wishes always. God bless you, and God bless America.
>
> Sincerely,
> Ronald Reagan

"My Nick" Dies

Maggie was attending another SFA banquet at Fort Bragg the next day when she received word that Nick Condos had passed away. He was seventy-four. In spite of his deteriorating physical condition, he had insisted that Maggie attend the annual SFA convention. He knew how much she loved the Green Berets and how they looked forward to her annual visits. Donald

Buchanan of Owensboro, Kentucky recalled her Fort Bragg presence.

> I met her for the first time in Fayetteville. Even though he was on his death bed, Nick told her to go to Fort Bragg so she could be with "her boys." She was at the convention when he died.
>
> My wife and I had the honor of meeting her. We found her a charming and very gracious lady.

Maggie stayed at Fort Bragg till the next day and then returned to California. It was Nick's wish, with Maggie's agreement, to be cremated. Their daughter, Melodye, took care of all the arrangements. Before Maggie got back to California, however, Nick's remains had been cremated. From that point on Maggie's relationship with Melodye and young Nick became somewhat strained.

Life Stops Moving

By this time, Maggie felt quite alone. Her parents, sister, and brother had all passed away. Now Nick was gone. Maggie kept his room the way he left it. In 1994, Lorraine Condos said to me, "Nick and Maggie were soul mates for life." They were. Maggie left a note on the chalkboard in her kitchen that said "God Bless My Nick," and she never changed the kitchen calendar from the month he died. I saw the note and calendar when I visited her in 1990 and again in 1991. They symbolized, somehow, that much of her life had stopped.

In 1988 following our Veterans group's annual "Christmas in August" dinner to raise funds for Christmas gifts and food for needy Veterans and their families, I had suggested that we invite Maggie to be our guest speaker for the 1989 dinner. I contacted the Ruth Webb Agency for assistance and received a copy of Maggie's "bio." It told us little that we did not already know...except for her home address. I sent a letter to Maggie and was pleased to receive a phone call from her secretary, Natalie Hope. Natalie said Maggie was unable to make the dinner but that she would send me an autographed photo of Maggie, which I now hang proudly on my wall. Meanwhile, our archival search for information about Maggie continued with little success.

When New York Democratic Congressman Mike McNulty was elected in November 1988, a letter was sent requesting his assistance in getting the medal for Maggie.

A Piece of My Heart

In searching for information necessary to substantiate key endorsements and recommendations for the PMOF, we did find a few articles in various periodicals. Most were in a somewhat casual journalistic style that made it difficult to distinguish hearsay from actual fact. Still, until we shifted our information-gathering approach to acquiring new primary sources from Veterans themselves, these articles did help us get some bearings.

For example, in the March/April 1989 edition of *BRAVO Veterans Outlook,* Henry Beckman wrote in a book review, "Did you know that comedienne Martha Raye was twice wounded, awarded the Purple Heart and commissioned a Lieutenant Colonel in the US Army? Neither did I, until I read *A Piece of My Heart.*" This book is a fine volume of reminiscences about women who served in Vietnam. The Foreword, written by Maggie, stated that she knew what those women experienced because she was there from 1965 until the end of the war. She noted that she spent over two years entertaining, nursing, and visiting units. Maggie felt that women went to Vietnam because American fighting men were there—and needed care—that's why *she* went. She felt privileged to be there. She wrote, "Few people realize that women were wounded in Vietnam: a few were killed. I was in many combat actions and was wounded twice."

Like our troops, these women never received recognition—which is exactly why Maggie became involved with the Vietnam Woman's Memorial Project and remained on their Honorary Council until she died. She said, "In Vietnam the troops let us know we were appreciated...Back in the U.S., everyone wanted to forget the war."

The *Army Times* (September 18, 1989) carried a story about John Wayne and the John F. Kennedy Special Warfare Museum at Fort Bragg. The story also mentioned that Maggie was an *honorary* Lieutenant Colonel in the Fifth Special Forces Group (Airborne) and that her Green Beret was on display at the museum.

After reading this article, I spoke with the museum's curator, Roxanne Merritt, who gave me more information about Maggie and suggested we contact Jimmy Dean at the Special Forces Association. Jimmy provided us with documents, some photos, more background on Maggie and an update on HCR 233 (which he said was going nowhere).

- She visited our troops during World War II, Korea, and Vietnam. (Of course, you already know this.)
- She spent more time in Vietnam than the average soldier. From 1965 to 1974, she spent a total of two years in-country. She not only did USO shows at the large bases, but went out to the bush and did shows for the soldiers.
- She was twice wounded and awarded two Purple Hearts for her injuries.
- She was given the honorary title of Lieutenant Colonel and a Green Beret from the Fifth Special Forces Group (Airborne), but no national recognition from our government.
- She preferred—and would answer only to—"Maggie" or "Colonel Maggie."
- She was at Pleiku, Chu Lai, Khe Sanh, Danang, Saigon, Quang Ngai, Cam Ranh Bay, Hue Phu Bai and Soc Trang.

- She often assisted medical personnel. She also spent time with the First Medical Battalion in Danang and the Seventy-first Evacuation Hospital in Pleiku.

Colonel Maggie's Drop-In

In 1989, we learned that there was a Veterans organization named for Maggie. "Colonel Maggie's All Services Airborne" was holding their annual "Colonel Maggie's Drop-In" over Labor Day weekend in Marina, California. After contacting them, we began hearing from many Veterans who have known Maggie for years.

Their response initiated our increasing reliance on a new area of primary source information: the direct experience of Veterans themselves! We spoke with several on the phone, and they sent us a lot of mail.

Jim Spitz and Chuck Darnell were especially helpful. This was just the beginning of a long friendship. They both insisted that we attend the "Drop-In" in 1990, almost a year away.

Jim, a Veteran and recipient of the Legion of Valor, was the group's president. He was instrumental in forming this Veterans' organization to include *all* branches of the military who served in Airborne units. Jim knew Maggie for a long time, and he put us in touch with members and friends who provided us with stories of their encounters with Maggie.

Maggie was revered not only by members of the Special Forces—she was important to all branches of the military. That's why a grassroots effort for the medal would have to include all branches of the Armed Forces, men and women, from all three wars—but especially in-country Vietnam and Era Veterans.

An Army Reservist myself, I turned to the *Army Times* for assistance. During 1989 I placed ads in the Locator column encouraging troops to send their personal remembrances of Maggie. The response was overwhelming. Belle, a former Woman Marine, placed similar ads in the *Navy Times* and Marine Corps publications. We wrote letters to the editors of the *Army Times, Navy Times* and *Air Force Times*. Veterans' publications were contacted. Some people not only sent us letters but even sent gifts for Maggie, which we delivered to her in person in August 1990.

For every letter we received, we responded with a packet of current information we had about Maggie and the medal campaign. We requested photos and asked recipients to sign and pass around our petition, which we would send to the White House.

"Medals for Maggie" Committee

In November 1989, Belle and I made a presentation—including passages from some of the letters—to the officers' board of our Veterans group. Before we could complete our allotted time, the board members voted to form an official *ad hoc* committee entitled "Medals For Maggie," with Belle and me as cochairs.

We made some wrong assumptions. We thought that getting Maggie honored was going to be an easy task. Second, we figured within six months we would receive a call from the White House inviting us to a Medal ceremony held in July. Finally, it never occurred to us that it would take four more years!

Unlike our futile library and archival research, the avalanche of new primary source materials from Veterans was a gold mine of information. We read stories and met individuals for whom personal contact with Maggie had been a deeply touching and memorable experience. She was not *just* an entertainer who went overseas to do a show. She became friend, mother, sister, aunt, and supporter who really cared about all service personnel regardless of branch, rank, or gender.

Our all-volunteer committee was named "Medals for Maggie" because we hoped Maggie would receive more than one medal.

Maggie was now seventy-three years old. The collection of letters and photos of Maggie from all three war eras was growing. We had initiated a petition campaign and hoped to have her recognized before her next birthday, August 27, 1990. Hey, dream *on!*

Roy Benavidez, God Bless Him!

The first major personal endorsement came from Congressional Medal of Honor recipient Master Sergeant Roy Benavidez of El Campo, Texas. Roy had met Maggie several times. He said, "Maggie is a true American. She gave all of her tomorrow's for our today's." Roy felt Maggie deserved three Medals of Freedom—one for each war. He also believed that she had more guts than General George Patton, Audie Murphy or himself!

In late 1989, Benita Zahn, a newscaster for NBC's WNYT-TV in Albany, taped us for her Sunday morning show "Forum." She interviewed and filmed three members of our committee while we worked on an upcoming mail project. The show generated many phone calls and more letters about Maggie. Suddenly my unlisted home phone number and my address were broadcast on TV, and my personal life soon shifted into the public domain.

Maggie is Stricken

On January 5, 1990, Maggie suffered the first of several strokes. She was hospitalized at Cedars-Sinai Medical Center in Los Angeles. The stroke that paralyzed her left arm and leg was compounded by four broken ribs when she fell during the episode. Jim Spitz called to tell us the news. He was understandably upset and thought she might not pull through. We prayed a lot. She did make it.

When Maggie returned home from the hospital, she had regained her speech although she spoke softly. She was continuing physical therapy at home and had round-the-clock nursing care. She also needed someone to prepare her meals, administer medications, and assist her in and out of bed.

Maggie talked many times with Jim Spitz. In March, he gave us Maggie's home phone number. Jim arranged for us to phone her immediately following one of his calls. Our first phone call with Maggie was lengthy. Belle and Richard Bushnell were with me listening through the speaker phone. I was awestruck to speak directly with this Hollywood legend and did not recall very much of what was said. They had to fill me in on everything! Belle and I spoke with Maggie often after that and became more relaxed about it.

February 1990 started with a bang. The Albany *Times Union* ran a story about our committee's efforts. UPI wire service carried the story and more mail came.

About this time, the following poem written by Belle Pellegrino was published in *BRAVO Veterans Outlook*. It summed up how Belle felt at the time.

Colonel Maggie

Since nineteen hundred and forty one
　　When Americans were called to carry a gun
A special woman heard her nation's call
　　And she went to share her love for all.

She sacrificed herself; her goals
　　To laugh with GI's in foxholes.
Wherever the military sent women and men
　　There too went Maggie to help again.

She nursed the sick, she held their hands
　　She joked or danced or sang with bands.
The chopper's call of "Mean Momma 1"
　　Told all who heard, they were due for fun.

From Europe to Thailand to Illinois
　　She tried to bring "her" troops some joy.
For those who fought or lived or died,
　　For each she joked or danced and cried.

Martha Raye, Colonel Maggie or Margaret Reed
Whatever name doesn't change the deed.
So, today, our hats are off to you
For what you constantly tried to do.

For your beloved troops you gave your all
Now we salute *you* as we stand up tall
To honor the one who passed the test.
Colonel Maggie, you *are* America's best.

Two of our committee members visited New York State's Albany County Veterans Alliance group, as well as both the Albany and Schenectady Chapters of the American Gold Star Mothers. At each meeting they made a presentation about Maggie and our quest to get her "the medals." Each group gladly gave their endorsement.

John Cardinal O'Connor, Archbishop of New York, knew Maggie well. He read a *New York Post* article about our committee, and he wrote an article for *Catholic New York*. He told of Maggie coming into the jungle, into little caves and lean-to's to visit a handful of troops, including him. She would talk, laugh, and clown around just to "bring a smile to the lips of one lonely marine or even a needed tear to the eyes of one soldier in pain."

> Martha Raye never philosophized about the war in Vietnam. She simply went there, time after time, when all seemed madness....She was trying with all her heart and at constant risk of her life, to bring a brief moment of "home," of sanity, of meaning to men without eyes, or legs, or even hope. No makeup, no spotlights, no billboards, no press. Only an aging woman who had once had a star on her dressing room, now in Marine camouflage utilities and jungle boots.

Personal endorsements were received from both Cardinal O'Connor and Bishop Howard Hubbard of Albany. Cardinal O'Connor added, "If her own days are dwindling down to a precious few, she deserves that medal a thousand times over, but she deserves far more.

She deserves the prayers of countless Veterans and of those who love them. She has mine." Bishop Hubbard wrote that his endorsement is based upon the extraordinary extent of her contributions to our soldiers and our country.

A Chaplain to Inmates

Harry Lee Morrison of Auburn, New York was an inmate at a New York State prison when he wrote. During the Vietnam War, Harry served as a Chaplain's Assistant (MOS 71M20) with the Army rank of Sergeant/E-5.

> I am now "The Chaplain" to hundreds of incarcerated veterans nationwide.
>
> Many of them know who Colonel Maggie is. Among her honorary ranks, I understand, is honorary Colonel for the 173rd Airborne Brigade. I never met "Maggie" while in-country. However, after returning, I served as a Servicemen's Representative to the USO and did meet her.
>
> You are somewhat correct. "She has not yet received national recognition." Speaking only for myself, I must wonder if "Colonel Maggie" *wants* national recognition for her service...I must wonder if she already *has* the recognition she wishes—the love and fond memories every GI has for her in their hearts.
>
> Mind you, I am *not* against your efforts. I fully *agree* she most certainly deserves the highest honors which we veterans can bestow. She has already received some... I also know of the honorary Airborne Wings, the Jump Boots, and the Combat Infantryman's Badge she wears.
>
> If it were in my authority, as a former "Holy Joe Assistant," I would grant her an "Honorary 71M20 Chaplain's Assistant."

Maggie Anchored Larger Concerns

Harry made an important point. Did Maggie *want* the recognition? No, we—the Veterans of our country—

wanted it for her. We wanted her to be further recognized nationally and publicly for her generous contribution.

Other issues were at stake. One of America's great treasures is our tradition of volunteerism. Volunteers receive no wages except their own personal satisfaction for contributing their time and energies to projects that primarily benefit others. Volunteer organizations, however, know that they have to use visible means to support and reinforce personal motivation—means such as public awards and medals. Gross oversight or neglect of significant volunteer effort can jeopardize others' willingness to give their own best efforts in the future.

Vietnam Era Veterans were especially sensitive to Maggie's being denied the Presidential Medal of Freedom. It reinforced the scorn many of them had experienced upon returning from Vietnam. Indeed, it might be seen as a setback in the still-fragile process of national healing over the Vietnam Era.

Maggie's longtime volunteer efforts were not only significant but had become highly visible to thousands of American troops and their families. By now, many knew of the grassroots movement to have her efforts affirmed and recognized at the highest public level.

More Endorsements

We were successful in getting both houses of the New York State Legislature to pass resolutions honoring Maggie. Strong support came from Assembly members Richard Connors and Catherine Nolan, and from State Senator Serphin Maltese. Partly in response to our committee's and SFA's initiatives, California, Rhode Island, Pennsylvania, and Florida passed resolutions honoring Maggie. Later the City of Los Angeles also passed a resolution.

The Medals for Maggie Committee was gaining more endorsements from various Veterans groups: the Northeast Chapter of the Korean War Veterans, Northeast New York Chapter of American Ex-Prisoners of War, American Ex-Prisoners of War, New York State Public Employee Federation Statewide Veterans Committee, Brotherhood Rally of All Veterans Organization (BRAVO), Regular Veterans Association of Texas, New York State Council of Chapters of The Retired Officers Association, *Globe* newspaper, and the American Gold Star Mothers.

Secretary of Defense Recommendation

We submitted the endorsements and some of the letters we had received to the Pentagon. By the end of April 1990, we received confirmation that the Joint Chiefs of Staff were behind the campaign, as well as the current Secretary of Defense, who sent this to President Bush:

> It is my great pleasure to nominate Martha Raye for the Presidential Medal of Freedom (PMOF) in recognition of her many outstanding contributions to this country and her unfailing support of U.S. service members around the World.
>
> Ms. Raye was an active celebrity volunteer of the United Service Organization (USO) for over forty years and devoted much of her career to visiting service members located in remote, hostile areas. Her span of service includes World War II, the Korea Conflict, the Vietnam era and peacetime.
>
> Attached are nomination letters....Many others have provided personal accounts of wartime encounters with Martha Raye and strongly support her nomination for the PMOF. A recurring theme of these accounts is Martha Raye's willingness to venture into dangerous war zones to lift the spirits of service members regardless of numbers, or employ her nursing skills by assisting in medical activities. She made repeated, extended wartime visits far beyond that of other USO volunteers, to Africa, Europe, the Pacific Theatre, the Republic of Korea and South Vietnam, despite great risk to her

personal safety, in order to do whatever she could to enliven and care for US service personnel. The media has documented well her close association with the Special Operations Forces as well as her complete dedication to all service members.

I believe that Martha Raye richly deserves this award. Her contributions are consistent with previous recipients of the medal. Presenting her with the PMOF would be a most appropriate way of expressing your gratitude for her many contributions to our country.

APRIL 1990

RICHARD CHENEY, SECRETARY of DEFENSE

Gold Star Mothers

Belle and I traveled to Utica for the New York State Convention of the American Gold Star Mothers where we made another presentation about the campaign. While we read some of the letters received, many tears were shed. The Mothers heartily voted to endorse the campaign and to take their endorsement to their National Convention.

After the meeting, many of them shared their feelings about the project. Some mothers wondered if Maggie had seen their sons before they died. They asked if it were possible that Maggie may have treated their sons' wounds. Some asked if Maggie had been to a particular location in Vietnam, as that was where their sons died. They were hoping that perhaps Maggie had entertained their sons or just sat and talked with them before their fateful day. Some simply embraced, hugged, and kissed us; words could not come out and we understood their pain of remembering.

Meanwhile Benita Zahn from NBC's Channel 13, WNYT, in Albany had contacted us to see how the project was going. Again she had us on "Forum" for the Mother's Day broadcast. Colonel Lib joined us for this program; she had seen Maggie in Korea and Vietnam. ABC's local Channel 10 WTEN shared an interest in covering our quest, but there still was no national TV coverage.

Not Again!

We took the campaign to Congressman Mike McNulty, a New York Democrat. On May 8, 1990, Representative McNulty, along with twenty cosponsors, introduced House Concurrent Resolution 322. HCR 322 was our project's first national resolution. We soon learned that, as with its predecessor (HCR 233), it was sent to legislative purgatory in the Committee on Post Office and Civil Service.

We knew how the Special Forces Association must have felt after their eight years of effort! HCR 322 would need 218 cosponsors in the House to be acted upon. We began writing and calling all members of Congress for their support. We also tried in vain—this time—to get a Senate Resolution.

Dear President Bush

We wrote to President Bush asking him to honor Maggie and to Mrs. Barbara Bush asking for assistance. The initial response to our letter to the First Lady came by way of a letter from the Office of the Assistant Secretary of Defense (OASD) at the Pentagon. That letter put us in touch with many influential people there who helped us, especially Lieutenant Colonel Kenneth Deutsch.

Mrs. Bush also responded on a more personal level. A letter was sent to Maggie dated May 9, 1990. She framed and hung it on her Team Room wall. It included an autographed photo of the President and Barbara Bush. The photo was placed on a desk in what used to be Nick's bedroom.

> George and I have just learned of your health problems. We are so sorry. May you be comforted during this

difficult time by the love and support of your family and friends. We are thinking of you, and you are in our prayers.

Warmly,
Barbara Bush

Many people called us. Reporters wanted to make arrangements to interview Maggie—she refused. "Reporters seldom write what you tell them. They write what they want to write."

Lieutenant Colonel Deutsch from the Pentagon asked me to keep him apprised of Maggie's condition. I spoke with Maggie's doctor (after he got her permission, of course), and he kept us informed of her health status. I asked Maggie if she would attend an awards ceremony if she were invited to the White House. Her answer was, "Hell, yes, I'd go in my wheelchair!"

Pancakes, Bingo, and Shirts

In May, The American Legion passed a resolution honoring Maggie. Meanwhile, we had selected a design for a T-shirt to sell to help cover committee expenses. The shirts were donated by a local Albany Veteran who had seen Maggie in Vietnam but who asks to remain anonymous. We were holding fund raisers to help meet the project's costs. We had a pancake breakfast with assistance of members of the William F. Wigand VFW Post 8444 and a bingo night with help from members of the Louis Oppenheim VFW Post 1019. We sold raffle tickets several times and were further aided by Post 8444.

Michael Hirsh, a film producer who had been working on a documentary about Maggie, wanted to include us in his film. He had been to Maggie's home and, with her permission, filmed her prior to her stroke. He was in the process of selling his film to a television network and hoped either the PBS or HBO would air his documentary. In June he came to New York to film us. I was on Active Duty at Fort Indiantown Gap, Pennsylvania, so he filmed Belle and Colonel Lib at Colonel Lib's home. Mike shared some of his collected information with us, and we shared some of our documents with him. As yet, his program has not been aired.

Jimmy Case of Ace Productions in Old Hickory, Tennessee, a musician who traveled with Maggie occasionally in Vietnam, also contacted us. He has a production company and represents many Country-and-Western singers. He gave us addresses, phone numbers, and fax numbers of many performers he felt would help spread the word about our endeavors. The only performer who responded was Lee Greenwood.

Drop-In 1990

After many phone conversations among Jim Spitz, Maggie, Belle, and me regarding transportation, accommodations, meals, and Maggie's condition, Belle and I flew to California in August 1990 for our first experience of the annual "Drop-In." (I hate flying!) Jim met and whisked us away to American Legion Post 694 in Marina. As we entered the building, we were immediately taken to Maggie's table. She was sitting in a wheelchair between her nurse, Oneata McDowell, and one of Maggie's best longtime friends, Lieutenant Colonel Rolande "Frenchy" Amundsen. We spent the afternoon and evening eating and talking. We had finally met "Colonel Maggie"!

The next day, we escorted Maggie in the local parade; then we returned to the Post for a barbecue luncheon and the "Drop-In." For us, it was a novel twist on an old phrase: this was an actual parachute "Drop" of numerous Veterans! Maggie was able to point out exactly where the parachutists were in the sky before anyone else in the crowd saw them.

While the men had their reunion in one room, the women had a party in another room to celebrate Maggie's seventy-fourth birthday. Her special "present" was a performance by Michael, a Chippendale dancer.

That evening there was a marvelous banquet with gifts and accolades for Maggie. Susan Christiansen made a presentation and spoke of the blind Veteran's encounter with Maggie. Belle and I presented Maggie with a life membership in our Albany Veterans' group, a jacket, and a plaque. We talked about the campaign's progress. We arranged to deliver the personal gifts and letters we had received for Maggie from other admirers.

The next morning we attended a steak and egg breakfast at the Post. Susan interviewed Maggie and us for *BRAVO*.

Maggie had invited us to stay at her home and told us where she hid her front door key, since we would be in Los Angeles before she could get there. We hated leaving Marina and all our new friends, but we were off to Los Angeles.

Marina, California—1990: The Drop-In. Seated L-R: Oneata McDowell, Maggie, Noonie, and Belle.

Maggie's Team House

We expected to find a mansion; after all, Maggie was a celebrity. What we found was a modest ranch-style home, not hidden behind a large security gate but separated from the street by only a sidewalk and white picket fence. This was the famous Team House we had heard and read about. (But we ended up spending the night at the Brentwood Holiday Inn because Maggie's key was not where she thought she had left it.)

Bel Air—1990: Waiting for Maggie at her "Team House."

The next morning Maggie was waiting for us. She gave us the keys to her Mercedes—a gift from Nick—which she never drove because she did not have a driver's license. She gave us full access to her home and invited us to look at everything, take photos, ask questions, watch movies, cook, talk—anything at all. What a thrill! I took pictures of the house, inside and out, and made pages of notes on our conversations. We spent many precious hours with her in her home.

Maggie let me go through her Rolodex and copy her friends' addresses and phone numbers. We made an inventory of the plaques on her walls and of those stacked on the floor. Maggie's den—better known to Vets as the

Team Room—was filled with military memorabilia. The walls were covered with plaques, photos, and awards that had been presented to Maggie over the years. Her desk, end tables, coffee table, and window seat were filled with letters, pictures, coffee mugs, and cigarette lighters in neat piles. In 1990 there were plaques leaning against the walls behind her sofa and loveseat in the Team Room.

The two items that identified her as a Hollywood star—her Oscar and a replica of her star from Hollywood's Walk of Fame—were the only Hollywood items in the Team Room. The Oscar was on a table in front of her picture window; the star was hidden behind her television. She obviously loved that room and all the memories it held. Her living room also had stacks of military plaques and other memorabilia.

Between her guest bathroom and the garage there was another small room where Maggie kept most of her souvenirs from stage, screen, and television days. Nick Condos had used the room as an office. There was a hidden doorway to a storage closet in which Maggie stored scripts, music sheets, and reel to reel film canisters from her professional career. When I first saw this room and closet, I thought it was strange that she would have those items out of sight. Maggie explained that was another part of her life and not to be confused with her commitment to our Armed Forces.

While we watched television with Maggie, we saw coverage on Desert Shield. Maggie began to cry and expressed how much she wanted to be there. Here was a woman who could no longer dress herself still yearning to be with our troops!

We Witnessed Her Amazing Memory

We described some of the letters we had received about her from troops she visited. Tears came to her eyes as she reminisced about those special people and occasions. We were amazed that she remembered so many of the people who had written to us. We would mention some insignificant part of a letter or a person's name, and she would fill in the rest before we could go any further. What a remarkable memory she had for the smallest details!

Melodye later reminded me that Maggie had to learn acting lines quickly. Nonetheless, without a photographic memory, it takes fervent and genuine commitment to remember the people, places, and things she did, and so well. This was 1990, but she showed no signs of memory loss from her stroke—at least not about her troops and their families.

Our visit came to a close much too soon. We had such a great time with Maggie, talking about her career, family, and experiences with her troops. We had been to dinner with her at Matteo's, her favorite Italian restaurant in Westwood. While we were there, an actor who appeared with Maggie in *The Concorde Airport '79* stopped by our table and spoke with her. We had been driven around Hollywood in a limo. We drove her Mercedes to food markets and cooked meals for her. We discovered what thousands of troops already knew: the more you were with Maggie, the more you loved her!

After returning to Albany, we wrote to over two hundred of Maggie's friends who were entertainers. Unfortunately, we heard from very few of them.

One evening I received an unexpected phone call from comedian Joey Bishop. Joey was with Maggie in

Vietnam in November 1968 when she collapsed from heat exhaustion. He could not understand why more of her friends had not responded to our letters. He said he would help spread the word of our project...and he did.

Whoopi Goldberg's secretary called. He said Whoopi had received our letter and information about Maggie. Unfortunately, Whoopi was overcommitted until February 1991 so she could not actively help us until after that. But, he also said Whoopi would try to spread the word about the project and wished us luck.

Rusty "Knockers Up" Warren wrote an endorsement in which she said, "Who deserves it [the PMOF] more than her?"

We also received letters from General William Westmoreland and Lady Bird Johnson.

Two of Maggie's best friends were Danny Thomas and his wife Rosie. Danny sent a personal written endorsement to President Bush and a copy to us.

> My dear friend risked her own safety many times to ensure our troops had a few minutes of entertainment. I just had to add my personal support of this great American, Martha Raye, and urge you to do whatever you can to see that she gets the recognition of the Presidential Medal of Freedom for she is so deserving this honor. I proudly add my name to all the other citizens.

When Danny passed away in February 1991, Maggie attended his funeral.

Sharing Documentation

During 1990 we shared some of our documentation with people who were writing books and who wanted to include Maggie in their manuscripts. Pete Billac of Alvin, Texas was writing a book about Master Sergeant Roy Benavidez entitled *The Last Medal of Honor.* He included a section about Maggie's efforts during Vietnam. Continuing through 1993 more and more of us pooled our experiences, shared photos, and worked on documentation for the medal.

Meanwhile, Lieutenant Commander Donna Fournier, U.S. Navy Reserve, of Chicago was writing a manuscript for the Department of Defense entitled *Military Women Serving in America's Defense*. It includes references to Maggie's role. Unfortunately, when the book went to Department of Defense for approval, permission to publish was refused. As of this writing, it is back at the Pentagon awaiting approval.

Following our first television appearance in December 1989 in Albany, we sought national television coverage. More publicity was needed than what we had received from newspapers and other publications. We wrote and called every talk show on the air; they were just not interested.

Chapter 14

Bureaucratic Inertia

"...Please be advised that your suggestion will be given careful consideration when future recipients are considered..."

Many letters, many signatures...same words
1969-1993

Would She? or Wouldn't She?

Would She? or Wouldn't She?

Presidential Medal of Freedom—1993: This official White House photo is the female version of the PMOF that was presented to Maggie, along with a certificate from President Clinton. Photo from The White House.

-14-

Shortly before Christmas of 1990, Lieutenant Colonel Deutsch called to report that he had just been on the phone to the White House. He apologized for not being able to share any of the details of that conversation, but advised us that very influential people were backing, supporting, and pushing for Maggie's PMOF. He spoke of his personal knowledge of her endeavors and said he felt comfortable about where the situation stood. We would hear from him in January.

In January he phoned to say that everyone was preoccupied with Desert Storm. He was not to contact the White House again until February 20 and told us not to expect anything until March.

On February 20, President Bush announced that he was giving a Medal of Freedom to Margaret "Maggie" Thatcher of England, but there was no mention of Maggie Raye.

Back in Hollywood

Good Old Days ran a story by Harry Wilkinson entitled "Looking Hollywood Way." He reminisced about his first encounter with Maggie way back in 1936 when he had reported, "A funny, funny lass with plenty of zip and zoom. A riot of fun. Watch her! I'm sure she's going far!" He certainly was "right on"!

His article described Maggie's Hollywood career and briefly mentioned her personal life. The article referred to her brother Bud and their act "Bud and Margie." Although Maggie never mentioned Bud, after her death we were able to verify that Bud, indeed, was her brother.

A great deal of publicity surrounded the USO's fiftieth anniversary celebration during February 1991.

Although Maggie was mentioned as one of the entertainers who often visited the troops, she did not receive nearly the publicity Bob Hope did.

During April 1991, we received a letter from Chuck Connors—"The Rifleman." He, too, had visited the troops in Vietnam. He ordered five of our Colonel Maggie T-shirts and wrote, "Martha Raye is truly a legend and for many years she has been loved by all."

Rosemary Clooney sent us a handwritten note suggesting that we contact Margaret Whiting, Kay Starr, and Helen O'Connell. She also suggested that we write to Actors Equity and the Screen Actors Guild. This lovely lady ordered twenty of our T-shirts.

During May we wrote to Ann Landers. She included us in her column, which generated more mail. We spoke with Maggie's former secretary, Ann Boddington, who gave us additional information for our research.

Steve Allen wrote that because Martha has "over the years given a great deal of her time, energy, and talent to entertaining American troops, she deserves all possible honors."

On June 10, 1991, Maggie had a seizure and another stroke, during which she broke her right shoulder. She was taken to the UCLA Medical Center where surgery was performed to place a pin in her shoulder joint.

New Faces on Capitol Hill

The November 1990 elections provided Washington with many new faces. A new Congressional session was underway. Maggie's Resolution HCR 322 had not been acted upon. If a resolution was not passed during one Congressional Session, it had to be reintroduced at the next session of Congress.

Congressman McNulty did not let us down; he presented another Resolution (HCR 100) to Congress on March 19, 1991. He had twenty-six cosponsors; unfortunately, HCR 100 was also sent to purgatory, the Committee on Post Office and Civil Service, where it waited for more cosponsors.

In July the Special Forces Association (SFA) reported the campaign's progress to their membership. They set September 10 as the day when all SFA members were to call the White House opinion poll to ask President Bush "to do the right thing" and honor Maggie with the PMOF.

Dan Cavanagh from New York State's Veterans Service Agency (Nassau County) and I had talked frequently since February 1991. I hoped to arrange an interview or phone call for him with Maggie. At this time, Maggie told me to act as her "East Coast Agent." I thought she was joking! But I interpreted this narrowly as limited to her role in Veterans matters.

Dan's agency had selected Maggie to receive their organization's Medal of Honor and planned a "Martha Raye Day" to be celebrated on August 24, 1991. I was to arrange for Maggie to be present. Since this was impossible, Dan planned to have a video hookup from her home in California to Eisenhower Park on Long Island where the presentation was to be made. This did not materialize. Belle and I had been asked by Maggie and Dan to be at the Park to receive the medal and take it to Maggie for her birthday. In November, Dan was able to deliver it to Maggie himself.

Bel Air—November 1991: Dan Cavanagh presenting the VSA Medal of Honor to Maggie. Photo contributed by Dan.

A Treasured Visit

In September, Arden Davenport and I spent two weeks in California where we enjoyed another fabulous visit with Maggie and the All-Airborne Drop-In. Once again, we had a great time with Maggie at her home.

We watched some old movies with her; she had them all on videotape. As Arden was preparing to put a tape in the VCR, Maggie remarked that the VCR had been a gift from her longtime friend, Rock Hudson; she commented that she missed him very much. She showed us a picture of the two of them taken shortly before he passed away.

Maggie's movies were fascinating, and she gave us a running commentary as we viewed them. She talked about one of the outfits she wore in *Waikiki Wedding* and joked about some of the scenes in *Navy Blues* and *Keep 'Em Flying*.

She also spoke of her trip to England and North Africa with Kay Francis, Mitzi Mayfair, and Carole Landis. She mentioned how the other three women could not help in the first aid stations; they kept getting sick, but Maggie was able to put her nurse's aide training to the test. We attempted to track down these old friends of Maggie's only to learn that Ms. Landis committed suicide and died on July 5, 1948; Ms. Francis passed away from cancer on August 26, 1968; and we were unable to locate Ms. Mayfair.

Maggie arranged for us to go to dinner to celebrate her seventy-fifth birthday. Her two nurses, Beryl Westby and Oneata; her physical therapist, David; her former secretary-friend and traveling companion, Ann Boddington; Arden and I had a great meal at Matteo's. While we were there, Tony Curtis stopped by our table to speak with Maggie. What a memorable evening!

I asked Maggie if she would be willing to be interviewed by Jane Wollman, a writer from New York City who had met Maggie through Steve Allen. The interview hopefully would obtain publicity for our committee's efforts. Maggie initially agreed to be interviewed, but only if I were there while Jane was interviewing her. Later she changed her mind and said she would not grant the interview, even though it might facilitate her PMOF. She hated interviews—unless the people were from the Veterans' community.

As Labor Day weekend approached, Maggie felt physically unable to make the trip to Marina for the Drop-In, so Arden and I headed up there. It was a pleasure to renew acquaintances at Marina, but it was not the same without Maggie. The parade was shorter and there were fewer spectators. There were also fewer parachutists Dropping-In.

At the banquet, the head table had large photos of Maggie taken over the years. Many gifts were presented for Maggie, and we took some of them to her. Others were delivered by Jim Spitz and Colonel Lewis Millette, another Congressional Medal of Honor recipient and friend of Maggie's. There were two very special gifts. One was a diamond and silver brooch in the design of the Parachutist Badge from the members of Colonel Maggie's All Services Airborne.

The other gift was the Golden Dog Tag Award from Coors Brewing Company. Maggie had been selected to receive this award after we provided much of her background information to Warren Hutchins, the Coors Veterans Administrator. The wooden plaque had gold dog tags on it, each engraved with the names of the various camps, firebases, and countries that Maggie had visited. Entertainer Ernest Borgnine had received this award several years earlier for his efforts within the Veteran community.

When we returned to Maggie's home, I took more photos and movies of her house. Maggie's only restriction was that we could not take photos or movies of her lying in bed.

During 1990 and 1991, Maggie and I spoke at length about her wartime activities. She openly discussed the things she did, places she went, and people she met. I reiterated that our main goal was the Presidential Medal of Freedom. Once that was accomplished, I wanted to write a book about her.

Maggie said, "If I get the Medal, you have my permission to write a book about me, but I ask only two things. Please tell the truth, as I have told you. You have researched my life and know more about me than even I can remember. Also, don't have it published until after I die. I don't want to embarrass anyone—especially myself—while I'm alive." This was a verbal agreement witnessed by Arden Davenport and Susan Christiansen.

Once again it was hard to leave Maggie and California. Maggie seemed so lonely, and she was disappointed that she could not attend the Drop-In. But Maggie was still very much "together," and she still possessed her truly remarkable memory.

Once Again...

The Special Forces Association, North Carolina's Governor James Martin, and Senator Jesse Helms all contacted President Bush to honor Maggie. After concerted efforts by Congressman McNulty, his aide Jim Glenn, and us, California Senator John Seymour introduced Senate Concurrent Resolution (SCR) 62 to the Senate on September 18, 1991, along with seventeen co-sponsors. SCR 62 was sent to the Committee on the Judiciary which—again—"filed" it, since it needed fifty-one supporters to be voted on. Once again all senators were contacted in our hope that the required number of co-sponsors would sign on.

Marriage Number Seven!

On October 1, 1991, I received a frantic phone call from Susan Christiansen who heard a news flash on

"Hard Copy" that Maggie had gotten married! Maggie shocked everyone she knew—including me, since we had just left her on September 5.

Sometime around September 11, comedian Bernie Allen brought Mark Steven Harris to Maggie's home and introduced them. Less than two weeks later, Maggie went to Las Vegas, with her nurse Oneata at her side, and married husband number seven. The ceremony was conducted by Rabbi Hecht at the Golden Nugget Hotel at three o'clock in the afternoon, September 25. Maggie was seventy-five years old; Mark was forty-two. I spoke with Maggie about her sudden marriage and she said simply, "He makes me happy."

I began getting calls from contacts in the Congressman's office, the Pentagon, and the White House. Everyone was asking me about how Maggie could get married again despite her tenuous health status. I didn't have answers.

On October 1, Army Archerd reported the wedding in *Variety*. He stated that Maggie had been hospitalized while in Las Vegas. Upon her return to Los Angeles, Maggie was taken to St. John's Hospital suffering from diverticulitis.

"A Very Big Heart"

We received letters and phone calls from more of Maggie's friends before the end of 1991. Margaret Whiting, Mrs. Jimmy (Marge) Durante, and Imogene Coca kept in touch. Marge and Imogene even sent us donations to help defray committee expenses. Imogene wrote from her New York apartment, "Knowing Maggie, I'm sure she contributed her energy and talent for the servicemen because she really *wanted* to give her best for them."

From New York, Margaret Whiting wrote, "I've known Maggie since I was a young girl in Hollywood just beginning my career. She's a great talent and a woman with a very big heart. She certainly did more than anyone else I know to help the Veterans of World War II and to entertain our troops all over."

In 1991 North Carolina local and state officials approved two resolutions honoring Maggie and asked President Bush to award her the PMOF. One was signed in the City of Morrisville by Mayor Ernest Lamby. Governor James Martin signed the State resolution.

Meanwhile...

President Bush awarded ten more Presidential Medals of Freedom on November 18. Among the recipients were Ted Williams, Betty Ford, and Thomas "Tip" O'Neill. Still no medal for Maggie. As mentioned earlier, he also awarded medals to General Norman Schwarzkopf and General Colin Powell for their efforts during Desert Shield and Desert Storm. (I was puzzled, since this is supposed to be a civilian award.) President Clinton presented General Powell with a second PMOF when the General retired in September 1993.

With all the mail, phone calls, and conversations that people were having with President Bush regarding Maggie, we could not understand why he had not yet awarded the PMOF to this great American. We continued pursuit of national talk-show exposure to discuss why Maggie should be honored with the PMOF. After Maggie's marriage, there was interest from some shows...providing we would talk about Maggie's personal life. *We* immediately lost interest in those programs.

By January 7, 1992, there were twenty-one cosponsors on SCR 62; HCR 100 had eighty cosponsors. That was a long way from the 52 and 218 needed to get these resolutions to the floor for a vote.

We kept plugging along. I spent more time on the phone and writing letters to senators and congress members. Many contacts reported they had personally talked with President Bush about the PMOF for Maggie. On January 18, the State of Illinois passed a resolution honoring her. Two weeks later, a proclamation in her honor was issued in Union City, California.

BRAVO Veterans Outlook reported that on January 28, 1992, military ceremonies were held in Maggie's Bel Air home. At that time she became the honorary Commanding Officer of the Army Reserve's 6325th Individual Mobilization Augmentee (IMA) Detachment. The article reported she was a former Army Combat Nurse, had received two Purple Hearts for wounds received in action in Vietnam, and held the rank of Lieutenant Colonel in the Army Special Forces. According to the article, Mark Harris stated that he felt this honor to Martha "might help her receive the American Freedom Medal [*sic*] that she most definitely deserved."

In April 1992, Senator Seymour's office notified us that there were twenty-six cosponsors on SCR 62, half the votes needed. We received a copy of the Senate Congressional Record dated September 18, 1991, which printed Senator Seymour's speech on the Senate floor.

In May, though she was still in a wheelchair, Maggie attended Memorial Day ceremonies at Westwood's National Cemetery in California. Her picture appeared in the *Los Angeles Times.*

Form Letters

In March we received the first of many letters from the White House. Much later, after comparing the letters we received between March 1990 and 1993 with those that other people received since 1969, the only difference was the person signing them! Form letters all said the same thing:

> On behalf of President ______, thank you for recommending Martha Raye for the Presidential Medal of Freedom. It was good of you to bring this recommendation to the President's attention.

> Ms. Raye is in distinguished company as a person whose contributions have earned the gratitude of the American people. Please be assured that your suggestion will be given careful consideration when future recipients are considered.
>
> With the President's best wishes.

The Democratic primaries were now over. Governor Bill Clinton was nominated to run for President of the United States against incumbent Republican George Bush. Already, we had written to both Bill and Hillary Clinton, as well as to Senator Al and Tipper Gore. We continued writing to Governor Clinton and Senator Gore in Arkansas, Tennessee, and their headquarters in Washington. We suspected that, if elected, they would be harder to reach in the White House.

Governor's Greetings

Governor Clinton sent a telegram to Maggie for her seventy-sixth birthday on August 27, 1992. The telegram said that if he were elected to the Presidency in November, he would present her with the Presidential Medal of Freedom. The story about Governor Clinton's telegram appeared in the New York papers two days later. Maggie's birthday party was held at the Friar's Club in Los Angeles. Many of Maggie's Hollywood friends were there, including Bob Hope, Caesar Romero, Dorothy Lamour, and Marge Durante.

At the annual Drop-In, another party was scheduled for Maggie to celebrate both her birthday and her latest marriage. Maggie could not attend. She was not as accessible to her Veterans now since someone had changed her phone number.

A New President

Bill Clinton became our new President. He took time on that important day to write a personal note. We had already received notes from both Clintons, but I was amazed that he took time on Election Day to write again. He thanked us for the Colonel Maggie T-shirt we had sent him with the fact sheet about Maggie. He also said he would enjoy wearing the T-shirt and appreciated our thoughtfulness.

Tenth Anniversary of The Wall

In 1992 Belle and I went to Washington for Veterans Day ceremonies celebrating the Tenth Anniversary of The Wall. We wanted to be with other female Veterans as they broke ground for the Vietnam Women's Memorial and to update as many as we could about "Medals for Maggie." We wore our Colonel Maggie T-shirts everywhere we went. Many asked us questions about how the campaign was doing. Most would tell their own stories about encounters with Maggie.

That day one soldier remembered his outpost being under attack while Maggie was there. Choppers were called in to rescue her, but it was a hot Landing Zone so they could only hover. Maggie came running out in a shortie nightgown, flak jacket, helmet and combat boots. The soldier and his buddy grabbed her where they could—there was no time for modesty—and hoisted her into the hovering chopper. It did not matter where their hands went, he said, as they wanted her safely off the ground.

We met former First Lieutenant Forman, a female nurse, who served at Qui Nhon and remembered Maggie helping at her Evacuation Hospital.

A former Green Beret said Maggie came to his area to do a show, but instead she worked in the Emergency Room. That area was "hot" and the entertainers with her were very scared— but not Maggie.

So Many People—So Many Stories

We told people about President-elect Clinton's promise to honor Maggie. We asked that they write to him while he was still reachable in Arkansas. After returning to Albany, we wrote President-elect Clinton to remind him of his promise and bring him up to date on Maggie's health. In a return letter, he thanked us for the letter and welcomed our ideas, which he said would be carefully considered. He expressed gratitude that we took time to write to him.

During 1992, President Bush awarded eleven Presidential Medals of Freedom. Recipients included Wal-Mart's Sam Walton, race car driver Richard Petty, Johnny Carson, David Brinkley, General John Vessey, Ella Fitzgerald, and Audrey Hepburn. President Bush presented his last Presidential Medal of Freedom to former President Ronald Reagan on January 13, 1993.

Following Election Day 1992, there was a new Congress. Resolutions HCR 100 and SCR 62 had again failed to be acted upon. On January 27, 1993, Congressman McNulty submitted yet another Resolution—our third one. This time he had no cosponsors for what was now called HCR 30. We never did find a Senator who was willing to submit a Senate Resolution in 1993.

Government of the People...*for* the People?

We had made many contacts in Washington, as well as across the country and around the globe. We just shook our heads when once again we received the same form letters from the White House. Each one was thanking us for recommending Maggie for the PMOF. The only difference was that now they were signed by someone new. Bureaucracy!

With a new Secretary of Defense in office, all documents had to be resubmitted to the Pentagon. In 1990 these submissions had been seen by the Joint Chiefs of Staff, approved by General Colin Powell, and forwarded to Secretary of Defense Cheney. This time the documentation also went to the heads of the Departments of Army, Navy, and Air Force. Once each office approved the documentation, their recommendations were sent to the Office of the Assistant Secretary of Defense (OASD). On June 4, 1993, the OASD requested that we provide new endorsements and documents. Once again, we contacted organizations and individuals for endorsements and documentation.

New endorsements did come from The American Legion, Air Force Sergeants Association, Vietnam Veterans of America Chapter 400, The Retired Enlisted Association, Department of Veterans Affairs, and the Blinded Veterans Association. We compiled those along with additional personal letters from people whom Maggie touched over the years and sent them to the OASD. We waited....

On June 14, Mrs. Clinton's office sent a letter in which she thanked us for reminding her about Maggie's important work on behalf of the men and women serving in the US Armed Forces. She appreciated our support for Maggie and our wish that she receive the PMOF. She was forwarding our information to the office that processed recommendations regarding the PMOF. She assured us our request would be given serious consideration. We waited....

Congressman McNulty sent a personal letter to President Clinton on June 15. He briefly outlined Maggie's background and asked that President Clinton consider awarding the PMOF to her. Six days later, Congressman McNulty received a response from the Assistant to the President for Legislative Affairs. It said that the Congressman's recommendation was forwarded to the Office of the Staff Secretary, who requested his recommendation be considered with the utmost attention. We waited....

Tennis great Arthur Ashe passed away earlier in the year from blood-transfusion-contracted AIDS. On June 20, President Clinton awarded his first Presidential Medal of Freedom posthumously to this marvelous gentleman for his humanitarian efforts in both the African-American and AIDS communities, as well as for his tennis prowess. It was presented to Arthur's widow, Jeanne Moutoussamy-Ashe.

Immediately afterward, we began a continuous mail and phone campaign to the White House. Maggie was still alive. Why should she be honored *posthumously*? She deserved to know that the President and the nation cherished her for what she did for Americans during her lifetime. We waited....

A letter came from Skila Harris, the Chief of Staff for Mrs. Gore. Dated July 20, it stated that the efforts of our committee were being heard by the White House and that Maggie was under consideration for the PMOF. It also said, "The warmth and sincerity of your tribute to Martha Raye brightened my day." That lifted my spirits. I even received a postcard from "Socks." Maybe *this* was the year that Maggie would be honored. We waited....

Governor Mario Cuomo

New York's Governor Mario Cuomo now made a pivotal contribution, somewhat like adding one more fuel pellet makes an atomic pile go critical and a chain reaction begins—while on the surface not much seems changed. He had been included in our writing campaign from the beginning but had not responded until after President Clinton was in office.

One day we received a phone call from Bruce Stuart of the New York State Division of Veterans Affairs. Governor Cuomo had asked him to check into our efforts, see what had been done and what he could do to help. I provided the documentation, and Belle spent over an hour with Mr. Stuart bringing him "up to speed."

Then, on July 28 this letter was sent from Governor Cuomo to President Clinton:

> I am writing to recommend Martha Raye for the Presidential Medal of Freedom. Ms. Raye is the embodiment of patriotism and bravery, and is deserving of our Nation's fullest appreciation.
>
> Ms. Raye is recognized internationally as an ambassador of good will and charity. As a starring member of Bob Hope's USO tour, she began entertaining U. S. troops abroad during World War II. She has performed in Pearl Harbor, England, Belfast, North Africa, Algeria, the South Pacific, the Philippines, Iceland and even on Navy warships—often at great personal risk.
>
> She later brought her cheer to Korea, and from 1965-1974, Ms. Raye worked her magic for our troops in Vietnam. Her combined visits to Vietnam totaled over 730 days—more than the average soldier served.
>
> Her service went far beyond mere entertaining; on many occasions she helped care for the injured and the dying. In fact, she herself was wounded twice and received two Purple Hearts.
>
> Martha Raye went well beyond what is expected of an entertainer. She believed in freedom and dedicated herself to making life a little easier for those who defend it.
>
> I cannot think of a more appropriate tribute than to award the Presidential Medal of Freedom to this tireless, selfless champion of freedom, Martha Raye.
>
> Mario Cuomo, Governor, New York

Viewed in retrospect, Governor Cuomo's intervention probably provided the necessary level of well-placed political clout to get the bureaucracy moving into higher gear. Not only had he "delivered" for President Clinton's election, but his counsel was valued by the Oval Office on so many critical matters. The bureaucratic back-scratching cycle could not ignore Governor Cuomo. Nor could it respond to *him* with a form letter!

Maggie's Condition Deteriorates

Meanwhile, due to her failing health, another Labor Day weekend passed without Maggie at the Tenth

Annual Drop-In. On October 12, Maggie was hospitalized once more. This time it was for surgery at Cedars-Sinai Hospital to amputate a toe on her left foot and to bypass blocked veins in her left leg. The following day, both *The Times Union* and a CNN newscast reported Maggie had about three months to live. We called everyone we could reach in the Pentagon, Congress, Senate, and White House. We spoke to each person several times about how quickly Maggie's health was failing. I talked so much I lost my voice.

On October 18, I called Lieutenant Colonel Deutsch at the Pentagon. He said all the services had concurred that Maggie deserved the Presidential Medal of Freedom, and he was waiting for a recommendation from Secretary of Defense Les Aspin. I also called Jim Glenn at Congressman McNulty's office. Jim suggested that we contact all the national Veterans organizations to try another big push on the White House.

Recommendation from the Secretary of Defense

By October 27, Captain Tracy Henson called from the Pentagon. She said that Secretary Aspin had signed a letter of recommendation for Maggie's PMOF and that it was on its way to President Clinton. Captain Henson faxed us a copy.

> It is with distinct pleasure that I nominate Martha Raye for the Presidential Medal of Freedom (PMOF) in recognition of her many outstanding contributions to this country and her unfailing support of the members of the US Armed Forces. She was an active celebrity volunteer of the United Service Organizations (USO) for over forty years and devoted much of her career to visiting military members stationed in remote hostile areas. From World War II to the post-Vietnam Era, she was a significant source of comfort, inspiration and joy for three generations of American Service men and women. A brief narrative of her service is...

Medal of Honor recipient Master Sergeant (Retired) Roy P. Benavidez, Archbishop of New York John Cardinal O'Connor, and former Chief Master Sergeant of the Air Force James C. Binnicker, among many others have provided personal accounts of wartime encounters with Martha Raye and strongly support her nomination for the PMOF. A recurring theme of these accounts is Martha Raye's willingness to venture into dangerous war zones to lift the spirits of Service members, regardless of numbers, or employ her nursing skills by assisting in medical activities. She made repeated, extended wartime visits, far beyond that of other USO volunteers, to Africa, Europe, the Pacific Theater, the Republic of Korea and South Vietnam. Despite great risk to her personal safety, she did whatever she could to enliven and care for US Service personnel. The media has well documented her extraordinary service.

Our Service members, past and present, have not forgotten Ms. Raye's exceptional dedication and sacrifices on their behalf. Accordingly, veterans organizations across the country enthusiastically support this nomination. Samples of their endorsements are...

I believe Martha Raye richly deserves this award. Her contributions are consistent with previous recipients of the medal. Presenting her the PMOF would be a most appropriate way of expressing your gratitude for her especially meritorious service to our country.

25 OCTOBER 1993
LES ASPIN, SECRETARY OF DEFENSE

More Surgery...

Maggie returned to Cedars-Sinai for another surgery on October 29. This time doctors amputated her left leg below the knee. She was now seventy-seven years old, had suffered several strokes, and had other serious health problems. Funeral arrangements were being discussed. My bags were packed in case I had to make a quick trip to Fort Bragg for her burial.

On November 1, we renewed the telephone effort, but *now* our calls got through to influential people in Washington. I spoke with Colonel Deutsch (who had been promoted) and Lieutenant Colonel Steven Chmiola (OASD) at the Pentagon. At the White House, we contacted Dee Dee Meyers, President Clinton's Press Secretary; Marsha Scott, Presidential Office of Correspondence; and Jim Dorskind, a White House staff official. We also spoke with Jim Glenn, Congressman McNulty's aide; Hershel Gober, Deputy Secretary of Veteran Affairs; Cindy Trutanic, working in Tipper Gore's office; and many others. Up-to-date news of Maggie's condition was shared with all.

Jim Dorskind promised to take this latest information to someone; he said President Clinton had been kept aware of Maggie's situation. Cindy Trutanic assured me that everyone knew of the situation's gravity and that they were moving on our request.

After so long and so much work by so many, however, nothing prepared me for what happened the next day—I will never forget it as long as I live!

Election Day, Tuesday, November 2, 1993

I was up early and went out to vote. I had nothing else planned for the day, except more phone calls. My telephone rang at 10:30 A.M. It was Jim Dorskind. He said it was very possible that President Clinton might award the PMOF to Maggie.

He needed to know her current health condition, location, and whom to speak with in Los Angeles about her status. I gave him the number for Cedars-Sinai Hospital and told him to speak with Ron Wise, spokesman for the hospital. I also gave him Maggie's home phone number, so he could speak with Mark Harris.

I phoned Mark to inform him of the call from the White House and for him to tell Ron Wise and Maggie's doctors to expect the call. Mark said he had already contacted someone about Maggie's condition. Information had been relayed to David Gergen at the White House that Maggie did not recognize anyone and that she was deteriorating rapidly.

Mark called me back with news that his attorney in Nevada had received a call from Mr. Dorskind, but that he (Mark) had not yet received one. The hospital apparently had given Mr. Dorskind the attorney's number.

Belle came over. We paced. Was this finally going to be the day we had waited for or was it going to be one more letdown?

At noon, Mr. Dorskind called again. President Clinton *would* award the Medal to Maggie, although he did not know exactly when it would be presented to her. He called back an hour later to say it was official, but we must wait for the White House news release.

Success!

Finally, Maggie would get her due! Belle and I cried tears of joy. Maggie would get the Presidential Medal of Freedom while she was still *alive!*

At 4:00 P.M., Jim Glenn called and asked, "Are you sitting down?" I said, "No, but I hope you know more than I already know." He had just received an official news release from the White House. Now we could tell whomever we wanted. It was *official!* Maggie would receive the Presidential Medal of Freedom. Jim faxed a copy of the press release. The next morning Mr. Dorskind faxed a copy of the citation itself.

I phoned Benita Zahn at Channel 13 WNYT-TV in Albany, the only person to put our story on television in 1989 and 1990. After the Medal was announced, newscaster Bill Lambdin of Channel 13 interviewed us.

Belle and I attended our Veterans meeting that night. We told the group "Maggie's going to get the Medal!" The council members cheered. When things quieted down, we told them what had happened since our last meeting. They were saddened by Maggie's health but elated that she was finally going to receive the Medal.

We called Ken Scharnberg at *American Legion Magazine*, Joe Bristol, Maggie's longtime friend, and Jimmy Dean at Special Forces Association. We also contacted Bob Michaels at the *Globe*, Jim Spitz in Marina, Brenda Allen in Nebraska, Dana Lynn Singfield at *The Gazette*, and many others. Jim Sharp at Channel 4, KPIC-TV, in Roseburg, Oregon, and Jane Wollman, who was then living in Santa Monica, both called the next day.

On November 4, Mark told me Maggie might lose her other leg. Her blood was not flowing properly due to arteriosclerosis. She was lucid, but unaware that the doctors had amputated her left leg. Mark told Maggie she was being awarded the Medal, although the presentation date had not yet been set. She did comprehend what Mark told her and was pleased.

Mark called to tell us an emissary from the White House would present the Medal to Maggie in her home on November 15 at 4:30 P.M.. On November 9 he called to say presentation arrangements had been made. The presenter would be Congressional Medal of Honor recipient Master Sergeant Roy Benavidez. Mark invited Bob Hope, Dorothy Lamour, Caesar Romero, Los Angeles Mayor Richard Riordan, Maggie's conservators, along with live coverage from "Entertainment Tonight." We were saddened we would not be there.

Vietnam Women's Memorial

We went to Washington with friends for the dedication of the Vietnam Women's Memorial on Veterans Day. Belle and I were treated to drinks with Hershel Gober, the Deputy Secretary of Veteran Affairs, and Brenda Allen, Maggie's friend from USO days. We had lunch with Jim Glenn, Congressman McNulty's aide, and dinner with Susan Christiansen. We were celebrating the unveiling of the Vietnam Women's Memorial as well as a successful conclusion to the Medals for Maggie campaign. Martha "Colonel Maggie" Raye was going to be honored by the President of the United States!

Washington, D.C.—1993: Belle Pellegrino, Susan Christiansen, and Noonie Fortin celebrating Maggie's receipt of the Presidential Medal of Freedom and the unveiling of the Vietnam Women's Memorial.

PMOF Presentation

Roy Benavidez called on November 14 to tell me he was making the Medal presentation to Maggie. He wondered who suggested his name and thanked me for everything I had done. I wished him a safe flight and asked that he give Maggie a hug from me.

Finally! On Monday, November 15, 1993, Martha "Colonel Maggie" Raye received the Presidential Medal of Freedom at her home in Bel Air. Master Sergeant Roy Benavidez had the honor of pinning it on her. The citation was read and presented to her by Major Leo Mercado, President Clinton's Marine Corps liaison.

I was so glad Roy was there! He was the first to endorse the Medals for Maggie committee, and he knew Maggie well. Since he was the last person to receive the Congressional Medal of Honor in 1981 (for his actions in Vietnam), it seemed so fitting that he should be the presenter of what could be the last Presidential Medal of Freedom for actions in Vietnam, as well as for Korea and World War II.

Our job was finished. The hard work, the *main* goal, finally was accomplished. But it was not over yet...

THE PRESIDENT OF THE UNITED STATES OF AMERICA
PRESENTS
THE PRESIDENTIAL MEDAL OF FREEDOM
TO
MARTHA RAYE

A talented performer whose career spans the better part of a century, Martha Raye has delighted audiences and uplifted spirits around the globe. She brought her tremendous comedic and musical skills to her work in film, stage, and television, helping to shape American entertainment. The great courage, kindness, and patriotism she showed in her many tours during World War II, the Korean Conflict, and the Vietnam Conflict earned her the nickname "Colonel Maggie." The American people honor Martha Raye, a woman who has tirelessly used her gifts to benefit the lives of her fellow Americans.

NOVEMBER 2, 1993
BILL CLINTON
PRESIDENT OF THE UNITED STATES

The Three Fighting Men

They Face The Wall

Washington, D.C.—1992

Vietnam Women's Memorial

Unveiled on Veteran's Day

Washington, D.C.—1993

The Other Side

Vietnam Women's Memorial

1993

Chapter 15

Points and Counterpoints

"She sensed my nervousness and, with her big smile, she hugged me and assured me that she had confidence in me."

Lieutenant Colonel William Russell
(Hampton, Virginia)

AWARDS AND HONORARY MEMBERSHIPS

Presidential Medal of Freedom—President Bill Clinton
Citation of Merit— National Ladies Auxiliary, Jewish War Veterans
Department of the Army—Certificate of Appreciation for Patriotic Civilian Service; Outstanding Civilian Service Award
Department of Defense, MAC-V—Certificate of Appreciation
Department of Defense—Distinguished Public Service Award
Letter of Commendation—Major General Lewis W. Walt, USMC
National Service Medal—Freedom Foundation
Armed Forces Day Award
Medal of Merit—Veterans of Foreign Wars
Woman of the Year Award—Veterans of Foreign Wars
Woman of the Year—USO
Special Award for Gallantry (twice))—USO Board of Governors
Distinguished Service Award—USO Board of Governors
First Annual Gold Heart Award—SERVE
Special Silver Helmet Award—AMVETS
Jean Hersholt Humanitarian Award—an "Oscar"
Outstanding Achievement Award—Screen Actors' Guild
The Dickie Chappel Award—Marine Corps League
The Susie Award (The Eddie Cantor Award)
Try A Little Kindness Award—Joey Bishop
The Circus Honored Saints and Sinners Award—PT Barnum Circus
Woman of the Year Award—B'nai B'rith
Entertainer of the Year —Non-Commissioned Officers Association
Award from the Association of the United States Army
Citation for Dedicated Service—American Legion
Medal of Honor—NY State Veterans Service Agency (Nassau Co.)
The Molly Pitcher Award
The Four Chaplains Award
Honorary Member—Non-Commissioned Officers Association
Honorary Woman in Air Force, Maguire Air Force Base, NJ
Honorary Flight Nurse—USAF
Honorary member—AD-Eighty-seven to Tenth ARVN
Honorary member—First Cavalry Division Assoc., Fort Hood
Honorary Lieutenant Colonel—U. S. Army Special Forces
Honorary Colonel—United States Marine Corps
Life membership—147th Fighter Group, Texas Air National Guard
Life membership—Albany Tri-Co. Council Vietnam Era Veterans

-15-

My work was far from over. So many people we had been in touch with over the past few years have become our friends. They called and wrote letters thanking us for our tenacity in pursuing the Medal for Maggie. Letters recounting personal encounters with Maggie continued to fill my mailbox. The response was overwhelming.

These letters also brought a significant body of additional primary source information, much of it included in prior chapters of this book. Several key items would have been especially helpful for evaluating aspects of our earlier Medal documentation research. In putting this book together, this additional information had been invaluable.

One of the most difficult things in writing a book of this kind is deciding what *not* to include and not to say. That is where a good publisher and editors make such tough decisions easier. Perhaps it is because they can view things from a perspective that is not as emotionally entwined with Maggie's story as mine is. This book is less than half the length of my first draft!

So, one of the Medal's first outcomes was to free me up from campaigning to shift gears into writing for publication. I had to reorganize information received earlier—but still incoming—from a *reader's* perspective. Would it be better to arrange it topically or chronologically, for example: which way would make it easier to follow Maggie's complex life as she juggled her career, her personal life, and life with her beloved troops. I had to do more research, acquire more evaluative resources.

More Good Outcomes

Through this project, some Veterans were able to locate friends or members of their old units. There were reunions for Veterans who thought friends had not survived Vietnam. Others had lost contact with their buddies when they returned to The World.

Callers wanted to be brought up to date about Maggie's health and her new husband. Many were curious about the suit Mark and Maggie had filed against Bette Midler regarding the movie *For The Boys*. Attorneys for Ms. Midler asked me to assist them in their defense. The lawsuit made its way to court in February 1994. The judge dismissed the case as without merit, stating there was no proof that this film was based on Maggie's life.

Follow-Ups from Wives

Military service members, wives, parents, and Maggie's Hollywood friends continued writing letters. Anne Sullivan of Dedham, Massachusetts admired Maggie. Although her husband Tom had written to us earlier, she felt she had to as well.

> We know that Martha Raye did not entertain the troops for recognition but because she knew how very much they needed her. When my husband served in Vietnam (his third war, second in combat) and Martha Raye appeared unannounced, I can just imagine what that did for his morale. He still claims that Vietnam was, for him, the loneliest country in the world.

Susan and Doug Chappina of Massapequa Park, New York both have fond memories of Maggie. Doug met Maggie while serving with the Fifth Special Forces in Ban Me Thout and An Loc in Vietnam. She brought both of them great comfort and support. Susan met her during

1972 in New York City when Maggie was appearing in *No, No, Nanette* on Broadway.

> We had this crazy idea to find out what time the play ended and meet—at least try to meet—Maggie at the stage door. So we hopped on the subway and carried with us numerous photos Doug had of her from Vietnam. Much to our surprise, our crazy idea worked! When Maggie came out the stage door, she was surrounded by admiring fans. We fought our way through the crowd, and she immediately recognized Doug and called him by his nickname "Chip!" She kissed him and greeted me. I couldn't believe I was standing toe to toe with THE Maggie. What happened after that was like a dream. The crowd seemed to disappear from view. In my eyes, there were only me, Doug and Maggie. She wanted to know if Doug was all right. She autographed the photo of Doug and her.

Ban Me Thout, Vietnam—Christmas 1971: Maggie with Doug Chappina. Maggie signed the original photo. Several years later Doug and his wife Sue had a copy made of it, signed it to Maggie and I delivered it to her in 1990. Photo contributed by Doug and Sue Chappina.

> She asked if we had seen the play yet. Of course, we hadn't—who had the money to see a Broadway play? She invited us to be her guests at a performance the following week. There would be two tickets waiting for us at the box office. I was very happy for Doug that she remembered him. She certainly went out of her way to place names and faces. We came to the performance and enjoyed the play because of Maggie.
>
> She also gave us her phone number while she was going to be in New York. The overall experience of meeting Maggie was overwhelming for me.

Maxine and Tom Gibbon believed Maggie deserved more recognition than any other person they could name. "She was out there pitching in and having some laughs with the guys." Tom was in the Seabees in Vietnam when he met Maggie. She called him an "ol' son of a bitch."

No One-War Stand

We heard from Veterans who served in two or three conflicts—World War II, Korea, and Vietnam—and saw Maggie more than once.

Colonel Amos Ewing of Lawton, Oklahoma first met Maggie at the 103rd General Hospital near Tidworth, England in 1945. Then in the 1960s, his unit provided electrical power for her show in Thailand. He also saw her in Vietnam when she flew out to remote firebases.

Chief Warrant Officer Thomas Sullivan of Dedham, Massachusetts saw Maggie during World War II in either North Africa or Italy. He also was in Vietnam in 1966 and 1967 when he observed an Army three-quarter ton vehicle straining through mud. It was the monsoon season.

> In the front seat sat Martha, dressed like one of us. Her visit was unannounced. She sang, clowned, and chat-

> ted to the delight of every man there in that crude shelter.
>
> She won many friends on that occasion, as she had in so many other areas of the world over many years of giving of herself.

Command Sergeant Major William Ryan of Melbourne, Florida first met Maggie in 1943 in Boston. He also saw Maggie in the European Theater during World War II but he missed her in Korea. Their paths crossed in Vietnam.

> I caught up with her during one of my tours in Vietnam. Like a dope, I asked her if she remembered the shopping incident [in Chapter Two] at South Station. Like the true "trouper" she was, she did not make me feel like a jerk. She told me that back in those earliest days, things moved so fast that she had very little memory of what happened. That was a nice way of letting me off the hook.

Bill added, "Martha never looked for or asked for glory. All she wanted to do was to help GI's get through a very difficult time by giving them a few laughs."

Major Virgil Goewey recalled seeing Maggie more than once during his tours of duty.

> I had the honor of seeing her from a distance in Korea. In Vietnam I had the distinct pleasure of meeting her twice, and not in safe places. First, I met her in a Special Forces camp, and then in mid-1966 in an advanced Marine Corps camp (Hue Phu Bai) as we were planning to expand out. She came into the tent, shook hands, and chatted jovially. That handshake will always be a treasured memory.

Sergeant Major Franklin Bryan saw Maggie in Korea sometime between March 1951 and February 1952 performing with Bob Hope, as well as on several occasions during the three and a half years he served in Vietnam.

> I know she was a definite morale booster and an inspiration to the troops. Everyone loved and admired her. She was a great lady...for her many tours to Korea and especially Vietnam. Jane Fonda could have learned a few lessons from Martha. No comparison! Martha flew around in our helicopters as if she was born to fly. Gutsy Lady!

Colonel Charles Thomann of Annapolis met Maggie three times—once in Korea and twice in Vietnam.

> The last time I saw Maggie was in a troop-carrying plane on the way to the Highlands of Vietnam. We had a nice chat, and she slept on my shoulder some of the way—obviously worn out. I've met many famous people who came to visit, but none who spent so much time with our fighting men. Most [younger soldiers] in the Vietnam Conflict weren't really sure who she was—but we let them know.
>
> They loved her. She always had a smile and a word of great encouragement—and a laugh. She would perform at the drop of a hat with anything as a stage and backdrop. All she cared about were those kids on the firebases and in the foxholes.
>
> Fame may have passed her by, but her star is still on the door.

Shortly before publication, Colonel Thomann informed us that he was now giving an annual "Maggie" award to the best drama student at Annapolis' Broadneck High School. When I read the colonel's note, it reminded me of Clayton Hough's nursing scholarship fund at a Holyoke area high school. Maggie would be so proud.

Lieutenant Colonel William Russell of Hampton, Virginia saw Maggie in all three war periods.

> I cannot hazard a count on the number of times in all three wars that I encountered this "Angel" in her tireless efforts to cheer the troops. I had an occasion in

> World War II, as a nineteen-year-old pilot, to have her on my airplane. I was a nervous wreck worrying that I might make a mistake, and we would lose a national treasure because of my flying. She sensed my nervousness and with her big smile, she hugged me and assured me that she had confidence in me. Then she immediately fell asleep to prove it!
>
> My heart went out to her in Korea and Vietnam, especially when she was exhausted but unwilling to show it.

Frontline Families

Wars are strange. Men are drafted, women volunteer. Family members often serve at the same time but rarely in the same place.

Colonel Lib told of her own experience with this family "dimension" in Vietnam. One day she happened to see her younger brother on a street in Saigon. He was a sergeant in the Army; she was in the Army Nurse Corps. She asked what he was doing there. He was preparing to go to a firebase. She said both of them could not be in-country at the same time, which was true, and that he would have to leave. He wasn't about to leave, he insisted. Colonel Lib reminded her brother that she outranked him. The next day, he was reassigned to the Philippines. He returned to Vietnam *after* his sister left the country!

Members of the same family saw Maggie. Brothers who served in different wars saw her. Master Gunnery Sergeant Charles Houts of Middletown, Rhode Island says that it wasn't until Vietnam that he met and talked with Maggie. His brother, also a career Marine, had the pleasure of meeting her years earlier in Korea.

> In 1968, I was Information Chief at the Danang Press Center when we got word that Martha Raye was going to be at the Freedom Hill Post Exchange that afternoon. Several Marine Combat Correspondents and I, along

with a group of civilian news media people, piled into a six-by and were driven to the Post Exchange.

We got there before the program started and Martha Raye was going around shaking hands with everyone. When she came to me, she stopped dead in her tracks and a huge smile lit up her face.

"Hey," she bellowed. "I knew you in Korea."

I explained that she had probably met my brother. She asked about him and seemed genuinely relieved when I told her he had retired. She ran her fingers across my name that I had stenciled on my flak jacket, and said, "You Houts boys really get around!"

I couldn't think of anything to say, but one of the civilian reporters said it for me, "*She's* the one who really gets around."

Nobody's Perfect!

Did Maggie ever have a bad day? Sure she did! Among thousands of letters and phone calls about personal encounters with her, only five people mentioned catching her on a bad day. One was a columnist who writes about celebrities for Sunday publications. He swore he would never attempt another interview with her. He even refused to write a story about her for us.

Lieutenant Colonel Carl Lillvik of Ocean, New Jersey had the opportunity to meet several entertainers while he was in Vietnam, and he talked to a number of the people who escorted them around. His unit was the Fifteenth Supply and Service Battalion, First Cavalry Division headquartered at An Khe in the fall of 1967 commanded by Lieutenant Colonel Robert Vaughn.

The commander volunteered to provide facilities for Martha Raye and her *Hello, Dolly!* troupe when they came to the area to do their USO show. I had been an escort officer for a small USO show a few months prior so I got the job to make the internal arrangements for billets and messing for the young men and women of the show. The troupe arrived at the battalion by two and a half ton trucks about 1600 hours, were assigned to their rooms and invited to attend a cocktail party in their—really in you know who's—honor in the officer's club.

While the troupe was talking to the officers and men of the battalion in the club—the enlisted men had been invited to be there between certain hours—Martha Raye was naturally surrounded by the battalion hierarchy and me, the action guy. She drank straight vodka on the rocks. Several. When she wanted a refill after taking her last gulp, she would say, "Get me another one!" Which I, or the Battalion Commander, got for her. Pushy and demanding! No "thank you," "please," or "excuse me." She didn't even attempt to join her troupe talking with the enlisted men.

One of the male performers stayed in my hooch and gave a similar opinion of her attitude as he had seen it. Apparently she was also a tough task master. He said the rules were very rigid and she enforced them. I have no problem with that. She could not move around Vietnam with a group of people like that without having rules.

My real view of Martha Raye is that she cared more for what she got out of supporting the troops than she cared about what she was giving them! I've seen Bob Hope on three occasions. The first in 1962 at Bupyong'dong, Korea—his first show of the Korean tour and it was terrible! But the man got out and made himself accessible and the troops loved him for it. Martha Raye ain't no Bob Hope!

Clifford James of Memphis was stationed aboard the USS *Repose* in 1967 through 1968 at Danang. He was in charge of triage. He recalled getting Maggie upset.

The Colonel [Maggie] was in the mess deck doing a short skit, which I caught at the conclusion. I walked up to her and said the wrong thing right away, "Miss Raye, I have laughed at you ever since I was a kid." I was, at

> that time, forty-four years old. She gave me a look that would cower a tough Drill Instructor and said something to the effect, "You S.O.B." She spun around and took off. I realized then I had committed the grave sin of dating her [age].

Bill Baril of Copperas Cove, Texas is a retired Army Master Sergeant now working at Fort Hood. He met Maggie while stationed in Vietnam. Bill was assigned to the Fifty-fourth Otter Company (Detachment One) in Can Tho in the Delta region during 1967. He was the Maintenance and Operations Chief of the detachment that flew Maggie on three missions. Among the sites they visited in the Delta were Dong Tam and Rach Gia. They also flew her to Saigon and Vung Tau. Bill said Maggie complained that the Otter had only one engine. She preferred twin engine planes, in case one engine stopped functioning. She also complained about the Otter's size and its cleanliness. Bill took offense because the craft's condition was his people's responsibility, and they did their best under the circumstances. He pointed out to her that a single engine plane is probably no more dangerous than a helicopter, and there were many places the Otter could fly to—and land—that other planes could not.

Special Forces arranged for Maggie to go to most places by whatever means were available at the time including jeeps, Otters, helicopters, C-130's, and almost any other vehicle that traveled by ground or air. When the USO sent her anywhere, they managed her arrangements; but when Maggie went on her own, she and Special Forces handled everything.

We all have bad days...even Maggie!

But overwhelming evidence shows that such days were rare for her. Who knows what had happened just prior to the few negative encounters reported to us, whether it could have been an insult or bad news from her stateside relationships or career? Maggie kept stretching herself to the limit on her trips to visit the troops, beyond the physical and emotional energy thresholds most of us have.

What surprised us in the massive amount of correspondence was that so few people exhibited the cynicism so many harbor about famous celebrities' *real* motives for their humanitarian acts.

Terms of Endearment

Chiefly through others, I came to know Maggie as though she were a member of my own family. The more letters I read and conversations I had with people about their personal encounters with Maggie, the more endearing she became. When I talked with Maggie on the phone or sat for hours in her Team Room listening as she reflected on her life with her troops, her stories moved me.

Maggie was a complex person. She did not want to talk much about her professional career, other than to say, "It paid the bills." Neither did she want to discuss her personal life, and we respected her wishes. She asked me to write the truth about her, and that is what I have done to the best of my knowledge.

But, There Were Discrepancies

After the medal presentation, we began finding some discrepancies between some letter writers' perceptions of Maggie—of her awards, especially—and what "official" records show.

Every detail in the stories sent to us was taken at face value...until some points did not check out. This section is a painful one to write because parts may disappoint some of her troops and burst a bubble or two about her larger-than-life *persona*.

After receiving so many letters about Maggie's exploits, we sought to verify some of those stories. Maggie had given me her Social Security number and her Service Number for her Dog Tags, which made our task somewhat easier. All Army personnel records are stored in St. Louis, and we began checking with the Army Personnel Center there, with the Department of the Army in Washington, and the Army Nurse Corps in San Antonio. There is no record of Maggie ever serving in the regular Army, the Army Reserves, or the Army Nurse Corps. Maggie confirmed this in later conversations.

This made stories about her that much more intriguing since our correspondents were so sure she was "one of us." Considering her rotation between her stateside career and time with the troops, it is inconceivable that she could have been regular military! Perhaps some assumed she was, from an earlier war.

We also received a letter from a retired Army Nurse Corps colonel, a Veteran of World War II, Korea, and Vietnam. She was a Chief of the Army Nurse Corps in the 1960s. She had checked into Maggie's credentials.

> This subject of verification as to whether Martha Raye was a professional nurse was pursued by me with her husband and family during the Vietnam War. The truth is that she has never completed a program in Nursing Education or received a licensure by requirement to practice Nursing. These facts were conveyed to the Chief of Staff and the U.S. Army-Vietnam staff in 1963 and 1964.
>
> According to her husband, she spent a few days one time observing in a hospital in order to play a part in a movie but never in a School of Nursing. As you well know, a requirement for appointment and commissioning in the U.S. Army Nurse Corps is that an individual must have completed a program in Nursing Education and be registered to practice Professional Nursing in a state or territory of the United States.

> Miss Martha Raye was an entertainer during the Korean War as well as World War II and in Vietnam. The rank of honorary Lieutenant Colonel was conferred upon her by someone; we were never informed of the author or procedure used.
>
> I have no feelings personally as to honors for Miss Raye but wanted to set the record straight. She did not administer to soldiers medically in Korea. As you know in the provisions of the Geneva Convention individuals not qualified cannot perform the duties of those qualified.
>
> I trust that I have clarified the fact that Miss Martha Raye was not a professional Nurse, nor did she perform such assignments in Korea, as I was Chief Nurse of the Far East Command.

Maggie had, indeed, received nurse's aide training at Los Angeles' Cedars of Lebanon Hospital where she volunteered her time. Dr. Sam Patton of Georgia saw her working there in that capacity. When I visited with Maggie in 1990 and again in 1991, she reiterated to me that she had been trained as a nurse's aide, but regretted she had never been able to complete training required to make her a licensed professional nurse. The soldiers she treated and the doctors who worked with her in Vietnam believed she was a nurse and Maggie said, "That's all that mattered."

One also must note, however, that states' formal licensing of *professional* nurses did not begin until the mid-1940s. For example, New York's first state exam to qualify Registered Nurses was conducted in 1945. Even today, in many states the title of "nurse" is an umbrella over a wide range of skill and educational levels.

In battlefield emergency settings where somebody *acts* like a nurse, *performs* like a nurse, *assists* harried medical professionals like a nurse, eyewitnesses are likely to regard her as a nurse—professional or not. To our knowledge, no one heard Maggie claim she was a *professional* nurse. She knew her way around an operating room in battlefield conditions and was able to assist with the wounded. That is a fully-confirmed fact.

Maggie's compassionate heart coupled with her formidable nursing skills, dedication, and experience probably exceeded those of some medics with more formal training. Even though she was a celebrity, she was willing to get her hands bloody, empty bedpans, clean up vomit, donate needed blood, and work hours on end to free up medical professionals for fuller use of their skills.

The stories of her exploits throughout World War II, Korea, and Vietnam are endearing and have helped make her a legend for those who assumed she had to be "Army." Because she related so well to them, she just had to be "one of us."

Myth and Reality

What little there was in print about Maggie often contradicted itself. Service personnel also relayed sometimes conflicting stories.

Myth: She *was* in the regular military—
Reality: No, she was *not*.

Myth: She *was* a real lieutenant colonel—
Reality: She was an *honorary* Lieutenant Colonel. Maggie told me she was not a "real" lieutenant colonel. Although she wasn't an "official" officer, her admirers felt she deserved her honorary military titles.

Myth: She was a *professional* nurse—
Reality: She was a nurse's *aide* in battlefield emergencies.

Myth: She was wounded—Many people wrote that Maggie had been wounded at least twice in Vietnam. This also appeared in several publications.
Reality: Maggie told us she never was wounded. She showed me her feet, ribs, and lower back to prove it.

(No, she did not display her buttocks!) There were no visible scars, except from the surgery done on her shoulder in June 1991. Both Ann Boddington, Maggie's former secretary and good friend, and Melodye, Maggie's daughter, said she had not been wounded.

It is quite possible that she sustained injuries in Vietnam, even that she was hit by shrapnel. But, given Maggie's nature and skills, it is also quite possible that such wounds either were not serious enough to report or were self-treatable by Maggie herself.

Myth: She received two Purple Hearts—

Reality: I could find no verification. Reportedly, Special Forces personnel presented her with two Purple Hearts. I saw no evidence of Purple Heart medals or their certificates displayed in her Team Room where she proudly displayed all of her military memorabilia

Myth: She was a full-fledged paratrooper, having jumped five times—

Reality: Maggie told me she wasn't a paratrooper. There is no reliable record she parachuted out of an airplane or helicopter. Some risky leaps from hovering choppers—yes!

Myth: Reported, but not confirmed—Maggie was given an honorary battlefield commission in 1964 before it became official in 1967.

Reality: She wore her uniforms with deepest pride and respect, especially her Green Beret...

Another reality: Maggie voluntarily spent over two years in battle zones of Vietnam.

Mythmaking

There are significant discrepancies regarding actual honors and titles bestowed upon Maggie. Myths sometimes surround a legend—especially someone as complex, caring, and brave as Maggie. One soldier "heard that Maggie..." and he passes it along. The rumor takes on the status of an assumed "fact." No deceit is intended. But, *why* does this happen?

The original root word for "myth" means the *significance* of an experience or event. A common thread woven through so many—if not most—letters we received is how significant their one-on-one experiences with Maggie were for troops in Vietnam. In the midst of their life "at the extreme" in Vietnam, she embodied The World with these troops for a few face-to-face moments or hours. The World of Mother, Sister, Aunt, Friend was there with them—as Maggie.

Each individual recognized how meaningful that encounter was for him or her. And so, when word was heard of a larger recognition of Maggie, that soldier or nurse was quite likely to welcome it and cherish the news because it "fit" their own experience with her. The medal, honor, or rank was also fitting because she or he felt Maggie *deserved* it.

Apparent discrepancies were limited to a small number of rumored honors and titles—few among dozens that are verified. With the probable exception of an airborne parachute jump, her exploits, travels, and contacts described in this book are confirmed.

Medals and Awards

Lieutenant Colonel Chuck Darnell (Retired from Special Forces) of Charlotte, North Carolina has been particularly helpful in our information-gathering efforts. Shortly after Maggie's stroke, he drew up an unofficial and partial list of her medals, citations, campaigns, titles, and awards.

Some he had seen cited in newsletters, some mentioned by military colleagues, and he has firsthand knowledge of several items on the list. Since so many of our Veterans referred to them in their letters, we went to work sorting out reality from rumor. We discovered that Maggie actually received most, but not all, of these items Chuck listed:

Medals—Bronze Star, Purple Heart with one Oak Leaf Cluster, Vietnam Service Medal, Vietnam Campaign Medal, Nurse Combat Medal, National Defense Medal, and Department of Defense Distinguished Public Service Medal.

Citations—Republic of Vietnam Presidential Unit Citation, and General William C. Westmoreland Citation.

Campaigns—Ia Drang Valley Operation and Tet Offensive 1968.

Titles—Honorary Colonel US Marine Corps and permanent rank of Lieutenant Colonel US Army Special Forces.

Awards—USO Distinguished Service Award 2/13/87.

We received many reports of Maggie receiving several *military* awards, but we were unable to locate documents to substantiate them.

All Maggie's awards received from the United States government were well documented. All were *civilian* citations, including those given her by the Departments of the Army and Defense and by the President of the United States. They were proudly displayed on the walls of her Team Room. If reported military awards actually exist, one would think they would have been displayed as well.

According to information I gathered from the Army Regulation 670-20, Incentive Awards, Maggie was eligible to receive some—but not all—of the above awards.

Whether Maggie served in the regular military or not, whether she was a professional nurse or not, and whether she was actually wounded or not does not really matter. The troops she saw and cared for made the larger-than-life legend of "Colonel Maggie" real to all of us.

Many people have asked me what took so long for our nation to honor Maggie properly. Let's not overlook the numerous awards and citations she received from the Defense Department, military leaders, and from national organizations that were very dear to her. She had received congratulatory letters from several Presidents. As Susan Christiansen suggests in her Introduction, perhaps authorities assumed she had already received a Presidential Medal of Freedom.

Bruce Jones provided documentation that he wrote to every President about Maggie since he returned from Vietnam, beginning in February 1969. Bruce may be the first Veteran or citizen to request that she be honored with the PMOF. Others sent us documents showing they had contacted Presidents Nixon, Ford, Carter, and Reagan to urge them to honor Maggie with the Presidential Medal of Freedom—*prior* to our project's efforts with Presidents Bush and Clinton.

Throughout President Reagan's tenure in the Oval Office, the Special Forces Association worked diligently in an effort to have Maggie honored with the PMOF. I began researching in 1987, and our committee's quest to have her so honored moved in earnest from 1989 on. Why did it take so long—thirteen years of organized grassroots effort—to get her the PMOF?

I don't have that answer!

Maggie's devotion to the troops could never be questioned. Her bravery and actions spoke louder than any awards, titles, or medals. Her generous heart moved her to open herself and her home to thousands of Veterans. Usually traveling at her own expense, she put her money where her big mouth was. She kept right on giving until deteriorating health forced her to stop. Maggie repeatedly put her life on the line, like any combat Veteran. But she was there by her own choice, voluntarily.

Strokes Had Taken a Toll

By 1991 the strokes had left Maggie debilitated. Friends seldom came by. She had become reclusive, venturing out of her home only for Veterans' functions. Many Veterans thought she wanted to be left alone to recuperate from her strokes. But Maggie missed them and wondered where they were when she needed them.

One factor may have been that within six months after her last marriage, Maggie's phone number had been changed, cutting her off from thousands of Vets who had used it over the years. Maggie was upset about this. She also wondered why she was not getting any mail from her Vets. Although she seldom answered mail after her first stroke in January 1990, she still enjoyed receiving it. She would read letters and cards from her Vets over and over.

Maggie would pick up her phone to call them just to keep in contact with her Vets. Sergeant First Class Kenneth Plante, Sr. of Baltimore was one of her Veterans who could no longer reach Maggie.

> I was with Maggie in Germany in 1969, and she also was at our camp in Long Hai, Vietnam in December of 1970. I corresponded with Maggie for over twenty-some years. I last saw her at the Special Forces Convention in Fort Bragg in 1988. I have written her several times over the past couple of years but haven't received an answer. Since she remarried in 1991, it seems she has been cut off from all of her old acquaintances.

What a gifted woman Maggie was! Her keen memory for names, faces, and places underscores a genuine interest and caring for people. So many of our correspondents marveled at her stunning memory for individual troops she had met. We tend to have the best memory for what we care deeply about. But, along with her passionate interest in the troops, what also endeared her to them was her spontaneity, lack of pretense, her bizarre sense of humor, her ability to act, sing, dance, and to love. All these talents and gifts were packed into one five-foot three-inch lady with a mouth that went from ear to ear and legs that seemed to reach up to her armpits.

Maggie was part myth, part legend, part reality. She was no pulp-fiction Pollyanna saint! But it may be sufficient to note that her mission with our troops has much in common with the complex lives of many "certified" saints throughout centuries past.

Chapter 16

Final Tribute

"Nobody contributed more of herself than that wonderful, generous woman."

—General Westmoreland

Previous page: *Fort Bragg, North Carolina—1994: Members of Special Forces carry Maggie to her final resting place. Photo contributed by Belle Pellegrino.*

Above: *Vietnam: Maggie visiting troops at an unknown outpost. Photo contributed by Charles Worman, curator, USAF Museum, Wright-Patterson AFB, Dayton, Ohio.*

-16-

Martha "Colonel Maggie" Raye passed away Wednesday, October 19, 1994, at Cedars-Sinai Medical Center in Los Angeles. The official cause of death was aspiration pneumonia due to multi-cerebral infarction and arteriosclerosis. She was seventy-eight years old and alone at the time of her death. Melodye tried to visit her mother in the hospital but orders were left she not be allowed in.

Maggie had once said of herself, "To be a clown is a gift." As much as she loved singing and dancing, Maggie enjoyed comedy more. When Bob Hope heard of her death, he said, "She was always bigger than life and will be missed." It is doubtful, however, that Hollywood will miss her as much as the Veterans of our country do.

The commercial press ran only one wire service article about her death and funeral. This was not the case with Veterans' publications! So many of them lifted up her life and its meaning for the Veterans.

It was Maggie's wish to be buried among "her troops" at Fort Bragg. Special arrangements had to be made long before to have her wish honored. Cemeteries at military installations normally are for Veterans and their families. Military cemetery burial of other civilians is not authorized.

Although Maggie was married at the time, once the hospital released her remains, the Army took over. There was a constant honor guard with her body from then on. A memorial service was held at Pierce Brothers Mollar-Murphy Mortuary in Santa Monica on Thursday evening. Among the mourners were comedienne RoseMarie; actors Red Buttons, Ann Jeffries, and Margaret O'Brien; and A.C. Lyles from Metro-Goldwyn-Mayer.

On Friday, following arrangements made by the Westwood Village Mortuary, Maggie's remains were flown from Los Angeles to Raleigh-Durham. The casket was met by the staff of Rogers and Breece Funeral Home and escorted by members of the Seventh Special Forces Group, then driven to Fayetteville.

Late Again…

Maggie was still running on "Maggie Time." During her travels visiting the troops, she could not be rushed. She stayed true to form even in death. The plane carrying Maggie's remains to Raleigh-Durham was delayed by weather. The wake, which was scheduled to start at five P.M., did not. Her remains finally arrived at seven P.M..

The Rogers and Breece Funeral Home was packed with Maggie's friends, soldiers, and flowers. Belle had flown down from New York, and I came from Texas. Many others came from all over the country to pay their last respects to this special lady.

The John F. Kennedy Special Warfare Museum staff had set up a display case with some of her momentos and photos. Flower arrangements from Veterans organizations and individuals were spread throughout the funeral parlor. There was a beautiful spray of flowers from singer Rosemary Clooney—the only Hollywood person to send flowers—and one from our own Veterans group in Albany.

Mark was there with one of his children, Stephanie. He said Maggie wanted to be buried with a Catholic ceremony but also to honor several of Mark's Jewish customs—a quick burial and a plain pine coffin. He told everyone to remember that Maggie was still a Hollywood star and beautiful; he then invited everyone to view her remains for the last time.

She wore a plain Army green dress uniform with no medals or name plate. If it were not for the Green Beret on her head, I would not have known it was Maggie.

Anthea "Dee" Gregory of Stedman, North Carolina asked Mark if she could put a small bottle of vodka in the casket. She remembered how much Maggie enjoyed vodka and said it was her send-off gift. Mark let her place it between Maggie's hands. Later, Dee told me a story about an evening during the 1980s when she was having dinner at a restaurant with Maggie.

> A woman approached our table. Maggie got that "you invaded my space look." The woman asked if she was Martha Raye. When she said that her husband knew Maggie in Vietnam, Maggie came out of herself and relaxed. When the woman told Maggie who her husband was, Maggie proceeded to tell her that she had been with him, told her how brave he had been. She knew about his death and explained how he had died honorably.
>
> Maggie's memory was awesome. The woman thanked Maggie profusely saying the government never told her what exactly happened—only that he had been killed in action. The woman left the table, sort of floating on air, knowing more than she had before and thankful that she had the chance to meet the woman her husband had told her so much about—Maggie.

Melodye flew in from California with her late father's sister-in-law, Lorraine Condos. They arrived at the funeral home after the casket was closed. She never got to see her mother's remains before burial. Cameras and reporters were not allowed inside the funeral home; however, they were waiting outside as people left.

Burial, With Honor

Saturday morning, Martha "Colonel Maggie" Raye was buried on a hillside among "her troops"—Veterans of World War II, Korea, and Vietnam. Melodye was there, accompanied by her Aunt Lorraine and three Special Forces officers. They were seated some distance from the head of the grave site. Melodye was unaware that she also had three bodyguards in civilian clothes, wearing bullet-proof vests and Secret Service ear and mouth pieces. Mark, his daughter Stephanie, and others sat at the graveside. There were hundreds of mourners at Maggie's burial. One was Joe Bristol from Michigan who had written us about his relationship with Maggie.

Maggie got her wish for a Catholic service. Actually, it was ecumenical. As the Eighty-second Airborne Division Band played "America the Beautiful," members of the Seventh Special Forces Group carried Maggie's flag-covered coffin to her final resting place. Members of the Special Forces Association stood at attention, saluting her coffin as it passed through their honorary pallbearers' line.

A Roman Catholic Chaplain began the service and presented a brief tribute to her. The band then played "Battle Hymn of the Republic." A Protestant Chaplain, Tom Mitchiner, continued the service and gave his tribute. When the band played "Ballad of the Green Berets," few dry eyes could be seen. A Jewish Chaplain continued the service and gave his tribute. The band played "Mr. Paganini," Maggie's theme song, to commemorate her Hollywood career. A lone piper played "Amazing Grace" as the Green Berets carefully folded the coffin flag. As the flag was handed to Mark, the Catholic Chaplain ended the service.

There was no bugler playing *Taps;* no firing squad shooting volleys. Those honors are for Armed Forces Veterans. Although she served her country through three war periods and peacetime, "her troops" gave their beloved Civilian the best send-off they could.

Maggie's troops stood in silence all around the hillside. They moved away slowly, visibly wanting to linger longer. As they passed her coffin for the last time, most—like Belle, Joe, and me—snapped to attention and gave her a final farewell salute.

The press was there too; however, they were kept away until after the ceremony. They were set up on a flatbed trailer outside the cemetery fence by the Randolph Street gate. When the ceremony concluded, they moved in for close-up photographs of the grave site and to interview people.

The world had lost Maggie, but for many Veterans of our country, her memory will live on forever. It will for me.

About a month after Maggie's funeral, I received a phone call from Melodye. She of all people knew what Maggie had given up to be with the troops. She thanked me for helping get her mother honored. She said that even though she knew how much the Special Forces loved her mother, she was overwhelmed by their final tribute to Maggie. While she and Maggie had differences over the years, she made it clear that she loved her mother very much and will miss her greatly.

Melodye said that the information throughout this book needed to be published to help its readers know just how much Maggie loved her Veterans and how much they loved her. She offered to help in any way and gave me her permission to gather relevant information about Maggie's life.

One theme ran throughout letters and personal conversations we had with people: what might have seemed an insignificant moment with Maggie meant so much to each person, including people who remembered encounters with Maggie way back in the 1930s and 1940s. The messages showed Maggie's compassion for people. After our trip to the 1990 Drop-In, Belle wrote the following paragraph, which summed up how we felt then and now.

> "Her troops" don't just *like* her. They truly *love* this special lady. As we spoke with Vets from all eras, their combat-hardened eyes filled with tears as they spoke of their Colonel Maggie. Tears of love, devotion,

adoration, and dedication to her, for her. From the young Sergeant, a Veteran of Panama, to the older Lieutenant Colonel Lou Millette, recipient of the Congressional Medal of Honor and Veteran of World War II—they all *love* the lady.

Maggie epitomized her favorite President's challenge to all Americans long before he made his now famous inaugural speech. She truly lived out President John F. Kennedy's words, "Ask not what your country can do for you, ask what you can do for your country."

I am thankful that I got to know Maggie, although it was too near her life's end. She was truly a great woman whose friendship profoundly enriched my life. Her memory will be blessed forever in the hearts and minds of so many Veterans—and their families!.

BLESS YOU, COLONEL MAGGIE!

Fort Bragg photo contributed by John Forde, Jr.

Appendixes, Glossary, and Bibliography

APPENDIX A—RADIO

1931-1935: The Chase and Sanborn Hour with Eddie Cantor
1934: The Bob Hope Pepsodent Show
1935: The Rudy Vallee Show
1935-1939: The Eddie Cantor Pabst Blue Ribbon Show
1936: The Edgar Bergen and Charlie McCarthy Show
1936-1939: Al Jolson's Show
1939: The Tuesday Night Party
1940-1949: The Eddie Cantor Show

APPENDIX B—MOVIES

1936: *Rhythm on the Range*—Paramount
College Holiday—Paramount
Big Broadcast of 1937—Paramount
Hideaway Girl—Paramount
1937: *Artists and Models*—Paramount
Double or Nothing—Paramount
Waikiki Wedding—Paramount
Mountain Music—Paramount
1938: *College Swing*—Paramount
Give me a Sailor—Paramount
Big Broadcast of 1938—Paramount
Tropic Holiday—Paramount
1939: *Never Say Die*—Paramount
$1000 a Touchdown—Paramount
1940: *The Farmer's Daughter*—Paramount
The Boys from Syracuse—Universal
1941: *Navy Blues*—Warner Brothers
Keep 'Em Flying—Universal
Hellzapoppin—Universal
1944: *Four Jills in a Jeep*—Twentieth-Century Fox
Pin-Up Girl—Twentieth-Century Fox
1947: *Monsieur Verdoux*—United Artists
1962: *Billy Rose's Jumbo*—Metro-Goldwyn-Mayer
1970: *The Phynx*—Warner Brothers
Pufnstuf—Universal
1979: *The Concorde: Airport'79*—Universal

APPENDIX C—TV SHOWS

1948-1953:	The Texaco Star Theater
1950-1955 & 1967:	The Colgate Comedy Hour
10/2/50:	Anything Goes
1951-1953:	The All-Star Revue
10/12/52:	The Bob Hope Show
1953-1956:	The Martha Raye Show
9/22/53-6/70:	The Red Skelton Show
12/13/54:	Dateline, Hollywood
2/27/55:	The Big Time
9/25/55-6/6/71:	The Ed Sullivan Show
1958:	The Steve Allen Show
2/58:	WABD-TV, NYC Telethon
2/59:	WNEW-TV, NYC Telethon
1959-1960:	The Big Party
4/14/63:	The Bob Hope Show
10/25/63:	The Bob Hope Show
1964-1970:	The Hollywood Palace
4/17/64:	The Bob Hope Show
11/3/65:	The Bob Hope Show
11/8/65:	The Comics
1966:	The Mike Douglas Show
11/9/66:	Clown Alley
1967:	Dateline, Hollywood
8/67:	The Jerry Lewis Show
9/11/67:	The Carol Burnett Show
1968-1975:	The Milton Berle Show
2/4/69:	The Joey Bishop Show
2/17/69:	The Bob Hope Show
1970:	The Lucille Ball Show
9/12/70-9/2/72:	The Bugaloos
10/5/70:	The Bob Hope Show
9/13/71:	The Bob Hope Show
1976:	Steve Allen's Laughback; also McMillan and Wife
12/5/76-8/21/77:	McMillan
3/20/77:	Bing!...A 50th Anniversary Gala
12/18/79:	Skinflint
1980's:	The Love Boat
1982-1984:	Alice
12/5/82:	Circus of the Stars
3/2/83:	Bob Hope Special: Bob Hope's Road to Hollywood

TV MOVIES

3/21/80:	*The Gossip Columist*
12/9/85:	*Alice in Wonderland*

APPENDIX D—RECORDS and ALBUMS

10/6/32—I Heard
  How'm I Doin'
5/27/39—Brunswick Label:
  Stairway to the Stars
  Ol' Man River
  If You Can't Sing It, You'll Have to Swing It (Mr. Paganini)
  Melancholy Mood
9/17/39—Columbia Label:
  Jeannie with the Light Brown Hair
  Body and Soul
  It Ain't Necessarily So
  I Walk Alone
10/8/39—Columbia Label:
  Once in a While
  Yesterdays
  Gone with the Wind
  Peter, Peter, Pumpkin Eater
3/20/42—Decca Label:
  Pig Foot Pete
  My Little Cousin
  Three Little Sisters
  Oh! The Pity of it All
Discovery Label:
  Ooh, Doctor Kinsey!
  After You've Gone
  Miss Otis Regrets
  Life's Only Joy
Mercury Label:
  Blues in the Night
  Close to Me
  That Old Black Magic
  Wolf Boy

ALBUMS

1951—Discovery Label: Martha Raye Sings
1954—Epic Label: Here's Martha Raye
1962—Columbia Label: Movie soundtrack, *JUMBO*
1969—Tetragrammaton: Together For The First Time [with Carol Burnett]

APPENDIX E—STAGE PERFORMANCES

Chez Paree, Chicago, IL
Loew's State Theater, New York City, NY
The Hollywood, Broadway, New York City, NY: *Calling All Stars*
Casino de Paris, New York City, NY
Casanova Cafe
Ben Mardene Riviera, Fort Lee, NJ
Winter Garden Theater, New York City, NY: *Sketch Book*
The Trocadero, Hollywood, CA
The Famous Door, Los Angeles, CA
Shubert Theater, Detroit, MI
Paramount, New York City, NY
Metropolitan Theater, Boston, MA
Faye's Theater, Providence, RI
Palace Theater, Albany, NY
Loew's State Theater, New York City: *Hold On To Your Hats*
RKO Theater, Boston, MA
Palace Theater, Albany, NY
The Palladium, London, England
Hotel Capitol, New York City, NY
Five O'Clock Club, Miami, FL
The Big Red Barn, Miami, FL: *Annie Get Your Gun*
500 Club, Atlantic City, NJ
Town & Country, Brooklyn, NY
Copacabana, New York City, NY
City Center, New York City: *Annie Get Your Gun*
Drury Lane, Chicago, IL: *The Solid Gold Cadillac*
Sombrero Playhouse, Phoenix: *Personal Appearance; Separate Rooms*
Pittsburgh Light Opera House, Pittsburgh, PA: *Calamity Jane*
Westbury Music Festival, Long Island, NY: *Wildcat; Call Me Madam!*
St. James Theater, New York City: *Hello, Dolly!*
Mill Run Playhouse, IL: *Goodbye Charlie*
Flint, MI: *Little Orphan Annie*
Chicago, IL: *Everybody Loves Opal*
Colonie Summer Theater, Colonie, NY: *Hello Sucker*
Storrowton Summer Theater, Springfield, MA: *Hello Sucker*
Shamrock Hotel, Houston, TX
Minsky's Burlesque Theater, Newark, NJ
The 46th Street Theater, New York City, NY: *No, No, Nanette*
Sardi's Dinner Theater, Franklin Square, NY: *Everybody Loves Opal*
Hamilton Place Theater, Ontario, Canada: *Pippin*
Colonie Summer Theater, Colonie, NY: *4 Girls 4*
Sahara Hotel, Las Vegas, NV: *The New 4 Girls*
Cal-Neva Lodge, Reno, NV: *The New 4 Girls*
Storrowton Summer Theater, Springfield, MA:*The New 4 Girls*
Dallas, TX: *The New 4 Girls*
Fort Bragg, NC: *The New 4 Girls*

APPENDIX F—
AWARDS AND HONORARY MEMBERSHIPS

The Susie Award (The Eddie Cantor Award): 1935-1939

Letter of Commendation—Major General Lewis W. Walt, USMC: 12/16/65

Citation of Merit—National Ladies Auxiliary of the Jewish War Veterans: 8/24/66

Department of the Army—Certificate of Appreciation for Patriotic Civilian Service; General William Westmoreland: 11/9/66

Department of Defense, MAC-V—Certificate of Appreciation; General William Westmoreland: 1/28/67

Woman of the Year—United Services Organization: 5/67

National Service Medal—Freedom Foundation: 1967

The Dickie Chappel Award—Marine Corps League: 1967

Woman of the Year Award—Veterans of Foreign Wars: 1967

Life Membership—147th Fighter Group, Texas Air National Guard: 2/12/68

Special Award for Gallantry—United Services Organization, Board of Governors: 3/68

Jean Hersholt Humanitarian Award—the Academy of Motion Picture Arts and Sciences (Oscar): 1968

Citation for Dedicated Service—the American Legion: 3/26/68

Armed Forces Day Award: 5/18/68

The Circus Honored Saints and Sinners Award—PT Barnum Circus: 9/68

Woman of the Year Award—B'nai B'rith: 1968

Try A Little Kindness Award—Joey Bishop Show: 2/4/69

First Annual Gold Heart Award—Servicemen's Emergency Recreational Volunteer Events, Inc (SERVE): 2/23/69

Honorary Woman in the Air Force—Maguire Air Force Base, New Jersey: 6/69

Department of the Army, Outstanding Civilian Service Award for period 24 October 68 to 7 January 69—General Creighton Abrams

Honorary Flight Nurse, United States Air Force—Lieutenant General K.E. Pletcher, Surgeon General: 1969

Special Silver Helmet Award—AMVETS: 4/70

Special Award for Gallantry (second time)— United Services Organization, Board of Governors: 3/25/71

Honorary Non-Commissioned Officer—NCO Association: 9/6/71

Award from the Association of the United States Army:10/25/71

Outstanding Achievement Award—Screen Actors Guild: 11/19/73

Medal of Merit—Veterans of Foreign Wars: 8/18/80

Department of Defense, Distinguished Public Service—Secretary of Defense Casper Weinberger: 4/86

Distinguished Service Award—United Services Organization, Board of Governors: 2/23/87

Medal of Honor—New York State Veterans Service Agency, Nassau County: 8/24/91
Presidential Medal of Freedom—President Bill Clinton: 11/2/93

OTHERS:
Entertainer of the Year—Non-Commissioned Officer Association
The Molly Pitcher Award
The Four Chaplains Award
Life membership—Tri-County Council Vietnam Era Veterans, Albany, New York
Honorary member of AD-87 to Tenth ARVN Division
Honorary member—First Cavalry Division Association, Fort Hood, Texas
Honorary Lieutenant Colonel—U. S. Army Special Forces (Green Berets)
Honorary Colonel—the United States Marine Corps

BACK COVER PICTURE CREDITS

Author's photo: Photowave Studio, Killeen, TX

GLOSSARY

ABC: American Broadcasting Company
Airdrome: landing field for airplanes; airport
AMEDD: Army Medical Department
AR: Army Regulation
Barracks: a building(s) for lodging soldiers; living quarters
Base camp: also known as the rear area; a resupply base for field units and a location for headquarters units, artillery batteries, and airfields
Billets: assigned lodging or living quarters
Bird: chopper; helicopter; colonel
B-rations: canned non-perishable foods that are heated in a field environment or mess hall for consumption
Cantonment: quartering area for troops
CBS: Columbia Broadcasting System
Chaplain: a member of the clergy attached to a military unit
Chopper: helicopter
CP: Command Post
C-rations: combat rations; preserved meals to eat in the field
Crappers: slang for toilet; also latrine
Debridement: cleaning of wounds
Disembark: to go ashore from a ship or airplane
DMZ: Demilitarized Zone; dividing line between North and South Vietnam established in 1954 by Geneva Convention; also divides North and South Korea
Dispensary: military aid station located at smaller bases and firebases; provided first aid treatment; manned by field medics
Dustoff: medical evacuation by helicopter; also called medevac
Ensign: the lowest commissioned rank in the U.S. Navy
Flagged: declined in interest
Flak jacket: a heavy fiber-filled vest designed to protect soldiers from shrapnel wounds
Front lines: where the majority of the fighting action is; in Vietnam there were no real front lines, battles erupted almost everywhere
GI: General Inductee; soldier in U.S. Army; also government issue
Green Berets: a highly trained and specialized corps in the U.S. Army, usually assigned to especially hazardous roles; the name refers to their distinctive uniform hat
Group: combined into a unit; more than two
Grunts: lowest ranked foot soldiers; infantrymen in ground combat units of the Army and Marine Corps
HCR: House Concurrent Resolution
Highline: mode of transportation between two Navy vessels while at sea; ropes are strung between two ships from which a chair hangs; the ropes are operated much like a clothesline

Hootch: also spelled hooch; a rural Vietnam hut or simple dwelling
Hot Landing Zone: a landing zone under enemy fire
Hot pad: area for planes or helicopters to wait while on alert status
Huey: nickname for the UH-1 series helicopters
I Corps, II Corps, III Corps, IV Corps: four military regions into which South Vietnam was divided, with I Corps the northernmost region, and IV Corps the southernmost (Mekong Delta)
In-country: serving within geographic Vietnam
Infiltration route: the route followed by soldiers to penetrate the enemy's line in order to assemble behind the enemy position
Interdiction: an action to divert, disrupt, delay or destroy the enemy's surface military potential before it can be used effectively against friendly forces
Jungle rot: raw open sores in the crotch and inner thighs
Khakies: yellowish-brown colored uniform
Kilometer: a unit of length equal to 1000 meters, 6/10 mile, 3280 feet or 1090 yards; ballistic measurement of distance used for map distances, contours, and elevation; also called klick or click
Laterite: reddish soil-like clay formed in tropical regions by the decomposition of underlying rocks; used throughout the tunnel structures at Cu Chi, for example
Latrine: a military toilet; sometimes referred to by number of toilet seats or holes available—e.g. two-holer
Lester bags: bag filled with water for consumption in the field; the bag had four to six spigots for drawing water
Life-line sling seat: a line with a chair or flotation collar suspended from a helicopter used to pick up people out of the sea or from a ship to carry them to safety
Line company: the company which is on the front lines or in a defensive position
LZ: Landing Zone; where helicopters land to take on or discharge troops or supplies
MACV: Military Assistance Command, Vietnam; U.S. military forces advising Republic of (South) Vietnam troops
MAF: Marine Amphibious Force
Medevac: medical evacuation from the field by helicopter; also called a "dust-off"
Mike Force: Mobile Strike Force Command consisting of a Special Forces 12-man A-team, several Civilian Irregular (e.g. Montagnard) Defense Group battalions, a reconnaissance company, and a Nung or Cambodian airborne company
Mine sweep: searching land or water for mines
Montagnard: a Vietnamese term for several tribes of mountain people inhabiting highlands of Vietnam near Cambodian border
MOS: Military Occupational Specialty
NBC: National Broadcasting Company

NCO: Non-Commissioned Officer
Nissen Hut: a shelter in the form of a metal half cylinder
OASD: Office of the Assistant Secretary of Defense
O-Club: the Officers Club
Paddy: a rice field, usually flooded
Perimeter: outer limits of a military position; the area beyond this belongs to the enemy
Phoenix Program: part of the 1968 Accelerated Pacification Program designed to identify VC, capture or eliminate them
Platoon: a subdivision of a company-sized military unit, normally consisting of two or more squads or sections
PMOF: Presidential Medal of Freedom
POW: Prisoner of War
POW/MIA: Prisoner of War/Missing in Action
Project Delta: code name for Detachment B-52 of the US Fighting Group operating in South Vietnam; trained units to perform recon, raids, battle damage assessment, etc.
Quay Wall: a wharf or landing place along edge of body of water
R & R: Rest and Relaxation; a three to seven-day vacation from the war zones for military personnel
Rear Area: the hindmost portion of an army; removed from the combat zone, responsible for administration and supplies
Recon: reconnaissance; going out into the jungle to (clandestinely) observe enemy activity
Red-balling: fast-moving; special convoy making depot runs to get spare parts
Regiment: a military unit usually consisting of a number of battalions
Round eyes: slang term used by American soldiers to describe another American or European, especially women
Sampans: a Vietnamese peasant's boat
Sappers: Viet Cong soldiers who were specially-trained to infiltrate heavily defended installations at night
Satchel charges: explosive devices containing several blocks of explosives tied or taped together designed to detonate simultaneously
SCR: Senate Concurrent Resolution
Scuttlebutt: rumor or unofficial information; often most accurate source of information about a pending event/action before it happened
Seabees: Naval Construction Battalions
SFA: Special Forces Association
Sick call: open period during day when soldiers with injuries or illnesses reported to unit's medical center for treatment
Six-by: a 2-1/2 ton standard military cargo truck
Sling cable: a cable used in hoisting freight or people by helicopter
Snipers: individuals who shoot at enemies from concealed positions

Soft covers: hats; fatigue caps; jungle hats
SPARS: Members of the Women's Reserve of the U.S. Coast Guard Reserve; created on 11/23/42; the word SPAR refers to "Semper Paratus—Always Ready," the motto of the Coast Guard
Squad: a small military unit consisting of less than ten men
Squadron: an operating unit of warships, cavalry, aircraft, etc.
Starboard: the righthand side of a ship or aircraft
Strap hangers: nickname for persons who accompanied a unit to field or air, but were not an official part of, or assigned to unit—usually performed no tactical purpose; some took helicopter rides in order to log in flight time towards air medals and awards
Strip alert: fully armed aircraft at a base or forward strip ready to take off within five minutes
Tactical zone: area under command and control of one headquarters
TDY: Temporary Duty
The bird; flipping the bird: a hand gesture using middle finger; also—helicopter
The Colors: U.S. Flag; service and unit flags
The Wall: The Vietnam Veterans Memorial in Washington, DC
The World: slang for normal American life, used while in-country
Tiger suit: camouflaged uniform worn mostly by Special Forces or Special Operations personnel; also called tiger-stripes
Tour of duty: an extended period in a military zone. In Vietnam, three phases were noted: 1—new troop in-country; basically fearful of the unknown, enemy's capabilities, his own limitations; 2—in-country for awhile; learned some survival tricks, more confident, callous, even a little crazy in his personal disregard for the dangers of war; 3—ultimate paranoia; knows enemy's capabilities and random factors controlling his life; does all he can to insure he survives his tour, knowing full well his limitations and vulnerability
Triage: the procedure of deciding the order in which to treat casualties
Turret: a long-range gun assembly on a battleship or fort
Unsecured: non-secured area, no defensive perimeter
USAR: United States Army Reserves
USCG: United States Coast Guard
USMC: United States Marine Corps
USO: United Services Organization
Utilities: Marine field uniform
Veteran: a former soldier or other service member
VIP: Very Important Person
Water buffalo: military water trailer with eight spigots for drawing water
0200 hours: military time for two o'clock a.m.
1600 hours: military time for four o'clock p.m.
2000 hours: military time for eight o'clock p.m.

BIBLIOGRAPHY

[1] Pyle, Ernie. *Here is Your War.* © 1943 by Henry Holt and Company, Inc. Reprinted by permission of Henry Holt and Co., Inc.
[2] Grant, Zalin and Claude Boutillon. *Over the Beach.* New York and London: W.W. Norton & Company, 1986. Permission granted.
[3] Jones, Bruce E. *War Without Windows.* New York: Vanguard Press, Inc, 1987. Reprinted by permission of Bruce E. Jones.

REFERENCES

Army Regulation 670-20: Incentive Awards.
Army Regulation 672-5-1: Military Awards.
Aros, Andrew A. *A Title Guide to the Talkies,* 1964 through 1974. Metuchen, New Jersey: The Scarecrow Press, Inc, 1977.
Baer, Beverly and Neil Walker. *Almanac of Famous People: A Comprehensive Reference Guide to More than 27,000 Famous and Infamous Newsmakers from Biblical Times to the Present,* Fifth edition, Volume 1, Biographies. Detroit, Michigan; Washington, DC; and London: Gale Research Inc, 1984.
Brooks, Tim and Earle Marsh. *TV's Greatest Hits: The 150 Most Popular TV Shows of all Time.* New York: Ballantine Books, 1985.
Brown, Les. *Les Brown's Encyclopedia of Television.* Detroit, Michigan and London: Gale Research Inc, 1992.
Buxton, Frank and Bill Owen. *The Big Broadcast 1920-1950.* New York: The Viking Press, 1972.
Clark, Gregory. *Words of the Vietnam War.* Jefferson, North Carolina: McFarland & Company, Inc, 1990.
Clarke, Donald. *The Penguin Encyclopedia of Popular Music.* New York: Viking Penguin Inc, 1989.
Davis, Luther and John Cleveland. *The Mayor of 44th Street.* New York: *Collier's,* December 14,1940.
Deans, Mickey and Anne Pinchot. *Weep No More, My Lady.* New York: Hawthorn Books, Inc, 1972.
Dimmit, Richard Bertrand. *A Title Guide to the Talkies: A Comprehensive Listing of 16,000 Feature-Length Films From October, 1927, Until December, 1963,* Vol I and II.New York and London: The Scarecrow Press, Inc, 1965.
Eisner, Joel and David Krinsky. *Television Comedy Series: An Episode Guide to 153 TV Sitcoms in Syndication.* McFarland.
Encyclopaedia Britannica, Vol 15. Chicago, London, Toronto, Geneva, Sydney, Tokyo, Manila, & Johannesburg: William Benton, Publisher.
Ewen, David. *New Complete Book of the American Musical Theater.*

New York, Chicago, & San Francisco: Holt, Rinehart & Winston, 1970.

Faith, William Robert. *Bob Hope: A Life in Comedy.* New York: GP Putnam's Sons, 1982.

Graziano, Rocky with Rowland Barber. *Somebody Up There Likes Me.* New York: Cardinal, 1955.

Grolier Inc. *Academic American Encyclopedia.*

Grolier Inc. *The Encyclopedia Americana International Edition,* Vol 27. Danbury, Connecticut: Grolier Inc, 1991.

Halliwell, Leslie. *Halliwell's Film Guide.* Great Britain: Harper Collins Publishers, 1991.

Halliwell, Ruth and John Walker. *Halliwell's Filmgoer's and Video Viewer's Companion.* Great Britain: Harper Collins Publishers, 1993.

Herbert, Ian, Christine Baxter, and Robert E Finley. *Who's Who in the Theatre: A Biographical Record of the Contemporary Stage.* Great Britain: Pitman Publishing Ltd, 1977.

Hope, Bob. *Five Women I Love.* Garden City, New York: Doubleday & Company, Inc, 1966.

Hope, Bob and Bob Thomas. *The Road to Hollywood: My Forty-Year Love Affair with the Movies.* Garden City, New York: Doubleday & Company, Inc, 1977

Johnson, LTC Richard S. *How to Locate Anyone Who Is or Has Been in the Military.* San Antonio, Texas: MIE Publishing, 1991.

Katz, Ephraim. *The Film Encyclopedia.* New York: Thomas Y. Crowell, Publishers, 1979.

King, Dennis. *Get the Facts on Anyone.* New York, London, Sydney, Tokyo, and Singapore: Prentice Hall, 1992.

Kinkle, Roger D. *The Complete Encyclopedia of Popular Music and Jazz 1900-1950,* Vol 1 and 3. Westport, Connecticut: Arlington House Publishers, 1974.

Landis, Carole. *Four Jills in a Jeep.* Cleveland, Ohio: World Publishing Company, 1944.

Langman, Larry. *Encyclopedia of American Film Comedy.* New York and London: Garland Publishers, Inc, 1987.

Lentz, Harris M, III. *Science Fiction, Horror & Fantasy Film and Television Credits,* Vol 1 and 2. Jefferson, North Carolina and London: McFarland & Company, Inc, Publishers, 1983.

Maltin, Leonard. *Movie Comedy Teams.* New York: Signet Books, 1970.

Marill, Alvin H. *Movies Made for Television: The Telefeature and the Mini-Series 1964-1986.* Westport, CT: Arlington House Publishers, 1980.

Marquis Who's Who. *Who's Who in America,* 43rd edition, 1984-1985, Vol 2. Chicago, Illinois: Marquis Who's Who, 1984.

Maxwell, Michael D. and Helen Wyatt. "The Duke's Pet Project," Springfield, Virginia: *Army Times*, 9/18/89.

Michael, Paul. *The American Movies Reference Book: The Sound Era.* Englewood Cliffs, New Jersey: Prentice Hall, Inc, 1970.

Moritz, Charles. *Current Biography: 1963, with Index 1961-1963.* New York: The HW Wilson Company, 1963.

Murphy, George, U.S. Senator. *Say...Didn't You Used to be George Murphy?"* Bartholomew House, Ltd.

Nash, Jay Robert and Stanley Ralph Ross. *The Motion Picture Guide,* all volumes. Chicago, Illinois: Cinebooks, Inc, 1985.

Noel, Chris and Bill Treadwell. *Matter of Survival.* Boston, Massachusetts: Branden Publishing Company, 1987.

Olson, James. *Dictionary of the Vietnam War.* Westport, Connecticut: Greenwood Press, 1988.

Parish, James Robert and William T. Leonard. *The Funsters.*

Quinlan, David. *The Illustrated Directory of Film Stars.*

Ragan, David. *Who's Who in Hollywood: 1900-1976.* New Rochelle, New York: Arlington House Publishers, 1978.

Ragan, David. *Who's Who in Hollywood: The Largest Cast of International Film Personalities Ever Assembled.* New York and Oxford, England: Facts on File, 1992.

Rigdon, Walter. *The Biographical Encyclopaedia & Who's Who of the American Theatre.* New York: James H. Heineman, Inc, 1966.

Room, Adrian. *A Dictionary of Pseudonyms and their Origins, with Stories of Name Changes.* Jefferson, North Carolina and London: McFarland & Company, Inc, Publishers, 1989.

Rust, Brian and Allen G. Debus. *The Complete Entertainment Discography: from the mid-1890s to 1942.* New Rochelle, New York: Arlington House, 1973.

Sadler, S/SGT Barry and Tom Mahoney. *I'm a Lucky One.* New York: The MacMillan Company, and London: Collier-MacMillan Ltd, 1967.

Shale, Richard. *Academy Awards: An Ungar Reference Index.* New York: Frederick Ungar Publishing Co, 1982.

Shapiro, Mitchell E. *Television Network Prime-Time Programming, 1948-1988.* Jefferson, North Carolina and London: McFarland & Company, Inc, Publishers, 1989.

Siegman, Gita. *Awards, Honors & Prizes.* Detroit, Michigan: Gale Research, Inc, 1988.

Siegman, Gita. *World of Winners: A Current and Historical Perspective on Awards and their Winners.* Detroit, Michigan: Gale Research, Inc, 1989.

Smith, Bill. *The Vaudevillians.* New York: Macmillan Publishing Co, Inc, 1976.

Smith, Elsdon C. *New Dictionary of American Family Names.* New

York, Evanston, San Francisco, California, and London: Harper & Row, Publishers, 1973.

Stein, Charles. *American Vaudeville as Seen by Its Contemporaries.* New York: Alfred Knopf, Inc, 1984.

Steinberg, Cobbett. *Film Facts.* New York: Facts on File, Inc, 1980.

Stevenson, Burton. *The Home Book of Quotations.* New York, New York: Dodd, Mead & Company, 1934.

Stuart, Sandra Lee. *Who Won What When: The Record Book of Winners.* Secaucus, New Jersey: Lyle Stuart, Inc, 1977.

Terrace, Vincent. *Encyclopedia of Television Series, Pilots and Specials:* The Index: Who's Who in Television, 1937-1984.

Terrace, Vincent. *Radio's Golden Years: The Encyclopedia of Radio Programs, 1930-1960.* San Diego, California and New York, New York: A.S. Barnes & Company, Inc, 1981.

Terrace, Vincent. *The Complete Encyclopedia of Television Programs 1947-1979,* Vol 1 and 2. Cranbury, New Jersey: A.S. Barnes & Company, Inc, 1979.

The Library of Congress. *Catalog of Copyright Entries,* Cumulative Series: Motion Pictures, 1912-1939. Washington, DC: The Library of Congress, 1951.

Umphred, Neal. *Goldmine's Price Guide to Collectible Record Albums 1949-1989.* Iola, Wisconsin: Krause Publications, 1993.

Van Devanter, Linda and Christopher Morgan. *Home Before Morning.* New York: Warner Books, 1983.

Walker, Keith. *A Piece of My Heart.* Novato, California: Presidio Press, 1986.

Walter, Claire. *Winners: The Blue Ribbon Encyclopedia of Awards.* New York: Facts on File, 1979.

Weaver, John T. *Forty Years of Screen Credits 1929-1969,* Volume 2: K-Z. Metuchen, New Jersey: The Scarecrow Press, Inc, 1970.

Westmoreland, General William C. *A Soldier Reports.* Garden City, New York: Doubleday & Company, Inc, 1976.

Wilkinson, Harry. "Looking Hollywood Way," Berne, Indiana: *Good Old Days Magazine,* February 1991.

Wollman-Rusoff, Jane. *And in the End.* Los Angeles, California: Los Angeles Magazine, November 1992.

ABOUT THE AUTHOR

Noonie Fortin has done an outstanding job of researching and gathering primary-source information about the love affair between Martha Raye and "her" troops. As co-chair of the Medals for Maggie Committee of the Tri-County Council Vietnam Era Veterans in Albany, New York, she successfully achieved her goal of seeing that Martha Raye was honored with the Presidential Medal of Freedom.

During those seven years of research and communication, she published her own *Maggiegram* for her many correspondents around the world and for Veteran publications.

Noonie is a Vietnam Era woman Veteran. From upstate New York, she frequently stays in Copperas Cove, Texas. She served over twenty years in the Army Reserves before retiring (having attained the rank of First Sergeant).

Her civilian career was with the New York State Department of Motor Vehicles for twenty years until she was disabled and forced to retire.

Her articles have been published in newspapers, journals, and magazines including *Forty & Eighter, BRAVO Veterans Outlook, The Scottish Rite Journal,* Canada's *199 News,* and *VIETNAM* magazine.

To Order Copies

If unavailable in your local bookstores, LangMarc Publishing will fill your order within 24 hours.

✉ *Postal Orders:* **LangMarc Publishing • P.O. 33817 • San Antonio, Texas 78265-3817**

Memories of Maggie

$15.95

Quantity Discounts: 10% discount for 3-4 books; 15% for 5-9; 20 % 10 or more copies.

Add Shipping: Book rate $1.50 for 1; 75 cents for each additional book. $3.00 for priority mail 1-2 books.

Call for UPS charges on quantity orders.

☎ 1-800-864-1648

Please send payment with order:

______	Books at $15.95		______
	Less quantity discount	-	______
	Total for books	=	______
	Sales tax (TX only)		______
	Shipping	+	______
	Check enclosed:		______

✂ - - If this is a gift, we'll include a gift card and message. - - - - - - - - - - - - - - - - -

Memories of Maggie

Name and Address for Order Delivery

____

____

____

____

Phone in case of question re. order ______________